THE FENCE-WALKER

WILLIAM HOLINGER

THE FENCE WALKER

A NOVEL

for Larry + Meg —
with admiration
and all best wishes —
Bill

State University of New York Press

Wm Holinger
Ann Arbor
August 8, 1985

Acknowledgements: Special thanks to those who so generously gave me their time and good advice while this novel was under construction. You know who you are. I also deeply appreciate the good will and support of the Michigan Society of Fellows; the Department of English Language and Literature; and the Department of Internal Medicine, University Hospitals—all at the University of Michigan, Ann Arbor. W.H.

PUBLISHED BY

STATE UNIVERSITY OF NEW YORK PRESS, ALBANY

© 1985 STATE UNIVERSITY OF NEW YORK

FOR INFORMATION, ADDRESS STATE UNIVERSITY OF NEW YORK PRESS, STATE UNIVERSITY PLAZA, ALBANY, N.Y., 12246

LIBRARY OF CONGRESS CATALOGING IN PUBLICATION DATA

HOLINGER, WILLIAM, 1944–

THE FENCE-WALKER.

1. KOREA—HISTORY—1960– —FICTION. I. TITLE.

PS3558.3477F4 1985 813'.54 85-2630

ISBN 0-88706-024-2

10 9 8 7 6 5 4 3 2 1

To Dorothy

ONE

I'VE FORGOTTEN HIS NAME BUT I can see his face as clearly as if he left the room a moment ago. He is my replacement. He sits on the edge of Harmon's bunk, leaning forward, forearms resting on his knees. Harmon is gone. Jack Evans, who moved out of this room to another a few weeks ago, is gone too. I'm packing. Tomorrow I leave for the States. This is sixteen years ago.

"Is it true, what Lieutenant Evans told me?" my replacement says. "That you've been to North Korea? And signed extension papers? And my God—did you really wrestle a North Korean?"

It's June and insects are buzzing outside the screens. In my right hand is a set of wool underwear, and my left holds open the mouth of a duffel bag. I am about to feed the underwear to the duffel bag. But his questions stop me. Are these things true?

Three years before, almost to the day—in June of 1966—I was graduating from college. I had marched against the war. Several times. The night before my first final I got drunk because my mother called to tell me that my father wouldn't make graduation: he had a meeting in Chicago. The next day I flunked the *exam. At the time it seemed important, catastrophic. Now as I pack, it seems like nothing, the equivalent at most of a sneeze or a pimple. How are such leaps, such transformations possible?*

I look over my shoulder at the second lieutenant who is sitting on Harmon's bunk. He has pale red hair, a round face, freckles. A small kid, short but muscular. "Evans told you this today? Before he left?"

"Last night. Late. You weren't here."

"He was packing."

"Yeah. Sure." He shifts uncomfortably. I don't take my eyes off him. He gets up and takes a cigaret out of a pack on Harmon's bureau and lights it.

"Listen," I say, squaring around and facing him. "Try to talk less. I don't mean any offense. You aren't going to learn anything around here unless you ask questions. But stick to business. Don't get personal."

"Yes sir."

"Don't call me sir."

"All right, um . . . ."

I stuff the long johns into the duffel bag and continue to pack. The bunk squeaks when he sits down again.

A few moments later the field phone on his bureau buzzes. I don't answer it. Seconds later it buzzes again, longer this time. He picks it up.

"Hello? . . . Oh yes sir, yes sir. . . . He's here, sir. . . . Okay, sir." He hangs up. "That was Colonel Brody. He wanted to know where you were."

Wool OGs. Boots. Field jacket liner.

"So it's true. You've been restricted to Camp Matta. You did go AWOL!"

I don't even turn around. "Get the fuck out."

He stands up. I hear the bunk squeak and his boots pass behind me. But then they stop. He says, "Up yours, Richardson."

I swing around. I am surprised to be looking him in the eye —he isn't nearly as short as I thought he was. He's giving me the finger. I take a good long look at it, consider reaching over to break it off, but it wouldn't be worth the trouble. He stands there waiting for me to make the next move, but I simply turn around and continue packing.

A moment later I hear him walk out of the room and down the hall. I think, He's learning fast, he'll do all right.

Our Boeing 707 reached Korea thirteen hours after leaving Seattle. The flight—most of it over water during darkness—was punctuated by turbulence, and by the time we began descending toward Kimpo Airport, we were very glad to be landing. A white sun rose above the mountains off the starboard wing of the aircraft. Below us the landscape looked flooded, covered by silver water and crisscrossed by a grid of earthen dikes patterned like fish scales. Our first rice paddies: hundreds of adjoining ponds, the water still, waveless. The paddy surfaces mirrored the sun, a glistening disk, and as we cruised toward a landing, the image of the sun leapt from one paddy to the next to the next, a flat white stone skipping on water.

As the plane lost altitude, the sun sank behind the terraced mountains. A factory appeared below us, chimneys smoldering, filling the air with brown haze. The morning sky turned dark, reversing the sunrise.

The intercom clicked on and a stewardess warned us not to take pictures of Kimpo Airport. "Photographing of military aircraft and installations is strictly prohibited," she droned. "Anyone pointing a camera out the window will have it confiscated and the film will be removed."

We flew over the outskirts of Seoul, and the factory and paddies gave way to houses and roads busy with activity. Off in the distance we could see buildings. We dropped still lower and the houses blurred and the nose of the aircraft came up and we began to glide, and the plane leaned back and then the runway appeared beneath us and we sank toward the conrete until finally there was a jolt, then the roar of reversed engines and we were thrust forward against our seat belts.

We were in Korea. It was May of 1968, and this was the Second Theater, the alternative to a thirteen-month tour in Vietnam. We were a plane-load of GIs who thought we had gotten a lucky roll of the dice.

The plane taxied for a long time, then finally stopped. One stewardess instructed us to remain seated while another opened the door. Moist air and an odor of fertilizer entered the cabin.

3

Two Army officers ducked through the doorway. They walked over to a colonel who was sitting toward the front of the first-class compartment. During the long trip, a rumor had gone around that he was flying over to pick up the body of his son, who had been killed on the DMZ. After a few words, the two officers escorted the colonel off the airplane.

The rest of us followed shortly, emerging dazed and disoriented and walking shakily down the steel steps. There had been about twenty officers in first class and perhaps a hundred and twenty enlisted men in coach. We walked stiffly across the tarmac toward a pair of huge hangar doors, following each other numbly, a wide column of sleepy, unwilling men.

Before we reached the hangar, the sun rose a second time from behind the mountains. It cast a crimson glow on a large sign that hung over the hangar doors.

Welcome to Korea

Land of the Morning Calm

Inside the hangar was the replacement depot. The huge room echoed with voices: voices shouting, amplified voices announcing, voices murmuring. There were desks with glass partitions, tables, cubicles, lines of men waiting and reams of paper to fill out and more lines, although the lines for officers were shorter and moved faster than the lines for enlisted men. Eventually I found myself in a line that wound toward a small cubicle defined by white curtains. The person inside the cubicle would holler "Next!" and the nearest officer would walk through the curtains. My turn came and I found a Spec-5 sitting inside holding a big black compressed-air gun for giving shots. He was a short, rather chubby man with a red face. Without looking up at me he said, "Welcome to Korea, sir, drop your drawers. This won't hurt a bit."

"I've only been here an hour," I said. "I'm going to get it in the ass already?"

Slowly he raised his head and looked at me. "I've heard it before, sir. I've heard it *all* before. Drop 'em."

I turned around and undid my trousers. He continued talking: "I've seen every pair of buttocks in this damn country, Lieutenant. American buttocks, that is. Private to general. I've seen more butts than a seventy-year-old whore."

4

"Interesting work."

He daubed cold alcohol on my ass. "I even know what the butt of the Eighth Army commander looks like. General Bonesteel. Do you believe that name, 'Bonesteel'? Not a bad handle for a general officer. Hold still now, Lieutenant. Lean back against it."

I felt the muzzle of the gun against my skin. Then the gun whined and my ass stung. I rubbed the sore spot and pulled up my drawers. "You been doing this long?"

He raised an eyebrow. "Lieutenant, I'm short. Fifty-four days. I've given shots to every plane load into Kimpo since my first week here. Count 'em."

I buckled my belt and buttoned my jacket. "What do you dream about?"

"I should have been born a woman. That's the way out." He pointed with the hydraulic gun.

"Thanks."

"Next!"

About noon, those of us assigned to the 3rd Brigade of the 7th Division were herded out of the hangar. We stood on the tarmac, perhaps thirty of us, squinting in the sunlight and wondering what would happen next. Way across the airfield an honor guard of six or eight men was loading a coffin into the hold of a giant silver jet transport. The red-and-white stripes of the flag were quite visible, even at that distance. Nobody said anything, but we all watched. The colonel was standing off to the side, by himself. All at once he saluted. The coffin disappeared into the black belly of the plane.

After a while we were loaded onto a military bus. The bus was a dark olive drab, and the distance between the back of one seat and the front of the next was less than on a yellow school bus. We left the airfield and headed toward Seoul. Someone passed around boxes of C-rations. The food on the plane had been so awful that I'd eaten almost nothing since leaving Seattle, so I was busy opening cans and eating, and I didn't see much of Seoul. The man sitting next to me was a staff sergeant, a black man with an unusual name: Love. While we ate, we talked. Sergeant Love had already done a tour in Korea, and he described it in glowing terms. "This place is a paradise," he said. "You won't believe the girls. Just don't get assigned to the DMZ. No sir—you don't want that."

We left Seoul on a two-lane highway going north. It was narrow. Bicyclists and pedestrians crowded both sides of the road, teetering on the brink of steep drops into paddies. There was hardly road enough for the bus, yet we whizzed along, barely missing the pedestrians and bicyclists. They all carried huge loads. Those who were walking had packs on their backs, and those who were riding carried boxes and crates strapped to the front and the rear of their bikes. It was a puzzle how the driver kept from knocking people off the road.

We passed one old woman who was walking alone, isolated from other pedestrians. She was wearing a black dress and black shawl. Her face was gaunt, and her weathered skin was stretched tightly across the bones of her face. Someone on the back seat swiveled around and pointed a camera at the old woman. She drew the shawl across her face and turned away from the bus.

We sped on, cruised through Uijongbu, and arrived in Tonduchon around six. The bus moved slowly through the narrow streets until we reached the gates of Camp Casey, where two MPs stood in a hut that looked like a tool booth. Stretching away in two directions, probably surrounding the sprawling compound, was a wire fence with great high masses of tangled barbed wire strung along the top. I had never seen a fence that tall.

The MPs waved our bus through the gate. Inside we passed soldiers dressed in fatigues. Most were armed with either a pistol strapped to their waist or a rifle at sling arms. All wore helmets.

The bus stopped in front of a pair of connected Quonset huts: 3rd Brigade headquarters. The buildings were painted in a camouflage design, dappled beige and green, and a pair of large pine trees flanked the main entrance. The driver shut off the engine. No one spoke. We could hear the wind in the boughs and smell the sweet pine pitch, and when I closed my eyes for a moment it almost seemed as though we had stopped in the middle of a pine forest.

But then a couple of NCOs emerged from the building, and we piled out of the bus, the enlisted men forming ranks and the officers milling about in a small group behind the formation. The NCOs took roll call. Then the officers were taken first to the armory, where each of us was issued a pistol and three clips of ammunition, and then to a BOQ, where we drew bedding and were assigned to empty single rooms. The sergeant who was directing us pointed out the mess hall and encouraged us to eat as soon as possible, explaining that supper was being kept warm especially for us.

I washed up and headed toward the mess hall. Outside, night had almost fallen. Bare light bulbs blazed from every doorway. The fence that surrounded the compound swung down from a low hill and ran along very close to the BOQ, then swung back up and away from the mess hall. Overhead the stars gleamed dimly from a dark purple sky.

The mess hall turned out to be the Brigade Officers' Open Mess, and a fine mess it was. The tables were covered by starched white linen tablecloths, and the tableware was real silver plate. The linen napkins had been heavily starched and smelled fresh. I was waited on by two Korean waiters. They were good waiters. The food wasn't bad either. The dinner hadn't suffered from having been kept warm, and I wondered again whether I was to be assigned to brigade headquarters or sent down to a line unit.

A captain and a couple of lieutenants whom I'd seen on the bus entered the mess hall and sat down at my table.

"Hello," I said to the lieutenants. "Good evening, sir," I said to the captain.

"Evening," they all replied. They were wearing their pistols strapped to the waists of the dark green jackets of their Class A uniforms, like MPs. I wondered why they'd brought weapons to dinner. During the meal, no one said much. I may as well have been eating alone.

After supper I went back to the BOQ. In the hallway I encountered a couple of officers in stocking feet, their dusty fatigue shirts unbuttoned, talking and laughing as they walked down the corridor. They ignored me and I made way for them as they passed.

My room was a tiny cubicle with cement-block walls. For furniture it had a small desk, two identical chairs, an army bunk, and a built-in wardrobe that contained drawers and a closet. I'd already drawn sheets, a pillow case and pillow, and two blankets, and I was looking forward to putting them to their intended use. But first I wanted a shower. I took off my clothes and gathered up a towel, soap, and toilet kit from my duffel bag and plodded in my bare feet up the long hallway to the latrine.

The shower stall was cramped and ugly, with exposed pipes, green paint peeling off its cement-block sides, and a canvas curtain thick with mildew. I climbed in and turned the faucet, expecting the worst. But the water was very hot, and the shower head was new, and when I stepped under the water it hit my shoulders and back with a gentle, penetrating force that felt luxurious after the miles I'd traveled. I soaped up and let the suds and hot water slide off me. The tension began to leave my body. I reached outside the stall for a bottle of shampoo, got ahold of it, and poured some of the green liquid into my palm. I lathered up my short hair. I put my head under the stream of water to rinse and it was than that all hell broke loose: shooting, screaming, a couple of explosions and then more shooting, all coming from up in the hills behind the BOQ. It was very close and I dived out of the shower onto the tile floor. I kept my head below the level of the open windows and I thought, Stay down. Get a weapon.

The ambush was evolving into a fireflight and the shots were light, high popping sounds that drifted down the moist night air and in through the latrine windows. I low-crawled out of the latrine and down the hall. Rooms lined either side of the corridor and my room was a long way down. Soap dripped into my eyes. The linoleum floor felt very cold and the hardness of it bruised my elbows and knees. I had to hold my butt high to keep my penis from scraping. I got to my room and reached up to my bunk, grabbed my .45 and a clip, jammed in the clip and chambered a round. I crawled out of my room and back up the corridor. I didn't know what I was going to do but I felt better for being armed. About halfway up the hall I heard voices coming from one of the rooms and then somebody laughed and another voice spoke and I thought, What's going on? A couple bursts of automatic weapons fire echoed down the corridor from the latrine, and then a burst of laughter erupted from inside the room.

What the hell?

I stood up and opened the door. The room was brightly lit. There were three guys sitting around in chairs and on the bunk. They were wearing fatigue pants, socks, and tee-shirts. The room smelled like beer and sweat and cigaret smoke.

"What's going on?" I said.

They looked up. I stood in the doorway naked, shivering, my chest heaving, my stomach and thighs and knees black with dirt and blood. Shampoo foam dripped into my stinging eyes and I rubbed it away. The shooting had stopped, and for a moment the only noise was the buzz of the fluorescent ceiling lights. Then all three of them began to laugh. They laughed harder and harder. One of them pointed at me.

"Look at him!"

"You're a little wet behind the ears, aren't you?"

"What a hero!"

"They train back there every night."

"Those are blanks! Don't you know blanks from live ammo?"

I looked at the pistol in my hand. Do I have to take this shit? I thought. I aimed the .45 at the ceiling over their heads and fired. In the small room the explosion was tremendous. It was followed by a peaceful silence void of derisive laughter. The empty brass cartridge spun across the lineoleum floor and hit the wall with a metallic *tink*.

"Show a little respect," I said.

My fellow officers stared at me, respectfully, waiting to see what I'd do next. Small white flakes of sound-proof ceiling tile snowed down on them. I backed out of the room and shut the door.

Taking a deep breath, I started up the hall in the wrong direction, turned and walked back to my room. I slipped the .45 under the pillow and padded back up the hall to the latrine. After I finished my shower I returned to my room, made up the bunk, set my alarm, and got into bed. I unloaded and cleared the pistol, put the loose bullet back into the clip, and put the clip and the weapon under the bed.

Somebody was bumping about in the room next to mine, and I thought I heard a woman's voice. From outside the open window, the sound of crickets and the occasional whine of a truck drifted in. I lay in the bunk with my eyes open.

I remembered a staff sergeant in basic training, a Drill Instructor, who had been drunk on duty one day. Our platoon was getting bayonet training. We were practicing on dummies with real bayonets on our rifles, and he interrupted the drill to give a demonstration. He called me out in front of the platoon, took my rifle, and proceeded to use me as his dummy. Lying on my bunk in Korea, I remembered standing in the hot Georgia sun and star-

9

ing down my nose at my own bayonet near my throat and realizing that this drunk sergeant could kill me as easy as swatting a fly. Easier. He held the bayonet at my throat—it touched me once—and talked about bayonet fighting and I could smell the booze on his breath at ten in the morning. I stood there and tried to decide whether to make a grab for the barrel of the rifle but I knew that it didn't matter what I did. I could die either way: standing there or making a grab for the rifle. My life was completely and totally in the hands of a drunk.

It was not long after that morning that I went to the company commander and volunteered for Officer Candidate School.

I got up and switched on the overhead light. A bare bulb. I rummaged around in my duffel bag until I found my journal.

First I wrote this:

May 2nd
I wonder what the repercussions of putting a hole in the BOQ roof will be.

Then I sat there for a while and thought about things. I thought about the flight over the ocean and the bus ride up to Camp Casey, and I thought about the questions I'd been asking myself lately. The questions were really beginning to bug me.

So then I wrote this:

I don't want to just "keep a journal." A journal ought to have a purpose. (Like everything else?) Sometimes people keep journals to record their "feelings." That sounds like something adolescent girls do. Other people keep journals to record what "happens." The operative word would seem to be *record*. The verb, not the noun. Once copied down, the record (the noun) is seldom referred to again. What good is the record if you never go back over it?

The *doing*, then, is finally revealed as the real purpose of the journal. To record. It's the writing down that accomplishes something.

Accomplishes what?

My journal will serve as a record. But in addition, the keeping of it may help me answer some questions.

Like what the fuck am I doing in Korea?

And more immediately, what are the consequences of putting a hole in the roof of the BOQ?

10

TWO

T HE FLOOR IN THE BRIGADE
commander's office was a linoleum checkerboard of big green and
white squares, clean, bright, glazed by a deep layer of wax that
glistened like the surface of a still lake. Colonel Larson sat behind
his gray metal desk and commanded the room and the furniture
as though he were on the reviewing stand of a parade ground with
the whole brigade spread out before him. He sat erect and emanated energy. His eyebrows were bushy and gray, and his blue
eyes blazed like miniature suns. On stands behind him were no
less than four flags. America was there, and Korea, and the
robin's-egg blue United Nations flag, and a deep purple flag that
probably represented the 3rd Brigade. A photograph of Lyndon
Johnson hung on the wall right above his head. That was heavy
support, but Colonel Larson didn't appear to need it.

I was standing in front of the desk in the 'at ease' position. It
occurred to me that Colonel Larson probably could levitate me if
he wanted to: there was that much power in his eyes.

"You blew a hole in one of my BOQs," he said flatly. "What
have you got to say for yourself?"

"I have no excuse, sir. I take full responsibility."

"Was it an accident?"

"No sir, it was not an accident."

"Well then why in the hell were you shooting at my ceiling?"

"The situation seemed to call for it, sir. I needed to get the attention of those men."

"Oh? Why?"

"Well, I'm not sure, sir. They were laughing at me."

"Laughing."

"Yes sir.

"Why were they laughing, Lieutenant?"

"Because I thought a training ambush was a real one. I couldn't tell the sound of blanks from real bullets."

"You thought we were under attack?"

"Yes sir."

"Did you think a North Korean was hiding in the crawl space between the roof and the ceiling?"

"No sir."

Colonel Larson peered down at the papers spilling out of the folder on his desk. He seemed to be trying to stifle a laugh. He took a good long look at the papers. At last he said: "Arthur Edward Richardson. That you name?"

"Yes sir."

"What in the hell kind of a name is it?"

I thought I'd try a little humor. "A long one, sir."

He was unimpressed by my wit. "Are you a WASP, Lieutenant?"

"Pardon me, sir?"

"Are you a WASP, I said. What's the matter, can't you hear? A white, Anglo-Saxon Protestant."

"Yes sir."

"You're a WASP, and an officer, and last night on your first night in Korea you blew a hole in my roof. Now what in the hell am I supposed to do with you?"

I said nothing.

"You want a job at brigade headquarters?"

"Wherever you need me, sir."

"What are you good for, Lieutenant?"

Again I kept my mouth shut.

"You must be good for something. You've been recommended for an Army Commendation Medal."

"I have?" I was completely surprised.

"Think I'd lie to you, Lieutenant?"

"No sir, of course not. I didn't know."

"You know about the *Pueblo*, don't you?"

"Yes sir."

"How many men on board?"

"Eighty-two, sir."

"Wrong."

"Yes sir. Eighty-three. Man by the name of Duane Hodges was killed when the ship was initially fired upon."

"Duane D. Hodges. How many American troops are stationed in Korea?"

"Fifty thousand."

"Exactly?"

"Give or take a couple grand."

"Take a few. We're way undermanned. Tell me: who cammands them?"

"Besides yourself, sir?"

"Who is the Eighth Army Commander? Do you want the goddamn question in writing?"

"General Bonesteel, sir." I grinned.

"What do you find amusing, Lieutenant?"

"Nothing, sir. I came by that information in a rather odd way. And the name. It seems so . . . right . . . for a general officer."

He lowered his head and glared through his eyebrows. "Any name is right for a general officer. Any name. Larson, Bonesteel. Except Richardson. That's a lousy name for a general officer. Tell me, Richardson, do you aspire to someday *be* a general officer?"

I hesitated, then decided not to lie.

"I don't really know, sir. I'm not even sure I'll have a future, much less know what to do with it. But I don't think I want to spend it in the army."

"What do you mean you're not sure you'll have a future?"

"Well, I could die over here, sir."

"You planning on it, Richardson?"

"No sir."

"Then you better plan on surviving." He leafed through my file, selected three sheets of paper, and briefly studied them. Then he put them down, rolled his chair back from the desk, and swiveled around sideways. "Sit down, please, Arthur," he said.

I sat down.

"You have a fine record here. Distinguished Graduate out of OCS, recommended for an ARCOM on your first assignment. It's an excellent record. You should know that; it's really quite excellent. You stack up better than most of the junior officers who come through this headquarters." He turned his head and looked at me. "At least on paper."

"Thank you, sir."

He slammed the palm of his hand on the desk. "Don't thank me, goddamnit. I'm telling you something you ought to know. But if you don't want to make a career of it, what are my choices? It's pointless to give you a staff assignment."

Oh shit, I thought.

"Besides," he went on, "field duty would do you good. Command time is essential if you decide to stay in. You do want to command a company before you get out, don't you? A platoon or a company of your own?"

I was full of candor. "No sir, I don't."

He snorted. "That's a damn shame, Richardson," he said sarcastically, "because you'll probably wind up in command of a company before you leave here. We're short of officers. There's a war on in Southeast Asia—you've heard? We're undermanned. Nearly every one of my companies is commanded by a lieutenant."

He returned to the papers on his desk and shuffled through them. Presently he looked up at me. "Tell me, just what *do* you want from your year here? What are your ambitions, what do you want to get out of it?"

His question surprised me. It confused me, too. No one that I could remember had ever asked me what I wanted.

"I don't know, sir," I finally said. "I'm not exactly here by choice. I was sent here. I hadn't really thought about the future. I didn't figure I'd have any say in it."

"Don't you have any goals or plans?"

"I don't think so, Colonel." I thought about my journal, about the questions I wanted answers to. "No sir. Nothing I could easily put into words."

"Perhaps not into words," Colonel Larson said. "But you made a statement last night when you put a .45 caliber hole through the ceiling of Lieutenant Shepard's bedroom." He straightened up and leaned forward. "And because you made that statement I'm going to assign your ass to a line battalion on the DMZ. The 1st of the 31st is losing some officers in the next few days, and they need replacements. Colonel Curtis is the battalion commander. You report to him."

"Where are they, sir?"

"Camp Matta. They'll send a jeep after you. My adjutant will arrange the details."

He stood up and so did I. He was very tall. The flags stirred as he walked around to the front of his desk. He shook my hand and stared solemnly down at me with his cold blue eyes, and then his mouth and cheeks moved, and something resembling a smile appeared on his face. "You'll like the DMZ, Richardson," he said. "It's a fascinating place. And you can shoot that .45 of yours all you like."

The 1st of the 31st sent a jeep and driver down for me and another lieutenant that morning, and we left soon after lunch. The country north of Casey turned rugged. The hills and mountains were steep, tall, and majestic, but they were more rock than soil. Vegetation was sparse, and the land was not green but gray and brown. The valleys seemed depleted: they were narrow and appeared to be all clay and rock. The land was both beautiful and bleak, magnificent yet barren. In the villages the pigs and goats were lean and the people wore drab clothing. Their small houses were pressed close together. The rice paddies here in the north were not yet green, and some of the paddy dikes were crumbling. Occasionally we saw paddies altogether untended: dry and unplanted. The farther north we drove, the scarcer arable land became: rocky hills and mountains took over, crowding the road and blocking out the sky. People became scarce too, and so did signs of prosperity. We were driving, after all, toward the DMZ.

The dirt road was dusty and full of holes. There were three of us in the jeep. The driver's name was Peters and the other lieutenant's name was Jack Evans. He had been on the flight over with me, and I remembered him from the mess hall the night before. Both of us had been assigned to the same battalion. We'd met before the jeep arrived; he'd been sitting outside brigade headquarters under one of the fir trees when I walked up with my duffel bag and suitcases.

"You going up to the 1st of the 31st?" I asked him.

"Yeah." He got to his feet. "Jack Evans."

"Art Richardson." We shook hands.

He gave me a long, hard look. "You the guy who shot up the BOQ last night?"

"Yeah, I guess so."

He thought that over. "Well," he finally said, "I'm glad you'll be on the same side of the border as I'm on."

"Why'd Larson assigned *you* to the DMZ?" I said.

"I asked him to."

"You volunteered? How come?"

He shrugged. "I wanted to be where the action is."

"So why didn't you volunteer for Vietnam?"

"Hey. Now I might admit to being a little on the gung ho side. But I'm not crazy." He laughed. "I wasn't the one who took indoor target practice last night."

Now he was sitting in the back of the jeep, bouncing around among an assortment of duffel bags and suitcases, while I sat in front next to the driver. Jack was big and very broad in the shoulders. He had blond hair, and his face was strong and good-looking. It was an appealing face.

The two of us pumped the driver for information about our new unit.

"It's an all right battalion," Peters told us. He spoke with a southern drawl. "As good as any, I reckon, but I've only been here three weeks. I ain't got much to compare it to."

"How's the CO?" Jack asked.

"He's a nice old man. Colonel Curtis. He's fair."

"Where you from, Peters?" I asked him, acting like an officer.

"Georgia, sir."

"Where are you from, Richardson?" Jack Evans asked me.

"Hartford, Connecticut."

"And I'm from Wisconsin. We've got half the country covered in one jeep load. How about that?"

Peters drove fast down the rough dirt road. The canvas top of the jeep was up, but the doors were missing and the air roared in and around the back of the jeep. It wasn't summer yet; the sun was bright but not warm, and I was chilly. Dust billowed into the air behind us. When we passed a vehicle going in the opposite direction, the dust would swirl in thickly, tasting dry and chalky. Once we roared up behind a troop truck and then couldn't get around it because of curves and hills. After we finally passed it, a thick layer of dust clung to our duffel bags, fatigue jackets, hats, faces—everything. Jack tapped my shoulder to get my attention and I turned around; the dust had coated his nose and lips and eyebrows, and when he saw me, he broke into laughter. "Look at you two!" he roared. "I didn't come here to join the circus." He took off his hat and started slapping at his fatigue jacket, filling the air with dust all over again.

We kept going and the land kept changing. The hills got higher and rockier for a while, and then they became lower again and more gentle and we crossed a couple of wide valleys. We could see mountains in the distance. So this is it, I thought. This is where they fought that war. And where I'm going: that's where it bogged down, stalemated. It's still not over. Panmunjom is somewhere just beyond a few of those hills.

Pretty soon the sky clouded up, and then it started to rain. Large drops splattered against the windshield, turning the dust to mud. The air turned cold and the rain began to blow in.

"Can we put the door on?" I shouted to the driver.

Peters was leaning forward and fiddling with the windshield wipers, which weren't working. He said something but I couldn't understand him.

"What?"

"I said we ain't got any, sir. Doors're back at Camp Matta." I swore.

"They wouldn't do no good, Lieutenant." He had gotten the windshield wipers to work—erratically—and he sat back in his seat. "We'll have to take the top off at Libby Bridge anyhow."

"How come?" Jack Evans asked.

"It's SOP, sir."

I turned around and Jack grinned at me. "That explains everything," he said.

By this time I was shivering. "Well," I said, "we may be cold and wet, but at least the rain's keeping the dust down."

We finally arrived at a village. Changpa-ri, Peters told us. He swung the jeep off the main road and we lurched down a muddy back street. Up until now, driving through villages, we'd kept to the main streets with their tiny shops and small public squares. I asked Peters where he was going.

"I got to pick up Lieutenant Anderson," he said.

"Who's he?"

"The fence-walker. I'm his driver."

"Oh. I see." What I saw was that Peters had a way of explaining things that left them totally obscure.

The narrow street we were on was defined on either side by a ditch two or three feet deep. I peered out of the jeep, and down. The ditch was running slowly with gray water, and it stank. Open sewers, I decided. Narrow foot bridges leading to the houses had been built across the ditches. The homes were gray, one-story, concrete block structures. The fancier houses were stuccoed. They all had very few windows, and the windows were very small. Some were barred. The roofs were strange and lovely: long, sloping, and peaked, they were made of rounded red slate tiles. At the edges the roofs didn't just end; the tiles swept upward toward the sky.

Most of the houses had outdoor courtyards attached to them. Their cement-block walls were streaked darkly with rainwater. They were tall—seven to ten feet high—and I couldn't see over them. A few had barbed wire running along the top, but along the tops of most of the walls were bright red and green and brown shards of glass, many shapes and sizes but all sharp, all lethal, the glass set into concrete—sharp edge up—broken Coke bottles, pieces of pottery, fragments of beer bottles with jagged sharp points glistening colorfully in the rain.

Peters drove slowly, made a few turns, and finally pulled up in front of one of the houses. The door opened immediately. A soldier stepped out of the door into the rain. The door immediately closed behind him. He was tall and his fatigues were washed out and faded. He wore a helmet and he was carrying a full laundry bag, a rifle, a PRC-25 radio, and a small AWOL bag. He approached the jeep on the driver's side in long, rapid strides.

"You're ten minutes late, Peters."

"Sorry, sir. It's a long trip to Camp Casey and back."

"I don't want excuses. Give me a hand with this bag."

Peters jumped out of the jeep and helped pile the stuff in back on top of the other gear. Anderson unfolded a poncho and pulled it over his head while he walked around the jeep. He looked in at Jack and me. "You the new officers?"

"Yes sir," Jack said. Anderson was a first lieutenant; we were second.

He spoke to me: "Get in back there, will you?"

I did not immediately move. There was a long pause while Anderson and I stared at each other. His face was thin and sunburnt, and he needed a shave. His eyes were red and had a glazed and empty look to them. He stood in the rain and stared at me, and the rain darkened the camouflage cloth on his helmet and splashed off his poncho into his face. He didn't seem to notice. I got out of the jeep and climbed into the back, settling myself among the luggage.

Anderson got in and we started off. I looked back at the house as we pulled away. The door had opened slightly and I thought I caught a glimpse of a woman looking out at us: dark hair, white dress or robe. But the jeep accelerated quickly and in the rain, I couldn't be sure.

We bumped and splashed out to the main road and turned north. "Step on it, Peters," Anderson said. "It's going to get dark early tonight."

The village ended abruptly at a bridge. There was concertina wire strung over the railings and all around the embankments at the entrance to the bridge, and cylinders of sandbags were piled high around a couple of machine gun emplacements next to the road. The check point at the entrance to the bridge was manned by American MPs. Peters pulled to a stop and one of the MPs walked briskly over to our jeep. He bent down and looked carefully at each one of us. Suddenly he straightened up and saluted. "Good afternoon, Lieutenant Anderson," he said. "You better get that top down, sir."

Anderson groaned. "Come on, Peters, let's do it. Quickly."

The two of them began stripping off the canvas top. The MP helped. Jack and I looked at each other as the rain began to fall on us.

"You have a poncho?" Jack asked me.

"No. You?"

"Christ no."

"What's the matter there, guys?" Anderson said, smiling thinly down at us. "Haven't you ever been wet before?"

Jack scowled at him. We pulled our field jacket hoods up over our caps. Anderson and Peters wedged the canvas top in behind Jack and me, between us and the spare tire. Then we started off again. Slowly we crossed the barbed-wired bridge. The river below was muddy and brown, and didn't seem to be moving. It was a couple hundred meters across. The rain was not heavy, and each drop that hit the water sent out rings that ran into other rings.

"Styx," Jack suddenly said.

"Pooh sticks?" I said, not understanding, reminded by the river and the bridge of a children's story my mother used to read me.

"No," said Jack. "The River Styx."

"That's the Imjin River, sir," Peters informed us from the driver's seat.

The dirt road on the other side of the bridge was in sorry shape. It had washboard bumps and potholes. The town of Chang-pa-ri did not exist on this side of the bridge: there were no houses, no rice paddies, no civilians. We picked up speed. The rain was blowing directly into my face. I had the visor of my baseball cap pulled down over my eyes and my field jacket hood tied tightly around my face. In the crowded back seat, Jack and I sat with our feet propped up on luggage and our knees jammed beneath our chins.

Anderson turned around and flicked on the big receiver/transmitter beside Jack. He waited for it to warm up and then twisted the squelch dial till he was getting plenty of static. He eyed us but didn't speak to us. The windshield was keeping the rain off him. He said to Peters, "You should have taken the trailer down this morning."

"I didn't know we were getting two of 'em, sir."

Anderson said to us, "It's only a half hour to Matta. It won't be too bad."

"I've got a raincoat in my duffel bag," Jack Evans shouted. "It's underneath all this shit. How about stopping so I can get it out?"

"No way," said Anderson. "I don't have time. Your field jacket'll have to do."

20

"What's this place like?" Jack said.

"What place?"

"Camp Matta. The DMZ."

"Terrible," said Anderson, and he turned around and faced forward again.

"You sound bitter," Jack observed. We were driving fast down a narrow dirt road between low, thick walls of unidentifiable vegetation. There wasn't a tree in sight. "The place looks just swell to me." Jack seemed eager to quarrel with Anderson. "It's a little wet, and cold, but if you'd stop for a moment and let me get a raincoat out of my duffel bag. . . ."

Anderson turned around. He was not smiling. "You got in yesterday, right? What's your name?" He read Jack's name tag. "Evans. Well, you're a clever guy, Evans. You're right. It's a great place. You're going to love it here. Wait till you've been here a few weeks. The place grows on you—like a fungus. You won't mind the rain. The rain'll be the least of your worries. You won't mind the snow, either. You'll be trying to stay sane. And alive."

"Sounds like you're glad to be leaving."

Anderson did not reply. He faced forward again.

We drove without talking for a while, and then the radio static cut out and a noise I couldn't identify came through the speaker. It was one long, drawn out syllable, like a moan or a belch. Jack jumped. "What the hell was that?" he said.

Anderson ignored the question. He stared out the jeep at the passing landscape.

Peters finally answered. "That's Short, sir."

"Who's that?"

"It's not a 'who.' It's what he said. Some guy gettin ready to DEROS, braggin about how short he is."

Jack and I exchanged glances. "Of course," I said.

The rain water dripped off my chin and Jack's, and the wind whipped past our faces and stung our cheeks. The jeep lurched and bounced, throwing us against one another. Nobody talked for a long time. Finally we turned off the main road, whizzed past another checkpoint, and continued on up a hill. After we topped the hill, we entered a shallow valley. Camp Matta lay spread out before us. Low hills surrounded the camp; the valley was taken up by roads, Quonset huts, shacks, military vehicles, antennas. A few of the green Quonset huts were sandbagged six feet or so up their sides. Off the road at the north edge of camp I could see two armored personnel carriers. They glistened in the rain, their smooth metal hulls shining, wet, and dark. Their .50 caliber machine guns were thin shapes like swords under dripping ponchos, and their radio antennas struck into the sky like lances.

We jerked to a stop not too far into the compound. "There you go," said PFC Peters. We all climbed out. L had difficulty standing up. It was still raining. Peters helped Jack and me with our bags. We had three apiece, and after we'd pulled them all out of the back of the jeep, we had a substantial pile of baggage sitting in the middle of the road.

I was so cold my teeth were chattering. "What next?" I asked Anderson, who stood off to one side, watching.

"Don't ask me," he said impatiently. "I'm not your squad leader. Come on, Peters, I'm late."

Peters said, "That's one of the BOQs up there, sir." He pointed toward a Quonset hut above us, part way up the hill. "You might bring your stuff up there and then that's the battalion headquarters, right there." He pointed to another Quonset hut just behind us, near the road. There was a bare flagpole in front of it.

"Peters!" Anderson was climbing into the jeep.

"Yes sir." Peters hopped in behind the wheel. He swung the jeep around and headed out away from Camp Matta.

Jack and I looked at one another. We were soaking wet.

I grinned at Jack. "Welcome to the 1st of the 31st," I said. "Friendliest battalion this side of North Korea."

He bowed and gestured up the hill. "After you, Lieutenant." We shouldered our duffel bags, picked up our wet suitcases and garment bags, and climbed toward the BOQ.

Jack and I changed into dry fatigues and then dropped off our personnel files at headquarters. The clerk told us the battalion commander wanted us to report to him after supper. We walked around the compound and found the mess hall without much difficulty: it was the Quonset hut with the long line. Compared to the relative splendor in which we'd dined the previous evening, it was a greasy spoon. The table cloths were plastic, the flatware stainless steel; the meat and potatoes and green beans all tasted like cottonseed oil.

By the time we walked back to the headquarters building, the sky had partially cleared and a few bright stars were visible in the purple sky between the clouds. We waited in an outer office. The clerk was still on duty, and so was the battalion sergeant major. They were busy shuffling paper and typing, but the sergeant major seemed curious about us and struck up a conversation. His name was Allen. He was a short, grizzly old soldier with a pencil-thin gray mustache above his small mouth. He asked us all the standard questions: where were we from, what units had we served with, what special training had we received, and had we by any chance run into Sergeant So-and-so who was stationed at Fort Benning just about the same time? He had a marvelous way of saying the word "sir" to a second lieutenant that made it a well-intentioned joke, something not to be taken too seriously.

Jack was sent in to see the battalion commander first. The sergeant major went back to his typing, and before too long Jack came out and I went in. What struck me as unusual when I shook hands with Colonel Curtis was what he was wearing. His fatigues looked brand new. They were dark green and fit loosely. His shirt was too big and heavily starched, and the shirt front ballooned out from his chest as though he had a large bust. He looked like an old woman with a crew cut. He didn't have an airborne patch or a CIB. He must have been sixty years old, and he sat behind his desk and looked at me with large, watery eyes and smiled beneficently.

"Sit down, please, Lieutenant Richardson. You must have had a long trip."

"I got drenched, sir. The ride up from Camp Casey was horrendous."

"Quite a downpour, I know. Well, you have to get used to that here, that's all there is to it. Tell me, how long ago did you leave the States?"

We talked for a few minutes: idle conversation. Colonel Curtis's questions did not deal with the military. He asked about my home, my father's occupation, the schools I'd attended, my college major and extracurricular activities. He didn't seem to be grilling me—we chatted as though we were at a cocktail party—but he got a lot of information out of me in a very short while.

A knock on the door interrupted us. A captain walked in.

"You sent for me, sir?"

"Yes. Norm, this is Arthur Richardson. He is just in from the States."

I stood up and shook hands with the captain. "How do you do, sir?"

He had hazel eyes that gazed at me steadily. "Lieutenant."

Colonel Curtis finished the introduction. "This is Captain Stewart, Arthur. He is our S-3." The Colonel turned to Captain Stewart. "There's a Lieutenant Evans in the other room, Norm."

"I know, sir. I just met him."

"Bring him in, will you?"

"Yes sir." Captain Stewart ducked out of the office and returned in a moment with Jack. We stood expectantly in front of Colonel Curtis's desk.

"Gentlemen," he said, "I want to brief you on our situation here. Norm, correct me if I'm wrong on anything or if you disagree. We are not in a good position. We're strictly on the defensive. That's a bad way to be and we've had trouble. The North Koreans seem to be able to come and go almost at will. We're not sure why. We've got patrols out every night, men along the fence, hilltop guardposts in the middle of the zone near the border. But it just seems like when they want to get through, they do. They get up to the fence and wait till some GI or Katusa falls asleep, and then they cut through and go. It's embarrassing. Our mission is to stop them. We aren't very good at it."

"Do we engage them on sight, Colonel?" Jack said.

"Oh yes, Lieutenant. We have orders to shoot on sight. But who sees them? They never travel during daylight, only at night. And that's one of the odd things about the situation. We almost never make contact at night either. They avoid contact almost entirely—unless that's their sole purpose. They've been known to ambush jeeps in or near the DMZ, but they don't do it often. Now Captain Stewart here thinks they might be digging tunnels under the DMZ. Don't you, Norm?"

"Could be, sir. I know you disagree, but that would explain why we make contact so seldom."

"Well, who knows, maybe you're right. Anything else to add?"

"No sir," said Captain Stewart.

We waited while Colonel Curtis put on a pair of glasses and

leafed through the files on his desk. Finally his watery eyes peered over the top of his glasses at Captain Stewart. "Well, Norm, I think we should keep both these officers at the battalion level. They have useful experience, Evans as company XO and Richardson in training. I know you need help so I'm going to give you both of them. Their administrative experience should come in handy. I think it's a good match." His eyes focused on Jack and me. "Gentlemen, Captain Stewart here, my S-3, will be your new boss. He's the battalion Operations Officer and a damn good one, too. He's been to Vietnam. I expect you to work hard for Norm and for this unit. We're a good battalion and our mission is extremely important. Pay close attention to what Norm tells you —you can learn a great deal from him, and you better learn quickly. There's no room for mistakes here. Any questions?" He peered over his glasses from one of us to the other.

We shook our heads. "No sir."

"All right. Good luck to you both. That'll be all."

"Thank you, sir."

"Colonel."

Jack and I saluted, about-faced, and followed Captain Stewart out the door. He walked briskly past the clerk and the sergeant major, through another door and out into the night. Jack and I followed. The sky had cleared and the air was cool. A few lights shone across the compound, and above us the sky was plastered with stars, all of them ages away.

We went next door. The TOC, the Briefing Room, and the S-3/S-2 office nearly adjoined the headquarters building. This Quonset hut was heavily sandbagged, making apparent the fact that it was one of the important buildings in the compound. We went through a door and walked straight through a couple of small rooms to a large office, which contained metal desks and file cabinets. Maps hung on every wall. The floor was bare concrete, and florescent lights dangled from the ceiling. The walls and ceilings were painted green. I noticed a bucket sitting on one of the desks, half-filled with dirty water. Either it was leftover coffee, or the roof leaked.

Doubtless he had inherited the place, not created it, yet Captain Stewart matched his office the way dog owners resemble their dogs. He looked as rough in texture and as hard as the concrete floor, and his blank facial expression was about as welcoming as the dull coldness of the florescent lighting and the gray steel desks.

He walked to the desk at the far end of the room, swung around, and sat down on the desk top. He wore a pistol belt, holster, and .45 caliber pistol strapped to his waist; a flak jacket, unzipped and hanging open at his chest; and a steel helmet with a dirty camouflage helmet cover. His insignia of rank, two parallel, vertical black bars, had been sewn on the front center of the helmet cover. His fatigues were a faded green, wrinkled and dampened no doubt by the same storm that had drenched Jack and me, and his old shirt had an 82nd Airborne patch on the right sleeve and a CIB over the left pocket. The red, weather-burned skin on his thin face was lined like the maps on the walls.

Captain Stewart took off his helmet and put it down; it clunked heavily on the metal desk. His hair was black and cut very short. Under the fluorescent lights, the white skin on the top of his head shone through the short bristles of his black hair.

He looked us over for a moment.

"First thing I want to do," he finally said, his lips barely moving, "is get you two squared away in your respective jobs." He paused and continued to stare at us. "The Colonel says you're well qualified. That may be. I haven't seen your files and I don't intend to look at 'em. I'd rather hear it from you."

He paused again. The silence dragged on. I wondered if he had asked us a question.

Finally he continued. "Now I have two slots open. I need an Assistant 3 and a fence-walker. Evans, the S-1 clerk tells me you outrank Richardson by four days. What's your choice?"

Captain Stewart's small hazel eyes peered intensely at Jack.

Jack glanced at me, then back to Captain Stewart. "I don't know, sir. Which job will get me closer to the action?"

The skin around Captain Stewart's eyes and mouth crinkled slightly: a smile. "What 'action' do you want to get closer to, Lieutenant?"

"North Koreans, sir. Quite frankly, if you don't mind my saying so, I'd rather be with a company. Patrolling. I'd like a chance to see action, engage the enemy."

"You explained this to Colonel Curtis, no doubt."

"Yes sir."

"Well, he made this assignment with your preferences in mind, so if I were you I'd forget what you want to do and concentrate on what you've got to do. Now I'll ask you once more, do you like to work, or don't you?"

"I don't understand, sir."

"It's simple, Evans. I mean just what I say. Would you rather work, or fuck off?"

Jack said, "I guess I'd rather work, sir."

"Don't bullshit me now, Evans. I'm giving you a choice. It doesn't matter to me. If you want to screw around, maybe wait and see if you can get transferred down to a company, I can arrange that."

"No sir. Just put me to work."

"How about you, Richardson?" He turned that gaze on me.

"I'd rather be busy, sir."

"All right. We'll see. For now, it seems you'd both prefer the Assistant 3 slot. There's more work involved, longer hours. And probably more time up at the DMZ, too. That means you got it, Evans. You're my new Assistant 3. Richardson, you'll walk the fence. Twice a day, every day. What you do in your spare time is your business. Just make those walks. If you miss one—just once —you'll be in more trouble than you ever imagined. You report directly to the battalion commander, not to me. Twice a day, after your walk." He paused. "Questions?"

"Sir," I asked, "who's got this job now?"

"Lieutenant Anderson."

"I was afraid of that."

"He's leaving tomorrow."

"Good."

"Go see him. Tonight. He'll fill you in on details. Tomorrow morning's his last fence-walk, so you go with him. You haven't got much time to learn your job, but it's not complicated. Just make sure Anderson tells you everything you need to know. Lieutenant Evans, you're going to come with me now. Other questions?"

"No sir."

"All right. Richardson, you're dismissed to go draw gear. I trust you can find the Supply Room without my drawing you a map. My driver's got a weapon and flak jacket for you, Evans. Helmet too. I'll give you a look at the DMZ tonight."

He shut off the lights as we left. A jeep was parked alongside the building, its motor idling. The driver's cigaret glowed in the darkness. Jack and Captain Stewart climbed into the jeep and the driver started off without a word. The jeep accelerated past the headquarters building and out toward the gate. Overhead, the stars seemed brighter than before, and farther away. The compound was still, and I could hear the spring songs of frogs and night insects. I walked back to the BOQ to find somebody who'd tell me where the Supply Room was.

May 3
BOQ, Camp Matta, Korea

This place is a shithouse. I don't even have a bed for tonight. No one in the BOQ has been friendly, like the fact that they've been here for a while makes them better than me. Fuck them. I don't see anything but a bunch of babies. Insecure kids trying to act tough.

I wish I knew what drove me into the infantry along with these dullards and jackasses—

I may owe my country something. But my life?

Why *shouldn't* I be one of the front-line soldiers, one of the infantrymen? If somebody's got to die for their country, why shouldn't it be me?

But why should it?

I would never have chosen to be here. Yet I'm here. I could die here. How'd I let myself get so fucked?

THREE

I LAY ON THE FLOOR THAT NIGHT
in the middle of a four-man room. People came and went into the
early morning, and a group of men talked and drank in the living
room at the end of the Quonset hut. Probably a going-away party.
After Colonel Curtis and Captain Stewart and Jack came in at
one-thirty or two in the morning, things quieted down.

I felt the toe of a combat boot in my ribs.

"Let's go, Richardson."

It was four o'clock and dark. I pulled on my fatigues, boots,
pistol, field jacket, flak jacket, helmet. Anderson was shaved,
starched and pressed. I wore the wrinkled fatigues from the day
before and didn't stop to shave.

On the road in front of the BOQ, Peters waited in the idling
jeep. Anderson and I walked down the steps, climbed in, and we
were off. The wind in my face was cold and fresh, and the moist
night air smelled like spring grass.

We left Camp Matta and turned north. The sky was clouded
over and visibility was almost nil. At a checkpoint, where a guard
saluted us, Peters turned off his headlights and switched on the
blackout lights. They cast a faint bluish gleam onto the road

in front of us. We drove for about twenty minutes, and then we seemed to arrive somewhere because the jeep stopped. I knew we must be near the barrier fence. We sat in silence. I expected Anderson to say something, to tell me about the place or the routine or my new job and its responsibilities, but he said nothing, just stared ahead. Peters lit a cigaret, hunkered down in his seat, and began to nod off. We waited. I didn't know what we were waiting for, but I was damned if I was going to ask.

It finally happened without my seeing it. The sky, suddenly, was no longer black. The clouds to the east turned pearl gray.

"Daylight," Anderson murmured. "Come on." He got out of the jeep and headed up a hill.

Then I saw the fence. It loomed in front of us; we had parked not six feet from it. It was much taller and heavier than that little thing at Tongduchon, surrounding Camp Casey. It was the tallest Cyclone fence there was, and in addition, it had triple concertina wire strung along the top. I couldn't conceive of climbing over. It was rusty and huge—it overwhelmed everything. There was nothing to be seen anywhere that was close to it in height, except for the hills themselves.

Anderson was walking steadily up the hill along the fence, and I slipped out of the jeep. The springs squeaked loudly, but Peters slept on. His chin rested on his chest, his eyes were shut, and his cigaret was burning down near his fingers. I walked around the jeep, grabbed Peters by the shoulder and shook him.

"Peters."

"What!" His eyes sprung open and he reached for his rifle.

"Your cigaret," I said.

He tossed the butt into the road. He stretched and looked around. "Where's Lieutenant Anderson?" he asked.

"He just started off." I pointed. Anderson had almost reached the top of the hill.

Peters grinned at me. "I wouldn't give him that much of a head start if I was you, sir. He's been walking this fence for a damn year."

"But why, Peters? *Why* does he walk the fence?"

He looked at me with amazement. "He's looking for holes, Lieutenant. Goddamn, didn't nobody tell you? The fuckin gooks infiltrate through here, that's what everybody's here for. Fence don't stop 'em; they cut right through it. Lieutenant Anderson checks it every morning. He double-checks the troops and the company commanders."

"Thanks!" I slapped him on the shoulder. "See you later."

I started off toward the east, up the first steep rise, picking my way among the rocks. I was out of breath by the time I reached the crest. At the top there were sandbags, a foxhole, and two soldiers manning the position.

"Morning, sir," one of them said.

"Nice day for a walk, eh, Lieutenant?"

And it was. I stopped, staggered by the view from the hilltop: valleys, hills, a stream, a marsh. To the north, mountains; to the east, the sky changing color from violet to pink; clouds breaking up, the sun almost visible at the horizon, a breeze, and birds wheeling on the wind.

Korea. Land of the Morning Calm.

And that fence. My God, I thought, how can such a thing be beautiful? But it was. It looked as if some giant fisherman had cast it like a fishing line, flung it over the undulating country and let it lie there. The fence stretched across the land and its rusted chain links caught the light from the morning sky and the light turned it red, and it became a soaring red curtain rising and falling, following the contour of the hills, draped over summits, stretched across valleys, running, turning, diving, then climbing in free flight across valleys and hills.

I saw Anderson below me, just starting across a low stretch of marshland, his head cocked to the left, watching the fence as he walked. I started after him and hurried to catch up. At the bottom of the hill, near a small stream, a sergeant, wearing a steel helmet and flak jacket, a rifle slung over his shoulder, stood beside a green wall of sandbags and sipped steaming coffee from a plastic cup.

How had he come by hot coffee way up here?

He saluted. "Morning, sir."

"Morning, Sergeant."

I crossed the stream and slogged over wet ground, tramping on boards that had been laid across the mud. Then up the next hill.

I hurried. I kept Anderson in sight, and I found myself jogging at times. But I couldn't catch him.

There were foxholes all along the fence, one or two soldiers in or near each one. In the low ground, near the stream and the marsh, there were towers, raised platforms with sandbagged walls and roofs. Boards crossed the soggy ground along the fence, and some split off toward the towers. East of the towers the ground rose and turned dry. Instead of towers there were foxholes. The foxholes were small, but every one or two hundred meters there was a much bigger hole surrounded by elaborate sandbag fortifications. Two or three men, one of them an NCO, occupied these squad or platoon command positions, which were equipped with telephones. There were occasional fighting positions, too: sandbag walls behind which nobody had bothered to dig a hole.

The dirt to the south of the fence had been worn bare by soldiers, waves of them I imagined, coming and going twice each day like tides at a beach. The earth just past the fence to the north was bare too. It was mined. I'd heard about this minefield in the States, during training: it was notorious because it was full of the new antipersonnel mines, little plastic ones, each with a small shaped charge that exploded upward into your foot. Just your foot. Or maybe it'd shatter your shin bone too or your knee if your heel came down squarely on it.

The sun rose and I began to sweat, and I still hadn't caught Anderson. I wasn't used to the helmet or the flak jacket, and my shoulders ached and sharp pains shot up the back of my neck. The helmet bobbed about on my head and the leather band held it too loosely and began to rub my forehead. I stopped and adjusted it, then hurried on. My flak jacket was heavy and hot over my field jacket, so I unzipped them both but then the cool air chilled my damp fatigues, so I had to zip up the jacket again.

I caught Anderson eventually, but he didn't notice. He cruised, walking fast and steady, confident of his footing. Up hills and down, with the sun rising over everything, Anderson's pace seemed never to vary. And all the way, his eyes remained fixed on the fence.

Finally it was over. There was Peters in the jeep at the bottom of a hill; there was the place where the ROK Army sector of the DMZ began. Abruptly, the fence ended; where the American sector stopped, so did the fence.

I climbed into the back seat of the jeep, aching and thankful. We pulled away from the fence. Anderson picked up the radio handset, pressed the push-to-talk switch, and the transmitter beside me began to whine.

"Six-eight, this is two-niner, over."

There was a pause. Then: "Two-niner, this is six-eight, over."

"Six-eight, this is two-niner. I have an 'up' for you this morning, over."

"Two-niner, this is six-eight." By now I had recognized the methodical voice of the battalion commander. "Roger, two-niner. Is this your last one, over?"

We were in motion, driving back toward Matta, and Anderson had to shout over the noise of the jeep tires on the gravel road. "Six-eight, two-niner. That's affirm, over."

"Two-niner, six-eight. Roger. Congratulations. Don't forget to stop by and see me before you leave. Is your counterpart with you, over?"

"Six-eight, this is two-niner. That's affirm on both counts, over."

"Two-niner, this is six-eight. Roger. Out."

Anderson hooked the radio handset onto the dashboard, removed his helmet, and ran his hand across the top of his head. "Jesus Christ," I heard him say. "Jesus Christ." He put his helmet back on and buried his face in his hands. He stayed that way, breathing deeply, and occasionally his back and shoulders jerked spasmodically.

By the time we got to Camp Matta, whatever had passed through him was gone. Though I wanted to, I didn't ask him any questions. I stayed away from him. When I looked at Anderson, it was like looking at myself. This was the guy whose job I'd inherited, and his reactions to leaving Korea and returning to the States were not what I expected. Why wasn't he excited about leaving? Why wasn't he ecstatic?

I didn't know what was troubling him and I didn't want to find out. I was afraid the same thing would happen to me. But I knew, too, that he'd never tell me, even if I asked. So I didn't ask.

He left shortly after lunch. I moved my belongings into his bureau and desk, and I put my footlocker at the foot of his bed. I made the bed up with my own linen which I had drawn from the Supply Room.

That evening, the fence-walk was mine.

May 4th

If Anderson scared me because he was my future, what does that say about me? Why should I shy away from what's ahead of me?

What *was* bugging Anderson?

There are forces at work in my life that I have no control over, that I am only now becoming vaguely aware of. That is what this journal will be, the vehicle of my search for the truth. The truth about myself and other people.

What is motivating me and making me do the crazy things I do?

Why am I here?

I've got a past but no future. I've got a present, too. This journal will be a record of the present, but more important, it will be a search through my past—and through the present too as I travel through it—a search for my future.

FOUR

OVER THE NEXT FEW DAYS I learned when I had to be someplace and how to get there, squared away my living quarters, and began to get to know the people I'd be working and living with for a year. I drew a poncho and other clothing, bought two pair of boots with cleated soles, and signed for six hand grenades and a hundred rounds of .45 caliber ammunition. The grenades I carried in the jeep, and the bullets were for practice. I wanted to learn to shoot better, and there was a range on the way to the fence.

I found out that I had additional duties. Curtis and Stewart apparently wanted to exploit my experience on the college newspaper: one of my jobs would be to write Hostile Contact Reports. Anytime anyone received fire, whether it hit him or not—shot at, wounded, killed, didn't matter—I'd write it up: interview witnesses, try to piece together an accurate chronicle of what happened. Go where the action was after it was over.

Some afternoons, when I had nothing to do, I'd go back to the BOQ and read or write in my journal or take a nap. I was fond of those naps; time flew. One hot afternoon, though, as I lay stretched out on my bed, in my underwear, asleep, the hoarse buzz of a field phone woke me. At first I didn't know where I was. Then I saw the phone on the S-2's bureau, and I got out of bed and picked up the handset.

"Lieutenant Richardson speaking, sir."

"Colonel Curtis for you, sir. Hold one, please."

I waited.

"Yes. Richardson?"

"Speaking, sir."

"Yes. We have a helicopter coming in from brigade this afternoon. Now I don't need the darn thing, and Captain Stewart doesn't seem to want it either, so what I'd like you to do is take it up, fly around a bit and familiarize yourself with the battalion sector. From the air. You're the S-3 Air, after all, and I know you've seen maps, but you really should get oriented from the air. What do you say?"

"I'd be glad to, sir."

"Fine. You meet that helicopter then. He's due in at fourteen hundred." It was a quarter of. "It'll land right outside headquarters."

"Yes sir."

"All right. Out here."

I pulled on fatigues, a pair of boots, and my cap; then I buckled on my pistol and hurried over to the headquarters building. I sat on the grass, in the sun, and waited. I daydreamed about summer vacations on the lake in Vermont with nothing to do but sail and play tennis and water-ski.

I looked around. The headquarters building was at one edge of Camp Matta, near the entrance. The low hills to the west were overgrown with weeds and low bushes. Right in front of me, across from the triangular concrete slab of the helipad, near the flagpole, was a Korean grave. Whoever lay there must have been important, once, because the grave mound stood alone, guarded by stone figures, and it stood on level ground.

The Koreans usually buried their dead on the hillsides; that was the use to which they put land too steep to terrace and cultivate. Burial sites—graveyards—were slanting grassy fields bulging with grave mounds. The graves were unmarked lumps of earth that looked like giant, sod-covered eggs.

But the solitary grave mound in front of battalion headquarters stood on level ground. Not only that; it was watched over by four tall stone statues. The gray, lichen-covered human figures resembled six-foot-high chess pieces. They stood facing each other with blank expressions, two statues staring across the burial mound at the other two. Four long, unblinking stares. I stared at them until the helicopter arrived.

The chopper was an old one, small, with a clear plastic bubble for a cockpit, a metal framework for a tail, and room for two or three people. It came into view over the hills behind the BOQ looking like a huge bumblebee, and it headed toward the concrete triangle that served as a helipad. As it approached, the American flag on the flagpole stirred lazily, then began flapping violently. With a rush of wind and a great roar and clatter, the machine settled onto the helipad. I ran out to the helicopter, ducked under the blur of the blades, opened the right-hand door. I'd never been in a helicopter before. I stepped up into the cockpit, sat down on the dry, cracked leather seat, and reached out with my right hand to swing the door shut. A hand gripped my left forearm. I looked at the pilot.

He wore a white flight helmet with a small radio mike that curved around from the side of the helmet to his mouth. He was light: blond hair under the helmet, bushy blond eyebrows, thin mustache, pale blue eyes. He was looking at me, but his eyes avoided my face. He was looking down. At my mouth? My throat?

He shouted at me: "Where is your Colonel?"

I knew, then, what he was looking at: my insignia of rank, the gold bar sewn onto the collar of my fatigue shirt.

"He's not flying today. I'm taking his place."

The pilot stared at me. He had expected a lieutenant colonel, and he'd gotten a lieutenant. I slammed the door shut and buckled the seat belt across my lap. The helicopter rocked gently from side to side. I struggled with the shoulder harness and finally snapped it tightly to the lap belt at my hips.

The engine roared, the machine vibrated and shook and rattled till I thought pieces of steel and plastic would tear loose and fly off, and then the ground tilted, dropped away, and our shadow began to move along the ground, and we were flying, gathering height and speed. The Quonset huts shrank and the sky loomed larger, and suddenly we were above the low hills that surrounded Camp Matta, and Christ, I could see everything from up there:

green rolling hills, blue mountains, gray haze at the horizon. Above us, the sun shone; below, birds swirled and wheeled in flocks, light specks against a dark green background.

Something hard struck my knee. The pilot was holding a flight helmet out to me, gesturing.

"Put it on!" he shouted.

I removed my cap and took the helmet from him. Like the pilot's, this helmet had a radio mike and wires leading to the instrument panel; its inside, as I slipped it over my ears, smelled briny, like an old shoe. And now I could hear the pilot's voice right beside my ear, speaking to me from the earphone in the helmet: "If you want to talk, hit that button on the floor by your left foot." I looked down at the steel floor and saw something that looked like an automobile dimmer switch, marked INTERCOM. I stepped on it with the toe of my boot.

"OKAY!" My own voice shouted in my ear. "Okay," I said quietly, "I got it."

We flew along, the machine swaying and rattling. I looked down: brown grass, thick green vegetation, small hills; a dirt road which I didn't recognize. Strange country: no trees, but wild, overgrown. No villages or houses, no rice paddies. Overhead: deep blue sky, streaks of cloud very high, radiant sun.

"Where are we going?" I said into the microphone. As soon as I said it, I realized it was a mistake. I should have told him where we were going. But I didn't know where I wanted to go. I didn't know the country from the ground, much less from the air. In this foreign element, I felt completely at the mercy of the pilot.

"We're going to the river," said the pilot.

I noticed a compass above the instrument panel. It was centered on 'S.' So he was heading south toward the Imjin River. "Why the river?"

He looked over at me, grinned behind the little microphone in front of his mouth. "Have some fun," he said.

And then there it was, right before us: a wide, curving river, muddy—a light tan color—sweeping in from the west, making a long S-curve in front of us, and then, in the distance, finally straightening out and continuing on to the east; but lazy—no sign of motion to it, no white water, no waves, looking in fact like a long curving lake, muddy and still.

Off to the east I could make out Libby Bridge spanning

the river, and beyond it the huts and streets and rising smoke of Changpa-ri. Beyond the village, to the south, were mountains, and that gray haze at the horizon.

Then we were over the brown water, and we made a turn and began to follow the river. I looked at the pilot; he was staring down at the river, his mouth set, his thin white mustache tense and bristling. What was he up to? 'Have some fun'? What did he do for fun over the Imjin River?

He dropped down toward the muddy water. The sun reflected off the river's smooth surface and created a dazzling white glare. We flew along rather slowly, I thought. The blond pilot was looking for something down there, looking for something in the river. What could he see beyond the sun, in all that mud?

He raised the aircraft a few feet, then he quickly banked, turned, settled in again, and we were flying back the way we had come, only this time, rather than chase the sun, we chased our own shadow—it flew along below us looking rather opaque, its border fuzzy, undefined. The shadow seemed to come to rest below the surface of the water, settling slowly and gradually in the cloudy water itself.

"There!" shouted the pilot. I jumped.

"Where?"

"There! Look!" He was pointing, beginning to circle and gain altitude. The river looked unchanged to me. "See? See?" he yelled. "There they go! *Look at those little bastards!*" His voice blared painfully in my ear. There was a tone to it that was familiar, but that I couldn't precisely identify.

Then he stood the helicopter on its nose, the bottom dropped out, and he dived straight toward the Imjin. The engine seemed to stop entirely, and as that light-brown river filled the plastic bubble in front of me I saw for the first time what that crazy pilot was after. In the water before us small dark streaks appeared, little black darts in the mud, dozens of them, a hundred of them, and they were moving slowly, lazily in unison.

The pilot pulled out of the dive, leveled off inches above the water, skimmed toward the school of fish and as we passed over them, he tilted the helicopter and plunged my side into the water. There was a splash, the river tugged at the helicopter, we yawed to the right—I thought we'd be dragged in, flip over—and then the skid beneath me came free of the river and we climbed, circled, and I could see the splash we had created, its rings widening. The fish had scattered and were darting back and forth, trying to regroup.

"Yeeee-hoooo!" yelled the pilot—but there was no smile on his face—and he wheeled the helicopter around like a stallion and dived back toward the fast-moving shadows in the Imjin's mud. Again he buzzed the fish, again he dropped my skid in the water right in the middle of the school, again we caromed up and away and whirled around to watch the fish scatter. But I was watching the pilot. Behind that microphone, beneath those bushy eyebrows and that thin mustache, beyond the jagged plane of his lightly tanned face I thought I could see shadows moving, little shadows darting back and forth just like those fish, and now I could identify the nature of the sound of those words he had uttered ("Look at those little bastards!"). It was anger. He was filled with some kind of self-destructive rage, and here I was sitting beside him—here to "have some fun"—and he was going to put all three of us into the river, me, him, and this ancient helicopter. But who the fuck was he? No one, a stranger, a maniac. A helicopter pilot, a WO1. I outranked the son of a bitch by at least three grades.

I finally found the intercom switch with the toe of my boot. We were hurtling downward toward the water.

"That's enough fishing for today," I said. "Turn back."

He gave me a furious look.

"Right now."

He didn't quarrel. He pulled the ship out of its dive, inches from the surface of the river. He pounded my skid into the Imjin River once more—muddy water splashed all over the canopy—and then we rose, circled, and flew high and swiftly back to Camp Matta.

May 18th
That pilot had complete control over me. I was at the mercy of a maniac.

What's important is control. Not power (control over others). Simply control over oneself, one's life. To plan and to carry out those plans. That's control. That's what I lack altogether. No plans, no control.

I need to find out how I wound up here on the Korean

DMZ, of all crazy places. Riding around with a suicidal pilot. And then I need a plan for the future.

The search:
An only child. Bloomfield, Connecticut. Father, an insurance executive. Mother, a housewife and volunteer. Private school in winter, a lake in Vermont in summer. I had it all.

I miss my parents. I miss the family kitchen, its warmth, the smell of cooking (bacon, chicken, roast beef), the clatter of pots and dishes and the rustle of Dad's paper. The way a sip of Dad's beer tasted. I miss the lake in the summer and the cabin. At dusk the deer would come down to the water and drink. And I miss crewing for Dad in sailing races; then as I grew up, losing to him in a borrowed boat; and finally beating him. I miss my bedroom, I miss the high school gym, and I miss the back seat of Dad's Olds and the smoothness of Suzy Wilson's naked back when I removed her bra at Lighthouse Beach in the spring of '61. She smelled incredible.

But when I got home that morning, around six, Dad met me at the front door in his bathrobe. "I thought it was the paper!" he snorted, and walked back into his study, the back of his neck pink with anger. He was mad at me often in those days, after I got my driver's license. I always wanted the car and stayed out too late. He gave me curfews and I did not observe them.

Once when I was little, at the dinner table, we were eating steak and I had a monstrous piece of meat impaled on the end of my fork and I was raising it toward my mouth when I heard his voice booming from the head of the table: "Cut it in two, Art, cut it in two!" I put the meat on my plate, sliced it cleanly in half with my steak knife, stabbed both pieces with the fork and crammed the entire mess into my mouth.

The morning of May 20th was cool and moist. The air at first light held the rich organic fragrance of springtime, and the world smelled like a greenhouse. I drew in deep lungfuls and savored the air, the substance of it, the moist texture of it. At first, walking felt good. Blood pulsed through my arteries, and as I walked I was aware of the pressure of blood in my fingertips. Climbing the third or fourth hill, though, I became short of breath and my chest began to ache. Farther on, my crotch started rubbing and then became raw and began to sting viciously because I had forgotten to spread Vaseline on the insides of my thighs. My left foot bothered me, the ball of it, a severe pain I'd had since basic training. It had become excruciating since I'd begun walking the fence, three or four miles twice a day. I was limping and I thought: Should I go on sick call and see Doc Lang about it?

Not likely.

I still was not accustomed to the weight of my flak jacket and helmet. The steel pot caused a sharp ache in the muscles at the back of my neck and between my shoulder blades. The hot pain spread as I walked. When I was done walking, my neck and back, my inner thighs, and my left foot burned and stung like crazy. I was an organism aware only of its own pain. I collapsed into the jeep, panting and thankful. That I'd discovered no holes in the fence seemed incidental; I was in such agony I didn't care. I called the Colonel and gave him an 'up.'

He sounded relieved to hear it. There had been an infiltration through the battalion on our left flank a couple of days before, and we had been jumpy ever since. Captain Stewart and Jack Evans and John Harmon, the S-2, had planned extra patrols and rear-area sweeps and ambushes. But no one made contact. So far we had been either a lucky or an accomplished battalion. There had been shooting along the fence practically every night, and reports of noises and movement. But no holes in the fence.

May 21

Something for the record:

The fence is located south of the DMZ. It's pure barrier. What if your family were on the other side? A split nation, divided. Separated. Lincoln. Davis. Kim Il Sung. Park Chung Hee. The Confederate States of Korea.

Imagine a fence stretching the length of the Mason-Dixon Line, today, in 1968, patrolled by blue and gray armies.

Wasn't Korea whole and complete for centuries? A union. And wasn't it divided not from within, not by its own rebellion and the will of its people, but from without? By foreign powers for foreign reasons?

Dissected the way a child might dissect a frog in biology class. Heart still beating, legs twitching.

The fence is 8' of cyclone fence topped by 3 rolls of concertina wire, the concertina about 3' in diameter.
Ways of getting through it:

> cut it and crawl through
> dig under it
> one guy put a board up against it
> and jumped over

But when you look at it from a distance—see it stretching across the countryside—it seems to move, to glide up hills, reach up and pull itself over the hilltops and zoom down, then run across the valleys like molten metal. In the wind it sings. It's a bristling, dangerous thing, anti-union, pro-separation. And yet when the orange light from a setting sun falls on its rusting links and posts, it can be beautiful.

That evening I saw my first deer. I sensed her watching me, and I looked up from the fence and she was there next to me, startlingly close, not ten meters away. The sun had already set, and in the twilight I clearly saw her profile: a slender head, one large brown eye, a long white tusk protruding from the side of her mouth. She was a little thing with no antlers, a doe. She was thin and looked very fragile. She had *tusks*. She was standing in a clump of scrub pine bushes in the A Company sector, and she was quivering slightly, watching me, her eye open very wide. Then in an explosion of movement she ran. She ran by leaps, seeming to bounce, tail bobbing, hind legs kicking up and fliging dirt. I caught flashes of her as she ran through brush that was waist high on me but was over her head, and every time she touched the ground she dropped from sight among the weeds and bushes, then immediately appeared a few meters ahead of where she had disappeared. She was out of sight before I fully realized I had seen her.

A doe with tusks: long curving teeth protruding like fangs from her mouth, slender white knives in the jaw of the most fragile-looking animal I'd ever seen.

May 22
For the record: The BOQ
The BOQ would make a terrific target for North Korean artillery. All the higher ranking battalion staff officers live

here. I assume we're plotted on North Korean maps as preplanned targets, small +'s. If they sent a barrage over at 3 or 4 in the morning, they'd stand a good chance of getting us all.

The BOQ is a Quonset hut with a latrine and a bunch of rooms. It has a small living room (five moth-eaten easy chairs and a plywood bar, empty, gathering dust), a large bedroom for the Colonel, and a hallway with single, double, and four-man rooms off it. It's a barracks with partitions and some privacy. You can go into a room here and close the door behind you.

I got the bunk by the latrine wall. The urinal flushes right next to my head. Harmon got the bunk under the window by virtue of the fact that he got here a few days before Jack and I did. There's a kind of *rank* associated with the length of time you've been in the country, like a seniority system, and Harmon takes full advantage of his seniority of a whole week or two. Plays the role of veteran to the hilt.

Dennis Sullivan is someone I rarely see or talk to. He's short, only another month or so left. He keeps announcing how many days he's got, and I don't listen.

Harmon and Jack Evans and Dennis Sullivan and I share the four-man match box at the end of the corridor. Harmon has to have his clothes and his bunk and his bureau arranged just so, his toothpaste and shampoo in the latrine arranged just so, his razor and shaving cream tucked away in his toilet kit just so every morning. I refuse to let him engage me in squabbles and bickering about his things:

"Richardson, did you take my Brasso?"

"Where are my jump boots?"

"I thought I had another fatigue shirt around here somewhere." He leans up close to my chest and peers at the name tag on my shirt. I have to refrain from putting my hand in his face. Things he does as S-2: plans all patrol routes and Guard Post reliefs. Both those things happen in the zone itself, yet he hardly ever leaves Matta, except to go in the other direction, into Changpa-ri.

Jack Evans is a nice guy. I like Jack. He is big and blond, blue-eyed, wide and muscular. He looks like a California beach boy but he's not, he's a Wisconsin farmer from Peewaukee Lake, or some such place, near Milwaukee. Nothing seems to bother him.

He has this quote hanging on the wall above his bunk:

Learn young about hard work and good manners—and you'll be through the whole dirty mess and nicely dead again before you know it.

—F.S.F.

FIVE

J UNE 1ST

For the record:

Pay day yesterday. We get combat pay ($65 per month).
The married guys get SEPARATION pay. Shit, I may not be
married, but I'm separated as hell.

What if I got separated from one of my arms or legs?

Some guys go crazy and buy Japanese cameras and watches
and stereo equipment down at the PX in Seoul, or custom-
tailored suits at the tailor at Camp Casey. Not me.

There's nothing to spend $ on here at Matta. Maybe I can
save enough so that I won't have to work for a few months
when (if?) I get back to the States.

But then what'll I do?

June 6

Sunny beautiful weather all day and tonight a star-filled
sky and my mood cannot be expressed. Most of the officers
hardly noticed, and some even affected a cynical attitude, but
I feel suddenly without hope. Especially after Harmon, that
asshole, said to me tonight: Good riddance. The fewer
Kennedys around, the better. He laughed. I don't know why I
didn't slug him.

Two Kennedys now, and King. Who next?

I went to the Green Door Hotel for the first time on Sunday, June 9. Jack, John Harmon and I rode to Changpa-ri in Harmon's jeep, down the dirt road between minefields marked by red triangular signs hung on single strands of barbed wire. It was a warm, sunny day; dust billowed into the air behind us. In Changpa-ri the narrow streets were crowded with chickens, children, soldiers, and women. One GI was walking down the street with a girl clinging to both arms, his hands on their rumps. Women sat in doorways and leaned from windows, leering at us.

Harmon leaned out of the jeep and shouted at one woman: "Hey, you fuckin skag! Gimme a break! Put a bag over your head!"

"I break you balls, cocksucker," she yelled back.

"Just don't look at me, bitch!" he shouted, laughing. Farther along, a woman in a doorway caught his eye, this one very fat, painted like a doll with pink cheeks and dark red lips. "Fuck you!" Harmon shouted at her. He gave her the finger.

She chased our slow-moving jeep and tried to clobber Harmon with her purse. She ran awkwardly in her high heels and tight skirt. Laughing, he fended her off, and she stopped and turned away, swearing and spitting. I watched her limp back toward her hootch.

The village smelled of dust and human sewage, and every so often a breeze would stir the air and we'd get a whiff of the river. We moved slowly through the cluttered streets, Harmon's driver being careful to avoid hitting people and chickens.

There was nothing remarkable about the Green Door Hotel. It was located on a quiet back street. The stuccoed walls had no windows, and no sign hung above the door. The door was not green. We walked through the door and found ourselves in a narrow hallway. There was a closet by the door, full of shiny black boots. If the owners of those boots ever had to leave in a hurry, they would all be wearing each other's footgear. I tied my laces together before I heaved my boots onto the pile. Then I followed Harmon and Evans down the dark hallway.

At the end of the hallway was a large living room, a dreadful-looking room with faded rugs, vinyl-covered metal furniture, a couple of worn couches and a few wooden tables. The tables were covered with round water marks from beer bottles and glasses. A small fan on a table pushed cigaret smoke around the room. There were some men sitting on the couches and chairs, and a few women. The men were Caucasian, the women Korean. The women were sitting on the men's laps and on the floor by their feet. They wore kimonos and the men wore bathrobes.

On one wall was a sign that said:

Make love *and* war!

There was a television going, a Korean program that everybody seemed to be watching. The image on the TV screen was the only thing in the room that seemed to be moving: a sobbing woman was trying to slap a man in the face. He caught her wrist in midair, before she struck him, and gave a sort of maniacal laugh. Then he smashed her in the face. She reeled back, flipped over a bed and crashed into a wall.

Just then a large, older woman entered the living room and hurried over to the three of us. She seemed to know Harmon, and she spoke to him.

"You late today, Lieutenant Harmon, you very late. All girls taken, we no have three more girls."

"Shit, Mama-san, I told you last week we'd be here."

"Only two coming, you say. Have two girls. You no tell me you bringing 'nother fella Green Door."

They all looked at me: the Korean Mama-san, Harmon, Jack Evans. "Hey, it's all right," I said. "I'll get Lesko to drive me on back. You guys go ahead."

"No no, stick around," Harmon said. He turned back to the woman. "Mama-san," he said, "come here a second." They went across the room and conferred.

Evans had already been to the Green Door with Harmon a couple of times. "They're busy today," he said, as though talking about a restaurant. He gestured at the people sitting around the room. "Sunday's always a busy day here. You get brigade officers and officers from other battalions with time to kill. This is kind of an Officers' Club. A whorehouse for commissioned officers only. It's small so it fills up quickly."

Harmon returned, looking exasperated. "Look, Richardson, since it's your first time here, Mama-san's agreed to go out of her way to accommodate you. She's going to find you someone, it'll take a little time is all, she'll have to send for someone. Give her some extra money. Not too much—a few dollars. Just relax for a while, have a beer, watch TV. She won't be long. I hope. See you later."

"Sure." But I wondered about the money. How much would be enough? Before I could phrase a question, Harmon disappeared down another hallway, and Jack winked at me and followed him.

I looked for a place to sit. There was a seat on a small couch next to an older man—a lieutenant colonel or a colonel, probably—who looked unshaven and sloppy and who wore a bathrobe so short it exposed his legs. He was a disaster. His legs, from his knobby knees down, looked like the legs of a frog, very thin and sinewy, his ankles thin, his slippers huge and hanging off the ends of two big frog's feet. He reminded me of Jeremy Fisher. He was drinking beer and watching television, and a Korean woman sat at his feet, her arms wrapped around his legs, stroking his calves and watching television. He looked like some bum on a tenement stoop, an old alcoholic, but the guy was probably a battalion commander or higher, perhaps a brigade staff officer or a brigade commander. Sitting in a whorehouse, drinking, watching a Korean soap opera, with a teen-age whore stroking his scrawny legs.

I went over and sat down. But not too close; I didn't want to touch those frog legs—they looked capable of inducing warts.

He turned and looked at me. The hairy stubble on his face was dark gray. I wasn't sure that I ever wanted to get that old. He turned his vacant, watery eyes back to the TV set.

"What outfit you with, Lieutenant?"

Had to be speaking to me. "First of the 31st, sir."

His eyes shifted over to me, and then away. "Is that a fact? Don Curtis's outfit? I never see him down here."

"Oh?"

"Nope. He must be a family man, faithful to the little woman back home." He looked at me again. "You married, Lieutenant?"

"No sir." I was staring at his bony legs and thinking of my father. He was about this man's age. Had he ever 'cheated' on my mother? Sat in a whorehouse while a teenager stroked his legs?

The old man droned on. "Nope. It's not the place for some married men, you know? A lot of them don't go in for this kind of thing. Now your battalion commander, Don Curtis, he seems like that kind to me. Faithful to the old lady, to the kids. Faithful to the idea of family. Me, I don't go in for that bullshit. Couldn't live that way. I figure a man gets over here, he gets horny, he's got to get some every now and then. A little separation compensation. Isn't that right, sweetheart?" He patted the girl on the top of her head. She ignored him. "Sure, I've got a wife back home, couple of kids, two daughters, both grown up now, one of 'em married. But what the hell, they're miles from here, you know? What good's a wife going to do a man when she's 10,000 miles around the globe, you know?" He looked at me.

"Yes sir, I know what you mean."

"That's why they give us separation pay, Lieutenant. I spend my separation pay right here. I'm separated, all right—10,000 miles and one year—but I compensate myself for it." His eyes focused on my face. "How long you been coming here, Lieutenant?"

"This is my first time."

"Thought so. Wondered why I hadn't seen you before. Been in the country long?"

"A few weeks, sir. Not long."

"Well, good luck, son. The DMZ's no picnic. But the old Green Door helps. Now me, I've been coming here for ten months, ever since I first arrived in Korea. Couldn't stand the country unless I got down here regularly. Got off the plane and came straight here."

Eventually the old man and his girl left. A pretty young woman came in, handed me a plate of something and a bottle of beer, picked up a few empties, and left the room. On the plate were some chicken wings. They appeared to have been fried.

I looked at the TV. A man was yelling at a woman and the woman was sobbing. It wasn't the first couple. I drank the beer and ate the chicken wings. Feeling drowsy, I turned sideways and rested my head on the back of the sofa and closed my eyes. I thought about the Kennedys, how they had gotten absolutely fucked, three brothers killed 'for their country'—hardly. The poor bastards. I was beginning to forget what I was there for, but finally Mama-san reentered the room. She looked around, spotted me, and came over.

"You come now," she said.

She led me down a hallway to a little room with pink plastered walls. I went in and Mama-san slid the door closed behind me. The room had no window, and it was dark. Four or five candles flickered dimly. The furniture was very dark—double bed, bureau, and wardrobe—teak, perhaps, or mahogany, black and deep brown. I was reminded of ancient rites taking place in torchlit caverns: the sacrifice of virgins. Could anything joyful possibly happen in this dark place?

I unbuckled my web belt and laid my pistol on the bureau. I pulled the tail of my fatigue shirt out of my trousers, unbuttoned and removed my shirt, and sat on the bed. I waited.

When she brought the girl, Mamasan opened the door and stepped into the room. Then she waited while the girl entered slowly, head down, looking at the floor. She was a thin little thing. She went and stood by the bureau, keeping her eyes down. Mama-san was standing by the door. I rose and took some bills out of my fatigue pants pocket. I pulled off a ten and handed it to her. She held her hand out. I pulled off another ten and handed her that one. She didn't flinch. A five. She looked me in the eye. Another ten. She pocketed the money somewhere in the folds of her wide skirt, bowed, and left the room. The door slid shut behind her.

The girl was lovely. She was young and slim, the smooth skin drawn tightly across the delicate bones of her face. She was holding the edge of the mahogany bureau with one hand; her hand was very narrow and her fingernails were cut short. She wore white pajama bottoms and a loose purple top that revealed no more than a hint of breasts. She looked like a kid.

June 9

. . . Did she arrive today straight from the orphanage? The orphanages supply the whorehouses with young girls, don't they?—and the whorehouses fill the orphanages with children. A self-perpetuating system. And I'm patronizing that system. She was such a small girl, so thin and delicate. I was afraid I'd hurt her. . . .

While I watched, she stepped over to the bed and lay down. She lay diagonally, leaving no room for me on the bed next to her. She made no move to undress.

I moved away from the door. I blew out the candles, all except one, went over to the bed and began to remove her clothes. I removed the slippers from her feet. I slipped off her pajama bottoms and then sat her up and helped her pull off her purple top. Her flesh felt very warm. Her bra slipped easily off her small breasts. Last, I removed her panties. She held her slim legs rigidly together and I had to tug to get them down, but I did. Her mouth quivered and she would not look at me. I wondered whether she had ever done this before.

I lay down next to her, still in my trousers and tee-shirt, and I ran my hand along her body, from her neck, across her flat breasts, down to her stomach. She looked very pretty in that golden candle light, this young girl—such smooth skin, soft and nearly hairless, small tight breasts, her belly sticking out a bit (was she already pregnant? Or was she merely still a child, her tummy plump in adolescence?), and though her lovely small body was desirable, I could not avoid looking at her face, at her trembling lip, at her large clear brown eyes which stared at the ceiling and registered neither pleasure nor pain but looked lost, and afraid.

Did I dare respond to that look? What sort of courage did it take not to act?

I kissed her cheek, and when she closed her eyes I kissed both her eyelids. Then I slid off the bed. I bent over and picked up her impossibly small and lightweight articles of clothing and handed them to her.

She moved gracefully to the edge of the bed and began to dress.

In the back seat of the jeep, on the way back to Matta, Jack poked me in the ribs and said, "Have a good time?"

"Yeah," I said. "It was great. I needed that."

June 13
    for the record:
    There's a Korean family with a pass that permits them to cross Libby Bridge. They have free access to the area between the river and the fence. They're a business, free enterprise at its best: they clear minefields for profit. Everyday they venture into the marked minefields south of the fence, strap on

the earphones of the home-engineered, jerry-built metal detector, and set about locating mines, digging them up, and then—so much fun—defusing them. They sell the disarmed mines for the price of the scrap metal. The family lives on the money they make from land mines they sell, a whole family supporting itself by clearing minefields. You see them now and then, off behind the fences that mark the minefields, their heads barely showing above the weeds and underbrush, the man wearing the earphones, the woman sitting off to the side surrounded by piles of damp, new-looking mines (they don't rust underground)—round mines, cylindrical mines, square mines: each one loaded with explosive and shrapnel. The kids play nearby.

Papa-san finds 'em and digs 'em up. Mama-san defuses 'em. Baby-san stacks 'em neatly. Good night. Sleep tight. Say your prayers by candlelight.

Walking the fence on a warm evening in mid-June, I spotted Sergeant Waters in one of the towers in the low ground in A Company. Sergeant Waters was a very large black man who always seemed to have something pleasant to say to me as I walked by. That evening he was cradling a large black object in the crook of his arm, apparently making adjustments on it. The object was tubular and metallic, and it looked about a foot long.

I stopped and shouted up at him: "Hey Sergeant Waters, what've you got there?"

"Starlight scope, Lieutenant. Don't you recognize it?"

"Never saw one before."

"Damn! I thought they *trained* you officers!" He shook his head. "Come on around here after dark, sir. I'll show you how to use it."

"I will. Thanks."

I ate supper and then called Captain Butler at his CP. Butler was an ornery bastard. Rumor had it that he'd been passed over for major twice. Fat and rather sloppy, he was the only captain commanding a company, and he got along with no one in the battalion but his own first sergeant.

I asked him if I could visit 27T that evening. He growled at me over the telephone. "What business you got in my company area at *night*, Richards? You trying to get yourself killed?"

53

I told him about Sergeant Waters' invitation.

"Ah hell. Why *my* company area?"

"Sergeant Waters—"

"*Fuck* Sergeant Waters! All right, you go down there and let Waters show you the starlight scope, but I ain't responsible for you. I don't like battalion officers in my company area, especially after dark. You take one peek through that scope and then you haul your ass outta there as fast as you can. Do you roger that?"

I told him I did.

The night was overcast and very dark. I made sure the troops on the fence knew I was coming. I shouted to them and told them who and where I was. I walked along a ridge from the road to the fence, and then I walked down the ridge to the low ground and carefully negotiated the planks in the mud. I arrived at the tower, sweating, without getting shot at. I climbed up. The pine boards smelled sweet, but their aroma was cut by the acrid odor of creosote.

A huge shape loomed up near the front of the tower and Sergeant Waters said, "Glad you made it, Lieutenant. Take a look." He handed me the scope. It was heavy, and awkward to hold. "You're supposed to mount it on a rifle," Waters said, "but I don't bother. If I see something, I just just line my rifle up with it. Or a grenade launcher. Then I pop a flare. If the thing moves, I shoot it. Go ahead, try it."

Standing beside Sergeant Waters, who dwarfed me, I looked through the scope. I saw nothing but green—light green and dark green. Bright, luminescent greens. I knew I wasn't holding it steady, so I leaned down and rested the starlight scope on the ledge.

"See anything, sir?" Sergeant Waters asked.

"Not much," I said. "Just a lot of green."

"Ain't nothing stirring tonight," he said. "Least not yet. But you ought to be able to make out that hill to the front of us. Or those bushes just down below there, or the fence."

Again I brought my eye close to the rubber-tipped eyepiece. The field of vision was a bright green disk with no depth. There was no clear way to distinguish one object from another: all I could see was a bright green circular field with brighter flashes of green here and there, lights and shadows, but no true images. No targets.

"Nope," I said finally. "I couldn't make out a *tank* if it was sitting out there."

"You got to learn to read it," he said. "Like a book. You got to learn to interpret the different shades, just like letters and words."

"Takes time, I'll bet."

"Yeah. Some. But it's worth it, 'cause when you get the hang of it you can make out anything. You learn to read those dark greens and light greens, and shoot, it's a miracle. You can see in the dark."

I gave the scope back to Sergeant Waters, and he continued his surveillance. I looked around the tower. It was an arsenal stocked with enough weapons and ammunition to hold off a company. Bandoliers of M-79 rounds hung from pegs in the walls, flares were lined up on the ledge at the front of the tower, an M-60 machine gun was standing in one corner, rifles and ARs stood in the other corners, and on a shelf below the front ledge stood a neat row of about two dozen hand grenades.

A moist breeze was blowing and I could hear the men on the fence yelling back and forth to one another. Occasionally a flashlight or a match flickered near the fence, but there wasn't much to see with the naked eye from the tower. Only to hear.

I had gradually become aware of a peculiar noise that seemed to come from the north. It was a droning sound that floated on the moist air, sometimes almost loud, most of the time barely perceptible. I concentrated on listening to it. After a while I thought I'd figured out what it must be: I'd heard that the North Koreans had set up a bank of huge public address speakers on their side of the MDL. That sound must be those speakers. I listened with that in mind, and sure enough, that was what it was. Huge speakers broadcasting propaganda. It sounded like English was being spoken, but I couldn't even be sure of that, much less make out the words.

"Sergeant Waters, are those the speakers I'm hearing?"

"Uh-huh. Yes sir, that's them all right."

"What are they saying?"

He sat back away from the starlight scope. "That's the Commander Bucher tape, sir. That there's the captain of the 'Pueblo.' You can't understand every word tonight, 'count of the moisture in the air and wind direction, but I've heard that tape maybe a hundred times. That's his confession you're listening to. He's confessing that he invaded North Korean territorial waters. Ain't that some shit now, Lieutenant?"

"Hm."

"I'll tell you one damn thing. That's one country I'd hate to be captured by." He leaned forward over the scope. "I don't think I'd ever surrender to those bastards. Rather be dead."

I didn't stay much longer. I was tired. It was late, and I had to be up at four. I thanked Sergeant Waters, then walked back to the jeep, and Peters and I drove back to Camp Matta.

That was the first time I was on the fence at night.

In my spare time, day or night, I often hung around the Tactical Operations Center back at Camp Matta. It was located in the sandbagged Quonset hut that also housed the S-3 and S-2 shops. The TOC was the nerve center, the cerebral cortex, the axons and neurons of the giant known as the 1st Battalion, 31st Infantry. At the TOC you could listen in on any radio transmission in the battalion, and hearing those radios, you got a sense of being tuned to the whole battalion and knowing everything that was going on. Also, there was always hot coffee at the TOC.

And I liked the three radio–telephone operators. They were entertaining. One of them was always on duty, and sometimes all three were there, bragging, complaining, telling stories. Unlike the officers, they only had time to kill.

The RTOs' names were Skinny Artie Shaw, Specks Morgan, and Crazy Carroll Mann. Between them and the radios, the TOC was a good place to pass the time.

One evening in June I stopped by and found Specks at the switchboard and Skinny manning the radios. Crazy Carroll Mann was off duty, but he was hanging around anyway. He had nothing better to do. He was sitting next to the coffee urn, his feet propped up on the field desk in the corner. The three of them were talking about how they had wound up in the army.

"What about you, sir?" said Specks Morgan. "You're not West Point, are you?"

"No. OCS."

"Enlist?"

"Yeah. Volunteered for the draft."

"No kidding. How come you landed in OCS, then?"

"Well, I volunteered for that too."

"How come?"

"It's hard to say. I seemed to have to keep choosing between the lesser of two evils."

"Never volunteer for *anything*," said Skinny Artie Shaw. "They taught you *that* in OCS, didn't they sir?"

"No," I said. "They teach you that in PFC school."

"Damn right."

"Shit," said Crazy Carroll Mann. "Army don't teach nobody nothin. Why the hell'd you go infantry, Lieutenant? Couldn't you of gone into a less dangerous branch of the service?"

"That," I said, "is the sixty-four-thousand-dollar question."

"Well you sure wound up in the wrong place."

"I'm not complaining. I could have wound up two thousand miles southwest of here."

Crazy Carroll Mann lit a cigaret. He was very large, and he spoke with kind of a lazy drawl. "Hey Specks," he said, "I still don't understand about your eyes. How'd you get in with them *eyes*? Shit—lemme see if I can see through those Coke bottles."

Specks handed him his glasses, then answered a call on the switchboard. At the same time, one of the big radios barked. We heard: "Shooooorrrrrt!"

"Who is that, anyway?" I said.

"Short is all of us, Lieutenant," Crazy said. "Short is any enlisted man who finds himself alone with a radio."

"Shut up, Crazy," Skinny said.

"Fuck you."

Skinny shook his head. "They'll never catch that son of a bitch."

Crazy put on Specks' glasses, and they made his eyes bulge. He looked like a goggle-eyed fish in a lens bowl. "Je–sus," he drawled. He took off the glasses and rubbed his eyes. "Hey Specks, how can you see *any*thing through these fuckers? I never thought they'd put a fuckin blind man in the *in*fantry, for Chrissakes." He handed the thick lenses back to Specks.

"My eyesight's correctible," Specks said. "But don't worry, Craze, I'm a noncombatant. If the North Koreans're going to come through here in force, they've got to get my permission first. I'm supposed to get time to clear out. That's why the Colonel keeps me around. That's how come I got assigned to Commo and got this cushy job."

"Cushy?" said Crazy. "You callin this a soft job?"

"Sure it is, Crazy," Skinny said.

"Well," Crazy said, "if these fuckin shifts of twelve and sixteen hours are *cushy*, then you two pantywaists belong in the fuckin WACs, not the army. I mean, why the fuck did you join up in the first place if you were looking for something *cushy*?"

"What?" said Skinny. "You're not making sense, Craze."

Specks Morgan looked over at me and winked through his glasses. "That's our boy," he said.

Skinny said, "Who the fuck says I joined up? I was drafted, sure as shit."

"So was I," Specks said.

Skinny said to Crazy Mann: "What about you, Craze? I suppose you fuckin enlisted, didn't you, you crazy bastard."

"You're goddamn right I enlisted," growled Crazy.

"That's crazy!" Skinny laughed. "Oh wow, I *knew* you were crazy!"

"What did you enlist for?" asked Specks.

"Joined up to get the fuck outta my house. Faked the physical, too," Crazy added, chuckling.

"You what?"

"You heard me."

"Shit," said Skinny, "I heard you, but I don't believe what I heard. You mean to tell me that you had an *out*, and you faked the physical to get *in*?"

"That's right, you skinny bastard, and if you don't like it, you know where you can shove it."

"Why did you do it?" said Specks.

"I had my reasons." Carroll Mann stubbed out his cigaret impatiently.

"What were they?" said Specks.

"Yeah," said Skinny. "We're not going anyplace."

Carroll Mann looked sheepish. He leaned forward. "Well, it has to do with my old man. Can't stand the bastard. Couldn't stand bein around him, had to get outta my fuckin house, you know? My mom was OK, but Pop? What a bastard. He never did

58

nothin but fight with my mom, ever since I can remember, unless it was to pick on me. They used to scream at each other—I never heard anything like it, never—and he'd always end up hittin her, or he'd come after me, sometimes with a strap. But then I got too big for that so he'd leave me out of it, and then finally about a year ago they split up. Just like that. I was gonna go to college. How bout that, Specks? Fuckin Crazy was on his way to college, I'd been accepted and everything, to the community college just a mile from the house, and you know what happened?"

I said, "What happened, Crazy?"

"My ol' lady ran off, that's what happened. She just took off with some guy, ran out on my father after he beat her up one time too many, I guess, and then she asked me to go to court with her, to testify that he'd hit her, beat up on her now and then, which he did, that bastard, I wouldn't lie for nobody, not even against my old man, and you know what he did when he saw me in court? He threw me outta the house. Said I wasn't his son no more. Refused to pay for college. Man, I had to join the army just to fuckin *eat*. And Pop told me to, he said there was a war on, go join the fuckin army. So I did. But I didn't do it cause he said so. I did it because if I didn't, I was going to kill that bastard. Who knows? Maybe I still will. I sure as fuck learned how."

"See there, Lieutenant?" said Skinny. "That's why we call him 'Crazy.' He's nuts. Isn't he, sir?"

"I don't think he's crazy."

"Hell no, sir. I ain't crazy. I'm just pissed off."

June 19

If I don't know what I want, how am I going to get control of my life?

What do I want?

Certainly not the kind of life Dad's worked for: big house in the suburbs, high pressure, big bucks, never home, long hours.

When I was in college it seemed like I had the whole fucking world, my whole life, ahead of me—but I didn't know what to do with it. Mom and Dad stopped telling me what to do, what to be. I couldn't decide, and I didn't apply to graduate schools because I had no idea what I wanted to do. I could have done anything, yet I couldn't imagine a future for myself.

I was going nuts. Graduation was approaching. I almost flunked out.

Because I never looked beyond college, college became a dead end for me. No wonder I almost flunked out: I didn't want to graduate. I had nowhere to go. Dad and Mom always stressed college—"Get that *degree!*" But they never told me what's supposed to happen *after* college. And I never decided for myself.

Then I decided to volunteer for the draft. I knew they'd get me anyway. I had no alternative. I was almost eager to turn my life over to somebody else: my parents, the army.

Winding up in the infantry wasn't difficult. The floor is tilted and everybody who doesn't have a plan—and a signed, notarized document from his recruiter—rolls downhill and winds up in the infantry. I just let myself roll down the fucking hill.

But that's too easy an answer. It's no answer. All right, so I had no plan. Why didn't I? Why didn't I fight to stay out of the infantry?

Because if I couldn't imagine a future for myself, I must not have wanted one. I must have wanted to die.

SIX

A FEW NIGHTS LATER, A PA-
trol from Company C shot and killed one of their Katusas. That
morning I debriefed the patrol members and wrote the report.
Long after they'd settled into their night ambush position, around
two a.m., this Katusa had to take a piss. He got up and wandered
away from his position. Completely unheard of. Coming back, he
walked into the killing zone and two men opened up on him with
an automatic rifle and a grenade launcher loaded with buck shot.

Tim Wilson took two Recon jeeps into the DMZ to pick up
the dead Katusa. Wilson thought he was going after an injured
man. His two jeeps rendezvoused with the patrol out near the
Guard Post, not far from North Korea, and when Wilson saw the
Korean lying on a bloody poncho, his legs and neck torn up the
way they were, blood everywhere, he panicked. He had his driver
race back to the fence at top speed, headlights full on, while he
applied first aid to the dead Korean. When they reached a medic
on the other side of the fence, near Charlie Company's CP, the
medic told Wilson that the Katusa was dead, but Wilson didn't
believe him. He raced all the way back to Matta with the body.
There Doc Lang convinced Wilson the Katusa was dead. Doc let

Wilson put on a stethoscope and listen for a heartbeat. He showed Wilson the raw, dark wounds in the Korean's neck that had long since stopped bleeding. I heard this later from one of the medics. Finally Doc Lang gave Wilson a sedative and sent him to bed.

That morning, after talking at length with Doc Lang and Major Nichols and Captain Stewart, Colonel Curtis relieved Tim Wilson of the Recon platoon. He arranged to have Wilson transferred to one of the reserve battalions at Camp Casey. So Wilson was gone before lunch, and I never saw him again.

Colonel Curtis also called in John Harris, the C Company Commander. They discussed patrols. What was a Katusa doing wandering around an ambush site? Colonel Curtis asked gently. We've got a language problem with those Katusas, Harris maintained. They don't understand a damn thing you tell them.

Colonel Curtis didn't relieve John Harris that morning, but he did appoint the S-4, Bobby Green, the new Recon Platoon Leader.

In late June I returned to the Green Door Hotel. It was a weekday afternoon, hot and humid. I was alone. There were only two pair of black boots in the closet near the entrance. Mama-san greeted me with a bow in the empty living room. Would I like to sit down? she asked. Would I like some tea? I told her I would. She left the room and I sat on a straw mat on the floor. A fan under a table behind me cooled the sweat on the back of my neck. In a few moments Mama-san returned, carrying a pot of tea and two cups on a tray. She sat cross-legged on the floor in front of me and placed the tray on the mat between us. She was fat, and sweat formed along the creases in her skin. There were dark stains under her arms. But she did not move awkwardly and the movements of her hands were very graceful. She tucked her large skirt beneath her knees and feet, smoothed some wrinkles in her lap, and poured tea for us both.

"Now Lieutenant," she said to me. "You not here just for tea. You want something else, eh?" She grinned.

"Yes, Mama-san."

"You would like to see young girl from last Sunday, week ago?"

"How old was she, Mama-san? Has she worked here for a long time?"

The smile remained fixed on the old woman's face. Slowly she raised her tea cup and drank from it. She said nothing. From deep within the tiny slits that were her eyes, I could see her brown irises gazing out at me. After a moment or two, she repeated: "You would like to see same young girl from before, Lieutenant?"

"No, Mama-san," I said firmly. "I don't want any young girls. Someone older, Someone who's been here for a while, who has experience."

"Experience?"

I sipped my tea. "Yes, Mama-san. A woman. No young girl. A woman who likes it here, who enjoys her work. A woman who looks forward to Saturday night. A professional, Mama-san. Skilled labor."

Again she led me down the dark hallway, the two of us padding along quietly, a buyer and a seller. This time she showed me to a large room with a queen-size bed, yellow walls, electric lamps. And she took less money from me, only twenty dollars.

I waited fifteen minutes. There was no window and the room was hot, and the heat and anticipation expanded the time. I stripped down to my boxer shorts and lay on the bed. There were cobwebs in the corners of the room. I sweated. When at last the woman entered she entered abruptly, throwing back the sliding door, stepping into the room without hesitating or looking at me, and closing the door decisively. I stood up and watched her. She returned my gaze without shame. She was the biggest woman I'd seen in Korea, tall and plump, not a trace of self-consciousness in her manner. Her kimono was not tied and as she turned from the door to face me, the kimono swung open. She was wearing only a bra and panties underneath. We looked at each other, meeting for the first time, both of us half-naked. She looked me up and down and smiled approvingly. It was also a seductive smile. She walked past me to the foot of the bed, bent over and reached down—her cleavage was aimed in my direction, naturally—and she pulled an electric fan out from under the bed, a Japanese fan with blue plastic blades. She placed it on the table at the foot of the bed, plugged it in, and switched it on. Her movements were quick and self-assured. The breeze hit me with a rush, and goose bumps rose on my slick chest and back. The woman, still standing by the fan at the foot of the bed, began to strip. With quick efficiency she bared her ample body while I watched. She was beautiful. What had I done to deserve this? Was it merely a matter of paying money? But the eager way she removed her few garments seemed a present to me, and her body a gift, unwrapped and revealed as her garments fell away: the kimono, dropped to the floor; her brassiere, unsnapped in back, then peeled from her large breasts and pulled down her plump arms (her breasts liquid, the nipples small and hard); and then her panties, pushed down over her dark bush, stepped out of gracefully and slowly.

She walked around the bed to where I stood and lightly ran her fingers down my chest and across my stomach; with practiced confidence she slipped both her hands into the elastic of my boxer shorts and slid them over my hips and down my legs, herself sliding down with them until she was kneeling before me and as I stepped out of my shorts her hand guided my erect penis into her mouth, a warm, busy, experienced mouth, and I remained standing, amazed, while she sucked my cock and quickly I came and kept coming until I was too weak to stand and fell backward onto the edge of the bed while she continued to stroke and suck me, drinking my sperm until there was nothing left of me and she stopped.

I swung my legs up onto the bed and stretched out, my head on the pillow. The woman picked up her kimono, put it on, and left the room. The fan was making a soft whooshing sound, and waves of cool air washed over me. My cock lay on its nest of pubic hair, limp and exhausted.

I dozed. Sometime later I heard the door slide open and then shut, and I looked up. She was standing by the door looking at me. Where had she gone? To rinse out her mouth? Again she dropped her kimono to the floor, and this time she was already naked. I looked at her large breasts and her small patch of black pubic hair. The bed rocked as she climbed onto it and her breasts swayed as she crawled toward me. Little beads of sweat stood out on her nose and forehead. With her hands and her lips she began to play with my cock, teasing it. She was strong and vigorous, and she had very long red fingernails. I was delighted by the confidence she had in her sexuality, by her power to excite me. It was clear she loved her work: the expression on her face was pure pleasure.

64

She played with my penis and kissed me all over my body. She said nothing, but every now and then she would moan pleasantly. Soon she climbed astride me. Now her face took on a more intense, businesslike expression. She raised herself up and slipped my cock inside her, and then she really began to concentrate. With her serious expression, with her eyes fixed on the wall above my head, she looked like a woman who would not have been content with being fucked, but who wanted to do the fucking.

That was fine with me.

She began to move. I grabbed ahold of her tits and hung on. She was no frightened little girl, no teen-ager who wasn't sure she wanted to be going through with the thing and had to be coaxed into it; she was a hungry woman, a mature sexual creature. She had no qualms, she did not hold back. She was on her way, with or without me, and I had only to lie there and feel the warmth of that large welcoming vagina, feel the fast rocking motion of her love-making, hear her breathing as it began to come quickly in deep gulps, as her forehead and chest grew slick with sweat, and finally she threw her head back, turned her face toward the ceiling, closed her eyes, and then her orgasm arrived and her whole body shuddered and she cried out and leaned down and hugged me, rocking gently and breathing very hard, kissing my face and my mouth and I thought: Now *that* is fucking.

Three hours and a couple of orgasms later (she was cunning, that whore, knowledgeable and persistent), I finally emerged into the late afternoon sunshine of Changpa-ri and found Peters waiting for me in the jeep. He drove to the fence and I walked it slowly and painfully. There was no strength in my legs; my knees shook and my balls ached. A couple of times I felt dizzy and had to sit down. I couldn't catch my breath. But I made the fence-walk and directly afterward I crawled into my bunk, trembling from waist to thighs. She was too much for me. Too much.

June 27
For the record:
The morning air as you walk the fence is white, viscous, almost solid with mist and fog. Before you: a blank white sheet

of air. Things are sensed or heard before they are seen. Your footfall echoes off a tower wall and you read the echoes like a bat. One by one the squat towers, the green sandbagged fighting positions rise darkly out of the white mist, gain substance, and grow. Approaching a hill, you hear voices coming from above you, shouts from almost straight up, but you can see nothing, only the mist, and the voices have no source, they are the cries of ghost soldiers raining down from an unseen sky. And then the barest silhouette appears, and suddenly the whole huge hill looms clearly up, up before you, reaching impossibly high. Can you climb it? You cannot see the top.

It is like the future, this mist, this hill, obscure until it is upon you, but you experience a brief warning, a premonition, a hint of the shape of the next moment before you begin to live it.

On a warm evening in early July, three of us sat out back of the Officers' Club, drinking beer and talking. It was a quiet night. Inside, somebody was playing Ping-Pong. Every door and window in the Officers' Club was open, but the place was a Quonset hut, all corrugated metal, and it heated up during the day like a charcoal grill and held the heat well into the night. So Harmon and Phil Roberts and I had sought the fresh air out back. The small patio where we sat was defined by flagstones with weeds growing up between them; scattered about was an assortment of metal furniture, painted white, rust-spotted. We sat on the chairs, tipping back, our feet propped up on round tables, and drank beer from cans.

Phil Roberts was a medium person. He was a man of medium height and medium weight, halfway between fat and thin. A little pudgy. He seemed tense most of the time, and he had the nervous stiff walk of a small poodle. But his voice was always relaxed and cool. It was an odd combination, that tense body and calm voice. His uniform always looked medium, not sloppy but bordering on it: a stain on the fatigue shirt, the trousers pressed but wrinkled, clean perhaps yesterday. I understood that he had a wife back in the States, and a couple of kids. Maybe three. But he spent a lot of time in the village. He was a first lieutenant, just about the only one left. He was senior to all of us, senior to a bunch of second lieutenants: medium senior.

The sun had set long before. Daylight of a deep purple color lingered in the sky. A band of orange light capped the northwestern horizon. There were no clouds. The air was dry, fresh and sweet-smelling, stirred by a slight breeze. The bugs were not bad. It hardly seemed like a combat zone at all. "It's nice out here," I said. "Cool and dry for a change."

"It's fine if you're drunk enough," Harmon said.

I looked around at the metal furniture, the low hills, the violet evening sky with its dim stars. The warm breeze cooled my sweat-dampened fatigue shirt. "Yeah, it's really pleasant," I said.

Phil Roberts scoffed. "Pleasant? Not with North Korea just two miles in that direction." He raised a finger from his beer can and pointed north. "*Un*pleasant."

I said, "But it's nice to forget North Korea, don't you think?"

"I never forget it," Roberts said. "I'm constantly aware of it. It's like a pain in my chest—like angina. My next heart attack sitting on my shoulder. I imagine gooks perched just beyond that first line of mountains, poised and ready to strike. They could be here in twenty minutes. In force, standing on this patio, guns smoking—the whole fucking North Korean Army. Thirty minutes max."

"Damn straight," said Harmon.

"Bullshit," I said.

"I'm not kidding," Roberts said. "We're the first line of defense here. People forget that, but I don't. If the balloon went up, our mission would be to delay and harass the enemy—while everybody else retreated faster than hell. Can you imagine that? Our backs are against a river and there's only one bridge. It's packed with demolitions and wired to blow. We're certain casualties if they invade. We don't have artillery, we don't have the Redeye, we don't have tanks. We don't have shit. We don't even have plans. That was something Anderson got involved in. Did you know Anderson?" Phil asked me.

"Yeah, I knew the son of a bitch."

"That's right, you took his job. Anyway, he was supposed to draw up contingency plans. For the battalion. I don't know if he ever did."

"Not that I'm aware of," I said.

Roberts took a swig of his beer. "When they come they'll hit us with everything. Air, artillery, tanks, mech infantry. Captured or killed, every last one of us."

"Most likely killed," said Harmon. He was playing the expert on enemy capability. "Northern gook assault troops don't take prisoners, according to the book. They'd go through us like a hot knife through butter. They'd squash us like bugs."

"Original, John," I said. But the talk gave me a chill. I imagined the roar of tanks, the shriek of MiGs. Invasion. First line of defense. Scattered after the initial assault, we would become the objectives of North Korean mop up operations. *Mopped up!* Disposed of like insects. Sudden and certain victims.

Inside the club, the Ping-Pong game had ended. Somebody had put coins in the juke box.

> *Sittin' here restin' my bones,*
> *And this loneliness won't leave me alone,*
> *Two thousand miles I've roamed,*
> *Just to make this dock my home. . . .*

"I'd run," said Phil Roberts. "I'd grab a jeep and try to make it across Libby Bridge before they blew it. Before *we* blew it. You wouldn't stand a chance this side of the river."

"Well," I said, "they probably won't attack tonight."

"I don't give a shit," Phil said. "I just can't wait to get the fuck outta here."

"You lucky bastard," Harmon said. "How short are you?"

"Hell, I'm not short. I've got five months yet."

"That's short, compared to me."

"It's not short. I won't be short till I'm on the fucking *plane.* Then I'll be short."

"Ah, fuck it," said Harmon with sudden vehemence. He threw his beer can across the patio and stood up. The empty can clattered on the stones, spun around a couple times, and finally lay still.

"Mr. Kim!" Harmon bellowed. "Another beer! Bring three Schlitz!" He turned to us. "What do you say we head down to the village. Come on. Let's go get layed."

"Shit, Harmon," said Roberts, "is that all you ever think about?"

"What else is there to do?" Harmon paced around the patio. He walked over to his beer can and kicked it off the flagstones into the grass.

Mr. Kim emerged onto the patio with three cans of beer. He was a small Korean man, and he served the beers with dignity. Phil Roberts paid for the round.

"Besides," Roberts said after Mr. Kim had walked back into the Officers' Club, "there're crabs going around down in the village."

"Crabs?"

"Yeah. You know who's got crabs? Green's got crabs."

"Ha! That's rich. Our new Recon platoon leader? Oh, I love that." Harmon laughed derisively and sat down.

"Yeah. He's already dumped his girlfriend. Says he doesn't want to find out where she got 'em."

"I wouldn't either," Harmon said. "Just get rid of the bitch."

"I wonder what Anderson would have done if he'd caught crabs." Phil Roberts smiled. "That would have been a real dilemma for him, wouldn't it?"

"Why do you say that?" Harmon said. "I didn't really know Anderson. He was gone a week after I got here. Sort of an asshole. Never talked to anybody."

"He was okay. Anderson was all right."

"Well, he never gave me the time of day."

"Me neither," I said.

"He had a girl," Phil said. "Down in the village. He got pretty attached to her. You ought to fuck her, Harmon. She's pretty. I understand she's available."

"Yeah, I heard about her. He called her—what the hell was her name?"

"Tammy." Roberts drank some beer. "Anderson spent a lot of time with her. Toward the end, he didn't have much time for anything else."

"Yeah," Harmon agreed. "I heard she almost nailed him."

From inside the Officers' Club came the sound of voices and the click of pool balls colliding with one another. No music. The night was pitch black now, the air still. Peaceful. From the open door, yellow light spilled onto the patio, but I couldn't make out the faces of John and Phil. Their voices were distinctive, though: Roberts' low-pitched and inflectionless; Harmon's a high whine.

"That poor bastard," Phil Roberts was saying, "he was in love with her. He really was. He almost married her and took her back to the States with him. Almost. We thought he would. He was all torn up; he sure did hate to leave that girl. I've never seen a man so heartbroken."

I couldn't imagine those things: wanting to stay; wanting to marry a Korean girl; wanting to take the girl back to the States. Gave me the willies to think about it.

Roberts continued: "He damn near extended, too, just to stay with her, but he was dying to get out of this place. Couldn't stand it. I mean, everybody hates it here, but Anderson positively loathed it. I don't know why, maybe it was his job. Is walking the fence that bad, Richardson?"

"I don't mind it. Twice a day is getting sort of monotonous, but I'm in shape now so it's not hard work. The land is beautiful. I could never extend, though. Too boring. I can't think of a reason I'd want to extend for."

"Anderson hated it, by the time he left. Yet he almost married that girl."

"She was after more than money," Harmon said. He laughed. "That sucker. She almost bagged him. She almost bagged herself an officer, didn't she, Roberts?"

"Yep."

"Some women really sink their claws into you," Harmon concluded. "Some guys haven't got a chance."

July 12

Letter from my father today. Asks me how it's going. Do I need anything? Talks about the weather and how the cabin looked when they went up to Vermont in June.

I've had a terrible relationship with my father. Kind of a non-relationship. I've never been able to *talk* to the man.

For example, here's the extent of his contribution to my sex education. In a few days I'm going off to basic training. I'm 21 years old. Mom and Dad and I are eating dinner and the phone rings and it's for Mom. She's talking in the other room. Dad says, "You know, Art, you'll meet some pretty sexy girls in the army."

"They drafting 'em these days, Dad?"

He turns red. "That's not what I mean. You just have to watch out for disease. Always wear something. Okay?"

"Sure. Okay."

First time he ever mentioned sex. If that's what he did.

Here's another example: only one letter from him since I got here. Today's.

When I left Hartford to fly to Fort Lewis, and then to here. Dad saw me off at the airport. Took time off from his busy schedule—rare. (Insurance! Imagine living your life for safety's sake, always playing the odds, betting you won't die.)

Anyway, Dad and Mom drove me to Bradley Airport and waited around in the glass-and-concrete building until they called my plane. I was in uniform—he'd seen my uniform at OCS—he couldn't make my college graduation because of a business meeting but he flew from Connecticut to Georgia for the OCS one. When I'd come home on leave, I'd change out of the uniform as soon as I walked in the door but now I was in Class A greens, a couple of ordinary ribbons, name tag (RICHARDSON, his name), and the gold bars. He loved my uniform.

Dad was agitated. I was thinking I might not come back and he was probably thinking the same thing. Finally he began to cry. He's a large man and he was wearing a suit and a tan raincoat and black wing tip shoes and his city hat, a gray one with a dark feather and a cloth band that looks like a ribbon.

Dad's eyelids were red and swollen, his eyes watery. He excused himself and went to the men's room.

"Your father doesn't cry often," Mom said.

"I know," I said.

"I've only seen him cry once before." She looked out the window at the airplanes. "That was when his mother died. He cried some then, but we couldn't attend the funeral." She continued to stare out the window, perhaps remembering when my grandmother had died. I thought, She's more upset by Dad's crying than by my leaving. But maybe that wasn't so.

They announced my flight before Dad returned. Mom and I started toward the gate and Dad caught up with us. We said goodbye in the concourse that led to the gates. Mom hugged me and managed to smile. "Have a wonderful year," she said. "Try to learn something every day. Stay out of danger and hurry home to us."

Dad was barely able to speak. "Goodbye, m'boy," he said. He solemnly shook my hand. He stared at me with his watery eyes.

"Goodbye, Dad," I said.

My father kept pumping my hand, gripping it tightly. "Goodbye, Arthur," he said. His eyes were red-rimmed and his lower lip trembled. I wanted to hug and kiss him but I

71

hadn't in so long. I wanted to tell him I'd be all right and he didn't have to cry and not to worry but he was so much older, wasn't he supposed to do the talking? He kept pumping my hand till finally I pulled away and he let go.

I hurried toward the gate, but I stopped and looked back. I didn't want to go, I wanted to stay with them. But they had turned and were walking away, their arms around one another, heads together, touching, both looking old and stooped. Already in mourning.

Like he was convinced I was going to die. Or wanted me to. He was so proud of my going into the army. Came all the way down to my graduation.

SEVEN

I ATE SUPPER WITH JACK AFTER walking the fence one evening and asked him what he did for a living. What he did, he said, was follow Colonel Curtis and Captain Stewart around all day and half the night and do odd jobs for them.

"I usually feel like the third tit," he told me. We were the only ones in the officers' mess. "They almost never talk to me. I'm just the *loo-tenant*, you know. But every now and then I get a project of my own, a detachment to supervise. Construction, or security of some detail, or reconnaissance. Something like that. That's okay; I don't mind that."

"What do you do at night?" I asked. "You come in real late practically every night. Crash around for a while. . . . Then your bed springs start squeaking."

Jack had a forkful of scalloped potatoes halfway to his mouth, and he stopped the fork in midair and laughed. Then he grimaced. "That's the worst of it." He waved the fork at me, spilling potatoes onto the oilcloth. "We go up to the Forward CP. The Colonel and Captain Stewart and myself. We get there after dark and sit around and wait for something to happen. It never does. You oughta come up sometime and have a look, Art."

"Sure, I'm up for a little boredom. How about tonight?"

"You're on."

The night was cool. We took Jack's jeep and driver, and we rode with the windshield down, me in back, the three of us wearing helmets and flak jackets, carrying weapons, the jeep with only its blackout lights on. Sounds: whine of the engine, roar of the wind in my ears, rattle of the jeep's loose suspension. We bounced and bucked from one pothole to another. Darkness. With the windshield down, the thick, damp air blew straight into our faces. Cool oxygen rushed down my throat and seemed to enter my bloodstream directly. A peculiar thing was happening: when the road climbed to the top of a hill, the wind became noticeably warmer. When we plunged down into a valley, the air turned cool and damp. I could feel the change in temperature immediately on my face, and Jack told me later that was the reason they drove with the windshield down: the glass fogged up so quickly as they went up and down hills that they couldn't keep the windshield clear enough to see out of. Especially with only the blackout lights on.

The road that ascended to the Forward CP was steep. The jeep strained. The air grew warmer. It was a brilliant black night; the sky was clear and we literally climbed toward the stars.

Two jeeps were parked in enfilade just below the south side of the hilltop and their drivers were sitting on the ground by one of the jeeps. I couldn't see their faces, only their dark shapes and the glowing tips of their cigarets, but I knew who they were: Lafeber and Lewis, the two L's. When our jeep stopped and we climbed out of it, they began to scramble to their feet—'military courtesy'—but Evans brought them up short:

"As you were, men. It's only us lieutenants."

"Oh, hello Lieutenant Evans," one of them said, and they sat down and leaned back against the jeep tires.

We climbed the path to the CP. The hilltop was broad, flat, and bare; the CP sat on the forward edge, a dark rectangle silhouetted against the night sky.

July 19
for the record:
The Forward Command Post is a fat box with sandbagged
exterior walls. It's squared off, rectangular, no roof, its sandbags stacked like walls of puffy green bricks. As you approach
it, it looms above you: its walls rise about ten feet from the
hilltop. That's because the floor is five or six feet off the
ground. When you're inside the thing looking out, the pine-
plank wall hits you just above the waist. The CP is roomy,
about twenty feet by ten, and it contains a few folding metal
chairs, a radio, a field phone, and assorted officers.

We walked across the top of the hill to the CP and clomped
up its wooden stairs.

"Good evening, sir!" Jack hollered. He had a way of greeting
people by bellowing at them, his voice an excited shout. "Good
evening, Captain Stewart!"

"Good evening, Lieutenant Evans," Colonel Curtis said.
"Who's that with you?"

"It's me, sir. Lieutenant Richardson."

"Oh, hello Arthur. Joining us for the night, are you?"

"Yes sir. I thought I'd try to rustle up a little excitement."

"You may have come to the wrong place. Everything seems
pretty quiet this evening. But the quieter the better, eh, Captain
Stewart?"

"That's right, sir."

I walked over to one wall of the CP. A warm breeze lapped at
my neck and face. I looked around, rotated my body all the way
around, 360 degrees. We were at the top of the world: the view in
every direction was unobstructed. Black hills to the north, their
peaks frozen in the night sky, and not a sign of life from that direction, not a single electric light, not a fire. To the south, the
lights of Changpa-ri twinkled on the horizon.

But it was the thing that ran along below and in front of the
hill that took my breath away. The fence. It glimmered for miles
in either direction, stretched to the horizon both east and west:
the glowing orange flame pots and the fluttering white sparks of
flashlights, a string of them—the lights running and curving like
a big-city boulevard or a sparkling diamond necklace draped over
the hills and valleys on this border.

And we could hear the fence. The breeze carried the sound of the men calling to one another. I heard the *chunk-chunk* as someone worked the bolt of his M-14. And somewhere somebody was singing. I couldn't make out the words, but the melody was upbeat.

An entire infantry battalion spread out at our feet. Miles of armed men, all of them controlled by a central headquarters, by one man. The man sitting to my right. The patrols, the Guard Posts, the barrier force—we couldn't see or hear all of it, but it was there. We knew the patrols were out there in the dark, we knew infantrymen manned foxholes as far as we could see. Everywhere around us the night hummed, the air vibrated. There was a sense of great energy, of motion and heat and breath and pulse. A giant in repose: the infantry battalion at night, restless, poised for a fight.

I was thinking those things, not quite consciously, I suppose, as I stood leaning on the wall of the CP and gazing at the lights along the fence. I took a few deep breaths of the warm evening air.

I turned to Colonel Curtis. "This is all yours, isn't it, sir?"

"Yes it is," he said. "And it's an awesome responsibility."

Colonel Curtis: the old gentleman; the reluctant commander. He was a nice man and a good administrator. Apparently he'd had two long Pentagon assignments, but there was some doubt as to his ability as a field commander. He'd been a lieutenant colonel for a long time, and his promotion to full colonel depended on this command.

He got up from his chair, walked over, and leaned on the rail next to me. He laughed softly and his hand swept the air in front of him. "Someday, son," he said, "this will all be yours."

I laughed. "Thanks anyway, sir, but I don't think so."

He was about to reply but the field phone buzzed and cut him off. Jack answered it. After a moment he hung up and said to Colonel Curtis: "That was the TOC, sir. Colonel Larson's on his way up."

There was mildly frantic preparation for the brigade commander's arrival. One of the drivers came in, carrying a broom, and swept out the CP. Captain Stewart and Colonel Curtis rearranged the chairs. Ten minutes after we got the call,

Colonel Larson arrived. It was too dark to see him, but his voice was distinctive—mellow and resonant. I was introduced to him.

"Oh, yes, Richardson," he said. We shook hands. "How's your marksmanship, Lieutenant?"

"It's all right, Colonel."

"You're the fence-walker, aren't you?"

"That's right, sir."

"What are you doing up here?"

"It's actually the first time I've been here at night. I'm visiting."

Colonel Larson turned to the battalion commander. "How are things going tonight, Colonel? Rather quiet, I presume."

They talked about military matters. I went over and sat down next to Jack. We sat quietly, killing time. The evening dragged. Conversation flared and flickered like a fire in a fireplace. We sat, talked, stood up and walked around. On the rough pine floor, our boots sounded like horses' hooves thumping against wooden stalls.

'Short' came on the radio, made his brief announcement, and then was not heard from again. Colonel Larson seemed to pay the breach of discipline no heed, but Colonel Curtis became restless. He got up from his chair and paced about, then sat down again. He started asking Captain Stewart and Colonel Larson questions. He called his company commanders a number of times on the land line, asking about their patrols and barrier forces, pressing them for reports of movement or noise. The presence of the brigade commander seemed to make him nervous. His career depended on the report Colonel Larson would write at the end of his tour of duty.

Then all at once someone on the fence below us began to shout in a loud, angry voice. The noise came from quite close, almost dead center in B Company.

"God damn motherfuckin cocksuckers! Pig fuckers! Assholes!" All of us simultaneously jumped up and moved to that side of the CP. If we'd been in a boat, it would have capsized. We peered down.

"Bastard motherfuckers! Go bugger your fuckin grandmothers!" Then a burst of automatic weapon's fire. Tracers zoomed up at us and cracked over our heads, the dry snap of the bullets sharp and clear in the night air.

Five officers never hit the floor so fast. The GI kept firing, and I thought, That bastard, what the hell's he so mad about? I stuck my head up over the wall and watched the tracers whiz toward us in straight red lines. I'd never been shot at before. The *pop-pop-pop-thump-thump-thump* and the bright red streaks of bullets zipping past our ears were beautiful. Best of all, no one had been hit.

"Get down!" A hand yanked my belt and jerked it hard, sending me sprawling. It was Colonel Larson. "Keep your head down!" he hissed. "This isn't the goddamn movies!"

He was crouching well below the top of the wall. He was right, of course: any one of us could get a bullet in the head. I stayed down. I sat on the floor with my back against the wall.

But I could still look up, away from the fence, and watch the red tracers rocket into the black, star-lit sky. I'd seen tracers before, of course, in the night sky over a rifle range at Fort Benning, but never this close, never whipping past just inches above my head. They arced up a long way before they burned out, and they were lovely, better than July 4th fireworks.

Captain Stewart was on the phone to Curt Davis. Finally someone, probably the platoon sergeant, got to the man doing the shooting and stopped him. He had emptied two clips of tracers at the CP.

We got up and brushed ourselves off. Colonel Larson was angry. As he left he said to my battalion commander: "Come on, Colonel Curtis. Get your goddamn battalion squared away."

July 20
The search.

Sometimes when I walk the fence I wonder: *What might have been?* What if I'd been born to different parents? In India, in China, in North Korea. Who would I be? How would I be the same?

If they have soldiers over in N.K. guarding some kind of barrier (they do)—if they have barbed wire, mines, booby traps, guys with rifles and flares—wouldn't they have a fence-walker too?

How are he and I alike?

He'd be young and compelled to fight. He'd rather be doing something else, was coerced into putting on a uniform. Some threat made against his family, not just against him. Like in

America: it wouldn't have gone well for Dad at the old insurance company if I'd skipped to Canada.

I was born into this world of theirs. I didn't make it. Someday, son, this will all be yours. Some inheritance! They keep trying to give you the chaff and keep the wheat for themselves.

It's the old generation—the generation with power and wealth, but without youth—that makes the threats, that sends us off to war, that gains from our dying far from home. These are their quarrels, not ours. What am I doing in *Korea?*

And my friend to the north: what do his old people gain by raising a massive army and sending him to guard their southern boundary? Security? Keep out the South Koreans? National unity? Meanwhile they're protecting themselves from their own young, getting them the hell out of the neighborhood and sending them south to the DMZ. It's almost as good a ploy as sending them overseas.

Jack put in for a short leave, and toward the end of July it was granted. We were all envious. He took a weekend in Seoul, and at lunch on the day after he returned we were popping questions at him like machine gun bullets, faster than he could answer, and he finally shut us up, saying, "Cool it guys, just cool it, let me tell you what *happened!*"

He told us he had met a girl named Christina, an American, a fabulous girl, very tall, well built, and lovely, whose father was a New York lawyer. He'd met her just by chance, a lucky accident: he'd gotten lost on the post and had asked her for directions. By the time she'd walked him back to within sight of the main building, they were friends. He took her out Saturday night.

"Did you fuck her?" Bobby Green asked.

Everybody laughed, including Jack. "No. But we danced real close and she was wearing this fantastic perfume. I took her home and kissed her goodnight."

Green said, "Which goodnight? The one between her legs?"

"Get your mind out of the gutter, Green," Jack shouted. He crumpled his napkin into a ball and bounced it off Green's head. It landed in Phil Robert's milk glass.

Roberts peered at it. "Nice shot."

Harmon asked, "Her father's a New York attorney? Where do they live?"

"I don't know. Long Island somewhere, I think."

"Is she Jewish?"

A look of anger crossed Jack's face. I had not seen him angry before. He had an absolutely cheerful disposition and a wise crack or an insult would roll right off him. But not this time. He didn't smile at all.

"What's it to you, Harmon?"

John paused. Then he raised his eyebrows. "Well?"

Jack stood up. Harmon was sitting across the table from him. "That's an obscene question," Jack said to Harmon. "You shut your face."

"What's the fuss about?" Roberts said, his mouth full of food. "The broad's named Christina. Does that sound Jewish?"

"I don't think the question's obscene," Harmon said. "To be Jewish isn't obscene."

I was sitting next to Jack, who was still standing. His sleeves were rolled above his elbow and his forearm was on a level with my eyes. I put a hand on his wrist. His fist was clenched. "Why don't you sit down, Jack?" I said.

"Yeah," said Bobby Green, "your mashed elderberry gumbo is getting cold, and Art's going to steal your crushed mogoo-nuts if you're not careful."

"I'll crush *your* mogoo-nuts, Harmon," Jack said, and sat down. "You're disgusting."

Harmon glared at Jack, but said nothing. His dark eyebrows were pencil-thin and his receding hair was slicked back, looking greasy against his pale skin. He continued to eat. He always ate slowly, almost primly, with great care. He chewed and swallowed carefully, and he never washed food down with water or milk. Always left food on his plate.

"So Jack," said Bobby Green, "did you make out with this girl or what? A little bare titty? A little nooky?"

"No."

"Too bad."

"It's all right. We had a great time." Evans glowered across the table at Harmon. "And the subject of religion never came up."

Mr. Lee served dessert. Phil Roberts and Bobby Green discussed a personnel problem—a driver in Recon had received a letter informing him that his wife was sleeping with his older brother. He was asking for an emergency leave. Green laughed. "I don't know whether he wants to go home to shoot his wife or his brother."

"Stop by my office after lunch," Phil told him. "I'll try to work something out."

Then Green teased Evans some more about the girl. "I can't believe your luck. She's really American? Why is she over here? She horny?"

They bantered back and forth, but I didn't listen. When Jack and I were finished eating we left the mess hall together.

"That fucking Harmon," Jack said.

"He seemed to be trying to pick a fight."

"But he backed down."

"Yeah, barely. Does he have any friends in the battalion?"

"Naw," said Jack. "He sort of hangs around with anyone. Has a steady in the village though. Spends most of his free time down there with her."

"Drives me nuts when he's around the BOQ. Always playing that damn stereo. He bought everything but headphones."

"You ought to come down to Seoul with me sometime, Art. We'll go down there together. Maybe Christina knows some other girls."

"An American girl. How long since I've seen one? Or talked to one. Almost three months. I'd love it, Jack. Just make sure she can speak English."

"I'll check her out personal. I'll test her, administer the SAT verbal. What kind of a score are you after?"

"Not that kind. But fluency in English is desirable."

August 4th

For the record: At the test-fire range.

Sergeant Waters climbs down out of the cab of a deuce-and-a-half and watches as the company barrier force lines up on the firing line at the test-fire range. The men prepare their weapons; some reach into a pocket and pull out ear plugs.

Waters: "Use those ear plugs now, men, your ears is all you've got tonight, eyes don't do you no good, you can't see nothin with those fire pots lit so use your ear plugs, you got to be able to hear. Protect your hearin, men. Lock and load but do *not* commence firin till I tell you. Don't fire your weapon without ear plugs, you'll wreck your hearin for a week, *don't* let me catch nobody shootin his weapon without *ear* plugs in his ears."

"*What did you say, Sarge?*"

"Who needs ear plugs? Who didn't bring ear plugs? Use em, men, use those ear plugs, you got to be able to hear tonight."

"*Can't hear you, Sarge, I got ear plugs in my ears.*"

"A comedian. Preserve your hearin, men, preserve your hearin, your hearin'll keep you alive on that barrier fence, it's all you got, you can't see nothin, you can't feel nothin, no pussy out there, men, you can't smell nothin, you got to use those *ears*. Okay. Everybody got ear plugs? Everybody got ear plugs? Who's missin plugs? Who don't have his plugs tonight? Everybody got plugs? Well, I'll be. You're surprisin me in my old age, men. Nobody need plugs? I'm goin to faint dead away from shock. I am becoming very impressed with the level of proficiency you all have reached within your own lifetimes. Welcome to the pinnacle of your military careers. Commence firin, men. Commence firin."

At the TOC not long after that, on a warm night in early August, Specks Morgan was hanging around, Skinny Artie Shaw was on duty, and both of them were bored, restless, talking to anybody about anything. Skinny was fantasizing a million dollars. "Man," he said, "what wouldn't I do with a million fuckin dollars."

"What *would* you do with it?" Specks asked him.

"A penthouse with a swimming pool," said Skinny. "That's the first thing. A different broad every night. We'd go swimming first. In the raw, and I'd look at her underwater. And I'd have a limousine with a driver that'd wait for me every place I went."

"You're a city boy, aren't you, Skinny?"

"Damn straight. I'd see any movie I wanted, and if it wasn't playing somewhere I'd have 'em bring it to my penthouse. Like Hugh Hefner's penthouse, that's what mine'd be like, only better. It'd be on top of the tallest building in New York, with a huge pool with round windows underwater and you could see the naked broads through 'em. I'd go to night clubs every night, topless and bottomless. Topless- and bottomless-a-go-go every night. I'd start a gun collection. I'd have the best gun collection in America. Rifles, tommy guns, pistols—I'd get one of those old buffalo guns that they used to shoot buffaloes with on the plains in the old west, those huge fancy things with scrolled metal on the butt and a barrel about an inch in diameter and a coupla yards long. And I'd have a Vette and a '56 T-Bird. That's all. Just two cars, a brand new Sting Ray and a '56 T-Bird."

"And the limo, Skinny. Don't forget the limo."

"Fuckin A. And the limo. Three cars. What about you, Specks —what would you do with a cool million?"

"I don't know. Maybe I'd invest it and live the rest of my life off the interest and dividends. Just take it easy, not do any work. Spend my life on the beach. Sit around and smoke cigars and drink beer." Specks shifted in his chair, shook his head. "Too bad I wasn't *born* rich. I wasn't that lucky. But if I did have a million bucks, I wouldn't be in Korea, that's for sure."

"Where would you be?"

"I don't know. Montana, maybe. In the country. I wouldn't want a penthouse. I'd buy a big old farm house, fix it up, put in air conditioning and picture windows and skylights, and then I'd plant a bunch of trees. I'd plant trees all over, fruit trees. So all I'd have to do was walk outside and pick fruit. Pick whatever I wanted to eat. Like I'd have a pizza tree out there, right outside my front door. And a cold beer tree—draft beer in frosted mugs! —and a bacon and eggs tree, and what the hell, I'd plant a pussy tree too."

We laughed. "A cunt tree," Skinny said. He sang: "My cunt-tree 'tis of thee . . . ."

"Yeah," said Specks, laughing too. "That's right. A pussy willow tree—all the pussy I could eat. An all-you-can-eat pussy tree. Unlimited seconds."

August 15
I've had things pretty good. Plenty of food, not many fights. Lived in a lovely suburb of Hartford. Three golf courses. Country club with swimming pool and tennis courts. Friends, people to take care of me—cook, mother, tennis pro, waiters at the club. Not much to fight about. Mostly I've lived without fear.

Then I join the army. Wind up in the infantry. Bayonet training, hand-to-hand combat, machine gun range, artillery demonstrations. What's this? Hand grenade. They kill people.

Then the long flight to Korea and suddenly I'm riding around in a jeep with hand grenades taped to the dashboard, Peters armed with an M-14 and me with a .45.

Nobody talks about fear. Fear is something you keep to yourself and mull over. You never know when something is going to happen. It might happen anytime. The enemy is just over the next hill. Maybe. You just keep doing what you have to do but you assume he's there because you have to be ready in case he is there.

Fear can be good. It motivates you to be ready.

There are different kinds of fear. Fear of getting killed. Fear of doing something badly, of doing the wrong thing. Being afraid for the other guy. The problem is, it can be hard to shake off at times.

August 20
For the record:

The most peculiar thing happened today. Peters was driving me back to Matta from the fence where a truck passed us going the other way. Curt Davis was riding in the cab, and there were men in the back, a patrol from Curt's company, just heading out. He hollered and waved, and his truck stopped so Peters stopped and backed toward the truck. When Peters stopped the jeep, I got out and walked back toward the truck. Curt was walking toward me. Then something hit me hard—something heavy—in the chin, spun my head sideways and knocked me down. One minute I'm six feet above the road and the next minute I'm lying on it, tasting dust. I picked myself up. Specks of dirt and gravel stuck to my palms.

I looked up at the men in the truck. I was dazed and surprised; I thought someone had thrown a rock at my head, and yet the notion seemed impossible. I looked up at the faces of the men in the truck—no expression—no snickering complicity or uncomfortable fear of being caught on any of those faces. They all looked sleepy and mildly puzzled.

What could have struck me? I touched my chin—it was sore, and there was one spot, a nucleus, that was numb. It felt swollen. I pulled my hand away and saw no blood. I looked at the ground—whatever struck me must be somewhere—and there in the gravel of the road, among the beige dirt and rocks, something gleamed golden-red—I picked it up—a pointed spheroid, a small rocket ship, copper-coated, a gleaming reddish-brown. It was hot to touch, too hot to hold, I had to flip it back and forth from one hand to the other while I examined it. A bullet. Curved rifling grooves etched in the copper shell of the lead bullet—a 7.62mm round. One of ours. Fired at the test range that lay on the other side of the big hill that loomed beside the road.

How had that bullet found me? Manufactured somewhere in the United States. Train to a west coast port city. Seattle? Lowered by crane into the hold of a ship, shipped to Inchon, delivered by truck to the 1st of the 31st. Distributed, loaded into an M-14 magazine, chambered at the test-fire range. Fired. Comes out spinning, skips off a pool of water, perhaps, or gets deflected by a leaf or a branch, ricochets up, over the hill, then comes tumbling down above the brush, toward the road; my jeep whizzing along beneath it, stops; I hop out; my jeep, myself getting larger, my steel helmet growing huge, my face, my chin. . . .

Being shot is like getting punched, or clobbered with a baseball bat. It feels like something very large and heavy hitting you. You suddenly get knocked down.

There's a big, sore knot on my chin, and I've got the bullet right here, copper jacket with lead insides, a heavy, sharp-nosed, nasty thing. Fell out of the sky and smacked me on the chin. Ricochet. Pure coincidence.

On the way back from the fence that morning, Peters and I saw two deer in the open, standing quietly in an old paddy, feeding. A peaceful sight: a buck and a doe, one slightly larger than the other, lovely creatures. Wary, though, nervous and alert. As we sped by they looked up, then bolted— but they didn't go far. They saw we meant them no harm, so they pulled up and continued grazing. I could see their tusks—white teeth curving upward from their lower jaws. Fierce-looking things. Then we were gone.

Sep 14
The record:
The land here is not different from land elsewhere, but we abuse it. We are not at peace with the land. We treat it as an adversary. We walk and drive across it, strip it away for camps, dig into it for bunkers and foxholes and latrines, drive stakes and fence posts into it, booby-trap it and blow it up. We light fires and burn off the fruits of its fertility: weeds,

85

wild grasses, brush. We do these things without feeling. We put back nothing. We plant nothing, cultivate nothing, harvest nothing. We have no permanence here, no attachment to the land, yet we're here. We resent the land because we are made to defend it even though it means nothing to us. We would as soon destroy it as defend it. It has no strong association for us, no meaning. We do not live here, we do not want to be here, we resent having been sent here.

In the ROK Army sector on our right flank, the Koreans treat the land differently. They do not strip it away and build sandbagged towers and buildings of imported metal and lumber. They shape the land and put it to use. Their bunkers have low silhouettes and are covered with soil, and the soil sprouts vegetation. A person cannot see the bunker unless he knows it is there. The ROK soldiers have woven straw liners for their foxholes, thick walls and mats made of grass they have cultivated. The straw serves to keep them warm in winter and dry in summer. The straw is grown in the sector that is defended by the soldiers who weave the straw and use it. They grow vegetables and rice as well as straw. They have many reasons to defend the soil they occupy.

They have no fence; they've created a continuous ridge line, and in crossing it a man must silhouette himself against the sky.

Nothing in the ROK Army sector is offensive to the eye; the land looks restful and at peace, tended and productive. The ROK Army sector of the DMZ looks not like a combat zone but like a farm.

The Koreans treat the land as a good doctor might treat a patient. 'First of all you must do no harm.' They are gentle and perform surgery only when absolutely necessary. They are careful to insure that when they are finished, the patient is better off than he was before treatment began.

September 16
For the record: Koreans in Korea

KATUSA: *Korean augmentation to the U.S. Army.* Korean privates and corporals attached to U.S. Army units. They are issued American clothing and equipment, but they are worse off than Americans. Because they cannot understand English, they appear stupid. They miss instructions, which are given in English, and therefore they continually fuck up. So they are given the shit details, the wet foxholes, the machine gun to carry rather than the grenade launcher, the bunk farthest from the oil-burning stove in winter, farthest from the window in summer. Demoralized, they move at half-speed, lag behind, 'maintain a low profile.' Approximately one out of every four soldiers along the fence at night is a Katusa.

What the Koreans do—
    KATUSA soldiers
    Clear minefields
    Construction
    Steal (village slicky boys)
    Night guard duty at Camp Matta (these guys are neither
soldiers nor civilians; they're some kind of security guards)
    Tend bar at the Officers' Club
    Wait on tables, mess hall
    Cook
    Houseboys (clean, wash, press, shine. Sell your socks in the
ville.)

They treat us with feigned respect and barely concealed disdain, with a kind of phony obeisance.

I'm a mercenary soldier from an imperialist state. I try to keep that in mind, to bury patriotic idealism and Good Samaritan bullshit. We aren't here to help *them*, we're here to protect our own interests. A dose of realism: I'm here because it's good for my country, not theirs—because it's good for me, not them. Because otherwise I'd be in Vietnam or Canada or jail.

EIGHT

Every so often, during the night, a report-that-shouldn't-have filtered all the way up from the fence to the battalion TOC. It would be phoned in to one of the company CPs from the fence, and the company telephone operator, rather than alerting the company commander, which he should have, simply relayed the message to the TOC. The report would come in by phone at two, three, four o'clock in the morning. The RTO on duty at the TOC would buzz Captain Stewart and the sound of the ringing phone would carry easily through the thin walls and wake up Evans, wake up me, not wake up Harmon, who seemed able to sleep through anything; and then Specks Morgan or Skinny Artie Shaw or Crazy Mann, whoever was on at the TOC, would give Captain Stewart the message, which was:

"Position 113 reports rocks being thrown at him."

"Tell the stupid son of a bitch to throw 'em back!" I heard Captain Stewart scream into the phone one night.

But walking the fence one morning I got to thinking about rocks. I could imagine my own ass on the fence at two o'clock in the morning and a stone the size of a baseball landing three or four feet from my position. I'd phone it in too. I'd make up any excuse to talk to somebody right then.

What if I were out there in the dark, well past midnight, and a rock lands near my foxhole? I'm a regular trooper, a rifleman. I've been up since three that afternoon; I climbed into a truck at five, test-fired my weapon on the way to the fence at five-thirty, arrived at the fence at six o'clock. I'll be on duty for twelve hours, perhaps longer.

The night turns dark. The fence-walker hurries by. Crickets chirp. I yell insults across to the guy in the next foxhole, and he shouts back. We light the flame pots. Maybe the company commander comes by, stops, checks my rifle (round in chamber, safety on), moves on to the next position. Platoon sergeant comes by. Smokes a cigaret. Moves on.

Four hours later. Midnight. I eat some C-rations. One o'clock. Tired. One-thirty. Two o'clock. Sleepy. Three o'clock. I'm nodding off.

Plink. What was that?

Everything's quiet. The fire pot has burned way down. I get up, sling my rifle across my back, pick up the can of diesel fuel, shuffle over to the pot. I unscrew the top, lift the heavy can, pour in the fuel. The fire flares up, bright yellow—a welcome rush of heat, but it's too bright. I'll have a difficult time seeing for a while. Screw the top back on the can, deposit can in foxhole. I walk off behind the foxhole, unbutton my fly, take a piss. Button up. Unsling my rifle, walk back to the fence. I walk up and down, peer through. Stare into the darkness looking for a face, for eyes staring back at me from the edge of the firelight. Back at my foxhole, I sit on the top of it. Time: 3:10. I lean against the sandbags. Nice. Hard, but comfortable. Sleepy. I nod.

Thump!

And then awareness begins to creep through my thighs, up into my gut, up my spine to the hair on the back of my neck.

There's somebody out there.

They're throwing rocks at me. They expect me to react if I'm awake. If I'm asleep . . . .

They're out there, and they can see me, and they want to come through the fence here, now.

They could have thrown a hand grenade.

But they want only to get through.

I stare out in front of me, past the fire pot, past the fence. There is simply blackness—I can see the earth perhaps five, perhaps ten feet beyond the fence. No more. Nothing out there but darkness—and someone who is as close to me as a stone's throw. He can see me and I can't see him. But he throws rocks at me. He throws rocks. I hear them land. If I were asleep—if I did not hear the rocks strike the earth—why, he would be here in seconds. Slip through the minefield (prodding, prodding with the thin stick he carries), up to the fence, big wire cutters (a rag wrapped around the head to muffle sound), small hole in the fence (nine cuts needed, no more) and he crawls through. Crawls past me—sleeping, perhaps snoring. Is he tempted to cut my throat?

Then he is gone. Nothing left but a few rocks around my foxhole, some footprints in the minefield, and a hole in the fence. A hole to be discovered later and reported by me, the soldier asleep at his post, or by the fence-walker.

We talked about that rock-throwing business: Captain Stewart, Evans, Harmon, and I. Harmon seemed to know a little about it. It happened in other battalion sectors as well as ours. It was a North Korean tactic used by infiltrators and spy trainees. The rocks were a message from the other side. The message said: I see you. It said: Are you awake? If not, I'm coming through. It said: I am out here, you American bastard —try to kill me. It said: Fire a few rounds in my direction and I will have passed my final exam.

18 Sep
For the record: night ambush patrols
The patrols go out through one of the three gates in the fence, the men wearing not helmets but soft caps, carrying heavy packs, their faces blackened (or greened, if they're black already), a rifle or grenade launcher in their hands. They move through the gate and spread out, spaced far apart yet walking together, not watching where they're going but looking up, down, side to side. They spend the night in the DMZ.
How come they never see a North Korean?

North Koreans:
are enormously crafty. Traverse minefields rapidly, float over them like spirits. Come and go like smoke, appear out of

the darkness and disappear in an instant. Can see in the dark. Are sorcerers and demons.

Now get rational. To negotiate the minefields they have probes, long steel rods that they probe with as they walk. It is an efficient method because they remain upright, walking, unlike us. When we go through a minefield, we probe with a bayonet from a kneeling position. Much less successful. The NKs are well trained and carry equipment designed specifically for the job.

But what about night movement? Their ability to come and go seemingly at will is phenomenal. Can they really see and hear better than we can? Can they move more quietly too? North Koreans are not accustomed to electric lights, flashlights, automobiles, street lights, neon signs. They can find their way over rough terrain at night because they've been doing exactly that since they were children. On the other hand, we were raised in cities, on farms, in towns; we never learned to walk in the dark. We're not used to keeping quiet. Our rock bands are so loud that we've suffered hearing losses. Our lights are so bright that we can't see as well as people raised without electricity. We've adapted so well to modern life that we're losing our senses. We're adapting ourselves toward extinction.

Exaggerated notions. Yet we aren't as well trained as they are. And it's *their* briar patch.

Norm Stewart thinks they're digging tunnels under the DMZ. Colonel Curtis disagrees and won't permit Norm to send patrols out specifically to look for tunnel entrances. Jack Evans has no opinion, and Harmon plays it both ways, depends on whom he's talking to. But I'm backing Norm: the NKs play those propaganda speakers awfully loud sometimes, and they could be covering the sound of digging or blasting.

In late September Dennis Sullivan returned to the States, and the QRF platoon leader, Jerry Knapp, was relieved. Colonel Curtis relieved Knapp because he went to the village without permission one night, and the forward two squads of the QRF were called out. The platoon sergeant was back at Camp Matta attending to some problem concerning the two reserve squads; a Spec-4 was in charge of the forward unit. So it was Jack Evans, finally, who took the QRF into an area behind the fence where somebody thought he had spotted something. They swept the area twice and found nothing. Jerry Knapp was relieved the next morning when he returned from Changpa-ri.

A new S-1 and a new QRF platoon leader arrived the next day, both transferring up from one of the mechanized battalions at Camp Casey. The S-1 was a West Pointer. He was a health food nut and wouldn't eat the stuff they served at the mess hall. He carried his own food up to the Officers' Mess: jars of grain, bottles of pills, cans of powder, boxes of crackers and cereal. His name was Ron Vandenberg. He had very smooth white skin and black hair. He wore thick glasses, yet he was in the infantry. With that smooth skin and those glasses, though, he looked like a personnel type, infantry or not.

The new QRF platoon leader was Dave Linderman. He insisted on drinking tea and wouldn't touch the mess hall coffee. He had a narrow build, tan skin, and brown hair. His blue eyes were large and dark, and when he talked to you he fixed them on you and stared. He was a quiet, sincere fellow. He knew his stuff. He had brought his platoon sergeant with him, a thin, black man named Small, one of those no-nonsense NCOs. He was as good a platoon sergeant as Dave Linderman was a platoon leader.

Walking up the steps to the BOQ after supper on the night Linderman and Vandenberg arrived, I could hear Harmon's tape deck booming out our window toward North Korea.

> Give me a ticket for an airplane,
> Ain't got time to take a fast train.
> Lonely days are gone,
> I'm a-goin' home,
> My baby just wrote me a letter. . . .

I found a bunch of guys sitting around my room: Harmon, Evans, Vandenberg, and Phil Roberts. Dave Linderman had eaten dinner with me, then headed toward the fence to be with his forward two squads.

I stood in the doorway for a moment. Guys were sprawled in chairs and on bunks, and they wore tee-shirts, fatigue pants, and socks. The scene reminded me of my first night in Korea, at Camp Casey, and it was nice to recognize their faces.

Harmon's tape deck was turned up loud.

Well she wrote me a letter said she couldn't live without me
*   no more,*
Listen Mister can't you see I got to get back to my baby once
*   more,*
Any way. . . .

The room was littered with beer cans, letters, jars and boxes of peculiar-looking food, ashtrays, magazines, and weapons. There were a couple of disassembled M-14s strewn about on the floor. Talk was about the girls in the village.

Harmon looked up and saw me. "So Art, how come I haven't seen you at the Green Door lately?"

"I don't know, John. Maybe because I haven't been there."

"Very funny. He's a clever fellow, isn't he? All that pent-up sexual energy going into wit. Getting horny, Art?"

"Don't worry, Harmon, I'll manage."

"Yeah, you'll manage. Listen, I'll fix you up with somebody special. I know just the girl for you. Hey Phil, don't you think Art's the proper stud for this girl?"

"You better watch it, Harmon," said Roberts. "You sound like a pimp."

Jack said, "You better find somebody quick, Harmon." Everybody laughed.

"What's the joke?" I asked. Green moved over and I sat down on my bunk.

"Harmon's steady has a friend she's trying to fix up," Jack said. "She's holding out on young John here till he comes up with a taker."

"Bullshit," said Harmon. "She does all the filthy things I tell her to. But she's bugging the hell out of me to find a steady for this friend of hers."

"You've got a steady and you still go to the Green Door?" I said to Harmon.

"Yeah. I like a bit of strange nooky now and then. What's it to you?"

"Doesn't your girlfriend mind?"

"What's she gonna do, divorce me? Besides, she doesn't know."

"Hey Harmon, how much do you pay this girl, anyhow?" Phil asked.

"None of your damn business."

"I'll tell you what," said Ron Vandenberg, the new S-1. "I wouldn't have a steady in Changpa-ri for two cents a month. You can't rely on these Korean bitches. They'll screw a battalion behind your back and then ask you for a raise."

"Maybe you don't pay 'em enough to begin with," said Harmon.

"I never had a steady," Vandenberg yawned. "Not in Korea. They're greedy little bitches. Sluts."

"They're sluts all right," said Harmon, "but they aren't bad if you pay them what they want. They understand money, that's all. They don't *have* to fuck; they're doing it for the dollars. They're more faithful than the little woman back home. The wife in the States is the opposite: she's got all the money she wants and no one to fuck her. She'll fuck for fun. She's the one you got to keep your eye on, eh Phil?"

"Bullshit," said Roberts. He turned red and twirled his wedding ring uncomfortably.

"You ought to try that," Harmon said to Vandenberg. "Give 'em their asking price sometime. Don't haggle about a few bucks for once, and see how they act. You want to start with Tammy?"

"Who?" I said.

"Tammy," John said. "Anderson's ex–."

"I didn't know that was who you were talking about."

"She's a gorgeous girl," Harmon said to me. "Get her for all night, try her out. What have you got to lose? Your virginity?"

"I thought she was looking to get married."

"Ah, bullshit. Give her a try."

"Did you ever fuck her, Harmon?" asked Bobby Green.

"No."

"Why do you care whether I do or don't?" I asked Harmon.

He grinned at me, showing crooked teeth. "I'm concerned about your health, Richardson. I'm telling you this for your own good, but shit, if the guy doesn't want a favor . . . ." He looked around at the others.

"I don't mean to appear ungrateful," I said, smiling.

"Look," said Harmon, "I don't really give a shit. But supposedly she's tired of one-night stands. She'll probably come cheap."

"I'll take her out," said Vandenberg.

I looked at him. He sat back in his chair, looking at Harmon, fingertips touching in front of his face. Under the fluorescent lights, his skin looked like rice paper, pale and shiny.

Harmon looked at me. "How about it, Art? You've got first refusal."

Coming from him this was surprising. It showed some loyalty to me. Maybe he wasn't such a bad guy after all.

"All right," I said.

"What do you mean, 'all right'?"

"I mean all right, I'll do it. You set it up and let me know when."

"Okay." He stood up and slapped me on the shoulder. "You won't be sorry, boy. She's a good-looking piece of ass."

"Well thank God that's settled," Phil Roberts said, standing up also. "Who's going to the Officers' Club? Is your driver still around, Art?"

"No. I gave Peters the night off."

They discussed whose driver to phone. Then they all got dressed. Jack Evans quickly assembled his rifle, and Vandenberg put away his bottles and boxes. In a few minutes they all rode off toward the Officers' Club.

I didn't go. I took off my shirt and boots and got out my journal.

22 Oct.
The Search
    I suppose the reason we write about our experience, about our past, is that we realize the past isn't merely "relevant," it's part of the present—the past is always present. Not only influential, but componential.

    I came home on leave before I was due to go to Korea. One morning at breakfast I asked Dad point blank what he'd done during WWII.

He laughed it off. "I got kicked by a horse," he said. "They wouldn't let you join the army if you couldn't get out of the way of the rear end of a horse."

"You told me that when I was little," I said, "and it didn't make sense to me even then. It makes less sense to me now. Were you hurt, or what?"

He laughed. "Something like that. They just didn't want me." He sipped his coffee.

"Why the hell won't you give me a straight answer?"

"Don't you speak to me that way, young man."

"This is important to me, Dad. If you didn't serve, I have a right to know why. I want to talk about it. Maybe I could learn something from you. But I don't know anything about you. You never talk about yourself."

He slammed his napkin down on the table and stood up. "Don't I have a right to eat my breakfast in peace?"

He put on his overcoat, grabbed his briefcase, and left the house.

Mom came downstairs and couldn't believe he'd gone without saying goodbye to her.

"What'd Dad do during the war?" I asked her.

"I don't know," she said. "He had an exemption of some kind. He worked for Travelers even then."

"What sort of exemption? How come he never got called up?"

"I don't know. He never talked about it."

"Didn't you ever wonder? I mean, he was only an insurance executive, for God's sake."

"Well. No. I guess I just thought we were both terribly lucky. It never occurred to me to stir things up."

The next morning I was sitting at my desk in the S-3 shop when the phone rang in the next office, Harmon's. I heard Sergeant Munoz answer it and tell Harmon that Colonel Curtis wanted to speak to him. Then I heard Harmon: "Yes sir. What? But sir, that's impossible! Right away, sir."

On his way out, he whipped past my desk so fast I had to hold the papers down. I asked him what was going on, but he didn't reply. The door slammed behind him and I knew it must be big —I'd never seen him move that fast.

He played the tape for me a couple of hours later; in fact, he played it over and over again for days.

They'd recorded it on one of the Guard Posts; it was a broadcast from the speakers in North Korea. The English was very good, and the recording was clear, so every word was understandable.

The message began typically: "Greetings from the People's Republic of Korea," and so on and so forth, all the usual bullshit at the beginning. But the tape rapidly turned chilling.

The voice addressed the soldiers of the 1st Battalion, 31st Infantry. It told us that our A Company was on our left flank, our C Company on our right. It went on to say that it hoped our company commanders weren't finding duty on the DMZ too hectic; it called them by name (George Butler, Curt Davis, John Harris) and then said it particularly regretted that John Harris, "an African Negro," had not "repudiated the capitalist cause and rebelled against the white tyrants" who had enslaved not only his ancestors but himself.

Then came the clincher.

"We are also pleased to welcome to the DMZ your two new officers, Lieutenants Vandenberg and Linderman. Lieutenant Linderman, we hope your trip from Camp Howze was not too arduous. Please take your time getting acquainted to your new assignment as platoon leader of the Quick Reaction Force. We recommend ten hours of sleep for you. And you never drink coffee, only tea, no sugar, and we are sure there is ample supply for you at Camp Matta.

"The People's Republic of Korea is flattered that the United States Army found us worthy of assigning a West Point officer to the 1st of the 31st. Welcome to you, Lieutenant Vandenberg. Perhaps you will die on the DMZ, although personnel officers seldom are killed in combat. The food here may not be to your liking, but we are sure that ample nourishment is available for you, especially since you brought your own supply of healthy foodstuffs."

Then they signed off. They'd gotten Camp Howze confused with Camp Casey, but otherwise their information was in order.

How could they know? Harmon worked on it for days, and the KCIA was called in. The mess hall staff and houseboys were questioned. Changpa-ri was turned upside down. But nothing —no spy—ever turned up. Aside from the closing of one of the whorehouses for health reasons, no one suffered consequences. Except, of course, every one of us. Word spread and everybody heard about the broadcast. It unnerved the battalion far more than anyone admitted.

NINE

LATE IN SEPTEMBER I WENT to Changpa-ri with Harmon. We left Matta after I'd walked the fence. It was a cool evening and we wore field jackets. We met Harmon's girl at her hootch, lingered briefly, and soon left on foot. I was carrying an AWOL bag. The village was closed and dark, but John's girl walked with assurance as our route snaked confusingly through side streets and alleys I'd never been down before. There were no streetlights. Everything was quiet. Gates were padlocked, doors were shut tight, windows were dark. We saw no one. Only a bedraggled chicken, asleep in a doorway, lifted its head from beneath its wing and clucked as we walked by.

At last we turned a corner and stopped in front of a dilapidated cement-block structure. The girl went to a barred window and spoke through it. Someone replied. Then the door was opened and we were let into a hallway. The girls drew a little away from us and exchanged a few words. John said to me, "Well, there she is. That's Tammy."

"I can't even see her face," I said. "It's too dark."

"She's good looking, take my word for it."

I peered over at the two girls. "I can't tell them apart. Is there a light somewhere? What does she look like?"

"Don't worry about it, Richardson, you're not gonna fuck her face."

"You never know. I might get lucky."

Harmon chuckled. "How're you getting back in the morning?"

"Peters is meeting me at the Green Door at 3:30."

"Okay. Well, have a ball. Don't get any on you."

"Right. And thanks. Maybe."

"You owe me one." He turned to the girls. "Come on, Kim. Let's go. Pronto."

After Harmon and his girl left, I looked down at the woman in front of me. She was taller than most Korean women. She stared up at me, but I could not see her face.

"Tammy?" I said.

"*Hi.*"

"I'm Art."

"Hello, Art. You take off your boots now?"

I knelt and unlaced my boots, and slipped them off. I stood up. "Do you have a light?"

Tammy disappeared for a moment and returned carrying a lighted candle. She was wearing a floor-length, white kimono. In the candlelight her face looked golden and smooth, a broad face with high cheekbones and large eyes: a lovely face framed by short dark hair and bangs. She stood still for a moment, not meeting my eyes, while I looked at her. She was afraid of me, I think. At last she turned away and I followed her up a narrow stairway. The air was warm and smelled of cooked fish. The wooden stairs beneath my stockinged feet had been worn smooth. At the top landing we turned down a hallway. I followed her through a door. The air in the small room was fresh and cool, and a breeze was coming in through a large window.

Tammy said, "You hungry, Lieutenant Art?"

"No. But I'm thirsty."

"You like beer?"

"Yes, I'd love a beer."

"I bring you a beer. Please, you get comfortable." The small room was dark, and she still held the candle, and her face was illuminated by its yellow light. She turned to go but I put out my hand, catching her arm. I pulled her toward me and blew out the candle. I put my arms around her and kissed her. The aroma of *kimchi* was on her breath; her lips were damp, small, and soft. Her hair was fragrant and her body felt hard and muscular. I kissed her for a long time. I was feeling a deep longing, not just to make love to her but to be loved by her.

She lay passively in my arms and didn't kiss me back. Finally she pulled away and left the room.

I looked around. In the darkness I could see that the large window facing the street was in an alcove. A bed filled the alcove in front of the window. It was a low bed built into the alcove only a foot or so off the floor, and I went and lay on the cool sheets, closed the window and stared out. The window looked down on the narrow street, the slanted tile roofs and small courtyards. The street was empty and the one-story dwellings opposite were dark, their courtyards deserted. There was no sign of life anywhere.

I thought of Anderson. Had he lain in this bed? How many times? Surely Tammy would think of him. How would I compare?

I took off my fatigue shirt and pants and laid them on the floor. I got the clock out of my AWOL bag and wound it and set the alarm.

I lay down again. I had showered after walking the fence and I felt fresh, though tired. A nice tired. I also felt excited, the way you do when you're about to be with a girl for the first time. Not scared, exactly. Pleasantly nervous and eager.

The door opened and closed. Tammy's kimono rustled as she crossed the room. She knelt by the bed and poured the beer into a glass. My eyes had adjusted to the darkness and I watched the foam race up the inside of the glass and spill over. She licked the foam away and handed me the glass. The bubbles made tiny popping sounds as the foam settled. I was thirsty and the beer tasted good. It was not cold, merely cool, but it was heavy and frothy, and the sharpness of the carbonation was a welcome sensation.

While I drank, she fussed about the room. She had suddenly found a million things to do: she opened and closed drawers, rearranged objects, straightened a picture I couldn't see, opened cabinet doors and closed them.

"Tammy," I finally said. I put down the beer. "Come over here."

She hesitated, and then she walked to the bed. She lay down beside me.

I slipped the kimono off her. She wore underwear beneath it, and I removed that, too. I touched and stroked her body slowly, gently. She lay still. It was like our kiss: she seemed to be just putting up with it. I made love to her for a long time before I entered her. All the while she neither spoke, nor looked at me, nor actively sought to arouse me. I did all the love-making and I had no idea whether she approved. But she was smooth and fragrant, and she did not resist, and she was so warm and soft that she made me feel welcome, almost wanted. Her body was comfortable and pliable.

I could barely see her face in the darkness, but I watched it, hoping for some sign of pleasure. But she hid her feelings—kept her face expressionless and said nothing. We lay together on her bed and I did what I wanted and she gave me nothing but cooperation.

When finally she spread her legs, it was with reluctance, I thought, not eagerness. She was tight and difficult to get into. She didn't help me. I pushed slowly because I didn't want to hurt her. I moved gently but I came almost as soon as I entered her. I made no sound. The entire night had been marked by soundlessness: no rustling of mattress and bed clothes, no sigh or gasp, no words, and at last a quiet, secret orgasm.

Then I was still. I lay on top of her, my face buried in her sweet-smelling neck. I lay there for a long time. Neither of us spoke. I brushed her hair away from her face. It was soft hair, damp at the edges, tangled. She let me stroke her hair and she didn't move. I adored her.

Finally I rolled off her. My penis, now shriveled, slid from her and spread its wet stickiness on her thighs, and when I lifted myself and tried to turn over, our limbs got mixed up, and we thrashed about for a few seconds before we separated our legs and arms. Tammy got up, put on her kimono, and left the room.

I lay on the bed, face down, cheek against the rough pillow case. A fly buzzed somewhere in the dark room, then hit the window with a sharp sound—*tick*. It buzzed again, hit the glass again. It kept on flying into the window, flying at it more and more frantically. After a few minutes it dropped to the sill, buzzed weakly for a moment, and lay still.

Tammy returned after a while. She was carrying a bowl in her hands that contained something I couldn't identify, probably soup, and she set it down beside the bed, picked up the beer bottle and glass and again left the room. I leaned over the edge of the bed. The liquid in the bowl was steaming. That felt good because the window next to the bed was beginning to radiate cold. I picked up the bowl, which was hot and burned my fingers. I held it by the rim at the top. It was made of brass or stainless steel (I couldn't tell which in the darkness) and it was large for a soup bowl. I sniffed it. No odor. There was no spoon, either. Should I sip from the edge of the bowl? I did. It tasted awful. I dipped a finger into the scalding liquid and felt something soft and rather large in there, like a dumpling or a piece of fish. I pulled it out. A washcloth. She'd brought me a bowl of hot water and washcloth, but she'd been too shy to wash me.

When she came to bed a few minutes later, she was wearing panties and a bra. I was nearly asleep. She pulled a blanket up over us and I held her and tried to fall asleep, but I was uncomfortable. In the past I'd slept all night in the same bed with a woman only a few times, and I'd never gotten used to it. Tammy's tight little body was warm and I soon became too hot and began to sweat. I gave up on the idea of holding her in my arms. After a few moments I turned away from her, toward the window. We lay with just the sheet and a blanket over us, and the cold from outside radiated in through the glass, cooling my damp skin. I fell asleep.

I awoke feeling that I'd overslept, that it was past dawn and I had missed the morning fence walk. Colonel Curtis would be furious and I'd be running an ambush patrol tomorrow.

I looked out the window and saw the darkness and knew I was all right. I looked over at the alarm clock; it was just past three. Tammy was asleep beside me. I could see her face: her closed eyes, thin eyelashes, fat cheeks. I kissed her. Her eyes fluttered open, focused on me, and sprang wide open. She got up and left the room.

Tammy was wearing a long skirt and a blouse when she returned. She handed me a small cup of tea which was very hot and did not contain a washcloth.

It was just 3:30 and still dark. Outside the air was cold and fresh. Tammy led me toward the Green Door through the waking village. We could hear people talking, see lights, hear pans and dishes clinking together. A couple of soldiers approached from up the street, peered at us, and saluted. Finally we turned a corner and I recognized the street. A couple of jeeps stood in front of the Green Door.

Tammy touched my arm lightly, stopped, and looked at the ground. "You pay me now, Lieutenant Arthur?"

I looked at her, feeling foolish. I would have forgotten to pay her. Part of me wanted her to have spent the night with me out of love.

I had the money ready. I put my overnight bag down on the dirt street, fished around in my pocket, pulled it out and handed it to her. She counted it. A ten and a five, fifteen dollars in M.P.C. She rubbed the bills between her thumb and forefinger like a bank teller looking for sticking bills. She counted it two or three times, shuffling the two bills from one hand to the other as though searching for more. Wasn't that enough? I'd given her more but I was trying to save money, and fifteen dollars was the going rate for an all-nighter. . . .

She looked up at me, and her expression was indignant. I thought she was about to say something. Instead she abruptly turned, and fled.

                                          I stayed out of the village for a while. I played poker at the Officers' Club, hung around the BOQ, went up to the Forward CP with Jack. Finally I decided to look up Tammy again. I went to the village during the day, between fence-walks. Whatever was good about the time I spent in bed with her that day was spoiled afterward. We were walking back toward the Green Door in the late afternoon. Sunlight slanted across the street and touched the red roofs. We had been together all day. As we approached the Green Door, Tammy pulled me into a doorway.

"You pay me now," she said.

I thought maybe what had happened between us could not be paid for. "You need money right now?"

"*Hi.* Yes."

I got out my wallet and gave her fifteen dollars.

"That's not enough. Please. I need more."

"I can't give you more."

"Yes. You have more money."

"How much more do you need?"

"Please, I owe Mama-san much money."

I gave her ten dollars. She looked unsatisfied. I had a few singles left, and another five. I gave her the five. She took it. Then she walked away.

I had been trying to put away some money for savings. I had so much else to give—I would give her anything. Was that all she wanted, just money?

I watched her go, a small girl in a blue jacket and a long black skirt, taking fast little steps down the dirt street. She walked in the shadows and the blue October sky above her looked very deep.

We had gone to the same room with the bed in the alcove, only now it was daytime and I could see the room with its pictures of movie stars from magazines and photographs of the orphanage, and a bureau and a wardrobe and the wide, hard bed in the alcove and the large window with the tile roofs and blue sky beyond it. We ate rice with meat and eggs, and then she pulled the curtain across the window, but it was white and translucent like a membrane and daylight came into the room. We took off our clothes and all her shyness from a few nights before seemed to be gone. She lay beneath me and I put my body on top of hers and lying on her I could feel all of her body, feel her skin warm and smooth and alive next to mine and some of the longing I felt went away and I was very happy. I stretched myself along the full length of her and felt her skin pressing against the tops of my feet, my knees, thighs, groin, stomach, her breasts against my chest, her cheek against my ear, her lips on my neck.

She began to squirm beneath me as though she were trying to get away, acting as if she hadn't quite made up her mind about whether she wanted to go through with this or not, like a school-girl. I looked at her face and her expression was impudent and she was smiling and I knew then what her squirming meant, and I accommodated her.

We made love most of the day, pausing to wash and eat.

And then later, in the street, she asked for more and more money. Driving back to Camp Matta with Peters, and then walking the fence, I mulled it over. I didn't think I wanted to see her again.

TEN

O CTOBER 6

It's fall. In the distance, the hills have turned red, yellow, and brown. Above them the sky is a clear and brilliant blue. All along the fence, smoke hangs in the air: the burning not of leaves in backyards, but of brush and grass behind the fox-holes. To start the fires, men splash diesel fuel on the ground and apply matches. There is no danger of the fires spreading too far and burning beyond control—what is there for a fire to consume in this place? Weeds. Mud. Rocks. The fires burn for a few minutes, at most an hour, and then go out.

Black smoke in the distance, plumes on the horizon.

At home, school has started. The football season must be in full swing. People spill out of the stadium and hurry home, kicking leaves on sidewalks. There are no leaves here. At home, in roadside stands, pumpkins and bushel baskets full of apples overflow wooden tables. Roasted chestnuts and hot mulled cider, homemade pumpkin and apple pies, and Indian corn sit on tables and hang from posts. Jars of honey and jam and cans of maple syrup line the shelves. But not here.

Here the food is the same and we've had no frost yet, but the air has turned cold, and the colors of the weeds and grass and brush are turning. Red, yellow, and brown. There are no trees, and no leaves. The season has changed but our routine has not. This is a piss-poor excuse for a nonwar.

One night in early October I was lying on my bunk reading. Colonel Curtis, Norm Stewart, and Jack Evans had not yet returned from the fence. Major Nichols was in his room, and John Harmon and couple of others were somewhere about, too.

There was a shot. It came from close by, outside the BOQ. A sharp explosion, unmistakable to me now—an M-14 for certain, no chance of it being a blank. For a moment all talking ceased. I was in my underwear, olive drab boxer shorts and tee-shirt, but I rolled out of my bunk anyway and grabbed a flashlight that I kept on the floor and followed the others out the door.

In the cool darkness outside the BOQ a group of men stood clustered together—Major Nichols, Harmon, and the others. Most were in their underwear too. A GI stood there, one of the drivers, Lewis. He wore fatigues and held a rifle. He was saying, "I told him to halt and he kept on walking, I told him to halt. . . ." Nobody did anything. They had all been talking excitedly, but then there was a sudden silence. In the background was a sound: a groaning that rose and fell in intensity like ocean swells. The sound came from the hill behind the BOQ. It was very loud. The only light source was a single bulb shining out the open door of the BOQ, so what I saw was a group of half-faces, like a cluster of half-moons in the darkness. One cheek, half a nose, one eye. The loud groaning continued. I went around the building and shone my flashlight up the hill toward the sound, but the thin beam was quickly lost in the dark. There was a tone of anguish in that wailing that filled me with a desperate urge to act.

I started running up the hill. Dried stalks of grass and small rocks stung my bare feet. I remember thinking that perhaps I could help. But would I get shot too? I wanted to silence that dreadful moaning.

My feet hurt and I was gasping for breath. Someone, a second voice from uphill, began to shout. The language was Korean, the tone angry. I answered the shouting:

"Don't shoot! American! Don't shoot!"

Suddenly I was on a little road. The gravel cut my feet. In the light of my flashlight now I could see a man standing over another man. The groaning was dying away. The man who was standing continued to shout at me. I couldn't understand a word he was saying. He was Korean and he wore fatigues with no insignia. He held a rifle in his hands, and now as I approached him, he began to wave the rifle in the air for emphasis as he shouted. I was afraid he'd shoot me.

The man on the ground stopped his pitiful wailing before I reached him. I ignored the standing man—what could I do for him? I knelt beside the man on the ground and shone the light on his face. Korean features: broad nose, large cheeks, small straight mouth. His closed eyes squinted in pain. He seemed to be breathing.

The thing that came back was what had been drilled into my head over weeks and months of dull, repetitive training: *Clear the airway. Stop the bleeding. Protect the wound. Treat for shock.*

I grabbed his chin, yanked open his mouth. It was empty, and his tongue (pink in the sudden bright light) was where I thought it should be.

The bleeding was next. Where had he been shot? The little white circle from my flashlight flickered up and down his torso. There. A hole in his shirt, just above his belt. I began to pull his shirt out of his trousers. What would I find? I loosened his belt and his zipper (odd thing, undoing another man's pants) and I tugged at his shirt. There it was, next to his navel: a small red disk. Smaller than his navel. *Stop the bleeding.* There was no bleeding.

I had thought that nothing could be more dreadful than the rising and falling moans that had come from this man. But this little red disk was worse. His stillness and silence when I reached him were worse too. And I knew that something even more awful was yet to come, because they had told us bullets do not merely enter a body. They go through it. And because a bullet tumbles and rips things up before it exits, the second wound is always bigger than the first.

Stop the bleeding. Protect the wound. So I had to turn him over and find the exit wound.

Someone arrived panting noisily behind me, boots cruching

on the gravel. "Help me turn him over," I said. I struggled with his butt and legs while the other man turned his trunk. "Careful of his head." As soon as we had him up on his side I could see it. "Hold him here." I leaned down close and stared. On his lower back there was a red protrusion of flesh, slightly larger than a silver dollar but jagged and shaped like a triangle. A damp, sponge-like wound, it mushroomed out from his back like a red piece of cauliflower. Again there was blood, but no bleeding. Only this large protruding red wound, this three-dimensional triangle of meat. *Protect the wound.* I straightened up hastily and pulled my tee-shirt over my head. I crumpled it up and was about to press it against the wound when I thought: Protect it from what? The tee-shirt was not sterile; it would contaminate the man's insides. I threw it aside and pulled his shirt tail down over the wound.

"Okay, let him down on his back." *Treat for shock.* I looked at the man next to me. Major Nichols. "We've got to keep him warm, sir."

"You're right, it's colder than a witch out here."

Someone else ran up, panting. "Evans called Doc Lang." It was Harmon. "They're sending an ambulance. Probably take all night, those bastards."

"John, we've got to treat this guy for shock. Get him warm." My voice was not steady, but it was loud. Harmon and Major Nichols took off their field jackets. When had they put them on? Had there been time? My whole body was shivering. I reached over and grabbed my tee-shirt and put it on. The Major stuffed his field jacket under the wounded man's feet while Harmon laid his jacket over the man's chest. One of them ran off down the hill.

I sat on the ground next to the Korean, up by his head. There was nothing more I could do. I was shaking now. The wounded man was breathing with difficulty. I reached out and touched his cheek. I stroked his short black hair.

This man is dying, I thought. He's alive now, but he'll be dead soon. A few minutes, it's a matter of time. He'll simply stop breathing.

I sat like that, my hand on his head. The other Korean began to talk again, fear in his voice now, not accusation. He seemed to be pleading. I didn't know what else to do because I couldn't understand him, so I ignored him. Time passed. Every now and then a cold drop of sweat would run from my armpit down my side.

The air rasped noisily in and out of the wounded man's throat. I waited for it to stop.

And then finally there was shouting from below and flashlights weaving back and forth, and the sound of a truck. Men were yelling in the darkness. The truck whined as it strained up the hill. Some soldiers arrived carrying a stretcher. One of them was Doc Lang. We put the man on the stretcher, the ambulance backed up to us, and we put the stretcher and the man into the ambulance. Doc Lang jumped in behind him. He already had ahold of his wrist and was taking his pulse. I shouted, "He's shot in the stomach!" Then Major Nichols slammed the rear doors and yelled to the driver, and the ambulance lurched off down the hill.

The others went back down without me. I took a few deep breaths and then picked up my flashlight. My feet throbbed painfully. I limped down the steep hillside toward the BOQ. I was alone. Already Camp Matta was quiet again, and from up there I could see most of the compound: rows of Quonset huts marked by bare lightbulbs; the TOC at the bottom of the hill, beyond the BOQ, brightly lit and sandbagged.

After a while a Huey flew in with a roar and they drove the ambulance to the LZ in front of the headquarters building. I could see the medics scrambling in the darkness. They put the wounded man into the helicopter and it took off, disappearing around behind the low hills to the south. So the Korean had lived at least that long.

At the BOQ, everyone was talking excitedly. I mostly listened. The man had been shot by a kid named Lewis, the XO's driver. Major Nichols hadn't needed him, so he'd been pulling guard duty at the BOQ. He had shouted "Halt!" at the Korean, who was walking down from the hilltop to take a smoke break. He repeated the command three times, and when the Korean kept walking, Lewis shot him. He kneeled down on one knee and shot him from that position, a hell of a shot in the dark, everyone agreed. What PFC Lewis did not know was the Korean word for halt, which is *chong-ji* and which everybody is told over and over when he first arrives. And promptly forgets.

I felt sorry for the poor bastard Lewis, having something like that on his conscience.

There was also speculation about Doc Lang. He was in trouble, Major Nichols asserted, because he had called in a medivac helicopter from I Corps. We weren't supposed to call in dust-offs for Koreans. The helicopters were for Americans only.

11 Oct.
   The search.
   I wonder what happened to me. Why did I act when nobody else did? Why was I the first one to reach the wounded man?
   What if those sounds had been coming from a resourceful and healthy North Korean?
   Nobody seemed to be aware of what my role in the incident had been, and I resented that. I would have liked some credit for what I'd done. Acknowledgement. Yet I didn't say anything about it. (What could I have said? Hey, you guys, I'm a hero, I saved his life.) What did I expect, a medal?
   But I sure didn't think of that when I took off up that hill in my bare feet.

   The next morning, after a painful fence-walk, I went to see Doc Lang about my feet. The sign he'd posted outside the aid shack read:

> *Flies cause disease.*
> *Keep yours closed.*
> *Be wise.*
> *Rubberize.*

While Doc worked on my feet he asked me what I had been doing on that cold hill in my underwear and bare feet.
   "First aid," I said. "I went up there to try to help the guy."
   "What'd you do?"
   "I pretty much left him alone. He wasn't bleeding or anything. We tried to keep him warm."
   "He wasn't bleeding?" said Doc.
   "No. Didn't you treat the wounds?"
   "Not enough time."
   "You mean he died?"
   "Nope. We saved him. Still critical, I hear, but alive. So far."
   I asked why neither of the wounds had been bleeding.
   "Strange, isn't it?" he said. "The body's reaction to being shot. That shows you what shock'll do to a person. The fluids seem to disappear, evaporate. We had six IVs started by the time

110

that chopper arrived. That was good, fast work. But he bled later, I bet. I bet he bled near to death on that helicopter." Doc began doing something very painful to the sole of my right foot. "What's this about 'wounds'? He was only shot once."

"My God! Didn't you see that hole in his back?"

"What hole?"

I couldn't believe what I was hearing. "The exit wound!"

"We were busy getting liquid into him," Doc said. "Never saw it."

October 14

Guys are taking a couple days leave and going down to Seoul. They say it's fantastic: American girls, real food, taxis, night clubs with bands (Korean bands: "I warra hoe your haaaan!").

Dating a girl! Going dancing with her on Saturday night, then taking her back to her apartment, folding her into your arms on the doorstep, giving her a goodnight kiss. Watching her front door close in your face. My God! Whose ingenious idea was it to bring these girls over here? Why didn't they ship their parents over too? All the forbiddance and sexual frustration of America, right here in Korea! All the comforts of home.

They're Red Cross girls. Donut Dollies. Harmon says they feel sorry for GIs, but they love officers. Their ambition is to marry one. (Talk about shooting low!)

Evans came back from Seoul yesterday and he was crazy, different. Grinning from ear to ear. "I made out with that girl, Tina," he said, "and I didn't lay her. Isn't that refreshing?"

Sometimes on those fall days or nights, along the fence or at the forward CP—any high hill would do if conditions were right—we'd get Vietnam on the big radio/transmitters on the backs of our jeeps. Some quirk in the atmosphere connected our radios to those of our counterparts in Southeast Asia, and we would hear the hiss of static, the garble of voices, and then very clearly, yelling: "Roger, four-niner, I roger that but I can't get in, it's too hot. . . ."

It was eerie to listen to a battle, to calls for air support and dust-offs, to casualty reports, to someone screaming *Contact! Contact!* But we listened anyway, a group of us gathered around the back of a jeep on a hilltop, spectators to a drama far more brutal than our own. We'd stand beside our jeeps somewhere along the fence, Peters, me, Jack, Norm Stewart, Linderman and his driver, and we'd listen, spellbound, and then one of us would shake his head and say, "Those fellows are catching some shit." What he meant was, "Those fellows are catching shit instead of us."

Sometimes we'd look at each other and grin, feeling good and lucky and smug, but other times we'd avoid one another's eyes altogether. More often than not, hearing those transmissions made us feel just plain guilty.

ELEVEN

One evening, mortar rounds started landing just in front of the fence in the B Company sector. There was no warning. I was walking toward the setting sun and I had just climbed to the top of a sharp rise and was starting down. I had a fine view of a long, curving section of fence. Where the ground leveled off at the bottom of the hill I spotted, just north of the fence, a man. This man was standing in the narrow strip of safe earth between the fence and the minefield. When I saw him, my immediate reaction was: 'There's one of *them!*' But he appeared to be wearing a flak jacket, and certainly that was an American helmet perched on his hed. He was not far from the gate at the bottom of the hill, and the gate was standing open. I stayed where I was and watched him, trying to figure out what he was doing north of the fence. He had something in his hands — perhaps a shovel — and he was bending toward the ground. Was he clearing mines? And then I remembered something I had overheard, perhaps in the BOQ or during one of the Colonel's morning briefings, and I realized that he had been sent out with a rake to manicure the ground so that if there were enemy activity during the night, on the following morning there'd be evidence of it in the smooth dirt.

And then a few meters north of the fence, not twenty meters from the man with the rake, there appeared a great gray cloud of dirt, followed, seconds later, by that unique noise, terrifically loud and quick: *CRACK!*

And here's the strange part: the man outside the fence glanced up, looked at the cloud briefly, and then bent back over his rake. He went on raking.

About twenty seconds later, the first mortar round was followed by a second one which landed a bit farther off—thirty or forty meters from the man—but then a third fell closer to him than the first one had, no more than ten meters away. The explosions came and went quickly: *CRACK! CRACK!* The man kept raking. That he was still alive was a fluke. From inside the fence, startled troops, who had either flattened themselves where they stood or leapt into the nearest foxhole, yelled at the Katusa. But he stayed where he was and continued raking.

I jumped into the nearest foxhole, shoved a man aside and grabbed the field phone. I picked up the handset and spun the lever as hard as I could.

A man at the company CP answered, "Yeah?"

"Get me the TOC!" I shouted.

"What?"

"The TOC! Get me the TOC!" I felt a shock wave jolt the ground beneath my feet, and then I heard another round: *PELT!*

"What in the hell do you want the TOC for, position 126?"

"This is Lieutenant Richardson. Get me the TOC now!"

"Yes sir."

"And stay on the line till they answer."

He made the connection and buzzed it. Nothing happened.

"Ring again!"

"Still ringing."

Another voice: "TOC here."

"TOC, give me the four-deuce platoon, quick"

"Yes sir." A bunch of professionals at the TOC. They rang mortars. Somebody answered:

"Heavy Weapons Platoon, Sergeant Brady—"

"Cease fire! Cease fire!"

"We just did."

114

"This is Lieutenant Richardson. Where's Lieutenant Peabody?"

"He's right here, sir, but he's pretty busy. He's talking to the Colonel on the radio. Can you wait, sir?"

"I won't interrupt. Do you people know you were shooting at a GI?"

"We were zeroing our FPF, sir."

"Maybe so, but your FO must be blind!"

"Did he hit anybody, sir?"

"No, but he couldn't have come much closer. Out here."

"Out, sir."

I put the phone back and turned to the soldier I had pushed. "Sorry I shoved you," I said. "Seemed necessary."

He was staring through binoculars at the man north of the fence. "That's okay," he said. "By the way, Lieutenant Richardson, that's not a GI out there. That's a Katusa."

"It is?"

"Surer'n shit."

I walked down the hill to the gate. The man was still out beyond the fence, raking. Soldiers around the area had resumed their evening tasks: setting out trip flares, filling flame pots, tying cans and bells to the fence. They ignored the Katusa; it was as if he didn't exist anymore. Which was almost the case.

I paused at the gate and then went through it. That alone felt strange. I'd been out to the guard posts, but that had been in a jeep. I'd never been north of the fence on foot.

I walked over to the Katusa. As I approached he glanced up and saw me coming. He stopped raking and stood up straight, looking at me uncertainly. I touched his arm. "Are you hurt?"

"No speak English."

"Did you hear those explosions?"

"No understand English."

"Don't you understand *mortar?*" I shouted at him.

He flinched and blinked his eyes. He looked very young. His face was dirty, and his dark skin was peppered with small pimples, little red cones with white tips. His large, watery brown eyes stared up at me.

"Come with me." I gave his arm a gentle tug. "Come on." We walked back to the gate and through it. I found the Katusa's squad leader, a thin, sandy-haired man named Brown. He looked tired and preoccupied. The rims of his eyelids were red, and he didn't look straight at me; his eyes kept darting away from me.

When I brought the Katusa over to him, Brown said: "Aw damn, sir, did Kim fuck up again?" He gave the Katusa a weary, fed-up look. "Kim, what the fuck have you been up to now?"

I told him what I'd observed.

"Shoot, Lieutenant, this Katusa's been out to lunch since I took over the squad. He ain't worth a shit."

"Tell me something, Sergeant Brown," I said. "When did he last take leave?

"Leave? I wouldn't know about that, sir."

"Does he have a girlfriend? Where does his family live?"

"Sir? Now where in the fuck would I get that kind of information?"

"Don't get testy with me, Sergeant. It's your business to know it. This is a person here, and he happens to belong to you."

"Yes sir."

"Now he needs help. Get him to the Katusa sergeant major. Tonight. I wouldn't want him in the foxhole next to mine, I'll tell you that."

"Yes sir."

"I'm going to talk to Lieutenant Davis about this man, so be sure to report to your platoon sergeant."

"Yes sir."

I hated those yes-sirs. A man could yes-sir you to death, and you knew he was telling you to go fuck yourself. I started to say something, but changed my mind. Sergeant Brown had more than enough to worry about. I turned away.

"Sir?" Brown said.

I turned back. "What?"

"I want to tell you one thing. I don't want you to think I'm a fuck-off." He finally looked me in the eye. "I got my stripes two days ago, and that's when I took over this squad. Before that I was in the third platoon. We came off patrol yesterday morning, and I was on the fence last night as squad leader. I've slept about five hours in the last three days. I just wanted you to be aware of that."

"Okay, Sergeant Brown, I understand. But you almost lost this man. Did you see those rounds land?"

"Yes sir."

"Why didn't you do something?"

Embarrassed, he looked away. "I don't know," he mumbled. "I think I yelled something. . . ."

"Okay, nevermind. It's over, nobody got hurt. Next time take some action. That's all. Just do something."

"Yes sir."

"And good luck with your new squad. Get to know them."

"Yes sir."

He even saluted.

At breakfast the next morning, John Harmon said: "Hey Peabody. I hear those mortars of yours took target practice on a Katusa last night."

"Yeah, we got a real fire mission for a change." Greg laughed and took a sip of coffee. "My best FO started calling in these rounds real near the fence. Conners. Claimed he was shooting at a UI. I think he wanted to go south, man. He sure did. We packed him off this morning, back to Casey. They might court-martial him, they might commit him, they might just reassign him. I never want to see that fucker again. But he was a hell of an FO. He's been in-country eleven months. Hey Art, I hear you called the fire direction center from the fence."

"I did. It was awful. I don't know why you didn't kill that Katusa."

"Man, I know! Weren't those rounds close?" He laughed. "Conners damn near dropped one down the back of his shirt, didn't he?"

"Peabody, what is so funny? You almost killed a Katusa."

"*I* didn't. Conners did."

"You've been here too goddamn long, Peabody."

"Fuck you. I've been here six months. Art, that's all. Six months and eleven days. Just a little longer than you."

Two men on patrol in Company A were killed by a hand grenade that night. The patrol was set in its ambush position and the grenade suddenly came in on one of the positions. Some of the other men in the patrol heard it hit the ground and bounce. They heard a scream and then the explosion.

That was all. The grenade exploded right between the two men and killed them both. No one had the faintest idea where it came from.

Before he left for Seoul *again*, that lucky bastard, Jack Evans and I talked. It was a blustery morning, windy and cold. I had walked the fence and then eaten breakfast in the warm mess hall, and when I returned to the BOQ I found Jack in his room, throwing clothes into an AWOL bag.

"How do you do it?" I asked him. "How do you get away with it? Doesn't Captain Stewart mind?"

Jack was digging around in his footlocker. "It's not that tricky. You just have to put in for it way ahead of time. Colonel Curtis doesn't care, and neither does Norm. He covers for me. I'm hardly indispensible." He threw a couple of pairs of black socks into the AWOL bag. "You ought to do it yourself, Art. I'll walk that fence for you."

"Twice a day, plus your own work? I wouldn't ask that of anybody."

"No sweat. I'd do that for you. I really would."

"Thanks."

"Don't mention it. I haven't done it yet."

"Besides, I'd rather go with you. You've been there before. Does Tina have any friends?"

"She has a roommate who's not bad looking."

"Let's head down there together sometime."

He grinned. "We'll both go next time. I'll ask Tina about it this weekend." He zipped his bag. "I am *gone*, Arthur. Sayonara and goodbye. If I'm not back by Christmas, forward my mail."

"Hey Jack!"

He paused.

"Drink a decent cup of coffee for me."

He laughed. "You bet." Then the front door slammed behind him, and the BOQ was suddenly a very quiet place.

Two days later, on Sunday night, Jack returned. He walked into the Officers' Club, sauntered up to where Bobby Green and I were sitting at the bar, and put an arm around each of us.

"I'll have a Schlitz, Mr. Kim!" he shouted. "And serve these two gentlemen another of whatever they're having."

"Hey!" I said. "How was it?"

"It was fantastic!" he bellowed.

"Did you fuck her?" Bobby Green asked.

Jack grinned. "If you think I'd tell you, you prick, you're crazy."

Bobby leaned over toward me, his face all teeth and freckles. "Hear that, Art? I told you he'd fuck her this weekend."

October 27th
Dream last night. I'm in an apartment in the city—bare white walls—except for a single watercolor, framed. I see a reflection in glass, my face—then a reflection of a nuclear mushroom-shaped cloud.
I look out a window and see a red fireball. It's a nuclear attack. Fires spontaneously erupt in buildings—I can hear people shouting and I feel a pervasive sense of dread. It is the beginning of the end of everything—there is no future imaginable

Later—
I've been walking around like an idiot with absentee ballots in my hand trying to get the enlisted men to vote. But they're all too young. The drivers, the commo platoon, all the support personnel and the combat platoons, Recon, QRF, the mechanics—none of these guys is old enough to vote. I've gotten some strange looks. Talk about disenfranchisement. We'll probably get Nixon.

At three o'clock one morning a squad leader in B Company was carrying a cup of coffee down to one of his men on the fence. The chow truck had just arrived from the company area, and the squad leaders and platoon sergeants were milling around in the dark, picking up hot coffee and rations for their men. With all the movement and noise, all the banter and bitching and commotion, no one expected anything to happen.

Sergeant Toomey was walking back toward the fence from the road. He walked carefully on a narrow path that he knew was not wired with trip flares. There was no moon or starlight, only the flickering orange glow from the flame pots, and Sergeant Toomey could barely make out the dim ribbon of path. As he walked he looked down, taking care not to leave the path or to stumble and spill the coffee.

Just before he reached the fence, as he was about to make a left turn, Sergeant Toomey looked up. The North Korean was squatting directly in front of him, just on the other side of the fence. The Korean's face, a round Mongol face, circular and flat, loomed out of the darkness like the moon itself. His squatting body, in black, was nearly invisible, but his moon-like face—though darkened by camouflage grease—caught the orange light of the flame pots and glowed, disconnected, as if illuminated by some inner source of heat and light. His glittering eyes stared unblinkingly at Sergeant Toomey.

Sergeant Toomey froze and gaped at this apparition. He was holding a cup of scalding coffee in his left hand and gripping his rifle in his right, and not fifteen feet in front of him crouched a North Korean, motionless, unarmed but for wire cutters, fully visible.

I'm gonna *bag* him, thought Sergeant Toomey.

He was gripping his rifle behind the trigger guard, muzzle down. His finger was not on the trigger. He brought the muzzle up smoothly, aimed one-handed at the Korean ("Can you believe it, sir? I tried to do it without spillin the fuckin *coffee!*"), and squeezed the trigger.

Click.

No round in the chamber. He didn't even see the North Korean take off. By the time he'd dropped the coffee and chambered a round, the North Korean was gone. Toomey got his whole squad up on line, had them fire flares; he got the xenon searchlight down there; he called in four-deuce flares and white phosphorous. Curt Davis went down to help direct the operation and Colonel Curtis alerted all three patrols in the DMZ, then sent Linderman and two squads of his QRF out in front of the fence to sweep the vicinity. They thrashed around in the dark for two hours and found nothing. In fact, only one sign of that North Korean ever turned up. In his haste to depart, he left his wire cutters lying by the fence. They'd been manufactured in Cincinnati.

I talked to Sergeant Toomey the next morning and then wrote the hostile contact report. Toomey seemed dazed; he was astonished by his own reactions.

"Jesus Christ it was spooky, sir, I thought it was myself lookin back at me, I thought I'd caught a climpse of my own face in a mirror—it was so weird to actually *see* somebody out there for once. And that face, that face. My God. I thought about it all night. I thought I dreamt it. . . . Oh fuck, I'm so confused. I'm not even sure it happened anymore."

"Take it easy, Sergeant Toomey. It happened all right. The wire cutters are lying in the next room in the S-2's office. It seems impossible in daylight, I know, but last night—"

"I mean I always have a round chambered, sir—*always.* I check on my men every night to make sure *they* have a round chambered. Jesus Christ, what an opportunity. What a fuckin PFC-thing to do. Maybe God is on their side, sir—wouldn't that be a bitch?

"And I didn't spill the coffee—can you believe that? I didn't spill the fuckin coffee. Not until the firing pin struck that empty chamber—then I dropped it—but before that, when I brought my weapon up to shoot that cocksucker, I did it kinda easy, can you believe that, sir? Some part of me wanted to keep from spillin that coffee."

November 17
For the record:
What we're doing here is somehow not to be taken seriously. We only go through the motions; it's like training. This is not a real war, part of us says. This is playtime. We're on an extended coffee break.

We live on the border between fantasy and reality. Sometimes our fears are more dangerous than any real thing. We're a greater threat to ourselves than the North Koreans are.

And sometimes our fears are justified. Ask a veteran of the Korean War. That one was undeclared too, and it has not yet officially ended. We use live ammo. So do the other guys. The enemy is not imaginary.

November 18
The search:
Granted, I would have been drafted—I had no choice.

But I did choose to become an officer. I worked my butt off for that gold bar. I made distinguished graduate, too. And it's okay. It's a better life than being an enlisted man.

But why the Infantry Branch? I could have chosen Armor or Chemical or Engineer or Artillery. Why *infantry*, where the odds are so much greater that I'll be "seriously killed or wounded"?

Because if I'm going to do it, I thought, I want to do it right, do it all the way. Get the experience, be in the real army. And maybe, I thought, if I become an infantry officer, I can do something worthwhile. Save somebody's life. Like the guard on the hill, or that Katusa. I doubt that I could do anything more worthwhile with my life than be heroic. Where that comes from I don't know—maybe religion or literature. Or a liberal education. Or from Boy Scouts or radio. The Lone Ranger. I used to listen to the radio every Monday, Wednesday, and Friday night at 7:30. I must have been eight or ten. "A cloud of dust and a hearty, 'Hi-yo, Silver!' The Lone R-r-ranger r-r-rides again!" I get goose pimples just thinking about it. What music! He was always right, always did the right thing. He sure saved a lot of lives.

They didn't have four-deuce mortars back in Lone Ranger days though.

Anyway, all that's rationalization, isn't it? I chose or wound up in the infantry. However it worked I landed here. I didn't think about dying. I didn't say to myself, my chances of dying in this branch of the service are greater than in any other branch. I didn't think that. Why not? But if I knew it—knew it deep down—why did I go infantry anyhow? Do I want to die? Is my life so devoid of a positive, imagined future that I'd rather be dead?

But I might just survive my three years in the army.

What *am* I going to do with the rest of my life?

I have no idea.

Nov. 19
Just for the record:

I saw Tammy again last night. God, she's sweet. I had an easier time parting with my hard-earned money. Glad to.

I've been thinking about 'going steady' with her. To know she's going to be there, only for me—that might be worth it.

TWELVE

December 17

For the record:

I did not see this, I only heard about it. It occurred yesterday in the battalion on our left flank.

This is how I imagine it:

On a bleak hilltop a sergeant is giving a training lecture to a group of soldiers. The late afternoon air is cold and heavy; dark clouds, swollen with moisture, race overhead, billowing close to the hilltop. The ground is barren, void of trees and snow, wind-swept and dusty. A colorless sun balances on the horizon.

The soldiers sit in bleachers and pretend to pay attention to the sergeant. They are bored and indifferent, tired—a company's night barrier force, about eighty men on their way to the fence. They have paused at the test-fire range to observe a safety demonstration on the .45 caliber pistol. They have seen it before.

The Staff Sergeant giving the lecture has been handling military weapons for seventeen years. He has given this lecture a hundred times, and by now it's like rolling off a log. He is dressed in cleaned and pressed woolen OGs, and his trousers are evenly bloused and tucked neatly into the high tops of his shiny black jump boots. His field jacket is starched and pressed, and he has nothing in any of his pockets, so his overall appearance is flat, smooth, immaculate. He wears no gloves and no hat or helmet. His hair is cut very short and stands upright in a stiff crew cut. Because the wind is moisture-laden and blows strongly into his face, the tips of his ears and nose and cheeks have turned pink. He has to shout to be heard.

"Once more, then: watch my demonstration," the sergeant yells. "To clear the .45, work the slide to empty the chamber; remove the magazine; and the weapon is clear, *so.*"

Only one man in the entire company catches the error. He is a Spec-4 whose father's hobby was guns, and guns are his hobby too. He sits forward, suddenly alert. He has never liked this particular sergeant. His eyes open very wide.

The sergeant puts the pistol to his head, smiles, and pulls the trigger. There is an explosion. Most of the opposite side of the sergeant's head bursts and blows about as red fragments. A sudden puff of gray smoke evaporates in the wind. The sergeant's torso collapses. Blood flows rapidly and spreads darkly. What is left of the sergeant lies on the ground, half-faced, its blood soaking into the cold soil.

And I imagine the troops staring in silence for a moment or two. At first they're shocked. They're shocked out of their lethargy: this is something special. It's the most engaging safety demonstration they've seen all year, perhaps the best. They'll remember this one. They break into uncertain applause. They begin to whoop and holler and cheer, and their applause becomes more enthusiastic, it grows and swells until it sounds like the crackling of distant small-arms fire, then like the thunder of artillery. The sound of each hand-clap is lifted and carried away, lost in the sigh of the wind and the roar of the company's applause.

Jack went down to Seoul again right before Christmas and Colonel Curtis wouldn't let me go. Said I was indispensible, the only one he could trust to do it right. I suggested Harmon. The Colonel gave me a pretty weird look. He did admit that Jack could be trusted to do it right, but that was another reason that he couldn't let us both go down to Seoul at the same time.

When Jack returned in the damp, cold darkness of Sunday

night, he dragged me out of my bunk and into the ugly little living room near the front door.

"Art, I gotta talk to you." He spoke quietly but eagerly. He was grinning from ear to ear. "Holy shit, this Tina's some girl. She's fantastic. You gotta meet her."

"You have a good weekend?" I yawned and tried to tie my bathrobe.

"Oh man, we had a great time. I can't believe it. It was just terrific."

"I guess so. You're glowing!"

"Am I? Jesus Christ. Art, I'm in love. I mean, this girl—she's fantastic. We did everything. We spent the entire weekend in bed. I took a shower with her, a *shower* for God's sake. What a body she has, Jesus. We spent two days in a hotel in bed and in the shower together—Jesus, it was great. I can't believe it. It was wonderful. *Wonderful!*"

"That's great, Jack."

He stretched, and grinned contentedly. He looked at me as though seeing me for the first time. "So. What'd you do?"

I told him about Tammy: that I'd seen her and that we'd made arrangements for her to be my 'steady.'

"No shit?" he said.

"No shit."

"You still want to go to Seoul, don't you?"

"Yeah."

"What're you paying her?"

"One-twenty-five a month."

"Ouch."

"Yeah, well. Turns out the best things in life aren't free after all."

"But a steady, for Christ's sake. Why'd you do it?"

"I don't know," I said. "I like that girl. I really do, and I just felt like it. I wanted to know she'd be there."

December 23
  For the record:
  Another death this afternoon, this time up on one of the guard posts. The man who died was 19 years old. PFC Klein, from A Co.
  Klein was shot by a kid named Robert Alfano. Alfano shot Klein at point-blank range. The bullet struck Klein

125

in the chest next to his sternum, passed through his heart, and continued out through his back. Klein was Alfano's best friend.

I took Alfano's statement. I asked questions and listened while he haltingly told me his story, which I transcribed.

//////////////////////////STATEMENT /////////////////////////////

At approximately 1300 hours on 21 December, it was my turn to rest and I laid down in my sleeping bag. I had all my clothes on except my boots. I slept for about 3 hours and woke up about 1600 hours. When I woke up Klein had our C-rations heated up and had hot water ready for coffee. I stood up in my sleeping bag and ate my C-rations off the edge of the bunker opening, which was at ground level and looked off over North Korea. We had both finished eating and Klein was looking out a little door of the bunker and playing with his rifle, putting it back together I think. I wasn't interested in this as I have been around guns for 13 years. I was looking out the front opening of the bunker at North Korea when I broke wind. Klein turned toward me and said, "You know what that means," or something to that effect. He picked up his weapon, which was in one piece, and took the safety off, and pointed it at me. I replied jokingly, "Two can play that game," or something to that effect, and picked up my weapon. I took my safety off also but I was standing with my side toward Klein and my weapon was pointing toward the floor. I don't know what he did, but his weapon made a noise and I jumped. When I jumped my feet got tangled up in my sleeping bag and I started to lose my balance and fell backwards. There were nails on the wall of the bunker that we used for hanging things on and as I fell back my back struck one of these nails. I flinched when my back struck the nail and my weapon discharged. The whole bunker filled with smoke. Jerry (Klein) didn't flinch or jump or anything. He just set his weapon down. "Oh Bob," he said. Then he fell over on the floor. When he fell down I thought he was kidding until I saw blood on his parka. I thought he was kidding because the guys were always playing jokes on me. Once on the Barrier Fence I was carrying a 90mm on my shoulders and started to turn around. The 90mm hit something and Jerry (Klein) fell down. I thought that the 90mm had hit him in the head, but it had only hit a fence post. When I saw the blood I heard someone yell for a medic. I don't think it was me. Then I began to holler for a medic.

///////////////////////END OF STATEMENT /////////////////////////

126

Dec 24
For the record:
The *Pueblo* crew was released. They were to drive through
our battalion sector if the weather closed in, but it didn't
snow, so they took Hueys out of Panmunjom and flew directly to Seoul. I didn't know they had that many Hueys in
this country; I thought all but about two or three were in
Vietnam. We could see them as they climbed into the gray
sky and headed south.

General Woodward orally denied the written document he
signed admitting U.S. encroachment into NK territorial
waters. Said in effect, This written statement is a lie, we
didn't *really* steam into their waters, but I'm going to sign
this anyway because it looks like that's the only way we're
going to get these boys home for Christmas.

And the NKs accepted the signed document and pretended
not to hear the oral retraction. Selective deafness.

It's unbelieveable. What a bunch of liars; what a pack of
lies. I don't know who's stupider: NK or the U.S.

Yet they both got what they wanted. So maybe they're not
so stupid. Why stick to principle (Do not lie) when it gets in
the way of achieving your goals?

December 30
The search.
Evening. Letter from Mom today. She says:

> You asked about your father. And his crying at the air-
> port. I don't know, Art, it was only the second time in my
> whole life I've seen him cry. I think he cried out of guilt. I
> asked him about it but he hates to talk about it. Please
> don't ever tell him I told you this, but we talked about
> why he never served in the war. Somehow he got someone
> to write a letter to his draft board about how he was doing
> important research, especially for insuring servicemen
> and making their families more comfortable if they were
> killed. But it apparently wasn't quite as defense-oriented
> as the letter represented it as being . . . Anyway, these
> things perhaps ought to remain unsaid, buried in the past.

So Dad got somebody to write him a phony letter, did he?
And so he encourages me to join up. So I'm *his* military obli-
gation as well as my own. I'm the family KIA.

Great. Terrific. Well, at least I know. It doesn't change anything but at least it answers a few questions.

Midnight, December 31, 1968
For the record: I have survived 1968.

One year less.

'Short' was at his best tonight: Harmon had a PRC-25 propped up on his bunk so he could monitor the battalion net, and we heard "Shortshortshortshortshort," and later, "SHHOOOOOORRRRRRTT!"

At midnight, the men along the fence cut loose. Everything: rifles, machine guns, grenades. . . . It was great. We could see and hear it all the way back at Matta. (Cold night: standing outside the door to the BOQ we could see our breath.) On the northern horizon: flares popping all up and down the fence, dozens of them drifting in the still air, swaying gently beneath their parachutes, their light illuminating the twisted snakes of their own smoke trails. The smoke hanging over the hills, then disappearing as the flares blinked out one by one. Tracers whizzing off toward North Korea. The quick explosions of hand grenades. Men cheering.

Happy New Year! I'm still alive!

"Richardson, turn that fucking light off and go to sleep, you bastard." Harmon. John Harmon, the nasty lad, the bully-boy from Baltimore. The pasty little creep.

Hard to know why he wound up in the infantry. I never talk to him. He's from Baltimore, went to a prep school but only got into Penn State. Did ROTC there. Maybe his branch assignment was dependent on academics or something, so without an outstanding record he couldn't transfer out of infantry. Didn't do Navy ROTC or Air Force for the same reasons not many others do: the commitment is two or three years longer than the Army commitment.

Sleeps nude. Takes a shit every morning at 10:00 sharp. Keeps a bottle of Jack Daniels in the bottom drawer of his bureau and thinks nobody knows it's there. Went down to Seoul and bought a tape deck, tuner/amp, and speakers at the PX. Sleeps under an electric blanket.

Electric blanket.

Let him freeze to death. I'm pulling his plug.

One cold night in early January I went forward to the fence and walked through A Company's sector. Captain Butler was long gone, DEROSed, and the new company commander, Bill Miller, a first lieutenant, had no qualms about my visiting his sector. Was delighted, in fact.

Going forward at night was no longer an unusual thing for me to do. The Officers' Club and the BOQ bored me. Even the TOC was boring. I preferred being on the fence to anything else, if I couldn't be in Changpa-ri with Tammy.

I visited Sergeant Waters in the tower at position 27T. Shortly after I arrived, Waters headed off to check his men. "Keep an eye on things, would you, Lieutenant? Thank you sir." Moving awkwardly in his parka and heavy winter boots, he heaved his large body out the door and climbed down the ladder. I sat down in his metal folding chair and laid the starlight scope on the ledge in front of me. Removed my gloves and made a quick check: lens cap off, switch on. Gloves back on. Looked into the cold rubber eyepiece, swept the scope slowly back and forth, and studied that green disk. There was the fence, at low elevation: a ghostly white web of crisscrossing threads, thick white posts, tiny white spirals of concertina wire. And there, a few meters beyond, three or four dancing white puffs: bushes. Farther out, a shadow: the small hill. Sweep the scope to the right, a dazzling flash with the intensity of the sun: a burning flame pot; and sweep left, another flame pot, bright, intense: the other boundary of the tower's sector of responsibility.

Sergeant Waters' voice drifted up to the tower: "Get your sorry ass outta that foxhole, soldier! Get moving!"

That's it Sergeant Waters, I thought. Motivate those young men. I was glad I wasn't in a foxhole. I swept the starlight scope back to the middle, then out to the bushes, sweep back, and forth, down to the fence, sweep slowly right, slowly left, out to the hill, and around, random observation, back to the middle, check the fence, left to right, out to the bushes, and so on. Nothing unusual. Boredom setting in. Before long I heard Sergeant Waters' boots scraping on the wooden rungs of the ladder. He grunted as he pulled himself into the tower.

"Did you see that deer, Lieutenant? Looks like a big one, a buck."

"Where?"

"Left of those bushes. Maybe forty meters. See if you can spot him."

I swung the starlight scope in that direction. It took me a moment, but I found him. Or rather, I found the flashes of luminescent green dots that represented him.

"Yeah, there he is." The deer was feeding quietly. Every so often it would raise its head and take a step or two toward the fence. Then it would stop and gracefully lower its head and continue to graze. The deer seemed removed from the earth, floating. When it moved, an after-image would remain momentarily in the green field of vision, a blurred image where the deer had been. It seemed to move in slow motion, or delayed motion, and the movements of its head and legs had an eerie quality to them. It seemed like two or three different animals in one. It was truly a night image: dream-like, ghostly.

Sergeant Waters spoke from close by my ear. "He's gonna step in some heavy shit pretty soon if he ain't careful."

"What do you mean?"

"Land mine."

"He's pretty close in, isn't he?"

"Yeah." He picked up his rifle. "Lemme see that scope for a minute, will you, sir?"

I got up and he squeezed past me and took his chair. He balanced both the scope and his rifle side-by-side on the icy sill. He peered through the scope. "I'll just kick up a little dirt close by and see if I can get him to mosey along." He found the deer in the starlight scope, then leaned back and aligned the rifle with the scope. He swung the muzzle of the weapon a few degrees to the right, clicked off the safety, and squeezed off a round.

I hadn't expected him to fire that quickly and the explosion made me jump. The muzzle flash blinded me momentarily, and my ears rang.

"Hear him, sir? Off that way." Sergeant Waters pointed toward the northwest.

I listened hard, but I heard only the ringing of my ears.

Sergeant Waters grunted. "Well, Lieutenant Miller'll be wanting a report on that shot right quick."

Sure enough, just then the field phone buzzed. Waters picked up the receiver. "Twenty-seven T, Sergeant Waters speakin sir."

"Hey Sergeant Waters, who fired that shot?" It was the RTO at Alpha Company's CP; I could hear his voice from the rear of the tower.

"I did, Warner."

130

"Okay, well, Lieutenant Miller says he needs a report on it right away."

"You can take this down, Warner. Ready?"

"Yeah, go ahead, Sergeant."

"Okay. 'Saw movement through starlight scope. Fired at unidentified individual. UI ran off. UI identified as deer.' Got that?"

"I copy, Sergeant Waters. Warner out."

Early morning, January 13th. During the night it warmed up enough to create mist, and the moisture condensed on the fence—the posts, the chain link, the concertina wire along the top—and froze. When the sun rose it turned the concertina wire into coils of galaxies, then melted the ice, star by star. I walked east toward the light, and the day seemed like any other. The ground was slippery, that was all; what was left of the snow was frozen.

A few meters along into Company C, I found a hole in the fence.

Links down near the ground had been cut, not many, creating a neat, diamond-shaped hole. There it was. Scuff marks in the minefield. Something shiny on the ground right where the fence had been cut. I removed a glove and picked it up. Copy of a Zippo, smooth, well worn. The North Korean had left a cigaret lighter in the dirt at the hole. I flipped it open with my thumb, then flicked the wheel. Windless day, and the blue and yellow flame flared high.

"Fuckin A."

I turned and saw a soldier standing behind me, his rifle half raised.

"Is that what I think it is, sir?"

"It's gotta be," I said. "First one I've seen."

"Oh man. My ass is in a sling."

"Where's the nearest field phone?"

"Right in that position there, sir." He pointed his rifle at a big foxhole.

"Thanks." I pocketed the lighter, walked down to the foxhole and called the TOC. Crazy Mann answered, and I told him I had to talk to Colonel Curtis right away.

"You have an 'up' for the old sweetheart, sir?"

"No. Cut the shit now, Mann, and get me the Colonel."

"If you say so, your honor. Lemme try and find him. Hold one."

He clicked off. I took out the lighter and played with it, flicking it on, flipping it shut. I couldn't imagine the mind of the person who would leave a thing like that in a place like that.

Colonel Curtis finally came on the line. "Yes, Art. What is it?"

"I'm afraid it's a hole in the fence, sir."

"I was afraid of that. Oh, gosh. Are you sure?"

"Well, you might want to have a look at it, sir. Maybe before you phone it in to Brigade."

"Where is it?"

"Charlie Company, sir. Position 608."

"All right. Wait for me. I'll be there as soon as I can."

"Okay sir. Out here."

Three or four GIs had gathered around the hole. I walked back and suggested they stay the hell away from it—someone might want to look at the markings, maybe get a scent for the dogs.

One of them said, "Uh-oh." He was staring toward the east, and I looked up. John Harris was walking our way, his eyes on the fence. A man carrying a radio followed him.

Harris was walking fast and reached us quickly. "Richardson!" he said pleasantly. "Find anything this morning?"

"I'm afraid I did."

John's face changed. He knew I wasn't kidding. He walked over to the hole and stared.

The men drifted away.

"Did you call it in?" he asked.

"Yeah. Just now." I suddenly wondered whether I'd done the right thing. "I didn't know if you'd been by or not."

"Motherfuckin son of a bitch."

"Don't worry about it," I told him. "Hey look, I *had* to call it in."

"No, it's not that." He continued to stare at the severed links.

"This happens, you know. Happens to the best."

"Motherfucker, did I crucify my ass." He looked at me, and I remembered the lighter. I took it out of the pocket of my parka.

"Message for you," I said, and handed it to him.

132

He took it without seeing it. "You know what I did?"

I shook my head.

"I already called in an 'up.'"

"What?"

"I got a late start and figured I ought to call. Spoke to Curtis ten minutes ago."

We stared at each other.

"What do you think'll happen?" he said weakly.

"I think that'll be it."

He nodded. "I reckon it will."

Jan. 13

for the embarrassing record:

Everything has changed. We look at each other differently. We've had an infiltration and we're not so proud anymore. Everybody's jumping through their ass. There's really hell to pay when somebody gets through. Nobody sleeps. The rear areas have to be searched and staked out. But the guy must have crossed the Imjin this morning. Hard to track him—most of the ground's frozen. Imjin's frozen and crossable. It's up to units south of the river now. Though I doubt Brigade will call us off soon—they'll just let us stay out hunting a day or two longer than everybody else, just to remind us who fucked up.

John Harris is gone. Steve Morrison already replaced him. And it looks as if Colonel Curtis is going. I think he's been on his way out for some time. He's well liked and I doubt if any of us will like his replacement nearly as much as we like him. He's a kind and honorable man. Major Nichols seems to love him.

Did I do wrong, calling Curtis before talking to Harris? What if I'd called John first? Would it have made a difference? He could have called Colonel Curtis about the hole, not me—or was it too late?

Harris is a lieutenant, like me. Yet I didn't think to call *him*—yet it was *his* company sector. And he's black; what if this had happened in Bill Miller's sector? Or Curt's? This was racial? But I'm supposed to report directly to the Colonel! *Fuck!*

A document. Needs to be drawn up. A "Priority of Allegiance." That's good. Who'd be at the top? My parents? Probably, but they're not here. My country? Jack and Curt. And

Tammy—what do I owe her, only money? How about myself? Colonel Curtis. Myself at the top? Curtis #2? Or Jack and those guys, Harris included? Then Tammy. Then Peters. At the bottom—who? John Harmon. But is Harris (was Harris) above or below Colonel Curtis?

What do I owe anybody? My country, my father, Mom. My allegiance, my life?

Maybe I don't owe anybody a thing. Colonel Larson asked me: What do you want? I've never been asked that before. What *do* I want?

January 14.
For the record: thick cloud cover, 20 degrees, ground frozen and slightly snow-sprinkled.

Sometimes I think I should have been born a girl. I mean, why not? It's 50–50 anyway. I would have been a fine woman. I would have had large, lovely breasts; I would have dressed sharp; I would have loved sex. I would have made some man a terrific wife. (But first I'd have fucked around like crazy.)

And I wouldn't have had to go to Korea.

Colonel Curtis is gone. Relieved. Hated to see him go. I didn't say goodbye to him, and he didn't look me up before he left.

The new colonel controls everything. LTC Brody. Tough bastard, insists on military courtesy to the letter. Everyone rises when he enters a room. No one leaves until he leaves. On the radio, he insists on being the one who terminates the conversation, the last to speak. He's got to be the one who says "Out."

Jan 15
The main problem is not getting through the day. It is getting up in the morning. We try to think of a reason for emerging from our bunk, and none occurs to us. So we lie there in the dark, and we wait. The act of crawling from beneath our warm blankets becomes ludicrous, an impossibility. But eventually it happens: some scale tips and our lethargy becomes more detestable to us than the prospect of the day ahead. By then we've reviewed the penalties of not arising. So, finally, in sheer anguish, we allow fear and disgust to force us to peel back the covers and step out onto the cold linoleum floor of our dark and miserable room.

THIRTEEN

P ETERS AND I DROVE TO THE VIL-
lage one morning after I walked the fence. He dropped me off at
Tammy's hootch.

She'd been asleep. Drowsy and warm, she met me downstairs
at the door; she tugged at my sleeve, pulled me in, kissed me,
helped me off with my pistol, parka, and boots. Slipped her warm
hands inside my shirt, rubbed my skin, whispered in Korean.

We went upstairs. She got the wok down from the cabinet
by the wardrobe and set it on the coal stove. Soon she had eggs,
rice, meat, and vegetables sizzling in the wok, throwing off a
white vapor. She warmed some milk and tea and dished up a
bowl of *kimchi*. A tall, slim, beautiful girl in a kimono frying
me breakfast. I lay on the bed; watched her; dozed. She brought
me tea. It scalded my throat and warmed my stomach. I closed
my eyes.

After a while the paper door slid open and another woman
entered the room. She was shorter than Tammy, more broadly
built. They conversed in whispers, giggling and looking at me.

"Lieutenant Arthur, this my friend Miss Kim. May she have
breakfast with us?"

"Sure. Why not?"

Tammy returned to her wok and Miss Kim followed her, stood next to her, talked to her absently. Kim was a lovely girl too: bright red cheeks, large eyes, fine black hair. She fixed those wide eyes on me as she chatted with Tammy, who concentrated on her wok, and then she gave me a big smile and voluptuously licked her lips. The whore. I grinned back at her. Like Tammy, she wore only a kimono, a blue satin garment tied at the waist. The deep blue complemented her dark brown eyes and olive skin, and I started thinking about what she might look like under that kimono, and I wanted to tear it off her.

Tammy got the mahogany table out from under the bed, scattered pillows around it on the floor, set out chopsticks and dished up bowls of food. We sat on the pillows—the floor now seemed a large bed with a table at its center—and we ate hungrily, hunched over the low table, sliding warm rice, soft eggs, fish and meat from our bowls to our mouths directly, using the chopsticks as pushers. We whispered to one another: *Salt, The* kimchi *please, You fast three days Lieutenant? Delicious, delicious . . . .* Why did we whisper? Where had this warmth come from, this friendship? I met Tammy's eyes: she gazed at me over her bowl with an eager playfulness. She seemed excited and carefree.

When we finished eating we lay back on the pillows. Tammy lit a joint, puffed on it, handed it to me. I passed it to Kim. The two girls passed it back and forth, avoiding the hot ash, sucking on the twisted end. They whispered a little, laughed, shifted positions on the pillows, their kimonos stretching tightly across a buttock, hanging loosely open at a breast. Kim moved over near me, lay on her back with her head next to my chest, one knee in the air. I began to stroke her arm. She looked up at me like a cat: wide-eyed, unblinking, expressionless. She *was* a cat, a female in heat. But a cat in heat makes a spectacle of herself, and Kim only lay beside me and let me stroke her.

Tammy put away the dishes, the wok, and the table. Then she stepped over to where Kim and I lay and knelt beside Kim. Slowly Tammy removed her kimono; then she removed Kim's, Kim willingly yielding to Tammy's small hands. Then they turned their attention to me: they removed my socks, my wool shirt and trousers, my winter underwear, my tee-shirt and shorts, the two naked girls giggling and fumbling with my clothing. Was

136

there ever a finer moment? To be free of that winter bulk, the marks of the clothing still on my skin (a pink-and-white band around my waist), to be nude with two nude women, to be the focus of their affection, to feel their warm breath on my legs and chest, and then to feel their mouths and hands everywhere on my body, my own lips and tongue touching salty skin, hair, an eyelid, a nipple, an ear. . . .

It seemed to go on for a long time. Two of us would make love to one and then it would be another's turn, and all the time Tammy's washcloth was close at hand, her brass bowl filled with steaming water, the white washcloth hard and rubby, and with it we massaged and cleaned our mouths, hands, genitals, foreheads, the hot rough cloth gently scraping our skin. Tammy would change the water, we would wash one another, and then we would begin again. We indulged and finally exhausted ourselves, and then we slept.

We woke up and I made love to Miss Kim, and then the two girls whispered excitedly between themselves. I was dozing off when Tammy snuggled up close to me, giggling.

"What is it? What's so funny?"

"She say you number one. She like you better than her steady. You more gentle. Bigger, too."

"Oh yeah? Who's her steady?"

"You know him. He introduce us. You not know? Kim is girlfriend of Lieutenant Harmon."

"What?" I sat up and stared at the woman lying next to Tammy. Miss Kim smiled back at me.

"I thought you know," Tammy said. "You met her once."

"Good lord." I started to laugh. I lay down again. "Come here," I said to Tammy. And to Miss Kim: "You come here too."

Someone is kissing my mouth. Someone's tongue is licking me. A hand is stroking the sole of my foot.

"Time for you to wake up, Lieutenant Arthur. You must put on clothes, eat, get ready. It is time to go. You must walk fence."

January 22

We've heard about Colonel Brody. That he's inflexible. That he's gung ho, a real worker. That he'll push you and drive you and work you to the bone.

He commanded a weird battalion in the south, four or five companies spread over miles. I'm not sure what their mission was—to guard emplacements of some kind, maybe storage areas for nukes. Command and control had been an appalling problem, he'd been in the air constantly, flying from one of his units to another. But he'd managed it, done so well that they'd given him Colonel Curtis's job and told him to pull this battalion together. He'd gained a fearsome reputation among his subordinates but he'd pleased his commander, and now he was being transferred to an even more difficult job: commanding a battalion on the DMZ.

I'll miss Colonel Curtis. He was always decent to people. I think we're in for a big change around here.

Colonel Brody's hair is chopped down to a short, short crew cut that looks ludicrous on an older man like him. It makes his big ears flap in the wind. He's thin, medium height. His face has a weathered appearance: tan, drawn in at the cheeks, wrinkles around the eyes and mouth. His skin resembles the surface of an old brick building: pitted, crossed by lines and scars. He might have been in a dozen fist fights. The belligerent expression he wears on that brick of a face makes him look like he just caught some PFC screwing his daughter.

When Major Nichols introduced me to him a few days ago, Colonel Brody's expression changed not at all. He said, "What do *you* do, Lieutenant?" (What's your excuse for existing?) I said, "I walk the fence, Colonel." Brody stared at me as if I were the PFC humping away on his daughter and said, "You what?" and I said, louder, "I walk the fence, Colonel." I don't think he's hard of hearing. He said "Oh," and turned away. Walked off with Major Nichols and no doubt asked him what the hell that lieutenant meant by "walk the fence."

Jan. 26

For the record: The men on the fence at night, dead of winter.

The snow fell dry and cold, and the wind blew and it was impossible to stay warm. Your ears had to stay uncovered and unless you turned away from the wind, the snow and wind would sting your face, swirl under your helmet and behind your hood and down your neck. The snow felt like needles on your cheeks and nose, and the wind blew the snow into your eyes. After a while your skin burned and finally your ears and cheeks went numb and you knew you had to do something or you'd get frostbite. So you huddled down inside your foxhole and didn't care if

Let the North Korean bastards cut through the fence, I've had enough, out here five nights in a row, hardly any sleep and now this god-awful weather. I don't want frostbite. Hell, maybe I do. Get a few days off. Anyway, let 'em cut. The motherfuckers, if they want to get through bad enough to try it in this weather, fuck 'em. Let 'em go ahead and cut.

One night in late January, a soldier in Company A fell asleep at his position. There was nothing too unusual about that—it happened increasingly often. But on this occasion, when the kid awoke and blinked his eyes, and stared toward the fence, he saw three people in the dim light between flame pots: dark shapes hunched over on the other side of the fence, working away at the links near the ground, cutting. Orange glow of faces, glint of white teeth. One of them appeared to have a weapon aimed at him.

The GI was sitting on the edge of his foxhole. His rifle was at the bottom of the hole, across from his dangling feet. Very far away, under the circumstances.

He did nothing for a moment. He didn't want to die, and he feared that if he moved, they'd shoot him.

But the fence! They were cutting the fence! They'd be through it in a minute, right in front of his position! So he took a chance, jumped into his foxhole, grabbed his rifle—an automatic—and pointed it toward the night sky. He pulled the trigger and held it, fired twenty rounds straight up. Waited a moment or two, then peeked out. Nobody there. Some other GIs came over, curious about the shooting, and asked what was going on.

They went up to the fence. Some of them had flashlights. It was all there: footprints in the snow in the minefield, a few severed links, a pair of wirecutters, a rag to silence them, and a thin metal rod for the minefield.

Colonel Curtis probably would have been happy that the infiltration attempt had been aborted. But not Colonel Brody. Colonel Brody was enraged when he heard about it. To him it was a missed opportunity, a couple of big ones that got away—and nobody to show for it.

It was around that time I had a talk with Donnie Lange, a lieutenant who'd been assigned to C Company in the fall. I saw him at the Officers' Club one evening, drinking beer alone, and I sat down on the bar stool next to him. We talked. Enemy activity was on the increase, and I wondered how Donnie was feeling about it. I asked him if he was ever scared on an ambush patrol.

"Not much anymore," he said. "I used to. Used to worry about everything: claymores, picking the right position, maintaining noise discipline—the works. But it's routine now; me and my guys have done it too often. And nothing ever happens. Nothing to be scared of anymore."

"But they *are* out there."

"Yeah, but they aren't going to walk into one of my ambushes. They're good soldiers. We're good too, don't get me wrong. I run good patrols. But we're not as good at night as they are." He took a swallow of beer.

I said, "Unless they fly, or use tunnels, the odds are that sooner or later they'll run into one of our patrols. They can't keep going from north to south and back without running into somebody."

"That's what I figure. They might stumble into us some night; that's why I don't fuck around."

We'd finished our beers, so I bought two more from Mr. Kim.

"Thing of it is, though," Donnie said, "it's frustrating as hell. I mean, I'm not aching to get shot at, don't get me wrong. I'm no lifer. But I can't think of a thing that's more tiresome than going out there, doing all that walking, listening to those goddamn speakers most of the day and half the night—and they're *loud* when you're practically on top of them, lemme tell you—but shit, we walk or climb all day, poke around, then select an ambush site and go in after dark, set up the claymores, and I check each and every position. I do it right, and it's hard work! But then you settle in knowing nothing's gonna happen. And yet you got to be ready! But nothing *ever* happens on a patrol, that's the bitch of it. That's what wears you out."

I looked at him. "And you don't get scared?"

"Nope."

"You sure?"

"Why, do you?"

"No, not really. Actually, I get scared sometimes," I admitted.

"I guess I do too. You hear a noise where there's not supposed to be one, or you think you see movement. But not often. I get more eager than scared. I'd really like to see a little action for a change."

"By the way, who is 'Short'?" I asked. "Do you know him?"

He smiled. "You mean the guy on the radio?"

"Yeah. The one who says 'short' on the battalion net all the time."

"Well he's lots of guys, isn't he?"

"But do you know anybody who ever actually said 'short'?"

Donnie just grinned at me.

Feb 3

I'm getting short. Four months. Today I got the re-up lecture from Major Nichols. "Worth a lot of money to you, Art. Bonus and all that. Good pay."

"Sorry, Major," I said. "Money isn't important to me."

Grinning, Nichols said: "What is?"

He had me there.

But there's no way I'd extend. I may not know what I'm going to be when I grow up, but it ain't a lifer.

I asked Tammy about the photographs on her wall. Four or five framed black-and-white shots of the orphanage: kids playing, kids smiling and looking up at the camera. Two pictures of a little girl.

"Who's this?"

"That's my sister."

"She's adorable. She much younger than you?"

"Five years. She's not at the orphanage any longer. I'm helping put her through school. In Pusan. Boarding school."

"Where's your mother?"

"She lives in Seoul."

"What's she do?"

"What I do."

"Do you ever see your father?"

"I don't know him. He's a ROK Army soldier. Mama never sees him anymore. Sister have American father."

"What's your sister's name?"

"Kim Lee. She and I very close. She's smart—going to be brilliant, maybe go to college in America."

Later: "What was it like in the orphanage?"

"It was all right. Not so bad. It was much worse to leave. My mother used to visit us once a month, but they didn't like her and didn't want me to go live with her. So I came up here, to a 'family'." She snorted. "It was no family."

One evening, Colonel Brody told me to spend the night on the fence. He told me to drive up and down the battalion sector and make random checks on the men. Peters and I were to stay forward until at least four o'clock. "You can sleep during the day," he told me. "Tonight's going to be very dark. Good night for an infiltration attempt."

So I spent the night on the fence. Sometime after midnight I walked the Charlie Company sector. I didn't inform their CP that I'd be down along the fence because I didn't want their RTO phoning everybody and telling them I was coming. As I walked from foxhole to foxhole, though, I made sure the next man down the line knew who and where I was. I shouted at him till he answered. I didn't want to walk up on a sleeping GI and surprise him; he might wake up shooting.

Apparently Colonel Brody knew what he was doing, because no one on the fence could see much. A heavy mist had settled in low over the snow, and the night was pitch black. The flame pots hardly dented the fog. It was a perfect night to go through, just as Colonel Brody had predicted. I was gaining respect for that man.

Somewhere along the line in C Company, I ran into this kid named Carter. I'd seen him many times before. He was sort of a sullen kid, slow and hunched over and always dirty: soot-smeared face, C-ration-stained parka, ripped field pants, scuffed boots. When I ran into him that night he was up out of his foxhole, near the fence, just standing there. As I approached him I could barely make out his silhouette next to a flame pot, and he looked odd for some reason. I wasn't exactly sure what was odd about him. The way he was standing looked somehow aimless. He was turned away from the fence; or rather, he actually had his back to it. Yet he didn't seem to be looking at anything.

I stared at what I could see of him in the dim light of a flame pot, and something about him bothered me. But I didn't know exactly what it was.

I walked closer—he turned and looked at me—I recognized him—he took a couple of steps, aimless ones, and looked away from me, stopped, stood there. Was he stoned? Wounded? I walked up to him, and finally it dawned on me.

"Hey Carter," I said, "where's your weapon?"

"Who wants to know?"

"Lieutenant Richardson."

"It's over there."

"Where's over there?"

"In my position. What's the difference?"

I raised my voice. "You're supposed to keep your weapon with you! What do you think they issue it to you for?"

"Oh bullshit, Lieutenant. You don't need a weapon here."

"What? You don't think so?"

"No. I been here six months. I been on patrol, I been on the GP, I been on the fence, and I ain't seen a goddamn North Korean yet. This place is rinky-dink. This place is nothin. I want to go to Vietnam. I put in for a transfer. I can't wait to get the fuck out of this hole."

I grabbed him by the front of his grease-smeared parka and threw him against the fence. Stones rattled in their tin cans. First time I ever touched an enlisted man in anger. I held him by the front of his parka and shook him.

"Now you listen to me, you little son of a bitch. You can go die in Vietnam if you want, but you aren't going to die in Korea! You keep that fucking weapon with you!"

"You seen any gooks lately, Lieutenant?"

"No."

"Well—?"

"I've seen plenty of dead Americans, Carter. You might be next."

Our faces were inches apart. I could see him clearly in the light of the flame pot. He wasn't looking at me. I let him go. "Understand?"

"Yeah."

"Yeah, *sir.*"

"Yes sir."

"Now go and get your weapon."

He did.

February 5

For the record:

Another dream last night:

a North Korean is coming at me. He's holding a rifle with a bayonet on the end. I shoot him; pistol works fine—

But he doesn't fall—I keep shooting him but he keeps coming at me. The bullets aren't hitting him—no mark on him—as though they're blanks—he keeps coming.

He knows I tried to kill him. I wake up sweating, terrified of what he will do to me now

North Koreans:

Their mission is entirely different from ours. They may be on orders *not* to engage us, *not* to fight unless absolutely necessary. That's the surprising thing. How many times have they skirted a patrol or cut through the fence and not lifted a finger against us? We're out to kill them, but they're not out to kill us.

Does that make *us* the enemy?

The winter nights grew longer and the men found it impossible to stay comfortable. When the wind blew, their sweat-soaked long johns turned ice cold and they shivered and clutched at their parkas and tried to keep the wind off their necks and throats. Each simple task, like setting a trip flare or arming a claymore mine, became a difficult chore and couldn't be done with gloves on. Pouring diesel fuel from a five-gallon can into half a 55-gallon drum filled with sand—a flame pot—took a large effort. Merely climbing out of a foxhole wasn't easy if a man was wearing thirty or forty pounds of clothing, equipment, and ammunition: long johns, shirts and pants, web gear, ammo pouches with loaded clips, helmet, grenades, flak jacket . . . . If his rifle happened to slip off his shoulder or out of his gloved, half-numb fingers, he'd have to bend down to pick it up, brush off the snow and dirt, and check the bore for blockage: time-consuming work that required bare hands and light.

Nothing was easy; nothing could be accomplished without pain.

In their efforts to get warm and avoid work, the men slipped toward inertia, toward hunkering down in their foxholes, finding a protected spot and staying put. This was a formula for sleep. The officers and NCOs resisted this tendency in the men, but it was impossible to supervise every soldier during every minute of the fourteen-hour night.

To compound the problem, the boredom and monotony that developed during the long winter nights became so deep that the men looked forward to action of any kind. They shot at every noise and shadow, and they would fire a flare or detonate a claymore mine just for the fun of it. Why not? They could always report that they'd seen movement or heard a noise.

Colonel Brody seemed uneasy. He could probably feel the battalion sliding out of his control. The men were sleeping on the fence at night—he *knew* they were sleeping, he had caught two of them asleep himself. Furthermore, an infiltration attempt had recently been successful in the battalion on his left flank, and he was aware that it could just as easily have occurred in his sector. He was worried, and he was scared, too, because if such a thing happened to him, he might not lose his command, as Colonel Curtis had, but it would affect Colonel Larson's opinion of him. Adversely.

He called a meeting. It was only for the three company commanders, the staff officers, and the top NCOs. Late in the afternoon we gathered in the briefing room in the TOC.

He started out calmly and rationally. "The danger is that things will fall into a routine," he told us. "The men's duties must never appear routine. You've got to constantly evaluate and change; there's *always* a better way to do things."

Before long, though, his talk came around to the soldiers he had found sleeping on the fence. He worked himself into a fury. "I want those Goddamn soldiers *alert!*" he shouted. "All fucking night long! Get out there and check on 'em! Get 'em off their butts! And another thing. This indiscriminate shooting has got to stop. Some of those noises that everybody is hearing all the Goddamn time might just be North Koreans, and the shooting's scaring them away! Tell your Goddamn troops *I want a body!* Let

145

the son of a bitches sneak all the way to the fence, let 'em get right up on the fence and start cutting—*then* do their ass in!"

Colonel Brody's weathered face had turned a deep red, and white flecks of spittle had gathered at the corners of his mouth. His small brown eyes sparked with rage and excitement.

"And another thing. If you catch a man sleeping on the fence, I want to hear about it. I'll court-martial the bastard. No sleeping! Is that understood? Don't let your troops get away with it. I'm holding every one of you personally responsible for keeping those troops awake. This is the most important thing they'll ever do, don't you see? And you too! This is the opportunity of a lifetime. To guard the Korean border. To kill a North Korean! How many Americans get this opportunity? Your troops ought to Goddamn well be looking for a clear shot at one of those cocksuckers. They should be fighting each other for the most likely spot, the position with the most sightings. Hell, I'll tell you what I'll do. A week off. A week off to the soldier who kills a North Korean! I will personally put him on the plane to Japan. Have you got that, Sergeant major? Am I within my rights on that?"

"Yes sir. You can do that. That'll keep these youngsters awake."

"All right. You heard that. A week off to the soldier—officers and NCOs included—who gets me a body. Falling asleep is out of the question. Out of the *question!* The next man who falls asleep, he's court-martialed, automatically! I'm not going to have any holes in *my* fence. Not one! Do you understand?"

He paused and glared around the room. We looked back at him.

"All right. Now, that's something, but it's not enough. We've got to stop this damn sleeping in the foxholes. Now you first sergeants and company commanders and staff officers are supposed to be smart. You're supposed to be leaders and problem-solvers, and I want some solutions. We've got a problem here and it's going to hurt us, hurt us bad. We haven't had an infiltration yet—not since I took over—and I commend you for that, it's not all luck and you should be proud and take credit. But our time's running out. We're overdue. So think about it. How are we going to keep these men awake? They're cold, they're bundled up, it's nighttime, they want to sleep. What can we do? Just think for a while. Don't talk; think."

There was silence for a few minutes. Colonel Brody, standing at the lectern, lit a cigaret and watched us think.

An idea struck me almost immediately. The solution was simple. Hundreds of fence-walkers. It took me a moment to think the thing through.

"Sir?"

"What, Richardson?"

Miller, Davis, Morrison, Sergeant major Allen, Captain Stewart, the first sergeants—everybody turned and looked at me.

"How about fence checks?"

"Explain that."

"Fence checks, sir. The only way we know for sure if somebody's gotten through is to make a fence check. The company commanders do it every day, and I do too. Why not have the troops making fence checks during the night? We could give each man a sector of fence, identify exactly which portion of fence is his responsibility. You have company sectors and squad sectors; give each man his own individual sector and have him check it every hour. Or every half hour. All they do now is maybe fill a flame pot every couple of hours. This way, you'll get them on their feet every half hour. Or fifteen minutes. Have them walk their sector, pull on the fence, shake it, make sure it's intact. Then have them report to somebody. And look, sir: if somebody does get through, we'll know it right away. Not two or three hours later or the next morning, but almost as soon as it happens. So we can go after him."

Colonel Brody dragged on his cigaret. He looked as though he was weighing the idea. Abruptly he said, "Well? What do you think? Miller? Davis?"

"It could help," Bill Miller said.

"Who'll the men report these fence checks to?" Steve Morrison asked.

"Yeah," Curt Davis said. "What about communications? How do we get the reports up the chain of command?"

"Christ, Davis," said Colonel Brody. "Where've you been the past six months? What's wrong with voice communications, land line, radio? The men could report their fence checks nine different ways. You can have your troops write you a military letter, for Chrissakes."

Colonel Brody was laughing. He was in a good mood now. He

crushed out his cigaret in the ashtray on the lectern. "Okay," he said, "we'll do it." He worked out the details with the company commanders, and then he dismissed us.

That was how everyone in the battalion became a fence-walker.

FOURTEEN

February 12—Abe's birth-
day.

For the record:

Terrible morning. Peters had to wait a long time in front of the BOQ, in the dark cold and the snow. I was late: split a sock while pulling it on, my whole body shivering, the stove out of fuel. Couldn't find another sock. I finally rifled my laundry bag and pulled on an old crusty one. It smelled like onions and it was stiff, but it soon softened up. All this thrashing around in the predawn dark and the terrible cold. Every inch of me shivering.

Here's what I'm wearing this morning: underpants (boxer) and tee-shirt, both olive drab in color; long underwear, tops and bottoms (white cotton and wool, itchy); a wool shirt; wool trousers with belt; field pants with big pockets and suspenders; two pairs of socks, leather boots with cleated rubber soles; an army-issue wool scarf, nice and long, olive-drab (what isn't? just the boots and long underwear); parka with fur-lined hood; driver's mask; flak jacket; web belt with shoulder harness. Steel helmet with canvas camouflage cover, and sewn to the cover, the black cloth bar of a first lieutenant. Hooked to the belt are four hand grenades and a leather holster, with pistol.

No radio. Anderson carried a radio. Communication isn't a problem; we've got radios and field phones all along the fence. The problem is weight.

I unplug Harmon's electric blanket. By the time I stumble out the door and down the steps to the jeep, snow has piled up on Peters' parka hood. He slams the jeep into gear and takes off almost before I climb in. It's pitch black, we're driving on blackout lights, and Peters is driving fast in the snow. He begins to have difficulty keeping the jeep on the road. He's going too fast. "Peters, slow down," I say. He looks at me and I know that at that moment he'd rather kill me than do anything else in the world.

One evening in mid-February I was at the TOC, talking with Specks Morgan and Skinny Artie Shaw, listening to the radios, waiting. Norm Stewart had asked me to "remain available." That meant stick close to a radio and have Peters stick close to me. But I'd borrowed the S-4's jeep and driver and told Peters to take the night off. The S-4's jeep was parked outside, and the driver was sitting at my desk back in the S-3 office, reading comic books.

Not much was going on at the fence and the TOC radios had been nearly silent. The predominant sound was the wind, which rattled the stove pipe and shook the storm windows.

At about 9:00 p.m., Ralph Sellers burst into the TOC. He slammed the door behind him. "Richardson, you asshole, I've been looking all over for you."

Talk ceased. Sellers stomped the snow off his thermal boots and clomped over to the stove. He put his hands out, warming them. He left his hood up, over his helmet, and didn't unzip his parka.

I watched him, saying nothing. After he caught his breath, he said, "Art, buddy, do me a favor, will you? Lend me your jeep and driver. I can't find a jeep to save my ass."

"What for?"

"I won't tie him up long. Forty minutes max. I just want to run into the ville. I'll get a ride back, no sweat."

"What about the duty jeep?"

"Christ, I can't find the fucker. I think it just went to Chang-pa-ri, I don't know. I'm in a hurry. It's my night off, you know?"

"I can't do it, Ralph."

"What?" He laughed.

"I've given Peters the night off. I don't know where he is. I wouldn't want to bother him."

"Is he out on pass?"

"I don't know."

"Call the barracks and find out, will you? See if he's around. He's probably taking R-and-R on his bunk. Get him on the phone there and tell him to get his jeep down here ASAP."

I looked at Specks, who was at the switchboard, but he avoided my eyes. He was writing on a clipboard. Skinny Artie Shaw was dealing solitaire by the radios.

I rose slowly and went over to the switchboard. I rang the barracks. Spec-4 Lewis answered.

"Lewis, this is Richardson. Is Peters there?"

"Yes sir, he's here."

"What's he up to?"

"Sir?"

"What is he doing?"

"He's racked out, sir. Asleep."

"All right, thanks. That's all." I unplugged the jack and turned to Sellers. "I can't do it, Ralph. Sorry."

"What, he wasn't there?"

"No, he's there."

"Well? What's he doing that's so goddamn important?"

"Nevermind. I gave him the night off. He's asleep, that's what. I'm not waking him. He's got to get up early enough as it is."

"Oh, bullshit. Let me have him for half an hour, for Christ's sake."

"Ralph. It's twenty minutes into Changpa-ri, twenty back. Maybe more in this weather. It's a walk to the motor pool, signing the jeep out, topping it off when he gets back. I won't do it. You asked, I said no. Just wait till the duty jeep gets back. It won't be long."

"How about the S-4 jeep then? It's right outside. Where's the driver?"

"No. I need it."

Sellers glared at me. "Well, you're an asshole, Richardson. A real suck butt."

He turned from the stove and slammed out of the TOC. The place was suddenly very quiet. One of the radios hissed; the phone rang. Specks answered it and Charlie Company gave him a negative fence-check report. For a few minutes nobody talked. That was unusual.

Finally Specks Morgan looked at me. His face was red and it had the most peculiar expression on it. I held his gaze for a moment. Finally I said, "What's up, Specks? What is it?"

"Now there is one lousy officer, Lieutenant Richardson. That man is one dangerous son of a bitch."

"I don't want to hear it, Specks," I said.

"Well, I'm going to tell you, sir. Somebody's got to say it, and you're going to hear it. That son of a bitch is going to get somebody killed. Everybody knows it. At least everybody in Alpha Company knows it. Nobody wants to go out on patrol with him—except for the fuck-ups. They love him."

I groaned. "Specks, go tell his company commander. Talk to the battalion commander. Don't tell me about it. What am I supposed to do with rumors?"

"Nothing, sir. Don't do anything. Why should you do anything? It's not your concern."

"You don't have to get sarcastic with me, Specks."

"Hey Skinny," Specks said. "What is it with officers? Why do they hound everybody with whips and clubs, and they use kid gloves on each other? Answer me that, will you?"

"Morgan, don't be a jerk-off," Skinny said. "What can Lieutenant Richardson do about it?"

"Blow the whistle on the bastard."

"I can't do it, Specks," I said. "All I've heard is what you've told me, and you're getting it second or third hand."

"I'm getting it straight from my friend in Alpha Company, and he's been on a dozen patrols with Lieutenant Sellers. He says there's no noise and light discipline, no site reconnaissance. Guys smoking at night. And he says—"

"Where did you learn patrol tactics, Specks?"

"I've been reading the manual, sir. They've got a couple dozen right back there in the 2 shop." He jerked his thumb toward Harmon's office. "I've got plenty of time to read. Sellers is doing just about everything wrong. For instance, they set up their ambush before sunset and never move after dark. Can you—"

"Specks, you told me that a few days ago."

"I wasn't sure you heard me, sir."

"I'll talk to somebody. I'll see what I can find out, and I'll mention it to someone."

"Thank you, sir."

February 18

I woke up this morning in Changpa-ri. Tammy was lying next to me in the dark. I rolled out of bed and lit a candle. She stirred, opened her eyes.

"You have to go already?"

"Yes." I kissed her. We looked at each other. Neither of us was able to smile, not at 4:00 in the morning in February in Changpa-ri.

During these dark winter months, Tammy seems to have aged. The skin around her eyes looks puffy, and there are wrinkles in her cheeks near her mouth. "I get up too, cook you something," she said.

"I'll get something at Matta. After the fence-walk."

"No, I do." She threw off the covers. Shivering, holding her arms tightly around her, she hurried over to the wardrobe. Looking at her, I felt no excitement. I've become familiar with her body: her breasts, ass, legs, the curve at the small of her back, her thin waist and tummy. I seldom get aroused anymore when I see her naked. How much longer will passion last?

Or if it's gone, how much longer will *we* last, without passion?

February 21

This morning at dawn, a patrol in Charlie Company found its claymores turned around, facing back toward itself.

What's wrong with our patrols?

The North Koreans know the night and how to use it. Most of them have lived without electricity all their lives. They wouldn't think of using a flare or a flashlight—those things ruin night vision.

Patrols.   The way they are:
12 to 14 men
officer-led

> *advantages*: lots of firepower
> *disadvantages*: noisy, easily detected, hard to control, lack mobility

—pretty ineffective:
easy for small teams of NK infiltrators to detect and avoid, UNLESS it's a perfect ambush, with alert soldiers maintaining absolute silence, and a NK team stumbles into them.

Are Ralph Sellers' patrols really that much worse than the others? Or are all our patrols incompetently run? I ought to talk to Bill Miller about Sellers.

The enemy uses small teams of really well-trained men. Three might come down to get one man through; the other two return north after one infiltrates. Two supporting one. How do you counter that?
Why not with three-man teams of our own?
(One-man teams??)
use starlight scopes
set up small teams along suspected routes of infiltration.
look for tunnels?
2-man teams
3-man teams with starlight scope.

NO NEED FOR THESE LARGE PATROLS

Why can't we send two or three competent men out into the DMZ with a starlight scope? Let 'em roam around at will in a company sector. Send the same team out each night for a week or two at a time. Pick good, experienced men. Volunteers. Treat 'em like celebrities.

You don't need the firepower of the large patrols, you need experience and discipline. And mobility: it's easier to move three men from one place to another than twelve, quickly and quietly, without being seen or heard.

Have 'em sit with a starlight scope and wait for the NKs, who we know have got to move to and from the fence somehow.

Unless tunnels really do exist.

A couple days later Jack got an evening off and mentioned to me at lunch that he was going into the village that night with Harmon. He tried to persuade me to go to the Green Door with them. He told me they'd be happy to wait for me. Said they always had more fun when I was along because they enjoyed watching me fall in love with a whore.

I had no plans to see Tammy, so I let Jack talk me into going. I hadn't been to the Green Door in some time. It was a Friday night and there was a good crowd there. Red and blue light bulbs glowed from the lamps in the living room and the furniture had been pushed back and the rugs rolled up. The record player was turned way up and people were dancing. The room was hot and smelled of perfume and sweat.

> *. . . and this loneliness won't leave me alone*
> *Two thousand miles I roamed,*
> *just to make this dock my home . . .*

The sound of laughter and ice clinking in glasses rose above the music. The atmosphere was smoky, humid, and electric. I ordered a shot and a beer and sat down with Jack and John. Most of the crowd were officers from other battalions. I recognized only one or two men from the 1st of the 31st. None of the girls was familiar to me. Our drinks arrived, and I paid the tab because they had waited for me.

"Well, down the hatch," I said.

"Cheers!" Jack bellowed.

I gulped my whiskey down and drank some beer. The room was very small and one of the couples dancing was in danger of tripping over my legs. I didn't move. The guy backed into me and stumbled over my feet; he caught his balance and gave me a dirty look. When he pulled away from his date to catch himself, I got a good look at the girl's face. I recognized her. She was the girl I had not slept with the first time I'd come to the Green Door.

Seeing her stirred up a lot of feeling. I felt my face turn red.

"Well come on, Rick," Harmon said. "Going to punch him out?"

"No, it's not him. I just saw a ghost."

"Don't swallow your shot glass," Jack said.

I drank more beer and waited till the song ended. Then I walked over to the couple. The guy dancing with the girl was a captain. He was about six inches taller than me. I tapped him on the shoulder.

"Excuse me, sir," I said. "I apologize for having my legs sticking out on the dance floor like that. I wasn't paying attention."

He looked at me, not angry, not even belligerent—just surprised. "That's all right, Lieutenant," he said. "No problem."

"I was wondering, sir," I said. "Is the lady taken for the next dance?"

He looked at her, then at me. She still had her placed lightly on his shoulder, but she had turned away from us both. She was a very delicate-looking girl.

"No," the captain finally said. "I guess not. Here, you can have her." He swung her toward me.

"Thanks." I took her in my arms. The music had begun again. "Hello," I said.

"Hello there, Lieutenant Arthur," she said.

I felt a rush of warmth and pleasure and squeezed her very tightly. She hugged me back. We began to dance.

After a few moments I said, "Let's get a room. Where's Mama-san?"

"Yes, I would like a room too. Come on."

We walked down the hallway. The room was lit by candles. Red decor. Cozy. She pulled my clothes off, then quickly slipped out of her own clothes. I wasn't sure I liked the change: what had happened to her modesty? Yet her compact little body was just as I remembered it, and she really was lovely. Her facial features were small and delicate, and her black hair was straight and hung all the way down her back. She was beautiful.

We smiled at one another and I wrapped my arms around her and laughed. I threw her on the bed and jumped on her. Perhaps her shyness was gone, her reticence, but who had liked those things in the first place?

We had good sex. I came quickly and she got me hard again, and then we made love for a long time. We lay together afterward and talked a little. She'd been at the Green Door for eight months, she told me, and it wasn't too bad. "When I first with you," she said, "it my first time. First time everything. You almost my first man."

It was soon time to go. When I told her good night, I had to bend way down to kiss her upturned face. I kissed her very gently on her mouth and on her closed eyelids. I promised her I would see her again. "I hope so," she said to me. "You very nice man."

It was a wonderful evening.

156

The following night, which I spent at Camp Matta, began as just another dull night at the BOQ. There were four or five of us hanging around, listening to music, writing letters, reading, cleaning a .45. Someone knocked loudly on the front door and then opened it a crack.

"Hey, sir? Hello? I think somebody ought to come out here." There was a frightened tone in the voice that alarmed me. I looked at my .45, which was spread out on my bunk in pieces — spring, barrel, and slide all shiny with oil. I shrugged, grabbed my parka and headed toward the door. Spec-4 Lewis stood outside in the darkness.

"What is it?" We crowded around the open door.

"It's Lafeber, sir. He's acting sort of strange. I think somebody ought to talk to him."

Lafeber was Colonel Brody's driver. "Where is he?" I asked.

"Outside, sir. He's heading toward the gate. I think he's gone nuts. He—well—he has a loaded rifle and he says he wants to kill some Communists."

Someone laughed. "Good for him!"

"Airborne!"

"Jesus," I said. I knew Lewis was a level-headed guy, a leader. He was due to get his sergeant stripes any day. If he couldn't handle Lafeber, then Lafeber was in trouble.

"Which way did he go?" I asked Lewis.

"That way, sir," Lewis said, pointing. "Toward the fence."

"Let him go," Harmon said from behind me.

"Come on, Lewis." We hurried down the steps and started up the road. I heard a couple of the others follow. We jogged toward the checkpoint in the direction of the fence. My eyes weren't accustomed to the dark. I shivered. An infiltrator on his way back north—or a whole team—could be anywhere. And I was unarmed.

"There he is, sir."

Not far ahead we could make out a figure walking down the middle of the road.

"Hey Lafeber, wait up!" I shouted. Didn't want to surprise him. He looked back over his shoulder without slowing down. I ran and caught up with him. "Lafeber! What's going on?"

He stopped "Nothing, sir."

"Where you going?"

"That way." He gestured with the muzzle of his rifle. The flash suppressor on the end of the muzzle wavered near my chest.

"Why?"

"I'm going to kill me some gooks," he said matter-of-factly.

"What did you say?"

"I'm going to kill gooks, sir. Now excuse me." He pushed past me and continued up the road. I ran around him and again stopped in front of him. He was holding his M-14 in both hands across his chest at port arms. The magazine jutting down in front of the trigger guard gave the weapon a lethal appearance. Did he have a round in the chamber? I wondered whether I could move fast enough to snatch the rifle away from him. What would he do if I grabbed at it and missed?

"Look Lafeber, it's too late to go out there now. It's dark. Why don't you turn around and forget it. Go to bed."

"I don't think so, Lieutenant. I'm gonna kill the sonofabitches. Now get out of my way, please."

"Lafeber, give me your rifle."

He didn't answer, just stared at me grimly. He held the weapon tightly against his chest.

"Lafeber, let me see your rifle, would you please? Is it clean?"

"I cleaned it."

"Yeah? Let me have a look at it. I want to inspect it."

"I don't think so, sir," he said indecisively. Then, in a menacing tone: "I'm not supposed to give my rifle up to nobody."

"Does Colonel Brody know you're out here? Or Lieutenant Roberts? They could drive by here any minute. Have you got a pass? You may be AWOL. Let's go back to Matta, what do you say? Come on. We'll get you a pass so you won't be AWOL."

He paused. Then: "I'm sorry, Lieutenant, but I gotta go. Now get outta my way." He went to move past me again, but I side stepped, blocking his path and I reached out with both hands and grabbed his rifle. I got a good grip on the stock and the butt and pulled. He held on. I held on too.

"Lafeber," I said. "Let go of the rifle."

"No." His voice was high and shrill. He tugged at the weapon.

"Give me the fucking rifle."

"I can't give up my rifle—not to no one!" There was complete hysteria in his voice now.

I adopted a loud and commanding tone: "PFC Lafeber, do you recognize me as an officer of the United States Army?"

"Yes sir."

"All right, I'm giving you a *direct* order. As an officer, in front of witnesses. Now give me your rifle!"

He yanked the rifle again and nearly tore it out of my hands. The muzzle swung toward my face. I held on to it with all my strength and tried to twist it away from him. "Lafeber! I gave you an *order!*"

Suddenly he stopped struggling. He sighed and relaxed his grip on the rifle, and then I was holding it. I pointed it at the ground, slipped the magazine out, reached over with my left hand and ejected a round into my right. I looked briefly at the bullet. It was the one he would have shot me with.

I gripped the rifle as hard as I could and tried to steady my breathing. It was all I could do to keep from smashing his face, driving the butt plate into his jaw and reducing it to bone splinters. One vertical butt stroke would do it.

I said to him, "Now go on, Lafeber. Go and get some rest. Lewis, take Lafeber back to your hootch and keep an eye on him. I'll get ahold of Lieutenant Roberts."

"Yes sir." He put his arm on Lafeber's shoulder and turned him around. "Come on, you fierce old motherfucker, let's go." He led Lafeber back down the road toward the barracks. I watched them start off, and from where I stood I could see the bare light bulbs of the barracks shining through the Quonset hut windows at Camp Matta. The two men—kids, boys—walked off together, the one with his arm around the other.

My mouth was dry and I couldn't seem to catch my breath. I became aware of the other officers standing around me. I looked at them—Nichols, Vandenberg, Harmon—and I felt embarrassed. "Let's get out of here," I said, and started walking. I slung the rifle over my shoulder and stuck the loaded clip in my parka pocket. "I don't believe it," I said, and spat. "Another report to write."

FIFTEEN

Mᴀʀᴄʜ 2

For the record:

Two nights ago a boy on a patrol from A Company was killed. The patrol leader was Ralph Sellers. A grenade exploded, killed one guy and wounded his buddy. No one on the patrol saw anything or heard a sound, just the explosion. The grenade came right in on their position. They're shipping the kid's body down to Seoul where they'll dig the shrapnel out of him and try to determine whether the grenade was Russian or North Korean or American.

The men I interviewed confirmed everything Specks had told me. Sellers' patrols were terrible. Sloppily run, no sense of mission, no security, no discipline—the patrols were perfect targets for assault, fertile breeding ground for accidents. My report drew no conclusion and made no recommendation; it merely rendered the statements of the surviving members of the patrol. And the men's statements told an unmistakable tale.

Upon reading the report, Colonel Brody contacted Colonel Larson and arranged for a replacement for Sellers. He called Sellers in and relieved him, told him to go start packing.

Then he called in Bill Miller. I don't know what he said to Miller.

Sellers will join a battalion down south, and we'll get another new officer.

Well and good. Where does this leave me? I could have done something. Specks told me. I promised him I'd speak to somebody and didn't even take the time to say something to Norm.

And now someone died.

Dad never did anything with me. We sailed together sometimes up at the lake. I finally beat him in a couple races, and he wasn't too pleased. Made excuses about the wind and the boat I'd borrowed. Said it was a faster boat.

At home he was always busy. If we'd do something on the weekend, it was work, not play. Big deal. He taught me how to mow the lawn and put up storm windows. Big fucking deal.

And I could never do it well enough. He would point out mistakes. Never a thank you, always a Well what about this? or Why didn't you trim that? He was impossible to please.

Because he was only happy with me when I was good, only loved me when I achieved something—an 'A,' an officer's commission—and when I fucked up, well, he wouldn't speak to me, just withdrew. I didn't exist for him when I wasn't pleasing him. That's what hurt. He wouldn't have anything to do with me when I failed.

So I did all these things to please him. College. Army. OCS. I think it's time I began to live for myself.

The day Sellers left Matta, he signed out at battalion headquarters around lunch time. I walked out of the TOC and saw him climbing into a jeep. His gear was piled in the back seat: a couple of duffel bags and a laundry bag. I reached the jeep just as it was about to pull away from the headquarters building.

"I heard you were leaving," I said. I put out my hand.

He didn't shake. "You wrote that report, you fucker, and you want me to shake your hand?"

"It didn't implicate you. Did you read it?"

"Yeah, I read it."

"It was damn accurate."

"But it wasn't fair to *me!*" he shouted. "You never came and talked to *me.*"

We looked at each other. There was a cold wind kicking up dust and I turned my back to it.

Sellers squinted. "You know something? I'm going to confide in you, Richardson, because you're all right. You never hassled me. You're gung ho, but that's forgivable. This bastard here though—" he gestured back over his shoulder toward headquarters—"this fucking colonel, Brody, he seemed to enjoy relieving me. You know what I say to that? I say fuck 'im. You think I give a shit? It's just what the fuck I hoped he'd do. I couldn't be happier. I mean who wants to die in this Godforsaken place, eh? Who even wants to *live* here?

"I wanted to get through my tour with the least possible hassle, you know? I mean, do I give a shit about Koreans? Do I care if one gook wants to go south and scope out the other gooks? What the fuck is that to me? Just leave me the fuck alone, that's all I ask. Go south, take your pictures and head home, but leave me the fuck *alone.* You don't bother me, I don't bother you. Over and out.

"That's the way I ran my patrols. We'd make a lot of noise, move into position before dark, eat chow. . . . It'd get dark and we'd stay put. *Fuck* it. I even popped a flare a couple times. *Here we are! Stay the fuck away!* I didn't want some slope infiltrator stumbling into my night ambush position by mis*take.* Somebody mighta got killed! It mighta been *me!*

"And the troops ate it up. They did! At least most of 'em, the ones that wanted to go on living, the ones who weren't so gung ho they wanted to kill a chink. One of my sergeants—an E-6, Richardson, a lifer—this staff sergeant came up to me on my third patrol. This guy was short, and I was on my third patrol. He'd been on close to a hundred patrols. He knew his fucking way around, believe me. We were out in the middle of the DMZ, right in the middle of it, about 200 meters from North Korea, and I was taking a piss, and he came over and stood next to me and started pissing too—we had security out, don't worry—and he said, 'Sir, you're the best Goddamn patrol leader I ever saw, next to myself.' That was my third patrol, and that's what he said to me, Richardson, I swear to Christ.

"And now look at this shit. Somebody got killed. But it sure as fuck wasn't *my* fault. That dumb bastard, he should never have thrown that fucking grenade, he was scared, I should have put him in the middle of the perimeter with me. He'd been here less than a month. That was his own fucking grenade, sure as shit, because I *know* no North Korean would have pitched one in on us. I *know* that, Richardson. We made a fucking *deal*. I didn't hassle them, and they didn't hassle me. They *knew* me, Goddamn it. Every third night it was Sellers' turn. *Every* third night. Rain or shine, on that third fucking night I'd be out there, and I did it the same way every fucking time. They *knew* that, and they left me alone. We had a fucking *deal*."

I couldn't think of a thing to say so I simply walked away from him. Headed toward the mess hall. Walking away seemed eloquent to me. He shouted at my back, but I kept going and finally I heard his jeep pull away.

I never saw Sellers again, but a few days later, Harmon, with a little prodding, showed me the classified report on the kid who'd been killed. The Eighth Army G2 had determined that what killed the kid were North Korean grenade fragments.

Late that night, Peters dropped me off at Tammy's. She wasn't there, and I had to let myself in. Not only was she not there, but the lights were out and the stove was almost dead. The room was freezing.

What the fuck? I lit some candles and looked around. The room was so cold it seemed vacated, but the bed was made and Tammy's photographs still hung on the walls.

I was irritated at first, but then I started to worry. Was she sick? Had she been called away? There was no note.

Then I considered the possibility that she was off screwing somebody else. I tried not to think about that.

I decided to wait. I didn't see that I had much choice, really. If she didn't show up, I wasn't sure what I'd do.

I put a charcoal brick into the stove. The stove was cylindrical, and so was the brick; it was made to fit snugly into the stove like a bullet into a rifle chamber. I had a hard time beause I'd never done it before. The fit was a tight one and the tongs were difficult to manipulate. Yet whenever Tammy did the same thing, the process looked simple and smooth.

I lay down on the bed in the alcove with my hands behind my

head. I lay that way for about an hour, doing nothing. The longer I lay there, the more hurt I felt and the angrier I became.

By the time Tammy arrived, I'd run out of patience. She came in and turned on the electric lights, but said nothing to me. She didn't even look at me. She went over and squatted near the stove. She wore no coat, just a kimono, so she must have been somewhere in the house.

"Where the hell have you been?" I said. I got up and went over to her. I was wearing fatigues over long johns, and I'd taken off my boots. I sat cross-legged on the floor. Tammy stared into my face and I got a good look at her eyes. She was deeply angry.

"Where *you* been?" she said. "Where *you* go the other night?"

So that was it. Well, shit. "I went to the Green Door Hotel," I said evenly, "and got layed."

She opened her mouth very wide and screamed. Her face seemed to crack; it became inhuman. Her mouth took over her face and the noise hurt my ears. Then she leaped up and ran around the room, pushing things onto the floor. She came to a pair of vases I had given her, and she picked one up and hurled it at me. I bent sideways and turned my face away, and it nicked the back of my head and thudded against something behind me without breaking. She raised the other vase high over her head and flung it from point-blank range. I ducked and it shattered on my knee. Something entered one of my eyes and I had to close them. She jumped on me and started hitting. We fell on the floor. Her blows didn't hurt, but my eye did, and then I felt her knees digging into my side. I shouted and flung her off me. Threw her across the room. She landed on the bed and stayed there. I got up and limped to the mirror. My knee was throbbing. I pulled my lower eyelid down and saw a chip of pottery on the rim and removed it with my handkerchief. That seemed to fix the eye. I turned and faced Tammy.

"What *is* all this?"

"You fuckin son of a bitch!" It sounded kind of funny in her Korean accent. But she was furious. She turned her back to me.

I went over and lay beside her. She moved away from me, toward the curtain. I slid over and took her in my arms. She struggled free and went over to the stove. She wouldn't look at me, but after a moment, she spoke.

164

"You can't do that. You not supposed to be with other girls. I'm your steady. You supposed to be with me, nobody else."

"Shit." I sat up. Why was what I did when I wasn't with her any of her business? That was exactly what I needed: a whore telling me what to do.

"I'll see whoever I want," I said. "I'll do what I please."

Now she looked at me. Still angry. She came over to the bed. Our eyes were about level.

"No!" she screamed. "You *not* do what you please! Not if you want to be with *me*. You go see other girls, I see other men. I go out when you not here. You want it that way, then you see what's gonna happen. I go out too. Fuck around. Make much money. Fuck all GIs in village."

She laughed at me. She tossed her head and turned her back. Her dark hair swung like a curtain closing.

Then suddenly she spun around and slapped me across the face.

It hurt. I felt like smashing her, killing her. I leapt up and she retreated to a corner of the room. I raised my hand to strike her. She seemed so small at that moment—it would be so easy to—

I lowered my hand. It was trembling. It wasn't even a hand anymore—I had made it a fist.

That made me even more angry. I couldn't even hit the bitch, she was so small. Yet she could hit me?

What could I do with my anger? I went back to the bed and sat down. Who was she to tell me what to do? And threaten me with infidelity. It was ludicrous. She was a whore! But the worst thing was my own rage—it made me furious to realize she could make me so angry! Soft little explosions kept going off inside my chest and stomach. I wanted to smash her, kill her. I'd never been that angry before in my whole life.

Tammy sat in the corner looking at me with accusatory, angry, self-righteous eyes.

It occurred to me that I might get up and walk out and never come back. That seemed like a fine idea. Just leave her sitting there being angry at nothing, at the space I had occupied. Goodbye, Tammy. You've been awful, so I'm leaving you. Have a nice life, you bitch. Stew in your own juices.

It sounded great. I thought I'd do it.

But it occurred to me that I had nowhere to go. Peters wasn't due to pick me up until 4:00 the next morning, and I wasn't about to wander the streets of Changpa-ri until then. I couldn't hitch back to Matta; officers didn't hitchhike. And the Green Door was out, too. I had about five dollars in M.P.C. on me. There was no such thing as credit at the Green Door.

So I was stuck here. With her. And with my own anger. What was I going to do with my anger?

I yelled at her. Called her a whore, a bitch, a cunt. What right did she have to tell me what I could and couldn't do? Was she laying down *rules* for me? I was *paying* her! I'd do what I wanted, I'd go where I wanted, I'd fuck who I wanted.

When I paused, out of breath, she said, "Then you don't want me anymore." She said it matter-of-factly. "You get yourself somebody else. That not what you paying me for. You want to make love to somebody else, you get some other steady. I not want to pick up other girl's disease. I not want other girls laughing at me."

Tears began to run down her cheeks. She said, "Other girls say to me, 'Hey Tammy, your steady been to Green Door. Whatsa matter? You number ten? He tired of you?' They all laugh at me. I not know what to do, you damn Arthur Richardson. I think you better find somebody else." She sat in the corner and cried.

The thought of leaving her filled me with dread. "I don't want to find somebody else," I said. And it was true. When I said it, it was true.

I went to her, bent over and helped her up. We spent the night in each others' arms.

March 6
The search
I finally wrote Dad today:
Dad:
I understand you copped out during World War II and got somebody to write you a phony letter that got you exempted from the draft.
Is that true?
I demand to know.
Art.
I mailed it to Dad's office address in Hartford.

166

March 10
Seoul soul sole Seoul
  Never go solo to Seoul / it's not good for your soul to be
sole in Seoul
            Though Doc may okay you
            the girls won't bouquet you
            they'll flay and filet you
            in Seoul

  Just returned from a weekend in Seoul. Never again, ne-
ver. Swear off that shit for the duration. When am I going to
learn? I should have stuck with Tammy.
  Well, I'm glad I did it. As soon as we left Camp Matta, I
knew what a bullet must feel like just after it leaves the gun.
(I'm *out!*) Now that I'm back, though, I know what that lead
projectile feels like when it hits concrete or bone.
  Jack was going down for the fifth time. Drowning. Same girl.
I'd be going out with the roommate.
  We left on Friday morning. We rode in Jack's jeep, and we
took Lewis as driver because he deserved a weekend in Seoul. I
walked the fence, then jumped into the jeep without changing my
sweaty fatigues—we were in a rush. I threw my helmet and flak
jacket on my bunk and grabbed my baseball cap, pulled on my
parka, snatched my AWOL bag (packed the night before) and
raced down the stairs to the waiting jeep. We took off immediately.
  Dave Linderman had agreed to walk the fence for the next
couple of days. "Be glad to," he told me. "I'm dying slowly of
boredom. Anything for a change."
  As soon as we crossed Libby Bridge and picked up speed
south of Changpa-ri, we relaxed. We felt the wonderful release of
being out: out of class, out of school, out of basic training, out of
OCS. Bullets leaving the gun. That feeling had followed me all
my life, the best times of my life, and here it was again: we were
out. Lewis honked the horn and swerved from side to side, Jack
and I laughed and whoooped and took punches at each other.
  "We're *out!*"
  "Holy shit, we're out *out OUT!!*"
  "Goodbye!"
  "Gone. Gone! Wah-hoooo!"

"Sayonara, DMZ! We are *out!*"

Blam! Jack knocked my cap onto the floor of the jeep. "Hah!" I stomped on it. "We're out!" I ground the silver bar on the hat into the floor with the heel of my boot.

Civilians. That was what Jack had promised. Red Cross workers in Seoul, Donut Dollies. American girls.

We drove too fast through Uijongbu, the road a gray swamp, the jeep skidding even in four-wheel drive, then out of the city, the road narrow, shoulders dropping off steeply into rice paddies on either side. We passed bicycles with amazing loads: a pyramid of tin cans tied down on the back of one, rising high above the cyclist's head. A pig strapped onto the rear of another, the cyclist —the pig's chauffeur—an old man, wizened, gray-haired. How much would he get for his pig in Seoul? Maybe a lot.

Farther on we saw a gang of Korean men working on culverts and a small bridge. Workers carrying loads of rocks on their backs sobered me up.

"Look at 'em," I said to Jack. "What sort of a life is that?"

"Don't get existential on me, Art. They're not us; they're them. Don't worry about it. We're only driving by."

And we did. We passed at a high rate of speed, and we reached Seoul in less than three hours. Seoul. It was a huge city: traffic, exhaust fumes, crazy little taxis—*kimchi* cabs—buses, and *trolleys*, for Chrissakes, with bells, and bicycles all over, and new, modern high rises standing next to shacks made of corrugated metal and tar paper. Contrast and confusion: chaotic incongruity. A city growing too fast.

Lewis got lost, but after forty-five minutes of high-risk driving, we found the Main Officers' Open Mess. It was a red brick building, three stories high and very long, sprawling over vast grounds, the lawns beginning to show some green, and a long curving driveway that swept toward a huge green awning with big white letters: M O O M.

We must have been a sight pulling up to the Seoul Main Officers' Open Mess. This place was fancy and we were right off the DMZ, the jeep plastered with mud, the top of the jeep still off (it was only 45 or 50 degrees out), Jack and Lewis and I looking windblown and wearing fatigues, dirty parkas, muddy boots. Armed. My hat crushed oddly, its silver bar scratched.

And then somebody yelled "Jack!" and here came this

woman dashing down the long flight of stairs from the front door of the MOOM, a lovely dark-haired girl with her coat billowing out behind her. She was a big girl and she ran straight for Jack and wrapped her arms around him and he lifted her and spun her around. Her feet flew out behind her.

"Jack! You hunk, how the hell are you?"

"I'm ready."

"I'll bet you are. You animal."

Lewis and I were standing on either side of the jeep, watching. Our eyes met. He shrugged and looked toward the sky, and I grinned.

The happy couple were kissing.

"Mmmm-mm!" said the woman. "Oh God, it's been forever, baby!"

Another woman had followed Jack's girl down the steps. She stood quietly looking on.

I walked over to her. She watched me. Her eyes grew large and she took a step backwards.

"Are you him?" she said. Then she blushed. "I mean, I'll bet you're Art."

"That's right."

"Hi, my name's Meg. I'm your date." She held out her hand and I shook it. It was tiny and quite cold. She was wearing a camel's-hair overcoat and a plaid scarf, and her cheeks were pink and her dark eyes shone. I thought she was just about the most gorgeous American girl I'd ever seen.

"Hello, Meg," I said, shaking her hand. "Sorry I didn't have a chance to clean up."

"Oh." She looked me up and down. "Well, that's all right."

Jack and I got our bags out of the jeep and dismissed Lewis. Then the four of us went in and had lunch at the Officers' Club. In the dining room the ceiling was very high and the tall windows had long, thick drapes. The carpet was soft and on the tables the starched, pressed white tablecloths were clean because the waiters changed them for each seating. Everyone in the dining room was wearing dress greens, and a couple of these office-bound officers said hello to the girls. Jack and I received strange looks. I didn't mind; I felt great. I knew where we were from and what we'd been through.

After lunch Jack and Tina went off in a *kimchi* cab to their

169

hotel room. Meg suggested I get a room at the club, and I did. She went back to her office for the rest of the day, and I went upstairs to get settled.

I wrote a couple of letters to friends in the States and then lay on my bed and stared at the ceiling. I felt relaxed and at peace, and yet at the same time I felt kind of anxious. I wanted to make the best of this short weekend, but I didn't know how. Getting time off was like getting a gift you've always wanted, a very special gift, and then not knowing what to do with it. You stop wanting it, and that feels strange. Getting what you want feels strange. There's a letdown. What do you do next? That was my problem. I had gotten what I wanted—time away from the DMZ—and I didn't know what to do with it.

I wasn't due to see Meg again till around supper time, so I went downstairs and bought a book called *The Naked Ape*. I brought it back up to my room, lay down again and began to read. After a while I dozed off, and when I awoke I thought I was in Tammy's room. I looked around and saw the bedside table, the small window, the green carpet on the floor, and I remembered where I was. I'd been asleep for a couple of hours. I wondered what Tammy was doing. Then I realized I'd have to hurry if I was going to shower before I dressed and went down to meet Meg.

There was a dinner dance at the club that evening. Meg and I ate with a bunch of her girlfriends and a couple of officers from Eighth Army headquarters, a lieutenant in the AG and an infantry captain. The captain had been to Vietnam and we talked about that for a while, but the subject dampened everybody's spirits, so we got off it.

Meg looked wonderful and her friends were not as pretty as she was, but they were funny and we laughed and had a good time. I ate and drank a lot, and after dinner I danced with all of the girls who had been at our table. There was no sign of Jack and Tina, and I expected them to stay away although I hoped they'd join us. But they never showed. Around one in the morning I walked Meg over to her apartment, the one she shared with Tina. She didn't ask me in. I went to kiss her goodnight, and she kissed me back. She kissed me warmly. I put my arms around her and held her, just held her against me and we didn't say anything and she let me hold her for a long time.

On Saturday morning I met Meg for breakfast, and afterward

we grabbed a *kimchi* cab and went off sightseeing and shopping. It was awkward at first. We seemed to have to start all over again, as if we didn't know each other. She seemed strangely unfamiliar, yet I had left her just nine hours earlier. When we talked, the conversation seemed superficial, all about Seoul and what we were going to buy and where we'd go next. When we didn't talk, the silences felt uncomfortable and full of failure. I began to think I'd forgotten how to talk to a women I was dating for the first time. *Dating*. What did that mean? It meant sex was a possibility but had to be ignored, put off till you got to know the girl. It meant you had to pretend that everything was important except the thing that was most important, and you couldn't mention that. It meant you had to avoid touching, at least intimately, for an unspecified period of time. Until, I suppose, you had talked yourselves half to death and there was nothing left to do but become physical because there were no more words and there was no more energy for thinking of words and no more energy for fighting the urges of your bodies—there was only exhaustion and loneliness and the other person and your own desire.

But we were far from that point on Saturday morning. Good Lord, I thought as the *kimchi* cab whizzed around one of Seoul's insane traffic circles, I have only this weekend, and only this girl, so we've got to cut through this shit, this awkwardness and reticence, and hit it off. Soon.

It did get better. As the day wore on we both seemed to relax. We entered a small restaurant for lunch and sat on the floor and they brought steaming washcloths to the table so we could wipe the dust from our hands and faces. Over lunch, the mood shifted. The tension fell away and was replaced by warmth.

"My mother never cooked rice in her life," Meg said to me. "Or fish, for that matter. I love the food here in Seoul. Korean food. This restaurant is a find—how did you do it? You just dragged us in here. I don't see any Americans in this place, do you? They all look like Korean businessmen. Have you ever seen so many suits in your entire life?"

I told her about Harmon and all the new suits in his footlocker, and she laughed. It was nice to be with an attractive American girl in a civilian setting. After lunch we wheeled around Seoul in another cab and I held Meg's hand. We had a fine time deciding where to go next. We visited a park on the outskirts of the city. It had a high hill and a stream with a waterfall, and a steep trail to the top of the hill with gardens on either side. At the top, the trail overlooked the city, and the waterfall fell off into the ravine near the park's entrance. When we arrived at the park, we passed a large group picnicking along the stream bed. It must have been a huge family. They were seated on straw mats and there was a huge quantity of food spread out in the middle. There must have been thirty or forty people in two long lines, everyone dressed for the cool spring weather. They were all different ages, from little kids to very old. At the ends sat two white-haired old people, one a man, the other a woman. Mama-san and Papa-san. There was much chattering and laughter—the sound drifted up into the ravine, louder than the splashing of the stream against the rocks and the rush of the waterfall. The children and adults were dressed in bright colors that stood out brilliantly among the dark greens and browns of the trees and bushes and the gray of the rocks along the stream. The group reminded me of someone I had known in basic training, an Italian kid we called Rosie, who had a big family that visited him nearly every weekend. His relatives would drive down to Fort Dix every Sunday from up near the city and they'd bring food and have a picnic in one of the picnic areas near the barracks. The guys in my platoon and I could smell the food from where we would sit on the steps of the barracks, polishing boots and belt buckles. The aroma of hot tomato sauce and clam sauce with garlic would almost—but not quite—overpower the sharp odors of shoe wax and Brasso. Rosie and I and six other guys shared a room, and Rosie was generous, and one by one he invited us to eat with his family. When my weekend came, it was everything I expected. The people were wonderful. The adults bossed the kids around and the kids raised hell, but only so much. They knew their limits. Rosie's aunts and uncles told him he was too skinny and what were they feeding him in the army that he looked so thin, anyway? Look at Arthur here, they said, he's big and don't look so wasted, are they feeding him the same as you? He's a big fella, Aunt Louisa, Rosie said. He's gonna go to OCS, become an officer. He's been to college and he played sports in college, which is why he's so big. That's right, I said, I was a jockey and rode the bench. They all laughed. Rosie and I were friends after that day and he invited me to the family's last picnic.

It was a somewhat somber affair: he'd already received orders for Vietnam. A few months later, while I was still in OCS, his mother wrote to tell me he was dead. He was an RTO and was killed in an ambush.

This Korean family seemed very much like his. They were a lively bunch and seemed to be enjoying the outing. The kids were not as rambunctious as Rosie's cousins had been, but they looked just as hungry and almost as well fed.

Meg and I climbed the long trail to the top of the hill and agreed that the view was beautiful. Seoul was nearly ringed by mountains, and though the air was dirty, the city looked dramatic the way it sat hugely in the midst of those gray chunks of earth and rock. Seoul itself was built on hills—we were standing on the highest—and they gave the city texture. There wasn't a bit of smoothness anywhere. The city's streets and buildings formed on the land a rumpled blanket that undulated for miles, ending only where the mountains blocked the horizon. It was like standing at the Forward CP in the daytime, only that view was the reverse of this. This view was of a thriving human colony, but from the Forward CP one saw only land that had been given up by humans. Mined and deserted.

Meg and I walked carefully back down the narrow gravel trail. People were walking past us, climbing toward the top. I wasn't paying attention to them; I was peering over the edge, down past the waterfall, oblivious to the climbers, trying to glimpse the picnicking family through the trees. Meg was in front of me. We had almost reached the bottom when from behind me somebody shouted:

"Hey Lieutenant!"

I turned around. Standing on the trail above me was a very large NCO. He had a great many stripes on his arm—a First Sergeant. I hadn't seen him pass us. A short Korean girl clung to him, and his face was very red.

"I *saluted* you. You better *return* that salute!"

I stared at him for a moment. Then I turned away.

"Hey Lieutenant! I'm *talking* to you!"

Was I going to have to confront this son of a bitch? Meg had stopped in the middle of the trail and was staring past my shoulder. I touched her lightly. "Come on, let's keep walking," I said.

She hesitated, and then I heard this rhinocerous puffing and crunching down the trail behind me. Meg didn't move; she stood and stared.

Then I felt his hand on my shoulder. The hand was large and heavy, its grip firm.

He said, "Look, Bub, I want an answer." I could smell alcohol on his breath.

He shouldn't have touched me. I turned my head and looked up into his beefy face. I kept my voice low, hoping Meg wouldn't hear me. "Sergeant, take you *hand* off me." He did, as if he'd been burned. I read his name tag and the insignia on his uniform. "Sergeant Johnson, I don't know what engineering outfit you're with, but when I find out— "

He interrupted me, shouting: "Blow it out your ass, Lieutenant! You fuckin looies are all alike! Walk around with your heads up your ass. You're worse than a bunch of *civilians!*"

He wheeled and walked off. Caught up with his Korean girlfriend, a shapely, heavily rouged woman, and charged up the trail without looking back.

I turned around. "I'm sorry, Meg, I— "

"Why did you just take that?"

"What?"

"Are you just going to let him go?"

"Sure. Good riddance. Come on, let's get out of here." I put my arm around her shoulder and she reluctantly started off down the hill.

But soon she stopped again and turned her face toward mine. "I can't believe you're just leaving. Just going to drop it."

I shrugged. "I'm on vacation here. Do *you* want to pursue this? I don't. Besides, what could I do?"

"*I* certainly don't know. Can't you report him or something?"

"No. Actually, yes, I suppose I could. But not now. There's nothing I can do about it right now."

"But why didn't you say something? Or do something? He had no right to talk to you that way. It was so . . . so . . . insubordinate. I mean, he may have been older and had all those stripes but he was only an enlisted man, after all."

"Let's forget it."

"But you just let him say those things. You just let him get away with it."

"Sticks and stones."

"Humph." She started to turn around, then looked back at me. "And that Korean woman he was with! She was a prostitute, wasn't she? She was a whore if I ever saw one!" She turned around and continued walking energetically downward.

"He was probably sensitive about that. Didn't want to be seen with her."

"Yeah, I'll bet! That's why he drew so much attention to himself."

"Good point. Perhaps he was reacting to my being with you."

"Why should he react to that?"

"He probably has a family back in the States. Maybe a daughter your age."

"God!" She stopped and looked back up the hill. "That'd be awful."

We walked in silence for a while. Then, without turning around, Meg asked, "What did you say to him?"

"It was nothing, really. I just told him not to make a scene in front of you."

"Well, he certainly didn't listen to you, did he?"

"No. He certainly did not."

SIXTEEN

I DROPPED MEG OFF AT HER apartment and got back to the MOOM around five o'clock. There was a message for me at the desk.

Art:
How's it going? Let's get together tonight. Cocktails, din-
ner, and a night club or two. A little jazz? Seoul awaits
thee, and so do I. Call me at the Chosun Hotel, 87-4222,
Room 8-113.

Jack

I took the elevator up to my room and phoned Jack. There was no answer. I undressed and got into the shower, and the phone rang. It was Jack. He was downstairs.

"Let's have dinner here," he said. "The girls want to go out later, after dinner."

"Are you sure?"

"Yeah, I just talked to them."

"Okay, have a drink and I'll be right down. Or come on up if you'd like."

"You about ready?"

"Yeah."

"Okay. I'll see you in the bar."

"Hey," I said.

"What?"

"How's it going?"

"Well, pretty good, mostly. It's been all right. Say, what happened with you? Some ruckus with an NCO?"

"Yeah, some old bastard blowing off steam. I'll tell you about it when I come down; I'm freezing here. See you in a minute."

"Roger." He hung up.

Meg and I had made definite plans for dinner, so I wanted to touch base with her. I dialed her number. Someone picked it up on the first ring.

"Meg?"

"No, it's Tina."

"Hi Tina, this is Arthur. What's up for tonight? Is Meg there?"

"Didn't Jack get ahold of you?"

"Yeah, I just talked to him."

"Well—?"

"Well, what are we doing? Can I speak to Meg?"

"Look, Arthur, we'll see you around nine. After dinner. You guys pick us up, all right?"

"Okay."

She hung up.

I put on my greens and met Jack downstairs in the bar. The room was crowded but Jack had gotten a table. He looked great: scrubbed clean and relaxed. I'd never seen him looking that way before, ever. His skin was dry, without that film of sweat everyone developed on the DMZ, and his eyes looked rested. As I sat down, he leaned back, opened his mouth, and yawned hugely.

I laughed at him. "Playing the bridegroom, I see. Sleep much?"

"Very funny. No. How about you?"

"Plenty of sleep. Too damn much." I rose and got a beer and brought it back to the table.

"So," Jack said. "No luck, eh?"

"No. It isn't working out. She's sort of holding back. I can't get close to her. And this first sergeant—I think he spoiled every-

177

thing. He started hollering at me and I think Meg thought I should have slugged him or something, or *reported* him. Jesus."

"Why didn't you?"

I looked up. "Now don't you start."

"Okay. What was his problem?"

"I don't know. I didn't see him, didn't return his salute. So he started yelling at me like I was some buck private or something. No, that's not right—it wasn't all verbal." I took a swallow of beer, remembering. "The son of a bitch put his hand on me. He grabbed my shoulder from behind and sort of swung me around. Makes me angry just to think about it."

"No kidding. You could have him court-martialed. Did you get his name and unit?"

"Just his last name. And his branch: he's an engineer. But there can't be too many engineer first sergeants wandering around Seoul, can there?"

"No. What are you going to do?"

I thought it over. "Nothing."

Jack smiled. "Good man. Wouldn't be worth it."

"No. It was really nothing. Just embarrassing in front of Meg, that's all. What about you? You didn't sound exactly in love on the phone just now. Is anything wrong?"

"Oh no. Everything's great."

"Really?"

He shrugged. "Actually, Tina's been acting sort of weird this weekend. I mean, the sex has been great. It's not that."

"Yeah? What is it?"

"I don't know. It's like she's not all there."

"Where's the rest of her?"

"How should I know? Timbuktu. She just isn't *talking* this weekend."

I grinned. "I have an idea. I'll spend the night with Tina and you can talk to Meg. She's a great conversationalist."

"Good idea. Tina will be thrilled. I'll mention it to her."

The joke had fallen flat. "Sorry," I said. We both drank. "I didn't mean to make fun of you. It's just that your position looks a bit better than mine."

Jack sipped his beer and thought for a moment. "I don't know what's going on. It's weird. Usually she has a lot to say. She's really sort of an interesting girl. She's been a lot of places. Knows a lot of shit. Her father's a lawyer in New York—a pretty interesting guy, apparently. Has a lot of celebrity clients, famous people. Me, I'm from Wisconsin. Big Ten education, you know?" He smiled wearily. "I don't know. She seems different this weekend."

"No conversation, eh?"

"Yeah."

"Just screwing?"

"Yeah."

"You poor guy."

We went into the dining room and ate dinner. We ordered filet mignon and a bottle of wine. I'd never eaten a meal that tasted so good. The meat was tender, the vegetables fresh, the baked potato moist. I ate two chocolate sundaes for dessert, and Jack ate three. It felt as though we had spent the past year in the field, like prospectors, and had come into town for a bath and a meal. A brief respite, cradled in the arms of civilization, and then back to the wilderness.

After dinner we grabbed a taxi outside the MOOM and picked up the girls. We were slightly drunk. Both of us were in uniform, which was the first thing Meg remarked upon when she let us into their small apartment.

"Uniforms," she said. "You're still in your uniforms."

"I know," said Jack. "Irresistible, aren't we?"

"Couldn't you wear something else, Art? I meant to say something. Don't you have some—you know—regular clothes?"

"It's all I've got, Meg."

Tina swooped into the room, dressed in a low-cut blue dress, pearls, earrings. She looked fantastic: sensual and elegant. Apparently she had overheard Meg, because she went to Jack and wrapped her arms around his neck.

"Now Margaret, I *love* their uniforms. They look splendid in them. Don't they?" She fingered the three ribbons over Jack's left breast pocket. "They don't have many medals yet, but you'll see. They'll get them."

We went first to a quiet night club. We talked. It was just small talk. We all seemed to be trying to sort out the mood, to find a pleasant plane and get up onto it. We all wanted to be happy, but I don't think any of us were.

There was a small American band playing jazz, and the place

was pretty crowded. It was a mixed crowd: Americans, some white, some black; and a few Koreans. Almost all the Americans were in uniform, army or air force. Some of the Koreans wore ROK Army uniforms. I didn't see any officers in the place, other than Jack and me. We were seated at a table near the back. A Korean waitress in a skimpy uniform and black tights took our order. She brought the drinks quickly, and Jack paid for them in *won*. He caught my eye a moment and flashed an open hand at me: five dollars for each drink. They were weak, too.

Tina lifted her glass. "Here's to the Army," she said. "To our boys in uniform."

"And to Korea," said Meg. "South Korea, that is. To being here in Asia and having adventures."

We all drank.

"My turn," said Jack. We looked at him. "Pardon me, Meg," he said, "but the hell with adventure. Here's to going home. Screw the Army and Korea, North and South alike." The girls giggled, and Jack and I downed our entire drinks.

"What about you, Art?" said Tina. "You've got to make a toast."

"No booze."

"Come on," said Meg. "You have to."

"All right then." I lifted my little glass with its sweaty sides and four ice cubes. "Here's to love."

Meg looked embarrassed, but Tina said "Aw, that's nice," and kissed Jack on the cheek. We all drank, Jack and I just draining our empty glasses. I put my arm around Meg and squeezed her shoulder, but she didn't respond, and I thought, Oh what the hell.

Soon our waitress brought another round of drinks. The music was moody, a kind of urban, upbeat jazz, and it was soft, really only background music from where we sat. We were able to talk.

"Well," Jack said, "I'm glad we made it. I'm glad Art finally got down."

"Yes. It's nice, isn't it?" said Tina.

"There's nothing like being here," I said. "I feel very fortunate."

"I've never met anyone stationed on the DMZ before," said Meg. "What's it like there? What do you guys do all day?"

Jack gave her a rather blank look, and I said: "Oh, we manage to keep busy. How's your drink coming?"

"Fine, thanks. But seriously. What do you do, Jack?"

"Jack works for the S-3," I said. "The operations officer."

"What do you mean, 'operations'?"

"Combat missions. He oversees special patrols, ambushes, searches. Work details, the barrier force. Stuff like that."

"And what do you do, Art?" Tina asked.

"I walk the fence."

"Yeah," said Jack.

"What's that? What fence?"

I explained to them about the fence. I would rather have been talking about anything else: masturbation, tactical nukes, anything.

"Don't you do something besides that?" Tina asked.

"Yeah, sometimes I do other things. Write reports. Or supervision, like Jack. I'm often on the fence at night."

"You have to be crazy to go nosing around the fence at night," said Jack, "but old Art does it. Knows every inch of it. Keeps those troopers awake."

"Is it dangerous?"

"Yep," he said. "Real bullets."

"No, be serious." Tina looked at me. "Is it *really* dangerous?"

I said, "Yes and no. Sometimes it really is dangerous. But it always *seems* dangerous, you know?"

"No," said Tina. "I don't."

"What Art's saying is that he's always scared shitless, but usually for no good reason."

I laughed. "That's it. That's it exactly."

"Oh," said Meg.

Tina said, "What do those North Koreans want, anyway?"

"Who knows?" I said. "They seem to enjoy stirring things up just for the fun of it. Aren't happy simply keeping to themselves."

"What do they do?"

"They send down reconnaissance teams, mostly. Three-man teams. Then one of them slips through the fence, the guy with the camera. Murder squads too, though. You heard about the Blue House Raid, didn't you?"

"Yes," said Meg. "Did they come through your fence?"

"No. Not our sector. But very close."

"But we weren't here for that one," Jack said.

"What guns do you guys carry?" Tina asked.

"Rifle," said Jack. "M-14."

"Art?"

I resented the grilling. "I carry a pistol. Sometimes hand grenades. Why don't we change the subject?"

"Have you ever been in any battles?"

"That's over with, for the time being."

"Did you ever throw one of your hand grenades?" The questions buzzed like hornets from Tina's red mouth. She was talking to me now, ignoring Jack.

"Yeah. A couple of times."

"Really? When? Where?"

"On the fence, at night. You hear something, you throw a grenade. It helps keep everyone awake. It's no big deal, really."

"But how do you know you're not blowing up an American?"

"You throw it *over* the fence. Nobody out there is going to be one of your own people."

"Did you ever get shot at?"

"Well yeah, sort of. By our own troops."

"Have you ever seen a North Korean?"

"Yes."

"Did you ever kill a man?"

I probably should have anticipated the question, but it was the first time I'd ever been asked it directly. I exchanged a glance with Jack, who looked away. Tina was staring at me. It took an effort to look at Tina.

"No," I finally said. "I haven't."

"Jack hasn't killed anybody yet either," she said. "Have you, Jack? Such a waste. He's such a good man. All those muscles. Such a marvelous specimen, aren't you, Jack? A beautiful killer. What a pity they didn't send him to Vietnam. But then I wouldn't have had you, would I?"

It was an unfortunate choice use of verb tense. Jack turned and stared off toward the band. His arms were crossed in front of him and he seemed not to have heard Tina. Next to me, Meg was sitting forward, and across the table Tina was leaning forward too. Tina's dress was cut low, and I could see far down it. The roundness of her breasts was terrifically erotic. Her eyes, and the pearls around her neck, gleamed like miniature moons. Her pulse throbbed along her slim neck. She was a lovely, sexy, bloodthirsty bitch. I thought, Maybe she'll wind up in Hong Kong or Australia, screwing guys on R-and-R from Vietnam. The Big Time in Donut Dolliedom.

God she was gorgeous.

Jack said to Tina: "Nobody's killed anyone up there in a long time. Except by accident. There've been accidents, but you don't see the enemy that often. You just don't."

The waitress came up to our table. "You like another round here?"

"Look," I said to everyone, "these lousy drinks are five dollars apiece, and this band is on break more than it plays. Can we go someplace else? Someplace where the drinks are cheaper and the music is a little more stimulating?"

"Yes," said Tina quickly. "There're lots of places." She conferred with Meg. Soon we were out on the sidewalk looking for a cab.

We drove through streets choked with traffic. The four of us had crammed ourselves into the back seat of a little taxi, and the windows had promptly steamed up. Meg was sitting on my lap; my hands were around her waist and we were kissing, and I was nuzzling her neck and ear.

I bit her lip, and she squealed. I whispered, "I love you."

"Sure you do," she said, and laughed. We went back to kissing and biting one another.

The cab stopped for the hundredth time, and the driver turned around and said something unintelligible. "We're there," Tina said. I rubbed some of the cold moisture off the window and peered out. I could see neon lights, and people milling about on the sidewalk. A few of the people were dressed in traditional Korean fashion, but most of the clothing was western. We piled out of the cab and I paid the driver. Up and down the street, neon lights flashed red, blue, yellow. We shouldered our way along the dirt street and ducked into a joint called, in English, The Firecracker Lounge. The neon sign over the door, of course, was a huge red firecracker. It had a fuse that would sparkle briefly, and then the thing would go off.

Inside, the place was a madhouse. It was packed and the music was very loud. Everybody in the place was Korean. Most were young, probably teen agers. The place smelled of sweat and beer and leather. Looking for a table, we struggled through the crowd.

People would not get out of our way. They'd stand still and block us, making no attempt to move. It was a struggle to squeeze through, and maddening.

At last we found four seats together at the end of a long table. The other party at the table, six adults, ignored us when we sat down. We took off our overcoats, settled back into our chairs, and looked around.

I felt uncomfortable. I wasn't sure why, at first. We were the only Americans in the place, but that didn't bother me.

I leaned over toward Jack. "You sure it's okay to be here?" The band had ripped into a rhythm and blues number, and I had to shout to be heard.

"Sure. I've been here before," Jack yelled. "We never had any hassle here."

I sat back and tried to relax, to enjoy the band, but I was feeling uneasy. I would look around, and people would either turn away or meet my look with a hostile stare. We had become the focus of a lot of energy, and I felt like a sort of lightning rod for hostility. Tina and Meg looked tense. Jack appeared relaxed and slightly drunk. We sat there with our elbows on the table, not talking, looking around apprehensively. Not one of the looks we got back was friendly.

We weren't served for a long time, but finally a waitress came over. She stared at us indifferently while we tried to order a pitcher of beer and four glasses. We did this by hand signal because none of us knew Korean, and even if we had, we couldn't have made ourselves heard over the band.

The waitress left and we waited anxiously for her to return. When she did, Jack paid her and tipped her very well. No reaction. I poured everyone a glass of beer and we toasted each other. I drank my beer straight down. It tasted terrible—a Japanese brand, highly carbonated and bitter. I poured another glass and started in on it. I felt strange, alienated. It didn't feel much different than wearing a uniform in the States had felt, though. You got mostly hostile stares there too.

Jack and Tina got up to dance, and the music was very loud so Meg and I couldn't easily talk to one another, but that was all right with me because by now I figured the evening was pretty much a bust. More talk wasn't going to salvage it. Perhaps another cab ride would, or a slow dance if the band got around to one. And I thought they probably would, because they were the only good thing about The Firecracker Lounge. Their varied repertoire made the music interesting. They played rhythm and blues, rock and roll, and even some Chicago blues numbers. They were good musicians. They played mostly instrumentals, with few vocals, and the instrumentals were very good.

After fifteen minutes or so, Tina and Jack returned to the table. They gulped down some beer. Tina looked flushed and out of breath and lovely, her hair mussed and her dress slipping lower, and Jack was sweating heavily, but they weren't smiling. Then someone came up to Jack. He was a young Korean male and he looked tough. His hair was very long and he wore a leather jacket with a lot of zippered pockets, and there was an ugly, sparse mustache on his upper lip. He leaned over Jack, close to his ear, and began to shout at him. I couldn't hear what the guy was saying, but I could see his throat straining and his jaws and lips working rapidly.

Jack didn't seem to understand. First he shook his head; then he shrugged his shoulders a couple of times and spread his hands wide, palms up. He seemed puzzled. He didn't look up, just sat there shaking his head.

Then the guy hit Jack. He hit him in the ear and mouth and chest. Jack looked surprised. The guy kept hitting him in the face with his fists.

Jack sat there while this guy pummeled him. When I saw his face begin to bleed I leapt up and jumped on the Korean. I grabbed him from behind and flung him off Jack. He was big and the muscles in his arms were very hard. He spun around and backed off a few steps. He steadied himself on the bar, glaring at me. I was backed up against some kind of post. There was an aisle between me and him, a distance of about five yards. The music banged on, obscuring all sound. He reached around behind him and grabbed a brown beer bottle off the bar, reared back, cocked his arm—

My mind sped up and time slowed down. I knew what was going to happen. Images flashed behind my eyes and I could feel a tingle in my fingertips, feel strength in my legs. The Korean threw the beer bottle hard and I dropped into a crouch and tucked my head to my chest. The bottle exploded on the post behind me. I felt glass rain down.

I rose to my full height and waited. He charged me.

Would he have a knife? My hands were empty. Something came back to me, a class in OCS, and I could hear the words as if someone were shouting: *Avoid hand-to-hand combat like the plague. There is always something strewn about the battlefield that you can pick up and use as a weapon: an arm, a leg. . . .*

I picked up a chair. I didn't do anything aggressive, didn't try to bash his head in. Instead I just held him off. I held the chair with its legs toward the Korean and he ran into the legs and I held him there. He couldn't get around the chair and couldn't hit me over the top of it. He struggled on the legs of the chair like a netted fish.

I suppose if I had clubbed him with the chair we'd have had everyone in the place on us. But that didn't occur to me then. I did what I did without reasoning. Things came to me and I did them.

I held the guy off and he feverishly swung at me and grappled with the chair, but nothing was going to make me let that bastard get around to my side of it. I seemed to hold him there forever. I thought, How is this going to end?

It ended when about five Koreans pulled the guy off me and threw him out of The Firecracker Lounge. I put down the chair and returned to the table.

Jack sat down at the same time I did. His face was cut and his uniform was disheveled. I had glass fragments all over me, and Meg began to brush them off my shoulders. I leaned over and brushed glass out of my short hair. A strange sort of dandruff.

"Sorry I couldn't help!" Jack shouted. "They were holding me, about five of them. We were slightly outnumbered!" He was grinning. "They followed your friend out the door."

"Why'd he come after you?" I asked.

"He wanted to dance with Tina. I said no."

Saturday night in Seoul City.

The band ended a number and paused between songs. I looked around at our group. Meg and Tina looked frightened: their eyes were large and their mouths were frozen in thin lines. "What do you say we get out of here?" I said. We started putting on our coats.

The woman sitting next to Meg, one of the people who had ignored us when we sat down, was middle-aged, heavy-set, and rather pleasant looking. Now she addressed us for the first time, and she spoke English.

"Don't go yet," she said. "You stay. Stay for a while." We stared at her, and we continued getting ready to go. But then I leaned down, close to her ear.

"Why not?" I said. I was angry. "Why the hell should we stay?"

"Better not to leave yet," she repeated. "He has many friends. A gang. They will be waiting outside. The bartender, he telephoned police already, so you stay here. They will be here soon."

I nodded. We removed our coats. "Thank you," I said to the woman. She bowed, and I did the same.

The four of us sat down, and I said, "Well, let's do something while we wait. Let's talk about something pleasant."

"Beer," said Jack.

"Yes, that's perfect," said Tina. "Let's have another pitcher of that rotten beer."

We ordered more beer and the band started to play again. In a few moments the police arrived. Six Korean MPs in sharply pressed khaki-colored wool uniforms walked into the bar and came over to us. They wore white gloves and white helmet liners, carried white billy clubs, and moved with a nervous quickness. They stood around us while we pulled on our coats, and then they escorted us outside. There were six or eight police cars in the street right outside with red lights flashing. A dozen or so more of the white-gloved MPs stood around talking, not really paying us any attention. Two of them flagged down a taxi; it was occupied, but after a few words from the police, the Korean passengers hastily got out. We got in no less hastily. We had a two-car escort back to the army compound. The police didn't go through the gate; they waited for us to make our turn, then sped off.

At the girls' apartment, Meg and I got out of the cab. I said goodnight to Jack and Tina, who would be going back to their hotel. Jack's arm was wrapped tightly around Tina, and she had her face pressed against his neck. She stirred sleepily, and Jack waved his free hand.

After the cab pulled away, Meg turned to me. "Will you come in for a drink?"

I replied quite sincerely, "I'd love to."

SEVENTEEN

I T WAS PAST ONE IN THE MORN-
ing and the compound was quiet. I could hear Meg's key as she
slipped it into the lock. Inside, we took off our coats and Meg
turned on a couple of lights. I unbuttoned my jacket and found
my poplin shirt damp with sweat, so I buttoned the jacket back
up.

Meg came out of the bathroom. "Sit down, Art, please," she
said. "Make yourself at home. What would you like to drink?"

I sat down on the edge of the couch. "Do you have bourbon?"

"Sure."

"That'd be fine. Just some ice, please."

Meg disappeared into the kitchen and I went to the bathroom. I took a piss, flushed the toilet and moved to the sink. I
stared into the mirror. My eyes were bloodshot but other than
that I looked about normal. I pulled off my jacket, tie, shirt, and
tee-shirt, then filled the sink with hot water and washed my face
and neck with a thick blue washcloth. I refilled the sink with cold
water and dunked my head, then let the water run out. I looked
for glass in the sink but didn't see any. In the cabinet I found a

plastic cup, and I drank three glasses of water. I could feel the tension leaving my body, but not all of it.

I put my clothes back on, except for my jacket and tie, which I carried into the other room. Meg had removed her shoes and was sitting up straight in one corner of the couch, her feet drawn up under her. "Come and sit down," she said. "Drink your drink. You look tired."

"I am." I sat down on the couch, not too close and not too far away. She handed me a drink. "Thanks," I said.

"You deserve it. You had quite a night."

"Yeah, we all did."

"I thought you were splendid in that bar," she said, looking up at me.

"Oh, it wasn't anything."

"Have you been in many fights?"

"No. A few."

"Tell me about them."

"I'd rather not, if you don't mind."

"Why not?"

"They're not my favorite topic of conversation."

"Didn't you win any?" She was smiling as she said it, but the remark sounded nasty.

"Yes, I 'won' some. If you can win or lose a fight."

"You looked so sure of yourself. You took over."

"Sheer instinct, nothing more. Tell me, how did you feel during all that?"

"I was terrified. But I was frightened for you, not for myself. It was like I was watching from a distance. Like I was watching TV. It wasn't happening to *me*, it was happening to you, and I didn't believe *I* could be hurt."

"But you know that now, don't you?"

"Yes. It sank in coming home. I started to perspire—did you notice?"

"No. But I noticed your hands shaking." I took one of her hands in mine. It was warm, and slightly moist. "Here, hold it out like this." I held my hand out flat, palm down, fingers spread. "See my hand? It's trembling."

She spread out her hand. It was a lovely hand, slim, long fingers, medium-length nails with no polish. It was shaking badly.

I took it in both my hands, brought it to my lips and kissed it, first the back, then the palm.

"Oh Art," she said. We embraced, kissed.

I could feel her breasts against me. "I want to sleep with you, Meg," I said.

"Oh no, please. We shouldn't. Please."

"Yes, I want to. Please come to bed with me."

"No, Arthur." She pulled away. "Please, no. I can't."

"Why not?" I put my arms around her and kissed her some more. "I want you so much."

"No Arthur. Please stop." She pulled away again, sat up, and grabbed her drink. The ice clinked against the side of her glass. She swallowed some of the amber liquid. She looked flushed, and mussed up. She was breathing fast. She turned away and smoothed her hair.

Looking like that, she reminded me of Suzy Wilson, my first real girlfriend. I'd been able to talk Suzy into just about anything, eventually.

Meg put her drink down, smoothed her skirt, turned and looked at me. "Arthur, I'm sorry. I didn't mean to lead you on. But really. Did you really expect me to jump into bed with you so quickly?"

"Why not?"

"Well, really. I mean, we're not dogs in heat."

"No. We're human beings."

"Yes, I know. That's exactly the point."

"Yes, it is the point. We're sexual creatures. Why wouldn't you want to go to bed with me?"

"We've just met!"

"So? Why else are we together? We know each other well— look what we've been through. Besides, we're adults. What's to stop us, if we want to?"

"Oh Arthur." She shook her head as though she felt sorry for me in my ignorance of things too complicated for me to understand. "Don't you see? I *don't* want to. I mean, of course I find you attractive." She patted my hand. "I find you very attractive. Tonight, you were—well, you were wonderful. But we're *people*, and we're supposed to act civilized."

"Well there's nothing more civilized—" My voice cracked.

"Please let me finish. The shame is that we have sex at all. It would be so nice just to get to know you—without sex interfering. You seem like such a nice person."

"If you want to get to know me so badly, then why won't you go to bed with me?" She didn't answer. "Are you a virgin or something?"

"That's none of your business!" She blushed.

"I thought so. You're probably waiting for your wedding night."

She leaned back, pressing deep into the corner of the couch. "Stop it, Arthur. Just please stop it. I can't take any more of this."

"I'm sorry. I'm being stupid." I stood up.

"Where are you going?"

"I think I ought to get back. Don't you?"

"But we were talking. . . ."

"We've talked enough."

She looked close to tears. "You only want one thing!"

I sat down next to her and picked up her hand. "Meg, look. I respect your position. I really do, and I can accept a 'no.' I'm not going to try to force myself on you, and I'm not going to lie and bullshit you. But you've got to respect my position too. I don't have much time. I'm only here for one lousy weekend. Who knows if I'll make it back? If I'd wanted to talk all weekend, I'd have stayed at Camp Matta. There're dozens of guys up there with nothing to do but talk. I wanted something more than talk."

She chuckled. "And I'm stuck down here in Seoul with dozens of guys who want to do it, and no one to talk to."

We both laughed. I hugged her. "I think I should leave," I said.

She looked at me for a long moment while she made a painful decision. Then she said, "All right."

I took a deep breath and looked around. The room seemed familiar and comfortable, like somebody's home. Comfortable easy chairs, end tables and lamps, the plush couch—it certainly wasn't a Quonset hut. I finished my drink and stood up.

She watched me pull on my jacket and overcoat. She seemed sad. "Please call me in the morning. Will you?"

"Sure. I will." It was the only time I lied to her. "Goodnight, Meg." I took her in my arms and we kissed. She pressed her body against mine and kissed me passionately. It didn't make very much sense to me. I got out of there fast.

March 9th
for the record:

In the dining room this morning I ordered the Sunday Brunch Special: steak, three eggs, hash browns, muffins, coffee, and a glass of pink champagne. I ate slowly and when I was done I wasn't full, so I ordered another. I ate that one too, every bite. When I finished I still felt hungry but I didn't want any more food.

What to do today? I've got lots of money saved up and nothing to spend it on. I sure don't feel like buying a ton of junk at the PX: stereo gear and camera and a watch, like Harmon. Or fucking suits.

When I get home, it'd be so great to buy a motorcycle and camping equipment, and take a trip across the country. A Harley and a tent. Great investments. Not that I'm all that enamored of camping out after three years in the infantry— Maybe I'll be able to afford motels.

That'd be *great*! Motor west, and south, or up to Oregon. See America.

At the newsstand in the lobby they didn't have the Sunday *Times* but they had Saturday's, so I bought that and brought it upstairs.

The news is all astronauts and Vietnam. The astronauts are in orbit above the earth, practicing for a landing on the moon. It's a big story and I didn't read it. What they're doing seems a waste.

In Vietnam, the NV are shelling cities. They're lobbing rockets and shells into district and provincial capitals, killing civilians. Somewhere, an assault on two American infantry units by 300 to 500 NV regulars resulted in 89 NV killed vs. no American casualties. I had to read that three or four times. That's what it says. At least, that's what it says a U.S. "military spokesman" said. I can't believe anybody would speak such impossibilities. Does he expect—*really* expect—anyone to take him seriously? *Does* anyone? How could the *Times* print that kind of shit? The army P.I.O. who gave out that story must have choked. Maybe his nose grew.

In California, a Navy court of inquiry continues its investigation of the behavior of members of the *Pueblo* crew. Everyone thinks they buckled too quickly. They responded to threats. To threats. ("Stand still or I'll blow you head off!") And then there's Lieutenant Harris, that poor bastard. He was in charge of the secret stuff that never got destroyed.

192

He'll be fucked for certain. They always fuck the lieutenants, lowest critters on the totem pole with any real responsibility.

Hal Holbrook is in some off Broadway play. He was great as Mark Twain.

Good Christ. Spring training has begun.

At Columbia, the use of marijuana is widespread and open, and at Vassar the students are voting on whether male visitors will be allowed in the dorms at all times. Gosh. Golly.

Not a word about Korea.

If. If the balloon goes up. If we're killed on a patrol or a guard post. Or crushed in a jeep accident or shot by a nervous GI on the fence. No one will ever write about us in the *Times* or erect a monument or read a Gettysburg Address over our graves. There's too much going on elsewhere; what we're doing is trivial by comparison. We'll never be part of the national memory.

Then again, we'd be dead anyway, so who gives a shit?

Lewis pulled into the driveway of the MOOM that Sunday at precisely 1300. Jack arrived in a *kimchi* cab a few minutes later, alone. We started the long trip back to Matta under windy gray skies that threatened rain.

North of Seoul, after we'd put the city well behind us, Lewis described his Saturday night in a Seoul whorehouse. He'd wound up with a woman who was at least a decade older than himself. "After we did it the first time," he said, "she starts telling me I put it to her too fast. Said she wasn't ready. Can you imagine that, sir? Twenty fuckin bucks, and she's givin me advice on how to get her hot!"

"Well, she's the expert," Jack said. "Did you listen?"

"Goddamn, sir! I wasn't payin her for *lessons!*"

Later, Jack turned around and asked how I had gotten on with Meg. I told him.

"Tough luck," he said.

"It doesn't matter. Thanks for fixing me up, though. It might have been nice."

We were quiet for a few minutes, and then I leaned forward and said: "Hey Jack. In that bar, when that guy was hitting you— why didn't you get up and punch him?"

He shook his head and grinned. "I don't know. I was too

drunk to feel much. Besides, I didn't have any quarrel with the bastard."

"I thought he was going to kill you."

"That would have made me mad."

After a while it started to rain. Jack pulled the collar of his fatigue jacket up around his neck. Then he turned around and gave me a big grin. "We'll have to take the top off at Libby Bridge."

"But Lieutenant Anderson!" I hollered. "I'm just in from the States and I can't stand getting wet. Can't we leave the top up just this once?"

EIGHTEEN

I WENT TO THE TOC MONDAY after walking the fence. I'd checked the schedule and knew Specks would be there. He was at the switchboard. He looked up when I walked in but I couldn't see the expression in his eyes because of his glasses. We stared at each other in silence for a moment. His irises seemed to shimmer behind his thick lenses. I finally went and poured myself a cup of coffee.

"I told you so."

I didn't say anything.

"I told you so, didn't I, Lieutenant?"

"Yes. You called the shot."

"What did you do about it? Did you do anything? Did you say anything to anybody?"

"No. Did you?"

"Shit."

"Specks—"

"Fucking shit. That's all. Just shit and fuck and piss. Shitfuck, and fuckshit. And cock. Cock too, sir. Cock and shit and piss and fuck and cunt. Shitfuck, cockcunt. Will you get out of here now please? I've said everything I have to say to you. I've got work to do. When I'm working the switchboard, I need peace and quiet. No distractions. Please? Goodbye."

"Look, Specks—"

He swiveled around toward the switchboard and shoved home a jack. "Are you working sir? Are you working?" *Click, shuck.* "Are you working, are you working?" *Click, shuck.* "Are you working, Charlie? Roger."

I put my coffee cup down and walked out of the TOC, back into the sunshine. Would Specks hold me responsible for that death? I didn't know whether I could work it out with him, or whether I wanted to. Who was he? A Spec-4 radio/telephone operator who'd been drafted after college. We were not really very different. Why hadn't he volunteered for OCS, taken a position of responsibility? It was he who had dropped out, not me. He'd dropped out long before. Fuck him. He was no less responsible than I was, and I was sick of his anger and moral outrage—let him dump guilt on somebody else. I was doing my job and doing it well. I couldn't be expected to prevent casualties or run the battalion. Hell, I didn't even run a platoon. I only ran myself.

On my good days.

I thought: I ought to go back to the TOC and say those things to Specks. Have it out with him.

But I didn't. I couldn't fight everybody.

Tuesday, March 11

The search.

Why *did* I fail to mention Sellers' patrols to someone? It's a failure, a fatal one. But after reporting the hole in Harris's fence—before speaking to him—So why didn't I go to Sellers? I hate that bastard. I should have turned his ass in to Brody.

Specks is right, it was my mistake. Pretty final, death. Maybe I could have prevented it. Maybe.

Does that make me responsible for it? Is it up to me to shoulder the responsiblility for all the things that can get fucked up in a military unit of approximately a thousand men?

After walking the fence last night I went to Changpa-ri. Tammy was waiting for me. I made love to her feverishly.

Is this love? We seem to need, more than love, one another. I don't think love between us is possible. We're separated by culture and language. Yet we're human and need each other desperately. Her body feels so *good*: her smooth hands and breasts are comforting. And she laughs. She nearly always smiles at me, and she laughs often. That's my favorite sound in the whole world, her laughter. My favorite sight, her smile.

I can't talk deeply with her but that's all right. I don't need to. It's enough just to touch her, to be with her and feel her skin on my skin, to hold her. It's all the communication I need. She holds me, and I feel all right.

What has meaning for me? Other people? Tammy? Jack? Mom, Dad? Who do I care for, what do I care about? What *means* something to me? What about myself—do I have meaning? What am I on earth for?

This is confusing and impossible, a comedy. Why do such questions arise? Does a deer ask itself what it's living for? Perhaps the questions come from feelings: longing, desire, rejection.

My life has been completely without purpose. I haven't even had to earn a living. God help me if I have to find some purpose on my own.

I hope the army will keep me busier. I don't want to think about my past or future or even the present anymore. I don't want another weekend in Seoul.

March 22, 1969

For the record:

This morning in the low stretch of marshland in A Company I saw a deer. There are few foxholes along that section of fence; the sector is covered by the two towers, 27T and 28T. The GIs in the towers were inconspicuous and the deer had free reign of the path (my path) south of the fence. She was right up close to the chain link. Fallow body on thin legs, about the size of a very large dog. Probably a doe. The fence rose high above her.

She trotted along the path away from me, came to the beginning of the next hill, wheeled and loped back in my direction, her head turned toward the fence. Her motions were rapid and jerky, not graceful but nervous, frantic. She seemed to be searching for a way to get through the fence, looking for a hole to slip through to go north. No doubt some instinct was urging her to migrate, but here was this fence, this vast fence, there was no end to it, she would never get past it. It sealed her off from everything she knew and wanted.

197

I kept walking and was within twenty meters of her when she bolted. She ran into the brush south of the fence and disappeared.

Along the fence the next morning, a single gunshot. I quit walking and listened for the chatter of an automatic weapon, the crack of a grenade. But there was no answer, just the single shot: the most unusual thing of all, along the fence. Probably an accident. I found myself wondering what poor bastard had bought the farm this time.

When I returned to Matta for breakfast, the deer was strung up by its front hooves on a pole near the mess hall door. The early morning sunlight streamed down obliquely and gave the deer a golden sheen. But even in that light, the deer looked very dead. Its head lolled to one side, jaws open, pink swollen tongue hanging sideways out of its mouth. Thin, black lips. Huge brown eyes, bulging, cloudy. The tusks protruding from its lower jaw gave it a look of malignant, carnivorous ferocity. It had small knobs of horns on the crown of its head. Its forelegs stretched upwards toward the top of the pole and the sky, as if in supplication. A strange odor. Blood still leaked out of it from somewhere. It was bleeding down its leg, the blood dripping off one sharp, black hoof. The sound of blood hitting the grass. Small turds lay in the grass beneath it, a dark, meager little pile.

Its light brown fur looked thick and soft. I reached up and touched its back, half expecting the deer to jump. The fur was rough in texture. I ran my hand down its side a couple of times, petting it. It didn't feel stiff.

The creature was not beautiful, not in death, but I had never seen an animal this size up close. What was it really like? How did it work? Maybe that's why men kill creatures, I thought: because they're fascinated and want a closer look.

I went in through the door of the mess hall. Colonel Brody was sitting by himself at the head table.

"Good morning, sir," I said.

"Morning, Richardson."

I sat down at a table not far from him. "Do you know anything about that deer out there, Colonel?"

"I really nailed that son of a bitch, didn't I?"

"*You* shot it?"

"Yep. One shot. That's a hell of a rifle, that M-14. Long as it's zeroed, it'll hit anything."

"But how come you shot him, sir?"

"*Her*, Richardson. That's a doe out there. Don't you know the difference?"

"I guess I didn't check out her genitalia, Colonel."

He gave me a nasty look.

"Why did you shoot her, sir?"

"Why? Why not? Because I wanted to, that's why. It was a tough shot. Had to be nearly three hundred meters. And I nailed her, too. Did you see where I got her?"

"No sir."

"Right behind the left shoulder. She dropped like a stone, didn't take a step—her legs buckled right under her. The bullet must have grazed her heart or ricocheted through it. Or bone splinters. Bone from her shoulder might have exploded her heart. I've never seen a deer drop that quick. Want to go with me next time I go hunting?"

"No, I don't fancy killing animals, Colonel."

"Oh, but of course. You're a man of refined sensibilities, aren't you, Richardson. Yet you're an infantry officer. That makes lots of sense. I suppose it's better to kill humans?"

"No sir, I don't think it is. It's worse. But it's a more even fight, usually. And there's usually a better reason."

"You're full of Goddamn shit. You ought to come hunting one of these days. Make you a better soldier."

"Where was the deer when you shot her?"

"Middle of A Company's sector, down in the hedgerow below the CP there. That old rice paddy. Know where I mean?"

"Yes sir, exactly."

"She wandered into a little patch of daylight and I got a clear shot at her from the road. Three hundred meters. Wham! Never saw it coming."

Later in the day, word came down from Colonel Brody: Officers Call at the Officers' Mess at 2000 hours. By that time the barrier force would be settled in and our patrols would be moving toward their night ambush positions.

The zone would be quiet for a while. All officers who could attend were required to. This would be a command dinner. A banquet.

Colonel Brody made all the arrangements. The deer's carcass was turned over to the Korean cooks, who were delighted. What meat they didn't serve the officers they could take home. Everybody would eat well.

We arrived at the mess hall in small groups: A Company officers, B and C Companies, headquarters platoon leaders, staff officers. We filed into the Officers' Mess quietly, all wearing fatigues, some clean, some stained with the day's sweat and dust. Sitting with Colonel Brody at the head table were Captain Lopez, the new battalion XO; Norm Stewart; the Chaplain; and the three company commanders: Miller, Davis, and Morrison. There were no NCOs present; not even Sergeant major Allen had been invited.

We sat and spoke quietly or not at all. The mess hall had been transformed: there was no florescent glare tonight, no pitted table tops and puke-green walls. The aroma of burning candle wax permeated the room; candles glowed dimly, eight to a table, one for every man. There was a warm, golden glow to every face. Hundreds of shadows floated across the four walls. The candlelight and shadows gave the place a ghostly atmosphere, like a cave or a church.

The tables were set with tablecloths. Tall bottles of liquor with Korean labels had been placed on the tables. The bottles were clear glass, and the liquid inside them was clear. There was a glass jigger at each place setting. The stainless steel flatware shimmered in the candlelight, and the glass pitchers of ice water sweated and reflected the flames of dozens of candles.

Mr. Lee had set up a large hibachi in the middle of the room. It sat on the oil heater, glowing and hissing; its smoke vented out the stove pipe. On a table near the stove, long strips of pink deer flesh marinated in liquid-filled pans. One by one Mr. Lee placed the strips of deer meat on the grill. They sizzled and crackled, and clouds of steam and smoke billowed up the stove pipe. Flames licked the edges of the meat and charred them black. Mr. Lee continually sprinkled a dark sauce over the venison. Lit from below by the orange glow of the coals and the bright yellow of the leaping flames, Mr. Lee's oriental face looked satanic. It brought to mind the sacrificing of animals and the burning of witches. Ritual killings.

We were a subdued bunch as we sat and waited for something to happen. No one drank, no one ate. Few of us said anything. Finally Colonel Brody slapped his flat palm sharply on the table. The low murmur of talking ceased, leaving only the hissing of sizzling deer meat. Slowly the Colonel pushed back his chair and stood up. He motioned to his right. "Chaplain, please," he said.

The Battalion Chaplain got to his feet as Colonel Brody sat down. He was a small man with narrow shoulders and short black hair, and he wore thick, black horn-rimmed glasses.

"Let us pray," the Chaplain said. We bowed our heads.

"Merciful Father, bless this food to our use and us to thy service, and make us ever mindful of the needs of others. Amen."

"Amen," came a few responding murmurs.

"That Chaplain's a real asshole," I heard Bobby Green mutter.

"Oh, he's all right," someone said.

"He's a fag."

"We need a psychologist, not a Chaplain," somebody said.

"That's right. The new religion."

The Chaplain had taken his seat, and Colonel Brody once again rose.

"Gentlemen, fill your glasses." Bottles clinked against jiggers as the clear liquor splashed and gurgled. "Please rise for a toast." We pushed back our chairs and stood.

"A toast, gentlemen." The room turned silent. "A toast to our commanders not present. To Colonel Larson, our Brigade Commander, and to General Bonesteel, Commanding General of the Eighth Army. And to our new Commander-in-Chief, Richard M. Nixon. May God give them good health, and the wisdom to lead us with—ah—with cunning and clear-headedness. May they lead us well." He paused, didn't seem to know what to say next.

Then he raised his glass. "And damn it," he said, "let's make Goddamn good and sure the next body around here is North Korean!"

He drank. We all drank, avoiding one another's eyes. The liquor was clear as water and very strong. From across the table,

Evans caught my eye and gave me a disgusted look. He said just loud enough for a few of us to hear: "A body, a body, my career for a body."

There were no more toasts. Colonel Brody sat down and we all followed suit. Mr. Lee and two other waiters began to serve the meal. The Colonel and those at his table were served first. They began to eat immediately, hungrily.

Seated at one of the long tables, I was sandwiched between Bobby Green and Greg Peabody. Harmon sat directly opposite me behind a couple of candles. His table manners had changed over the months; he ate with a kind of shoveling motion, bread in one hand, fork in the other, scooping at his food with both hands. He slumped over his plate, both arms on the table, head down, shoulders hunched as if he were protecting his meat from circling vultures. I looked down the table at the line of glowing faces. I saw mouths working rapidly, chins and jaws pumping in the candlelight, foreheads shining.

"Oh God, this is fantastic."

"Delicious."

". . . gamey . . ."

"Kind of tough, isn't it?"

"Yeah, Mr. Lee must have slipped a pair of Colonel Brody's boots into this mess."

"Best thing I've tasted in weeks!"

Bobby Green, next to me, picked up a piece of charred meat with his fork, stared at it, and then launched into one of his monologues:

"Reminds me of the day at home when we cooked and ate the family cat. Damn animal tasted like its own damn litter box. Mother was the only one who ate it. She *loved* it! Couldn't get enough. After she'd devoured her portion, mine, and my brother Freddie's, she sent Father out for more cats. But all he came up with was the neighbor's dog, a nine-year-old mutt, a mangy bitch, but we cooked her anyway and fed her to Mother and she said it was the tastiest morsel she'd eaten since her grandfather's house burned down and she ate the entire the second-story landing. 'Now *that* was a meal!' she said." Bobby disdainfully tossed the chunk of venison on his fork over his shoulder. Somebody behind him gave a yelp, but Bobby ignored it and continued eating.

I sat there and stared at the meat in front of me: strips of

charred flesh on a white plate. ("Cut it in two, Art, cut it in two!")
I felt sad and a little nauseous. What were we celebrating?
Granted, starving people had been known to eat their relatives,
but I wasn't starving, and I'd been seeing deer along the fence for
months. I felt something for them.

The vegetables came around and I helped myself. They filled
the plate and made the venison a little less conspicuous. I nibbled
at my peas and potatoes and tried to make a decision. The men
around me were eating hungrily and talking.

This is ludicrous, I thought.

I cut a small piece of venison, put it in my mouth, and
chewed. It was tough but very tasty. Had kind of a deep, sharp fla-
vor, almost nutty. I took another bite. The marinade and charcoal
flavors were rich and strong. I cut off another piece and chewed
rapidly.

Goddamn, I thought, this is all right.

"How d'you like it, Art?" Jack shouted.

"It's terrific!"

"Don't talk with your mouth full," Green said. "'S not po-
lite."

March 29
Finally an answer from Dad:

Dear Art:

*There is a tone of toughness and bitterness in your recent
letter that I didn't realize you felt but that in your present
circumstances I am sure is justifiable. You want the whole
story of my draft-exempt status during WW II and I think
you are entitled to it. But it is a long story and I want you to
know not just bits and pieces but everything. Some of these
facts and circumstances you know already but I doubt that
you've put them together the way I'm about to arrange them
for you. I trust things will look different to you once you see
them in the following context.*

*Neither Mom's family nor my family had the affluence
you've known as you grew up. I know that many a winter
Grandmum didn't have a coat warm enough to get around
in and still she had to get to and from work. Her older
brother had to quit school early to help earn money for the
rest of the family to live on. My father, who of course you
never knew, arrived in this country from Portsmouth as an
immigrant and for many years had a struggle that we as*

*children realized as we grew up. But through hard work and
sincere effort he became successful in his field, and he
passed up many who earlier had ridiculed his devotion to
his work. He worked for everything he got and used it to provide for his family. I chose to follow his creed. During the depression and even before that in high school, college and
early training I worked summers, Christmas vacations and
during school at various and sundry jobs—bus boy, waiter,
house manager at the fraternity, stock boy at a music store,
"bouncer" at Harvey's downtown, drug store clerk, runner
and messenger boy, cutting the neighbors' lawns, etc. What
money I didn't absolutely need for my education went to the
family. We men were providers and we were proud of our
ability to earn a decent wage. We knew that education was
the only sure way to improve our wages, which is why your
mother and I have always stressed education with you and
paid for it without complaint. We have reached a state of affluence that I never dreamed possible when I was in school.
I hope we have used it wisely to raise you in respectable and
culturally favorable surroundings and to provide you with
the advantages of a good education.*

*Almost 30 years ago, however, in 1940 and '41, our en-
tering the war seemed inevitable. Your Uncle Pete, your
mother's brother, who was quite young when the war
started, was drafted almost immediately (he was unmarried
and not in school) and was killed in the Pacific early in the
war. So by 1942 I had two sisters, my mother, and my
mother-in-law (your Grandmother Corey) to support. My father had died in 1935, and Pop Corey passed away in 1938. I
was sole support for two generations of Coreys and
Richardsons; the only exception was your Aunt Eliza, whose
husband was in the Navy and on whose salary they had to
support the three children (your cousins) and themselves.*

*At the time I was advancing at The Travelers and making
a very decent salary for a youngish (I was 26) executive. On
the money I'd have made in the service, I don't know how
those people dependent on me would have gotten on. Any alternative seemed to me better than deserting them. Since
then—given the perspective of time—I've realized that of
course they wouldn't have starved—that the worst that
might have happened is that they might have had to find
jobs, perhaps even had to ask the neighbors for occasional
help. But at the time it seemed unthinkable to me to desert*

204

them and leave them to fend for themselves if I could find a way to avoid military service. It was a clear-cut dilemma, you see: my duty seemed to lie not with my country, but with my family.

I set about trying to honorably avoid the inevitable call of the draft board. Being the sole supporting member of the family was not a deferment. And I was in good physical health. But deferments could be had, I knew, if one were involved in work vital to the war effort. It took some foresight, planning, and politicking, but I got transferred into a section at The Travelers where preliminary work was being done on GI Life Insurance. It was a concept just being developed at the time, and I pioneered some of the original statistics. It was our office that came up with the standard $10,000 life insurance policy for all U.S. Servicemen. It wasn't hard to get my boss to write the appropriate letter to my draft board, and his letter did the trick.

I think there are probably some widows around the United States today who would agree with my old boss that my work was vital to the interests of the nation.

For all the pain I'm sure it's caused you, your mother and I are extremely proud of your service record. You are suffering so that others may not; you are giving of yourself, sacrificing so that others may live in an atmosphere more secure and free from fear than otherwise would be possible. Your mother and I pray every day that you are not called upon to make the ultimate sacrifice. Art, I am speaking to you not as my boy, but as a son with whom I can talk on an equal level. Please understand it that way and keep your back straight and your chin up. We have great pride in you—you've earned it in our eyes.

May God bless you—

Dad

March 30
Dreams last night, nightmares. Dad armed with a PPS. Suzy missing, unable to find her. Empty dormitory rooms.

I've been here a long time.

Age is not a matter of how the skin is arranged on your face, it is how you feel when you wake up in the morning. Do you look forward to the coming day? Did your dreams disturb you?

You go through life and accumulate the past, take it with

you from place to place like old books and clothing and junk you store in the basement and forget about until one day you trip over it as you stumble around in the dark.

And not just your own past but your whole family history. Like a police record, you can't get rid of.

Dear Dad:

I got your letter. It's good to know finally why you never served in WW II. I don't blame you; it seems to me that you made the right choice, and the smart one.

But I sure don't know what I'm doing in Korea. I thought I was patriotic, but I don't know what I'd be dying for here if I did die. I could see defending Hartford, but what in the world is the point of my fighting here? So some S. Korean can build a factory and make and sell enough cheap boats so he can buy a Cadillac? Kim Il Sung never shat on me. I'm being used! By you, by Nixon, by the rich in the U.S. and S. Korea. And I hate it Dad—I hate it.

But I'm doing my fucking duty just the same.

Love to you and Mom—

Art

Colonel Brody came down with pneumonia, but March finally turned to April and the weather got warmer, the sun shone, and Brody got better. After a week in bed he was all right.

In early April enemy activity increased, yet nobody got through our sector. Nobody'd gotten through since Harris was relieved in January. The Colonel was frantic for a body, though. He was having real difficulty tolerating all the reported noises, all the shooting, and all the sightings—without a body. He became louder and more abusive during the morning briefings.

One morning in the briefing he announced that he wanted a tunnel dug. It would be near the left flank, over toward the road to Panmunjom. That was a very active sector of A Company, where a couple of our guys had been shot at. The terrain along the fence there was hilly, and the Colonel wanted the tunnel dug through a low hill that was hard clay, where the land wasn't so steep and rocky. The tunnel was to run under the fence and surface beyond the minefield. His idea was to send out a couple men every night and have them set up close to the fence where a team of infiltrators would not expect them.

Brody assigned the QRF, Linderman's mechanized platoon,

to dig the tunnel. You could hear Mortars and Commo and Recon all breathe a sigh of relief when he announced that assignment during the briefing.

Linderman came up to me after the meeting and asked me to tell him more. "Why does he want to dig a tunnel under his own fence?"

"Well, he's crazy," I told him. "Start with that." We were standing outside the TOC and nobody was within earshot. "It gives him something to tell the brigade commander. Also, he just seems to want a tunnel. He figures the north's got 'em, and he can't find theirs. So he wants one of his own."

That was another of the changes that had occurred when Brody took over the battalion from Curtis: he became a believer in the existence of North Korean tunnels. He had told the patrols to keep alert for anything resembling a tunnel entrance.

"Yeah, and we've got to dig the damn thing," Dave said, shaking his head. "Some Quick Reaction Force. Quick with a shovel. The men'll be exhausted. What a waste, making this platoon dig ditches. After the way we've trained."

"You've been training?"

"Yeah. At Matta. They don't just sleep when they're back here, you know."

"Say something to Brody. It won't do you any good to say it to me. Or are you rehearsing?"

"Naw, fuck it." Linderman removed his helmet and wiped his forehead with his sleeve. The band in his helmet left a stripe around his head. "I can't say those things to Brody. But I had to say it to somebody. Anyhow, I've been thinking of volunteering for patrols in the DMZ. This sitting around sucks, and digging'll be worse yet. Sergeant Small can supervise the digging. And if I get a patrol and he wants to come with us—well, that's fine too."

I knew Linderman's platoon sergeant. He was a good man. "Sergeant Small might not appreciate staying south of the fence if you're out on patrol."

"Well, we'll see. He likes having the platoon to himself. But I've had enough sitting around and supervising shit details. Dig a tunnel? Man oh man."

April 6
An explosion today from somewhere between Matta and the fence. In a minefield. The Korean family that clears

minefields lost a member, a whole member, not just a leg or an arm but a complete person. It was the woman who got it, the wife/mother. The kids—two of them, both pretty small—were standing there shocked, holding hands, not crying, staring at her body all legless and white.

Peters and I drove by on the way to the fence, saw the aid vehicle, stopped, walked over, looked at the charred depression in the ground, nothing we could do but feel the depression. Scrape her up for scrap. Late for the fence-walk so we hurried off. Nothing to be done. Kids staring at their mother. Why didn't anybody cover her up? Should have covered up the body. Take cover. Now they'll have to cover for her. Where was her husband? Probably talking to Americans. Or off vomiting in the grass. If you're not careful, you'll get it too—though they were well out of the minefield itself. She must have been defusing one; still, it was her legs that got blown off. Maybe these minefields aren't well marked after all. Grave situation. Build her a mound. He won't mound her any longer. But she won't mound. Mounds are the negative image of graves. Reverse depressions. Jubilations. A tunnel is a long, slim grave. God, those kids, hands linked, staring. The littlest one put her other hand in her mouth.

April 7, 1969

For the record: the DMZ.

There are no trees here, and no leaves, because all the trees were blown away during the Korean War. In the minefields the rain clings to grass stalks like beads of sweat. Rivulets of water etch gullies in the hills and the mines wash up out of the soil and lie at crooked angles among the rocks. Some of them look like toy tops, others like tin cans. Soldiers on patrol skirt the minefields, look past the rusty barbed wire and wonder whether that treacherous ground isn't a sanctuary for North Koreans. The rain drips from their helmets, slides down their cheeks; on their lips it tastes of salt.

NINETEEN

IT STARTED THAT NIGHT WITH
sporadic shooting up and down the fence. I was at the Forward CP
with Colonel Brody and Norm Stewart. Jack had the night off.
There was activity all along the fence: a couple of shots here, a
burst of automatic fire there, the *whoosh* and *pop* of hand-held
flares both east and west. Now and then an explosion would rip
the seams out of the atmosphere. Weather conditions had created
a night that was ripe for an infiltration attempt: the air was
warm, the sky overcast and black.

Furthermore, one man or two—nobody knew for sure how
many—had infiltrated through the battalion on our left flank just
three days before, so everybody was worked up, nervous. We
knew someone was crawling around in the rear, south of the
fence, trying to get back north.

The Colonel was furious. He thought no shooting was justified unless it produced a body for him. He got all of the company
commanders on the land line at the same time and screamed: "If
you can't control those Goddamn men, I'll relieve your Goddamn
ass *tonight!*"

But the men were seeing things. Not just hearing them. That

was the message the company commanders sent back to Colonel Brody: We can't "control" our men because they're not just jumpy —they really are seeing things.

"Bullshit! I don't want them shooting at noises and shadows! You tell 'em to wait for a *target!* Wait till the gooks get up on the fence and start cutting! *Then* do their ass in!"

Out. End of message. Don't bother me with reality.

We sat around for a while, waiting, and activity below us along the fence quieted down. The flame pots burned dimly; flashlights twinkled every ten or fifteen minutes during fence checks; and radio traffic on the battalion net took on a routine quality. The night began to get boring.

And then an incident erupted in B Company, four or six hundred meters east of us. We heard everything. First there were two shots, then three or four more. Then a burst of automatic weapons fire, very rapid. Then more shooting, automatic and semi. Tracer bullets arced up and away from us, on line with the flame pots.

We had all jumped up at the first shots, and we stood along the east rail of the CP and watched the tracers cut the blackness. Some bullets appeared to be flying right up the line, parallel to the fence and just behind it.

"What the hell are they shooting at?" Captain Stewart said. "They'll hit somebody in Charlie Company."

"God*damn* it!" Colonel Brody muttered. He reached for the phone.

We saw a flash and heard a huge explosion, a grenade: P-E-L-T! Then another grenade, P-E-L-T! And finally a third, this time slightly muffled: W-H-U-M-P-H!

Colonel Brody slammed down the phone and took two long strides to the radio. He shouted into the handset until he got hold of Curt Davis, the B Company commander. "This is three-four. Now what the Christ was that? What's going on? I told you to control those men!"

When Davis's voice came on the radio, he was shouting over the noise of his jeep engine: "Three-four, this is six-two. I'm on my way to check it out. I'll report as soon as I know. Over."

"This is three-four. Make it fast! Out!"

We waited. The Colonel fumed and steamed like an old radiator turned full on. He sat down and got up and clomped back and forth along the length of the wood floor. We waited five, ten, fifteen minutes. Nothing stirred on the fence. It was past midnight, approaching one o'clock. Not a word over the radio.

Colonel Brody spoke. "Richardson, get Davis, see what the hell's keeping him."

I went over to the radio. It was at the front of the CP, and below me I could see the string of yellow flame pots rising, falling, curving with the fence in both directions.

"Six-two, this is five-one, over."

A pause. Then the uncertain voice of Davis's driver: "Five-one, this is six-two bravo. Six-two isn't here right now. Over."

I turned to Colonel Brody. "What do you want me to tell him, sir?"

"Tell him to get Davis to the radio *right now.*"

"Six-two bravo, this is five-one. Three-four wants six-two to report to him immediately. I say again, have six-two report to three-four immediately. Over."

"This is six-two bravo. Roger. Out."

Another ten minutes slugged by, and then the radio started up again: "Three-four, this is six-two, over."

Colonel Brody sat still. He didn't move a muscle.

"Three-four, this is six-two, over."

Colonel Brody sat in his corner and spoke in a low voice: "Well go ahead, Richardson, answer the goddamn thing."

The guy was nuts. I walked over to the radio. "Six-two, this is five-one. Go ahead, over."

"Five-one, six-two. What is three-four's location, over."

"This is five-one. We're at the Foxtrot Charlie Papa, over."

"Five-one, six-two. Roger, I'm on my way up to talk to three-four. We've had a positive sighting of a UI, over."

I turned to Brody. A "UI" was an unidentified individual, a North Korean.

"Tell him to move his Goddamn ass," Brody said.

"Six-two, this is five-one. Roger, we'll see you soon. Out."

Colonel Brody stirred in his chair like a bull in the chute. "Give him the message, Richardson. What's the matter with you, you deaf?"

I picked up the radio handset again, pressed the push-to-talk switch. "Six-two, this is five-one, over."

Davis came up on the radio again, shouting over the noise of his jeep: "Six-two, go ahead five-one, over."

I spoke slowly, distinctly: "Six-two, this is five-one. I have a message from three-four. He says move your Goddamn ass. Out."

There was a pause. I imagined the guys in the TOC, back at Camp Matta, gathered around their radios, cracking up.

I went back over to my chair and sat down. Colonel Brody fumed in the corner—I could almost feel the heat of his anger, radiating like a stove. He said: "Put the QRF on alert too, Richardson."

I called the TOC on the field phone. Crazy Mann was on, and I told him to alert the forward two squads of the Quick Reaction Force.

Crazy said, "Should I tell 'em to move their Goddamn ass, Lieutenant?"

"Just put them on alert, Crazy," I said, and hung up.

After a short while we heard Davis's jeep straining up the hill, and soon he strode into the CP, excited and slightly out of breath.

"Sir—? I can't see a thing. Colonel Brody?"

"Over here, Davis."

"I think they saw somebody, Colonel. I just talked to Sergeant Toomey and Sergeant Love, and they said the guy returned fire and everything. They think they might have hit him."

"Bullshit," said Colonel Brody. "Where's the body? They're exaggerating."

But I thought Brody was wrong this time. I knew Toomey and Love well. They were reliable.

"No sir," Davis said, "I think somebody's back there. I think we ought to go in after them."

Captain Stewart spoke. "Where'd this happen, Davis?"

"Right behind 146 and 147, sir. There's a gully back there, a little ravine. The ground rises toward the fence. Sergeant Love always puts six or eight trip flares down in that gully. Somebody tripped one. Love and Toomey both claim they saw him. They shot at him and he fired back. They said he threw grenades."

"Sounds like they're working their way back north," said Captain Stewart. "Perhaps we could send the QRF in, Colonel."

"Bullshit. They're shooting at shadows, or a deer, maybe. They're going to kill our own people back there."

"Sir," I said, "Toomey and Love are good men. They can be trusted."

"Perhaps *you'd* like to lead the QRF in there, Richardson."

"Sir?"

"Well *think*, Goddamn it. My QRF platoon leader is somewhere in the middle of the DMZ, said he wanted to lead a patrol. Isn't that right, Captain Stewart?"

"That's right, sir. He's got the Charlie Company patrol tonight."

"But I've got to send an officer in with the QRF. Don't I, Richardson?"

"Yes sir. I'll take it in. Let me do it."

"Just wait a Goddamn minute. Davis, you're sure those NCOs saw someone? I don't want to commit my QRF on a false alarm. It's the only reserve I've got."

Curt was leaning against the wall of the CP. The thing was out of his hands, and he looked relaxed. "I believe they saw someone," he said.

"If we send in just two squads," Captain Stewart said, "we can move the other two forward from Matta."

"That's what I'll do, Captain Stewart. Richardson, you'll take the forward two squads in. Right now. Get moving."

"Norm," I said, "may I have a look at your map?"

"Here." Captain Stewart spread out his map. He and Curt and I quickly coordinated the operation. Then Captain Stewart phoned Sergeant Small at the forward QRF position and gave him the coordinates of an assembly point on the road behind 146 and 147. A few seconds later we heard the diesel whine of the armored personnel carriers starting up below and behind us.

"Give him the xenon searchlight, too," Colonel Brody said to Norm Stewart. "You want that searchlight, don't you, Richardson?"

"Yes sir."

Captain Stewart radioed the light jeep and sent it off to the same place as the tracks.

"Now get your ass in gear," said Colonel Brody, and I walked out of the CP and down the hill toward my jeep.

Curt Davis caught up with me.

"Colonel Brody's a loud-mouthed bastard, isn't he?" he said.

"He sure yells a lot."

"I don't let it bother me," Curt said. "I think of Brody like the weather. When it rains or snows, you carry on, right? I let him

scream all he wants. Then I do it the way I'd have done it anyhow."

We were almost down to the jeeps. "They really saw somebody, didn't they?" I said.

Curt stopped and looked at me. "They did. No doubt about
it."

"I thought so." I turned away downhill. "See you."

"Good hunting," Curt said.

I found Peters in the dark and we took off immediately. On
the way down to the assembly point I breathed deeply and tried to
stay clear-headed. Get the searchlight in position. Coordinate
with Toomey and Love on the fence, find out what they saw and
exactly where. And then deal with Sergeant Small and his platoon. I somehow had to get the QRF to do exactly what I wanted
it to do. That was the problem: control. I didn't know those men,
they didn't know me—together we could screw up this simple
sweep without any effort at all, get somebody killed. The trick
would be to have everybody doing the same thing at the same
time, like a school of fish.

Silence would be unnecessary; we weren't about to *sneak up*
on one or two men, twenty of us. We could make all the noise we
wanted. That would make everything much easier.

But leading a unit I hadn't trained with, and at night . . . .

Against a real enemy.

I tried not to think of that, tried not to imagine what could
happen, how men might be killed. Tried instead to focus on what
I was going to do. The QRF, the xenon light, the men along the
fence—I had to coordinate everything, keep the men from shooting each other, set it up quick and get it done before whoever was
out there had a chance to bolt.

The jeep reached the bottom of the hill and Peters turned east
toward B Company's right flank. We crossed an intersection and
ran into dust that hung in the moist night air like fog. The APCs
were already somewhere up ahead of us.

When we reached the assembly area, the two tracks were
standing motionless on the side of the road, their diesels idling.
They were huge hulking things, big rectangles of blackness loom-
ing in the dark. I told Peters to pull over behind them and wait for
me there. "Stay awake and listen for your call sign on the radio.
Don't go to sleep."

"Yes sir. Will do."

The men had dismounted and spread out along the shoulder of the road. They waited quietly, kneeling or sitting, facing in toward the area we'd be sweeping, an interval of four or five meters between each man. Perfect.

"Sergeant Small!"

"Yes sir." A thin figure approached me from around behind one of the APCs.

"I'm Lieutenant Richardson. Remember me?"

"Yes I do, sir."

He was taller than I, and black, and as I looked up into his face I couldn't make out the expression on it.

"I'll be taking you in tonight. Understood?"

"Yes sir. You're gonna be acting platoon leader."

"That's right. There may be one, possibly two UIs in this area. We're going to go in and make a sweep, but first I want to go up to the fence and coordinate with the men up there. So they don't shoot us. Leave a man in charge here and come with me. And get rid of those tracks. Send them back to your forward area, okay?"

"Yes sir."

I walked over to my jeep and got ahold of Captain Stewart on the radio. I told him the light jeep hadn't showed up and asked him to locate it and get it over here to the assembly area. "That's a roge," he said. "Out here."

The tracks whined past my jeep and clattered off down the road. Sergeant Small returned and we started up the hill toward the fence. As we walked, the sound of the armored personnel carriers grew distant and the night became quiet.

I knew the terrain behind 146 and 147. The fence was on high ground along there; it ran across a long, low hilltop, and the ground sloped back downward gently, away from the fence toward the road. The road made a loop around the bottom of the hill, curving out three or four hundred meters away from the fence, then hooking back toward it. On the map, the curve of the road looked like the profile of a woman's breast. The hillside within that curve was not too big to be searched by two squads, even though the grass and brush averaged a foot or two in height and provided plenty of cover for a man.

Out past the road, to the south, there was nothing but wilder-

215

ness for a few klicks, and then the Imjin River. Once they crossed the road, they were long gone. I was hoping they'd already crossed the road. I could have put the APCs down there at the nipple of the curve to block them, but later on I didn't want those .50s opening up on us.

Sergeant Small and I climbed the hill without talking, our feet making a sweeeping sound in the tall grass, but now we were approaching the fence. I started hollering: "Sergeant Toomey! Sergeant Love!"

"Yeah!"

"Over here."

"We're coming up!"

"Come on ahead!"

"It's me, Richardson. Two of us."

"Come on up, sir."

They were excited. They had seen somebody. "Shit, sir," Sergeant Love said, "that motherfucker shot at us. Threw grenades, too."

"Okay. Tell me this. How many of them are there?"

"One."

Sergeant Toomey said: "Might be two of 'em. They had a lot of fire power, threw a lot of grenades."

"Yeah," said Love, "but we hit that son of a bitch, I know it. I heard him grunt."

There was a pause. I said, "Do you men know Sergeant Small here? Sergeant Small's platoon sergeant with the QRF."

"No, I don't believe we've met."

"Sergeant."

"Pleased to meet you." They shook hands.

"Okay," I said. "Sergeant Small and I are going to take two squads in behind you. We're going to walk up behind your positions in file, come up parallel to the fence, and then do a right face and sweep south, away from you. Tell your people we're coming up in back of them. Keep them facing forward, toward the fence, north. Don't have them shooting at us. We're starting soon, five or ten minutes. Is that clear?"

"That's clear, sir."

"Okay, Lieutenant."

"Right. Hurry up and get the word out. We'll be coming up in five minutes."

"Sir?" It was Sergeant Love.

"What is it?"

"Oh, nevermind."

"Go ahead."

"Well, listen here, Lieutenant. That son of a bitch was on full automatic, an' throwin hand grenades. . . . Me an' Sergeant Tom, we're lucky to be alive. But we hit him. I know it. And he's still out there. He's out there sure as shit, an' he's gonna be one angry son of a bitch."

April 10
dreams last night—I committed suicide—drank something—KILLED MYSELF—never wake up—another dream—a ship sank under me—Pueblo? My father sent me off to war—the one thing I did he was proud of—OCS graduation—so proud of me—sent me off to die—he never joined up, cried when I left for Korea.

I saw a lot of mothers out demonstrating against the war in Vietnam, before I left for Korea—and a lot of vets and young men and girls—but I didn't see any fathers out there. Fathers don't want the war to end. They let it go on. Good for business.

And less competition: fewer men going after the goodies back home.

The best thing you can do for your country while you're young is die for it. That's the only way you can gain respect. It's the dead who are most highly honered. The living are forgotten.

On the way back down I explained the thing again to Sergeant Small. I'd be at the front of the file, he'd be at the rear. "When we turn south for our sweep," I told him, "the trick's going to be keeping everybody on line. Four or five meters between each man. Keep them spread out and on line. Move slow. Got it?"

"Yes sir."

We walked downhill in the darkness through the tall grass. I had my .45 in my hand. Sergeant Small was carrying his rifle at port arms.

All at once he said something, but I couldn't hear him.

"What?" I asked him.

"I said I don't like it. I don't like it one bit. There's no telllin where this guy is, no tellin where he's gone to. He could be sittin

217

there waitin for us to come in after 'im. He could be listenin to me right now. Can't see jack shit out here. You could be troddin on his hand, you'd never know. If he's hurt bad, he won't be expectin to see daylight. No sir. He'll have one thing on his mind. One thing."

"Yeah."

"That's right. Takin one or two of us with him. An' you know who he's gonna be lookin for too, don't you, Lieutenant?"

Of course I knew.

Down at the assembly area, Sergeant Small got his squads together while I positioned the light jeep. I could hear him talking to his men: "Lock and load a round, but do *not* take those safeties off. Leave those safeties *on!*" I heard the clicking of bolts and safeties, and then the searchlight operator started his generator and I could hear nothing else. I went over to my jeep. Roughly fifteen minutes had passed since we'd arrived at the assembly area. I called Colonel Brody.

"We're all set. We're starting in," I told him.

"This is three-four. Get moving. Out."

I checked once more with Sergeant Small. "Have you got a medic?"

"Yes sir."

"Keep him with you. I'll take your RTO. Where is he?"

Someone at my elbow spoke. "Here, sir."

"You on the battalion net?"

"Yes sir."

"Okay. Let's move out."

We started up the hill, a long file of us, point man first, then me, the RTO, and the rest of the squads, Sergeant Small somewhere near the rear.

The hill wasn't too steep, but it was late and I'd just climbed it, and I'd walked the fence twice that day, and I was tired. Drained. Yet I was alert in a nervous, strung-out sort of way. I directed the man in front of me now and then, told him to go left or go right, and I watched the grass to either side. As we moved up and away from the light jeep, the roar of its generator faded behind us. We could hear crickets and peepers. We could see plenty, too. Not great, but okay. The blue-white xenon light turned the place into a ghost landscape. The eerie blue light streamed overhead, catching the moist night air and turning it silver-blue. But the ground itself was mostly shadows. Black and silver. The terrain looked as spooky as it felt. I was shaking with exhaustion and excitement, and my teeth were chattering, but I don't think it showed. My voice sounded calm.

"A little to your left. Go slow."

The point man silently changed direction, heading more toward the fence. I wanted to get in close behind the foxholes before we turned to sweep the area.

The hill was leveling off. I could see flame pots now.

"Okay, straighten out. Parallel to the fence. Slow it down."

We walked a few more steps. Then, behind me, somebody said:

"Hey sir, what about him?"

I turned, looked. I saw only the men behind me.

"Who?"

"Him." It was the RTO, right behind me, who had spoken. He was looking toward the fence. He had stopped, and the whole column behind him stopped too.

"Who?"

"Him!" he said urgently. Then he pointed. I looked again. All I saw was grass, silver-blue and black. There was nothing else there, no movement, nothing. . . .

"Where?"

He was still pointing. "Right there, sir. There's somebody there."

I followed the line of his arm and finger. And then everything wheeled and froze, like the changing of a slide on a projection screen, and I saw it, stretched out among the weeds not ten meters away, barely distinguishable from the dark vegetation, a man. I pointed my pistol at him. He didn't move.

I thought: What now? What?

I spoke quietly to the RTO: "Go down the line. Tell everyone to hold his position, set up security."

"Yes sir."

"Tell Sergeant Small I want him to stay put till I call for him. Then get back here. Go on, move out."

He moved off down the column. I gestured to the point man to cover the area in front of us and to the south. Then I moved back to the next man in line. He was kneeling on one knee and staring at the figure in the grass. He held his rifle balanced on his thigh.

"You see him?" I asked softly.

"Yeah."

"All right. Keep your rifle on him. If he moves, twitches, does anything, *anything*, shoot him three or four times. Got it?"

"Got it."

I holstered my pistol. I was thinking, *He's faking. His buddy booby-trapped his body. The other one's going to open up on us any second.*

I knelt in the grass and thought for a moment. A rope. No. A rifle sling. No. A belt. I unbuckled my belt, pulled it out of my pants. I ran the end through the buckle and pulled the loop tight around my hand. Then I lay down on my stomach and began to crawl toward the . . . ? I didn't know what it was—body, man, weapon, corpse. I crawled slowly. It got bigger. I could see a couple of legs stretched out toward me. I kept crawling.

Then I suddenly stopped. The weirdest feeling came over me —a terrifying feeling of separation. I was cut off from the QRF, crawling toward something completely unknown and dangerous. I'd never felt so alone. I looked back over my shoulder and there above me was that soldier, silhouetted against the electric blue haze of the xenon light, in a perfect kneeling position, his rifle level and aimed over my head. He was holding that weapon perfectly steady—it looked like part of him, man and rifle inseparable, chiseled from a single rock. A warm feeling flowed through me. Whoever that GI was, I could have hugged him.

I turned and resumed crawling. The thing ahead of me was face down, heels in the air. I approached a boot. I reached out and nudged the sole with my fingertips. Then I grabbed the heel of the boot and shook it. I expected the thing to move, but nothing happened. Pressing my face into the dirt, I took hold of the ankle tightly and yanked on it. Still nothing. I took the belt off my hand and slipped the loop around the toe of the boot and up the ankle. Tightened the loop. I crawled backwards, out to the end of the belt. Then I tugged. I held the belt with my right hand and pulled away backwards with my left, dug my elbow, knees and feet into the earth and heaved. I could barely budge it. I was expecting an explosion any second. Christ, it was heavy. I yanked and pulled and it moved grudgingly. I expected it to explode, its buddy having planted a live grenade under it so that when somebody rolled it over. . . . So I dragged that huge dead weight backwards, off the grenade I hoped, and I kept my head down, face buried in the moist dirt, helmet toward it so I wouldn't catch shrapnel. I dragged him eight inches, a foot, a couple of meters. Five meters. Nothing. Ten meters. We were safe.

Was he dead? Or merely wounded and unconscious?

I stood up. "Send the medic up here." My voice broke a long silence. "Medic!" I shouted. The GI with the rifle let out a long sigh. He lowered his weapon. "Keep your eye on him," I said.

Behind me, the point man asked: "Who is it, sir?"

"A North Korean."

"No shit?"

The medic came jogging up the hill, puffing hard. He was thin, gangly. He carried a pouch of some kind, but no weapon. "What is it?"

"Over there. Check him out, will you? See if he's alive."

The medic was an older man. His gaunt face looked deeply wrinkled in the indirect blue light. He strode up to the North Korean and rolled him over. One of the North Korean's arms ended just below the elbow. The shredded limb seemed to blend into the man's torso, which looked chewed, as though by dogs. The medic said something that I couldn't hear.

"What'd you say?"

"Did himself in. Pulled the pin and put the grenade to his chest."

"He's dead?"

The old medic snorted. He pointed down. "That's his heart right there, hanging out of his chest."

In the tangled mess of his chest I could see nothing that looked like what I imagined a heart would look like. But I wasn't going to admit it.

"See there, Lieutenant?" He prodded a thigh with the toe of his boot. "Wounded. Shot in the leg. Killed himself to avoid capture."

I saw something in his mangled chest that looked curious. I reached down and tugged at it. It was slippery and long, like a noodle.

"What's this?"

"Artery."

"Oh." I wiped my hand on my trousers. "Okay, Doc. Stay here with him. I'm going to sweep this area. RTO!"

"Right here, sir."

"Let me see that radio."

"Here ya go, sir." He handed me the handset.

I put it up to my ear and pressed the push-to-talk switch, but then I paused. We'd been chasing a UI all night, an "Unidentified Individual." Now he'd been identified. The Colonel had a body at last. How could I say that on the radio?

"Three-four, this is five-one, over."

Captain Stewart answered. "Five-one, this is two-niner, go ahead, over."

"Two-niner, this is five-one. I've got a Delta India here. We found a *Delta India*. Over."

There was a pause. "Five-one, this is two-niner. Do not understand your last transmission. Say again, over."

"Two-niner, this is five-one." How to put it? I wasn't carrying my code book; Peters had it. "I say again, we found a Delta India. Not a Uniform India, a *Delta* India. Over."

Another pause. Then Colonel Brody: "This is three-four. Five-one, what the hell are you talking about? Over."

I knew the whole battalion was monitoring this conversation, had been following the operation since Curt first reported a sighting. The men in the command bunkers on the guard posts; Crazy and Specks and whoever else happened to be in the TOC; the soldiers in the Company CPs: they were all tuned to the battalion net. The North Koreans were probably listening too.

"Three-four, this is five-one. We've got a *dead individual* here, a DI, a Delta India. A body. One of theirs. Over."

When the Colonel next hit his push-to-talk switch, I could hear cheering. "Five-one, this is three-four. Good work. Have you finished your sweep, over."

"Three-four, five-one. Negative, over."

"Five-one, this is three-four. Roger that. Go ahead and complete your sweep. Let me know when you're done. Over."

"Three-four, this is five-one. Roger. Over."

"This is three-four. Out."

TWENTY

Aprıl 12th, 1969

For the record:

The DMZ is a mirror. Our enemies are reflections of ourselves. North Koreans merely do what we do. We call it aggression, but it is imitation. We kill them, they kill us. Two mirrors facing each other, reflecting images infinitely, a chain of hostility and outrage with no apparent end.

The score is six of us to one of them. We're more dangerous to ourselves than we are to the North Koreans.

We don't just resemble the enemy, we've surpassed him. The worst has happened: we've grown more loathsome than the thing we loathe.

But I don't suppose anything unusual has happened. We've changed, adapted. Anybody is capable of anything.

I had a fleeting thought about my bunk back at Camp Matta, a wish: ordinarily I'd be there by now. We were going to have to go into the tall grass and flush the other one. This one had been mean enough to kill himself. What would the other one do?

I sent for Sergeant Small and we talked briefly. He went back to alert the men that we were moving out. I went over to the medic. "Doc, stay right here. If you hear shooting, you join us quick."

"I'll come with you, sir. This one ain't goin nowhere, not with his chest open thataway and his heart hangin out."

"No, stay here. I want to be able to find him. And I want you in one piece, too."

"If you say so, Lieutenant."

I walked back to the column. I could see down the hill a short ways, could see four or five soldiers poised to move, their rifles and grenade launchers ready. I was looking downward against the light, and the men were outlined against it. Black, humanoid shapes against that blue-white electric haze, illumination like a lightning bolt nobody turned off. The black shapes looked strangely uniform, evenly spaced and identical. Sentries in a nightmare.

"Let's move out," I said to the point man. We resumed walking in file, crossed the crest of the hill, and started down the other side. After a few steps I noticed that my pants were falling down. I'd left my belt back there, fastened to the ankle of the North Korean. Holding my pistol in my right hand, I had to walk along holding up my trousers with my left.

Because of the searchlight we could see fairly well on the reverse slope of the hill. When I could make out the road, I stopped the column. "Okay, we'll start our sweep," I said to the point man. "Turn right and walk slow." I passed the word back down the column. "Turn right and walk slow. Stay five meters apart. Stay on line."

They passed the word down. I heard a few safeties click off. We moved forward into the tall grass.

We could barely see. We moved slowly, but it felt like running.

Every so often I shouted: "Spread out! Catch up, stay on line!"

But mostly I stared ahead and tried to look everywhere at once and waited to be shot. I had one hand for my pistol and one hand for my trousers. Sweat rolled down my face and down my back. Even my knees were sweating, the backs of them, cool drops sliding down my calfs. I concentrated. I expected him to pop up in front of us, PPS blazing, grenades flying. . . . I'd never concentrated as hard on anything as I concentrated on looking for a man to shoot.

But then my concentration lapsed, just for a second, and I

imagined what it would be like to be him, the other North Korean: pressing close to the earth, listening to the approach of twenty armed men. To be on the wrong side of the DMZ, to hear the enemy calling to one another, hear the swish of their boots in the grass as they came closer. . . .

I was *feeling sorry* for the bastard I was out to kill.

"Stay on line!" I shouted. "Keep your interval! Five meters! Concentrate! Watch out for this son of a bitch, he could be anywhere!"

We made it to the road uneventfully.

Back at the jeep, Peters handed me my canteen. I unscrewed the top and drank. The water tasted stale, but I drank the whole quart.

Colonel Brody and Norm Stewart and Curt Davis soon joined us at the light jeep. Sergeant Small and I walked them up to the body. Someone had a camera—Norm, I think—a small plastic Kodak with a flash. The Colonel posed everyone with the body, kneeling behind it, himself included, with his rifle. The whole safari bit. I stood back by the guy with the camera, but Colonel Brody motioned to me.

"I don't want to be in the picture," I told him.

"You found the fucker, didn't you?" he growled. "Get your ass over here."

"No sir, I'd really rather stay out of the picture if you don't mind."

"Get over here, Richardson. Now."

I went. A GI took the picture. The flash blinded me for a few seconds. The Colonel was in a terrific mood. I was exhausted but remembered to get my belt off the body. Before I went back down to my jeep, Curt pulled me aside. He thanked me for backing up Toomey and Love, and himself, earlier at the CP. And then for finding the body. He shook my hand and told me I did a great job.

April 13

The body of the North Korean infiltrator—what will become of it? Will they lay it out in a public square in Seoul? Take photographs of it? Will President Park Chung Hee himself pose for the gathered press with the body of the dead North Korean infiltrator?

What will the authorities do when it begins to stink? Bury

225

it? Where? Grave or grave mound? Will they provide a marker?

On the hillside, at first light, whose poncho will the body be wrapped in? Will blood soak into the poncho, staining it? Later, will an American supply sergeant scrub the poncho, trying to remove the stains and make it serviceable again? Will he eventually give up and throw the poncho away?

Or will the poncho rip, spilling the stiff body onto the concrete slab by the rear entrance of KCIA headquarters?

Will some soldier in Company B—a PFC—be made accountable for his poncho, despite his contention that it was lost on the field of battle?

What was the dead North Korean's mission? Did he photograph southern installations? Which ones? Camp Matta? Did he photograph me? What kind of camera was he carrying, and where was it purchased? By whom?

Was the North Korean a volunteer? If he had not wanted to take this mission, could he have refused it? What did the North Korean dream of? Killing Americans? A long life, a woman, children?

The North Korean pulled the pin and pressed the hand grenade to his chest. What did he feel just before he died? Just after?

What has become of the fingernails of the hand that held the grenade? Where will the dead North Korean's PPS submachine gun end up? Will it ever again be used as a weapon?

Who will pick up the pieces of lung and intestine and windpipe that soaked into the earth and grass beneath the freshly dead North Korean? Insects? How long will it take the rain to wash the clots of blood from the weeds or beetles and ants to eat them? Or the sun to decompose the flesh and the shreds of shirt front and shirt sleeve?

Would the government of North Korea have harassed, or killed, or 'relocated' members of his family in North Korea if he had not killed himself, but instead had fallen into American, and subsequently South Korean, hands? Why would that government have done so? Will the dead man's family in North Korea be ashamed because their husband, son, and father failed his mission? Or will they feel proud because he took his own life in order to avoid capture, thereby saving themselves untold humiliation and loss of privilege and esteem? Will a monument be erected to the dead man?

Why did the *Pueblo* crew give up so easily? Are Americans

unable to subordinate their individual selves to a larger, collective self? Is that admirable, or pathetic? Is America a weak nation? What is strength? Suicide?

Will the soul of the North Korean infiltrator ascend to heaven?

I got to the village hardly at all in April; I saw Tammy rarely, once or twice a week when I was lucky. The Colonel gave me dozens of jobs, most involving supervision of his projects. He had details spread all over the battalion area: details driving engineer stakes deep into the ground along the fence to prevent the North Koreans from crawling under the chain link; details in the DMZ clearing brush and looking for tunnels; details on the guard posts digging bunkers and trenches and laying barbed wire; and details digging foxholes and building fighting positions behind the fence.

Then of course the QRF was digging a tunnel. Sergeant Small had one squad digging eight to ten hours a day.

The entrance to the tunnel could be seen above the road in A Company's sector. It was a round black hole perched on a pyramid of its own tailings, the tailings spreading below it down the hillside toward the road. The entrance looked like a black disk balanced on the point of a brown triangle.

On the morning of April 18th I drove over to check the QRF's security. Peters stopped the jeep on the road and I got out and started up the hill. The soldiers saw me coming and one of them yelled into the tunnel entrance; a moment later Sergeant Small emerged like a bird from a birdhouse. He brushed himself off, took the rifle somebody handed him, and walked down to meet me.

"Good morning, Lieutenant."

"Sergeant Small."

We exchanged salutes.

"How much time you got, sir?"

"Forty-eight days." I grinned. "It's nice to see you again."

"Thank you, sir."

"How's the digging going?"

"It ain't for shit, if you want to know the truth. The clay is very hard. And there's a lot of rock. It's tough digging."

He was a tall man, and he was a very dark color. His features —nose, lips, and ears—were tiny, almost miniature, but his eyes were large. His fatigues were sweat-stained and dirty. He wore no helmet, and his short black hair, as well as his forehead and cheeks, were smeared with light brown clay. His rifle was slung over his shoulder and he was gripping the sling with a tight fist. His black knuckles were encrusted with clay, and there were scabs and raw gouges on the back of his hand.

"You look like you've been digging it all by yourself," I told him.

"No way, sir." He ran his hand across his forehead and flicked the sweat off it. He chuckled. "Some people get dirty, some don't. Me, I like to get in there and show the men how to do it. Show 'em I ain't afraid to get dirty."

"What have you got for security?"

He told me he had three men on a rise forward of the fence, and he pointed them out. They were a long way off, up a hill beyond the minefield, and I could see only one of them. He'd also placed a man on the other side of the road, away from the fence, who was out of sight behind a rice paddy berm.

I asked Sergeant Small about patrols.

"Yes sir, I got all the patrol information. I got overlays from the S-2. I get that every day, and Lieutenant Linderman and I go over it the night before. Now today, we ain't goin to see any patrols today, sir. Not north of the fence. None comin, none goin. I told the men, anything they see, it ain't ours. So shoot it."

"Good." We looked at one another. I think with mutual respect. We had been through something together.

"So how do you feel about the other night?" I asked him.

"Well, sir," he said. He shifted his rifle from one shoulder to the other, then pulled up his trousers and tucked in his shirt, talking as he did so. "I feel pretty good about it. We got the job done. But it's frustratin to get all keyed up like that an' then not get into it."

"I know."

"Anyhow, that's gone and forgotten. Past."

From behind Sergeant Small, I could hear the men in the tunnel cursing, hear the *chunk* and *thwack* of shovels and pickaxes. Occasionally a bucketful of dirt and rock would spew out of the hole and tumble down the pyramid of tailings.

"I keep going over it," I said.

228

"Going over it?" Sergeant Small squinted at me. "How come?"

"I'm not sure. Probably because I was scared. I was really scared."

He grinned. "That's nothin to be ashamed of, sir. Everybody gets scared." He was looking at me with mild amusement. He suddenly appeared old to me, and I realized that he must be at least ten years older than me, perhaps fifteen or twenty. Sure, he could be 40 or 44 years old.

"No," I said, "I mean I was *really* scared. I've never been that terrified in my life."

Sergeant Small chuckled. "Well then, why'd you do it, sir?"

"What? I couldn't have told Brody I wasn't going to."

"I mean, why'd you volunteer for the job?"

"Leading your squad in, you mean?"

"Lieutenant Linderman told me Lieutenant Davis said you volunteered to take us in."

"Well yeah, I did. Somebody had to take you in. I figured, better me than somebody else."

"But you said you were scared."

"That came later. It was a surprise."

"Well, look here, sir. You functioned. I mean, you didn't *act* scared, you did the job, right?"

"What about you, Sergeant Small? You said you were scared, you told me so. Didn't that bother you?"

His eyes slid away from me again, glided on over toward something I couldn't see. "Shit, Lieutenant," he said, "I been scared all my life. Fear ain't nothin new to me. I'm good friends with it. We're on speakin terms."

"I suppose I'll get used to it too, someday."

"Used to it? Hell, you can do better than that. You can use it."

"Use it?"

He grinned and shifted his weight from one foot to the other. "It's good for you. Sharpens your senses, quickens your reflexes. Don't fight it. Takes energy to fight it, so put it to work. Deep fry it. Let it boil in oil till it hardens into anger. Get mad!"

I had heard that sort of talk before. "People are afraid of their anger," I said. "Afraid to get angry."

"The sheep of the world, sir," he said. "If you can't get angry, you can only get afraid."

April 18
Three days ago they shot down one of our planes. An unarmed recon plane with 31 men on board. Very vulnerable: no armament, no escort. All dead.

Like the *Pueblo*, but worse. Brutal, unexpected. Like they don't like our rules so they're changing them.

Late in April, one of our patrols spotted a good-sized North Korean infiltration team on our side of the MDL, during daylight hours. They engaged it. They fired everything they had—rifles, grenade launchers, M-14 automatics—but they couldn't hit anybody. I talked to the patrol leader after he came in—Gary Packard, B Company—and he was exasperated. He even laughed about it. When he laughed, his lips curled back and revealed his teeth and gums. He said he remembered watching one of his riflemen shooting at an enemy soldier who was crawling as fast as he could toward cover. The rifleman, shouting excitedly, fired until he'd emptied two clips—"I can't hit him, sir! I can't hit him!"—while bullets kicked up dirt behind the distant man's scrambling feet.

And of course, it turned out that they were shooting at one of our own patrols: Bravo Company shooting at Alpha.

Later, when I briefed him on the incident, Colonel Brody said he felt rather mixed about the fact that no one had been hit. He pointed out that it was the first time our ineptness had paid dividends.

Then, on the night of April 23–24, a man was killed on patrol in A Company's sector. Another grenade. Another dead rifleman.

A day or two later I discovered a work detail in the DMZ taking a lunch break without having put out security. It was a squad from Recon, two jeep loads of guys under an E-5. Their orders were to spend the day in one small area clearing brush and searching for tunnels. I found all seven or eight men sitting in their jeeps, eating C-rations. No security. I chewed that E-5 up one side and down the other, got red in the face, shouted, waved my arms, paced up and down, slammed my hand on the jeep hood. I was getting good at that sort of thing: I was getting mad.

230

When Bobby Green heard what I'd done he went straight to Colonel Brody. Brody called me in later that afternoon.

"What's this I hear about you chewing out Sergeant Carpenter in front of his own men?"

"That's right, sir. That's exactly what I did. He was leading the detail you told me to check on this morning. I found him and his men sitting around eating lunch with no security. I lost my temper."

"Good for you, Richardson."

"Sir?"

"I said good for you. I sent Green packing." I could hear the anger in Colonel Brody's voice. "He came and told me he didn't want you yelling at his NCOs. I told him I was the one who sent you out there in the first place, and if his NCOs didn't know enough to post security, they damn well needed yelling at. He said you'd taken it too far and I told him you couldn't have taken it far enough. He realized about that time that he was losing the argument, so he shut up. I let him go after awhile. You might hear from him, but I doubt it."

"Thank you, sir."

"You're welcome." He paused.

"Will that be all, sir?"

"No." Brody was leaning back in his chair, apparently thinking. He had his hands locked behind his head and was staring at the ceiling. "Call Norm in here, will you?" he said. Then: "No, hold on." He picked up the phone and had the operator ring the S-3 shop. Captain Stewart was in, and Brody told him to come right over. "And bring what's-his-name, Evans, with you."

The two men walked into the room a couple minutes later. Colonel Brody told us to pull up chairs. He said he wanted to talk strategy. We got settled.

"Tactically speaking," Colonel Brody began, "I'm unhappy with our performance. We've got to improve. Now let's review things. First, I think there's real evidence that the North Koreans have built tunnels *somewhere*. Just because we can't find them —and the fucking *dogs* can't find them either—that doesn't mean the tunnels don't exist. Second, our patrols are terrible. All they've done is kill people. Our own people. If I had my way I'd shit-can the patrols today, this minute, but I've got to go on running them because Eighth Army wants them, and that's that. It's one of our missions, plain and simple, irregardless of how ineffective they are. And they will in fact give us some measure of early warning if the balloon goes up. But those Goddamn patrols are not doing what we want them to do, which is to intercept infiltration teams. They're probably tunneling underground and surfacing somewhere between the MDL and the fence, coming up south of our ambushes. Isn't that right, Norm? Aren't most of Harmon's ambush positions way the hell up near the MDL?"

"Yes sir, that's where he's got 'em. That's because of the early-warning concept. The thinking is, the farther north, the better because of the earlier warning."

"You see? Those sons of bitches have tunneled under our patrols! No wonder we're not catching anybody in our ambushes. Norm, you make sure Harmon changes those routes as of tomorrow night. Have him plot the ambush sites far to the south, as close to the fence as possible. One terrain feature away. Tell him to bring his overlays in to me tomorrow before he sends 'em to the companies. That's number one. Number two is our own tunnel over in A Company, which is almost finished. That's good—that just might surprise somebody. Now, number three." He leaned forward on his desk and said slowly: "Has it occurred to any of you that we don't know whether our patrols are going out at all?"

For a moment no one responded. Finally I said, "I've seen them go out, sir. And come back in. I see one or two every day. And Harmon debriefs the patrol leaders. He talks to all of them."

Colonel Brody gave me one of his disgusted looks. "Of course they go out, Richardson. That's not what I mean. I mean we don't know what they do once they get the hell outside the fence. We don't know where they *really* go because we have no means of supervising them."

"That's true, Colonel," said Captain Stewart. "But that's why we've got officers leading them."

Brody snorted. "That's not enough. Look what that Goddamn Sellers was pulling before I relieved him. Maybe there are others doing the same thing. I want more supervision. I want Evans here, and Richardson, to go out on a couple patrols and report back to me on what they observe. I want to know what the hell is going on, why we have grenades falling into our ambush sites, why we have one patrol firing on another. We can't do anything out there but step on our own dick. I want to know why. Got that, Richardson? Evans? Now you get ready to go. I'm sending one of you out tonight, the other tomorrow night. Evans. Take the first one. Both of you can cover for each other as far as other duties are concerned. Questions?"

He paused. Jack said, "Who do you want me to go out with, sir? Which patrol?"

"I'll let you know. Just go get ready. Norm and I'll talk it over and let you know. Any more questions? All right, you two are dismissed. Norm, you stay here."

Jack and I walked over to the BOQ. He was excited. "A fuckin *am*bush patrol!" he shouted. "Combat, Art! Hot shit! Man, it's about time!"

I helped him get his gear together. He took the sling off his rifle and started taping the metal on his equipment with black tape. He sent his driver after camouflage paste and a piece of cork, telling him to check with Recon or the QRF if the S-4 didn't have any. He swiped a book of matches off Harmon's bureau.

Captain Stewart called and said he wouldn't need me at the FCP that night. Then he wanted to speak to Jack. Norm told Jack they were sending him out with the Charlie Company patrol. Donnie Lange was leading it, and they were scheduled to head out in an hour. Jack was about to hang up when he suddenly said: "Hey sir! What the heck am I looking for, anyhow?"

I didn't hear the reply, but after Jack hung up I asked him what Norm had said.

"He told me to look for Lange to fuck up."

"Great," I said.

"Yeah. Say Art, we're going to be mighty popular fellows around this battalion pretty soon. Don't you agree?"

"Yes. Cherished by our peers. It's a great life."

Jack got his gear together quickly and left, his spirits somewhat dampened. I checked my pistol and equipment for the fence-walk and thought about what I might do that evening. The weather was fine and I considered going into Changpa-ri to see Tammy, but I felt I'd be deserting Jack.

After I walked the fence, I went back to Matta and ate dinner. Then I had Peters drive me up to Charlie Company's CP. Steve Morrison was there. He'd turned out to be a good company commander. We talked. He didn't seem to mind Jack going out on one of his patrols.

"It doesn't make any difference," he said. "Lange runs good patrols."

"He's been doing it for a long time. Maybe too long," I said.

"No, he still does a good job. A guy can't afford not to. There's nothing wrong with the way patrols are being run. There just aren't many North Koreans out in no man's land, that's all. How often can you expect to make contact?"

"What about the grenades we've taken? What do you make of that?"

He shrugged. "I don't know. You may have a point. They may be able to locate our people simply by noise—a twelve-man patrol has a hard time moving silently."

"I know. And if they send just one man out there, no way are twelve going to hear one."

"Yeah," Steve said. "It all depends on who's already waiting when the other comes along. If they're just sitting all day or all night, waiting for us to come along—only one man, you know, or two—then we're in trouble."

"You think they've got tunnels?" I asked.

"Nah. No way."

"Colonel thinks they do."

Morrison laughed. "He's been wrong before."

The CP bunker had been dug into the back side of a hill overlooking the fence. Its walls were dirt, and large wooden beams supported a low plywood ceiling. It was illuminated by candles and Coleman lanterns, and furnished with a couple tables, a few chairs, and two cots. The radios sat on one of the tables and hissed continuously. On the beams hung maps. Donnie Lange's patrol route had been grease-penciled onto the acetate which covered a large map of the DMZ.

Lange radioed his position to the company CP every hour, and when he did, the RTO would mark the spot on the map. He did that at seven, eight, and nine o'clock. Nothing out of the ordinary occurred, and Steve Morrison went to bed around ten. He told his RTO: "Call me if anything happens, *anything*. Especially if someone spots Brody in the company area. Got it?"

"I got it, sir."

"And make sure you get the fence checks on time. If you

don't hear from one of the platoon sergeants, wake me up and *I'll* call him."

"Right sir."

Steve turned to me. "How long are you staying?"

"I don't know. Do you mind? I'll take off if you want."

He grinned up at me from his cot. "Don't worry about your buddy. Nothing's going to happen. Believe me. But I don't mind, stay as long as you want. Don't bother waking me to say good-bye."

"Thanks."

Morrison was asleep within five minutes. I heard the ten o'clock report from Donnie Lange, and I waited around for the eleven. Lange made it right on time. He reported that the patrol had moved without incident into its primary ambush position. I went outside, found Peters, and we returned to Matta.

I was at the gate in the fence the next morning at 10:30 when Donnie Lange's patrol came in. I said hello to Lange and gave Jack a lift back to Matta.

"How was it?" I asked him after we pulled away from the fence where the men were climbing into a deuce-and-a-half.

"It was okay. No big deal."

"What happened on the patrol?"

"Not a thing. Actually, it was boring as hell."

He looked exhausted, and we drove the rest of the way in silence.

April 20, 1969

It is a landscape of nightmare, this wasteland of a demilitarized zone: artillery craters, barbed wire, minefields, grave-yards, the skeletons of villages and the remains of rice paddies. The earth has been shelled, mined, overgrown, booby-trapped, burned and abandoned to grow wild yet another time. Its very name is a lie, it was never demilitarized. Military men enter it every night, seeking out other military men. The dead chase the dead. We're zombies, awaiting the final call from the other side of the DMZ.

Colonel Brody decided to attach me to a patrol in A Company, the sector where most incidents had occurred. It would be the first patrol to set up an ambush near the fence.

The patrol leader would be Al Crandall. Crandall had dark hair and a hard, square-jawed face. I'd eaten some meals with him because A Company shared the Headquarters Company mess hall with us, but I'd seen Crandall most often at the Officers' Club. Two or three times we'd sat at the same poker table, and what I knew about him I'd picked up there. He rarely talked, but when he did he talked with a great deal of self-assurance. He also played poker well; he could bluff outrageously without giving himself away. I'd once called a bluff of his, winning a large pot, and three hands later someone else tried the same thing and Crandall beat him badly.

Crandall had run patrols for six months without incident. And perhaps that was why Colonel Brody sent me out specifically with him: the Colonel *wanted* incidents, not the sort we were used to—accidents and killings—but the right sort. A nice, productive ambush, for example. A couple of bodies. Or a tunnel entrance.

Patrols run without incident made Colonel Brody skeptical, even suspicious.

Crandall knew this, or at least he guessed it. When I met him at the company, the first thing he said to me was: "So I'm going to be spied on, is that it?"

"Come on, Al," I replied. "It isn't that bad. I'm really just going along for the ride."

"And then reporting everything to Brody."

I stared at him. "Look, this doesn't have to be difficult. Let's try to get along. I don't have any doubts about your ability to run a patrol, and I'm not out to burn you."

Crandall looked at his watch. "Well, come inside. I better check your equipment. This your first patrol?"

"Yeah."

"You'll want to draw a weapon, something besides that .45."

I followed him to the company armory and drew a grenade launcher. I signed for a bandolier of HE rounds and one of pellet shells. Al examined my gear and found everything in order.

"You got camouflage grease?" he asked me.

"Yeah, plenty."

"Okay. Let's check the men. Sergeant Williams should have formed them up by now."

We went outside. The afternoon was overcast and humid.

Crandall checked the formation, then gave a quick briefing. He told the men where we'd be going and read them the weather report. Light rain was expected. Then he explained that I'd be coming along as an observer. I'd be a functioning member of the patrol but not one of its leaders. Sergeant Williams would be second in command. The men listened attentively. Then they piled into a truck. I rode in the cab with Crandall.

By the time we reached the fence, the truck driver had his windshield wipers going. We got down out of the truck. Nobody had a poncho—ponchos made too much noise. We wore field jackets and soft caps. We checked our weapons and darkened our faces and hands and necks with camouflage grease and burnt cork. We put on black gloves. The light drizzle continued to fall steadily. Finally we lined up and started through the gate. It was exactly 1400 hours. I'd seen patrols moving out like this countless times, and part of me had always wondered what was in store for them. I'd wanted to go on a patrol for a long time.

4/25

I seem to have lost the will for the search. I'm here because I'm here. Nothing else matters, not my past, not my future. I don't give a shit about anything else. Vietnam, my parents, a job when I get home—fuck it. Today, now—that's all. Nothing else matters.

TWENTY-ONE

As THE PATROL MOVED
through the gate and into the DMZ, we picked up our interval
and loaded our weapons. Everything was done without spoken
orders. I did what I saw others do. Crandall was third through
the gate, I was fourth. I selected an HE round for my grenade
launcher. At nightfall I'd switch to a shotgun shell.

While daylight lasted we walked slowly and took frequent
breaks. We were in no hurry. Our packs were heavy and the rain
chilled us and weighed down our clothing. Crandall treated me
like a VIP. He explained what he was doing every step of the way,
showing me where we were on his map, pointing out landmarks,
explaining SOPs he and his men had developed over the months.
He followed the patrol route exactly.

The farthest point north on our route was a low ridgeline
practically within spitting distance of North Korean soil. We
reached the spot an hour or so before supper, and we laid up there
for a few minutes. We could see activity in North Korea, a vehicle
on one of the distant hills. The RTO called it in without being
told to. Crandall pointed out the North Korean speakers to me:
three rows of them, about four speakers to the row, huge circular

things aimed right at us. The whole bank of them must have stood two or three times the height of a man. They looked like a series of bull's-eyes and made a tempting target, well within range of the M-14 Crandall carried. "Did you ever take a pot shot at them?" I asked him.

He laughed. "They'd crucify me," he said. "It'd be all over Panmunjom the next morning."

"So you've thought of it."

"Hell yes."

Crandall also pointed out the border. "See that barbed wire? That's the physical MDL." The rusted strand of barbed wire was visible because white ribbons hung from it at wide intervals. The ribbons hung straight down in the rain. "It's down in some places, rusted through. On the darkest nights, you could cross over and never know it. It's happened."

After our break we turned back south, and Crandall started working me into the routines of the patrol. When we halted for supper, he suggested I take a stint at security. I said I'd be willing, so he posted me and another man on a hilltop for half an hour. The other man was a black named Baines. Baines had large, very white teeth that constantly nibbled at his lower lip. The lip was gouged and chapped. I recognized him from the fence, where I'd seen him the in A Company sector many times. He was a nice kid. We talked softly, mostly about nothing: where we were from, whether or not we thought we'd see action that night. Consensus was we wouldn't.

We split the landscape into two sectors and each took half the circle, 180 degrees. Our sectors overlapped somewhat. It was a lot of territory to keep under surveillance. The terrain was hilly, with low vegetation offering plenty of cover.

As we ate our C-rations, I noticed that Baines could open a tin can without making a sound, and could eat without looking at his food.

We could see for at least a mile in every direction. Off to the northwest, a hill loomed up and blocked the sunset. The guard post where Klein had died sat on top of it, and I could see the bunkers from there, see where the foliage had been stripped away, making the hill an ugly, bald dome. It was an imposing hunk of real estate; it looked solid and steep, and it commanded the entire sector.

Baines and I sat there, and everything was very quiet, and I said so at one point. "I'm glad it is and you ought to be too, sir," Baines said without taking his eyes off the terrain in front of him. "If they had those speakers on right now you couldn't think straight. They'll give you a damn headache. And when they're on, you know the gooks're up to something. They use 'em to cover the sound of their movement."

"Or digging," I said. "You think they've got tunnels?"

"No I don't," Baines replied. "They ain't that crazy."

Three or four times I thought I saw something—movement, a human figure—but I hadn't. I was glad when we were relieved after half an hour.

The patrol continued south after six. It was getting dark. The rain stopped and the breeze picked up, and it got colder. We walked stiffly. There were no trails, and we walked through underbrush and short weeds up to our ankles, sometimes to our knees, but it wasn't bad walking. By now, though, after the long break for supper, and with the wind rising, the cold and the stiffness made it painful just to put one foot in front of the other. We were getting tired. After twenty or thirty minutes of walking, though, our muscles and joints warmed up and we moved faster. It was twilight. The sky filled with birds, black shapes wheeling against the silver-gray ceiling above us. The wind blew, but the clouds were so thick they seemed not to move at all.

Then the birds were gone and it was night. Our pace slowed again. I followed Crandall and watched his back. Soon all I could see were the two pieces of luminous tape sewn onto the back of his soft cap. I followed the two glowing rectangles and listened for noises that didn't sound like us. All I heard was the wind in my ears and the thudding and scraping of the footfalls of the men behind and in front of me.

Every so often Crandall would halt the patrol and Sergeant Williams would come forward. He and Crandall would whisper a few brief words. Williams was counting paces, and Crandall held the compass; they'd compare notes and figure our position, and then we'd start off again, usually in a slightly different direction. Williams would stand and count heads as the patrol moved past him. Then he'd take up his position again at the rear of the patrol.

After a couple of hours we halted and stayed put. Crandall

whispered to me: "Assembly area. Security out. Pass it back." I turned around and whispered the identical words to the next man. Crandall sat down, and I sat next to him. Williams joined us. They took out some snacks left over from the C-ration supper—crackers and chocolate—and unwrapped them. "Ten-minute break," Crandall whispered to me. "Then we'll do a site reconnaissance."

We were halfway down a low ridge. The ground slanted steeply here, but we could sit comfortably, leaning back into the hill. The wind was gusting. When the wind fell off, the night was very quiet. The speakers had started up, but we were a long way from them now and the sound reached us only occasionally. The words were unintelligible: they were Korean, and they came and went on the wind.

Crandall slid over closer to me and began to talk. I could smell the chocolate on his breath. He said the site recon was the only time he ever split the patrol. It was admittedly dangerous, he said, but necessary. He didn't want to take the whole patrol into a good ambush position without first checking it out. He said he wanted me to go with Sergeant Williams and another man and find an ambush site about 200 meters down the hill. There'd be something suitable. A lot of that low ground, he said, might be used by infiltration teams.

"So take five minutes," Crandall said quietly. "Then go with Williams. He does these all the time. Do what he says. There'll be three of you. Leave your pack and take your weapon."

"Okay," I said.

Crandall sighed and leaned back. He stretched out his legs. "Coming in," he said, "listen for the command to halt. Don't miss it. Then you'll hear the pass word. You know the second part?"

"Yeah. 'Broom' and 'firefly.'"

"You got it. Just don't miss the command to halt. You walk through that, you're dead."

"I'm all ears."

Not much later the three of us set off: Williams, then me, then the third man, who turned out to be Baines. After a few minutes we reached level ground. Williams stopped and turned around. He whispered very softly: "What to take the point, sir?"

"Why not? Sure."

"Okay. Go first. Look for a place without vegetation. Good fields of fire."

"I can't see a fucking thing," I whispered.

"Don't matter. Nobody else can either."

I started walking. It was so dark that I could have closed my eyes and not known the difference. I was going by the feel of the ground under my boots and the sound of the wind in the grass and bushes. I tried to walk silently. I put my toe down first, then my heel. I moved forward three or four steps at a time, feeling the earth with my feet, then stopping and listening, trying to sense the vegetation and the slope of the terrain. I stopped every few steps.

After about five minutes I felt a hand on my back. "Move faster if you can, sir. We want to get back before daybreak."

I started to say something, but Williams said: "Don't worry. Nobody out here but us."

All right, I thought, and I picked up the pace. The wind gusted in my ears and the speakers droned. We walked for three or four minutes. Then I felt a hand on my shoulder.

"Shhh," very softly.

"What—?"

"Sh!"

We stood still, listening. The wind fell off and the speakers quieted down.

Was that a step?

I stood still. I heard nothing. Then the wind picked up again and all around us the grass started rustling. Noises came from every direction.

Way off to our left a machine gun chattered. A couple of tracer bullets whipped far over our heads, and then came the faint light of a flare over the fence. Sergeant Williams' hand was still on my shoulder, and I could see Baines' teeth. The three of us looked around. We were in a small valley. To our right the ground stretched away for a hundred meters or so before it began to rise. The fence was somewhere beyond the high ground to our left; that was where the light was coming from. Behind us was the ridge where we'd left the patrol, and in front of us the valley stretched away into darkness.

The light from the distant flare faded, and the night seemed darker than before.

Williams squeezed my shoulder. "Let's head back."

"Did you hear something?"

"No."

"I heard something, Sergeant," Baines whispered.

"What?"

"Heard a man moving."

"Sure?"

"Could've been."

With my gloved hands I was squeezing my grenade launcher as hard as I could. I had my thumb on the safety and my finger on the trigger.

"All right," said Williams. "Go slow on the way back. Baines, take point."

"I've got it," I said.

"No. Please. Baines, go."

"I'm gone, Sergeant," Baines whispered.

I turned and followed Williams. We set off in the direction of the patrol. I took eight or ten steps and then stopped. I heard or smelled something peculiar, and then I *knew*, but it was too late. Something loomed up on my right and I swung my weapon around switching off the safety but he clubbed me in the face and leapt on me and my weapon was gone so I wrapped my arms around him and we crashed to the ground hugging each other, his weight on top. He reeked of garlic and sweat, and his clothing smelled of damp earth and dank, musty air. I hit him with my gloved fists, I kneed him and he did the same to me, but I couldn't feel it. His face was close to mine and I tried to gouge his eyes but couldn't for the gloves. The stubble of his beard scratched my cheek, we were both wheezing—lord how he stank—and I kicked and struggled, tried to damage him with my hands and fingers, tried to climb on top of him, to get free, to hold on. I didn't want him to get an arm loose to grab a weapon and then I thought of my pistol, but I thought better of letting him go. It occurred to me that Williams or Baines might kill us both. We kicked and rolled on the cold ground, neither of us able to retrieve a weapon. I could feel a submachine gun on his back, he had grenades too but they were useless to him. Then it occurred to me to use his gun so as we rolled and kicked I found the trigger and squeezed but it didn't budge. I didn't know where the safety was. Harmon had taken the dead infiltrator's PPS out to the test fire range and tried it a couple times using the ammo we'd found on the body and now I wished I'd gone with him. Where was the safety? I pulled on the weapon and tried to gouge his back with it but his coat was too thick.

We clung to each other like lovers, grappling and twisting and kicking. There was the loud sound of our breathing. He worked his legs up my legs and then wrapped his legs around my stomach, embracing me. He began to crush me. I knew then I was losing. He squeezed his legs together and crushed me and I was barely able to breathe. Why didn't Williams or Baines do something? His legs were like steel and I imagined him squeezing my guts out, imagined my guts coming up out of my mouth and I could no longer breathe, couldn't inhale, and white sparks went shooting off behind my eyelids. Then my fear turned and I wanted to kill him. I not only didn't want to die but much more, I wanted to kill the stinking bastard who had his legs wrapped around me, I'd enjoy crushing or stabbing or shooting him. My hands were around his neck and I pulled his face to me, pulled on his neck until I could feel his cold cheek. My lips touched the thorns that were his whiskers and I opened my mouth and my teeth dug into his flesh and now it was *my* turn to clamp down. And I did. I felt warmth and wetness in my mouth, tasted salt, blood. He grunted and released me. He struggled, I relaxed my arms, he pulled away. I drew my pistol, cocked it, listened, tried to see. I heard him run.

"Sir? Sir?"

I tried to speak but had to spit. I shouted: "There he goes!"

Somebody fired twice. The muzzle flashes were blinding and the explosions were close and monstrous and I felt dirt kick up in my face. I rolled over and covered my head with my arms.

"Shit! Don't fire!"

There were no more shots, and I sat up and listened, but I couldn't hear anything. The North Korean had disappeared, probably gone back into a tunnel, if they existed. I was sure now that they did—I had smelled it—but I also knew the man was gone for good, tunnel or no.

"Lieutenant?" Sergeant Williams said quietly. "You all right?"

I took a couple deep breaths. "Yeah."

"What happened?"

I holstered my .45, took off my gloves, and felt the ground all around me. "Fucking guy jumped me," I said. I found what I was looking for and put it in my field jacket pocket. "He almost killed me." I got up. "Where are you?"

"Right here," said Williams. I reached out and felt his hand.

"I didn't know what the hell to do," he said.

"Me neither," said Baines. "I was afraid I'd shoot the Sergeant."

I gripped Baines's shoulder and squeezed it. "You did the right thing, both of you. Let's get back. Help me find my launcher. It's around here someplace."

We looked for it but couldn't find it, so we rejoined the patrol and told Crandall what had happened. He led us into a secondary ambush position without reconnoitering it. Everybody was alert all night, but nothing further happened.

The next day Colonel Brody got the bloodhounds from I Corps and took them into the DMZ. Crandall and I went with the party, which included elements from Recon and the QRF. We found the place where the earth had been chewed up and the grass beaten down. We found my grenade launcher. But the dogs picked up nothing, no odors, no trail. We didn't find any North Korean footprints. And we found no sign of a tunnel opening. The tunnels still eluded us, if they existed at all.

April 29

For the record: the following things have happened during the past two days:

1. A Recon jeep rolled over on the way to one of the GPs. The two men in it had to be medivaced down to Seoul.

2. In the B Company barracks one soldier threatened another with a loaded rifle.

3. Company C: a Katusa went berserk and shot at Steve Morrison. Busted into Steve's office and shot at him three times with an M-14 before he was disarmed by Steve and another Katusa.

4. The new officer who's supposed to take over A Company after Bill Miller leaves accidently shot out his jeep windshield with his .45. He cleared it the same way that sergeant cleared his during the safety demonstration. Didn't put it to his head, that's the only difference.

5. A man in Company C intentionally shot his own foot.

Spring came. The sun turned hot, and during the day its light warmed my shoulders. It rose earlier in the morning than it had during winter and set not in late afternoon but in the evening, and there were long stretches of day between my fence-walks, and short nights. I didn't sleep many hours at night, and I didn't sleep during the day, either. I was feeling pretty strung out.

One night I left the Officers' Club well after one in the morning. I fell into my bed at the BOQ without undressing, and Peters woke me at four. I walked the fence, and Peters drove straight from the fence to the village. I spent the day with Tammy.

When I arrived at her place, she made me a cup of warm milk. "Go, lie down," she said. I don't think anyone had ever made warm milk for me before. She helped me take off my dusty fatigues. I drank the milk and Tammy crawled into bed with me, and I fell asleep holding her.

Tammy had become completely familiar to me: the taste of her, the feel of her breasts, the firmness of her thighs, her odors, the sound of her voice. I didn't see how I could live without her.

May 2

We are an old couple now. She knows when to expect me and she reads my mood as soon as I enter. She knows what I need, what I want. She decides quickly whether I need soothing or upbraiding. She decides either to put on the tea or take off her clothes, either to take down the mats and unroll them, spread out the pillows, remove her kimono—or to let me remove it. And I read her too, when I walk in. Immediately I know whether the food will be good or bad, whether she wants to make love, whether she will ask me to repair something or give her money.

We don't talk much. There's a sadness between us. I'll leave soon. She asks me when I'm going, and I tell her I don't know. But I'm waiting for orders, and it's going to be soon.

246

Often during that time I found myself sitting at the small table in Tammy's hooch, eating breakfast or some other meal, staring at the wall or out the window at the red rooftops and not talking, thinking about how long I'd been in Korea and how soon I'd be leaving. Not knowing what I was going to do with the rest of my life and not caring.

Tammy would sit next to me and she'd be silent too.

May 3

Twelve months gone, one to go. What's left is easy, the same shit day in, day out, only thirty days left, no new problems, no challenges. I've seen it all.

What will become of Tammy after I'm gone?

We talked about it sometimes.

"You'll be leaving me soon," she once said.

"Yes, that's right. Who will take care of you, Tammy?"

"I have friends. Family, too."

"Your mother?"

"Yes. Kim Lee, too."

"But she's at school in Pusan."

"She'll be out for the summer soon."

"What friends have you got?"

"I have Miss Yi," she said, "and Miss Kim, and also Mama-san."

"Mama-san from the Green Door?"

"Of course not," she scoffed. "That's not my Mama-san. I have my own Mama-san."

"Oh."

I didn't know how she would get along after I left. But I knew she would. I supposed she would find another man. Maybe it was that simple.

A few days later, Peters and I drove out of Camp Matta in midmorning and headed toward the village. We'd gone about a mile when a call came over the radio. There had been an explosion in the headquarters company mess hall. A stove—something—had blown up and there were casualties. How many? we heard Colonel Brody ask. That was still unknown. A few.

Peters and I looked at each other.

"Let's turn back," I said. "Quickly."

We breathed our own dust as Peters turned the jeep around. He drove fast. The jeep skidded as we swept through the checkpoint, and as we passed the TOC and the BOQ, I could see soldiers milling about in the road ahead of us. We pulled up to them.

"What's going on?" I asked someone.

"Hand grenade, sir."

I got a feeling in my gut. "Again?" I said.

There were bodies stretched out on the road in the sun. They were lined up side-by-side. In a neat row. Five. The bodies were covered from the waist up by ponchos, and the legs and boots were twisted at peculiar, rubbery angles. Dark blood oozed from under the ponchos and formed smooth puddles. The puddles spread out in the brown dust of the road.

I ran up the steps to the mess hall. Inside, the floor was slippery with blood. There were pieces of flesh and a fine spray of blood on the walls so that it looked like beets and potatoes had exploded out of a pressure cooker. A large hole had been blown through the partition separating the enlisted and officers' mess. Tables and chairs lay every which way.

A Korean brought a wet mop and a bucket out from the kitchen and began to mop the floor. He pushed a wave of blood along the floor in front of the mop. I walked back outside, into the sunshine. I could look down and see everything: soldiers standing in the street not knowing what to do; Peters backing the jeep out of the way; Doc Tonne tending to someone on a stretcher in the road near the bodies.

I went down and walked over to Doc Tonne.

"Who are they?" I asked him.

"I don't know. A Company, that's all I know." One of his aidmen ran up with a jar of something, and I stepped out of the way.

I went over to the bodies and pulled down the ponchos, one by one. I had to know. Only two had enough face to be recognizable, and one of them, his eyes closed, his lower lip chewed and gouged, was Baines.

Colonel Brody drove up. He had on his helmet and flak jacket, so he must have come from the fence. He started asking questions and I saw his tan face turn pale. I'd never seen anyone turn pale like that, and I thought he might faint. I was about to go over to him but just then Doc Tonne said, "Get this man to the helipad fast. Chopper's coming." I grabbed one of the stretcher handles and four of us lifted him.

"Take it easy," said Doc Tonne. "Keep him level. But hurry. Dust-off's due any minute."

We walked fast. The man was heavy. We were carrying him feet first and I was back by his head. His face was right in front of me. He was upside-down but when I looked at his face carefully I felt a shock run through my body. It was Sergeant Waters.

We carried him up the road at a fast walk. Every so often his eyes would open and his irises would float upward like a fish rising in a pond. He'd look at me and at the man next to me and then his eyes would sink back down where they'd come from. His face was blank and looked old, as if he'd aged. His ears were bleeding and the blood ran down from inside them, red on brown, and formed dark splotches on the olive-drab canvas of the stretcher.

"You're going to be okay," I said to him. "You'll be all right. You'll be fine."

We carried him up to the headquarters building and set him down on the grass near the grave mound with its four stone guardians. A breeze stirred the flag on the flag pole, but there was no sound. I looked at Sergeant Waters. He lay quietly. I was kneeling by his head. His eyes stared upward at nothing, blanks. He was breathing. Then I heard the helicopter, the dull rotor-thud of the Huey echoing off the low hills, and then the huge metal thing came roaring into view, fast and low, spun around, hovered tentatively for a second, then set down on the pad. Even idling, the roar of its turbine hurt my ears. We jogged toward the open door carrying the stretcher. I was bent over, running, my back straining, my face hovering a few inches above Waters' face.

"You'll be okay," I shouted. "You'll be okay."

Tears welled up in his eyes and rolled down his temples into his ears, mingling with blood. His lips moved—he was speaking to me—but I couldn't hear him.

We passed him up to the aidmen in the Huey and got out of there. I held my ears as the chopper took off.

A grenade exploded in the mess hall. Five men died. The men had come off patrol early that morning. They went back to their barracks where they turned in their ammunition and weapons and then they walked up to the mess hall for chow. They were cocky and jivin each other and hacking around and this one black dude was juggling a grenade he'd taken the detonator out of. He was tossing it around in the chow line, having a good ol' time and teasing his buddies, I'm goin to blow you the fuck away, motherfucker, I'm goin to frag your ass, and Sergeant Williams told him to go turn the hand grenade the fuck in before he killed somebody. By this time he had drawn considerable attention to himself and had made a lot of GIs nervous because he was the only one who knew the grenade was disarmed. So when Williams, whom he didn't like anyway, spoiled his joke by telling him to turn in the grenade, he pulled the pin and let the handle fly and then watched and laughed, watched some men freeze in shock—like Baines—stood there watching other men duck under tables and dash out the door, stood there and laughed and held the grenade in the palm of his hand and then tossed it over his head and caught it with his other hand to keep it away from Williams, who lunged for it, then laughed at Williams and the guys in the chow line—"See?" he said. "No sweat motherfucker, no—"

They lined up the five bodies in the dust on the brown road below the mess hall in the sun and his was the body that had no arm from the elbow down.

May 6
A hand grenade exploded in the mess hall today and killed five people. Five people. Killed Williams and Baines. Sgt. Waters was injured and I carried him to the helicopter. *He was not me!* I watched the helicopter take off and clear the low hills to the south, behind the BOQ, the hills where the Korean security guard was shot. I don't know what to do with myself.

SHIT! Fuck that bastard, the self-destructive, suicidal, murdering son of a bitch, that bastard, fuck him, I hope he burns in hell. The dumb shit. The wrong grenade, how could he do it? The dead bastard motherfucking cocksucker, I'm glad he's dead.

It was hard to go into the mess hall to eat after that. The hole in the partition was patched with thin plywood. I'd go in to eat and my stomach would feel queasy. The plywood reminded me, and I couldn't keep what I had seen out of my head. I lost weight.

May 8

Why have I survived? To do what? I don't think I will ever be able to do anything frivolous again.

The score: 11-1. Eleven of us killed; one of them.

We killed most of our own.

Their side: one infiltrator—wounded, then suicide. They killed their own. With one exception, all the dead—our dead and theirs—committed some form of suicide.

War is not murder, not even homocide. It is suicide perpetrated upon the young by the older generations. Can suicide by perpetrated? That's a contradiction but it's the truth. The real enemy are our fathers, who sent us here.

TWENTY-TWO

Norm Stewart went home. It was hard to say good bye to him; he was a good man. Competent, fair.

Colonel Brody gave the S-3 job to Jack. A lieutenant in a major's slot. Jack moved into Norm's desk at the office and into Norm's room at the BOQ, and that evening Jack and I sat in his new room and talked. It was about 6:00 p.m. and outside the sun was setting. Jack sat on the bed, slumped down, his back against the wall and his dusty boots on the floor. I sat in the easy chair. It was a luxury to be able to close the door for privacy. We were drinking reconstituted orange juice. Straight. I would walk the fence soon, and afterwards I'd either meet Jack and Colonel Brody at the CP or head into Changpa-ri to see Tammy.

"Good for you, Jack," I said about his new job. "It's really a compliment."

"It doesn't mean shit." He laughed. "They don't have anybody but you and me."

"No, they've got plenty of people. They'd have brought in a captain or a major from somewhere else in the division if they thought they needed to. Colonel Brody has a lot of confidence in you."

"Maybe. Maybe not. I just don't know if I can handle the whole thing."

"Of course you can."

"What the hell makes you say that?"

"I know you."

"And then there's the Colonel. He's a maniac. You never know what he's going to come up with. And I'm supposed to be his right-hand man, you know? I'm with him twenty-four hours a day. He's in his office right now. I know that. I'm like his aide, or his other self. I just do what he says."

"That's right. That's what an S-3 does."

Jack sighed. He tipped his glass and drained the orange juice. I watched his Adam's apple bob.

"I can't believe Norm's gone," Jack said. He leaned forward and set his glass on the floor. "I'll tell you, Art, I loved that son of a bitch."

"I know," I said.

"I'm not sure I can get along without him."

"Of course you can. You'll do a fine job."

"He sure knew his stuff."

"He'd been to Vietnam. He was a lifer."

"You can bet I'm not."

"Look," I said, "forget about Norm. He's gone. You've got to work directly with Brody, but it's nothing to worry about. He's no dummy. He knows you, even knows your limitations, probably better than you. You'll learn—he'll teach you."

"That's easy for you to say." He grinned. "How would you like to be my assistant?"

"I wouldn't," I said. "No offense."

"Come on. I could arrange it."

"Look, do me one favor, will you? Don't do me any favors. Leave me be. Don't go telling the Colonel I'd make you a good assistant. I'm short. I want to stay right where I am. I don't want a company or the Recon platoon or the Assistant 3 slot, I just want to walk the damn fence. I'm good at it and I get a lot of time off. I've got less than a month. I could stand on my head for a month. I don't need any favors.

"By the way," I said, "you heard from Tina lately?"

Jack had gotten a Dear John from her shortly after our abortive weekend in Seoul. He'd gone down once more, by himself, and had patched things up with her, he thought. But since then she hadn't answered his letters, and he'd been unable to reach her by phone.

"No. Nothing. It's over."

"Too bad."

"Yeah." He shook his head. "She was kind of superficial, you know? I never did feel she knew who the hell I was." Then he grinned. "But she sure was gorgeous, wasn't she?"

"She was beautiful. And sexy."

He laughed. "She knew it, too. She used it. She got whatever she wanted."

"Must have been nice, being wanted by her."

"While it lasted. It was great while it lasted. And then it was just gone and there was nothing I could do to bring it back."

"What are you going to do when you get out?" I asked him.

"I've given it some careful thought. I'm going back to the farm. Work with my Daddy, and study. When I'm ready I'll take the LSATs again and apply to law school. Work with my brain instead of my hands."

"I suppose you know what kind of law you want to practice."

He chuckled. "Well, I have a notion. Agricultural law, maybe eventually politics. Specialize in land-use law and legislation."

"You've got your whole life mapped out, Jack."

"Naw. Only the next ten or fifteen years. You come up with any career plans yet?"

"Not really."

"You sure don't have the difficulty writing that I have. Aren't you going to do something with all that journalism you did in college? The *Daily* and all that?"

I shook my head. "Newspapers are for shit. They print only bad news. Maybe I'll become a novelist. Write romances, science fiction. Create sweet dreams."

"Escapism, Art. You ought to try to effect change. You can't run away from the world. It'll catch up."

"I know. But I just haven't made a decision. Who can think beyond tomorrow, up here?"

"Harmon does." Jack laughed. "You keeping track of all the crap he's buying?"

254

"Hardly. What's he going to do when he gets back? Open a pawn shop?"

Through the screened window we heard a jeep pull up. I knew it was Peters by the sound of the brakes.

I stood up. "Maybe I'll see you at the CP later on."

"Yeah, okay."

I picked up my helmet and flak jacket and left the BOQ. It was on the way to the fence that I realized Jack was my new boss. I hoped it wouldn't change things between us. I didn't think it would.

That night at the CP I found that I missed Norm Stewart too. He had been a calm and rational man, and he had served to stabilize things at night at the CP. He'd been a soothing influence on Colonel Brody; he'd tempered him.

Brody was in a foul mood and was nasty to Jack. He swore at him and made him broadcast trivial radio messages to the company commanders. He treated Jack worse than an RTO and humiliated him, and it was clear that Colonel Brody missed Captain Stewart too.

Things were quiet along the fence, but there was a lot of radio traffic on the battalion command net. Most of it was routine, but around eleven old Short started up. We sat through two or three long, resonant shorts and then finally he broadcast sort of a bugle-call short, and that was followed by a Broadway-musical rendition à la Ethel Merman: "There's *SHORT* business like *SHORT* business. . . ."

That was enough for Colonel Brody.

He got up and strode over to the radio. He keyed the handset. "Short, this is three-four. Now you listen to me. You know who I am. I want you to stay *off* this radio net. What you're doing is unconscionable. It's a breach of security, of radio security, and you're disrupting radio traffic. We can't conduct business on this net with you groaning every ten minutes! It's illegal and disobedient and I want you to STOP IT!! Do you hear me? You're undermining everything we're doing here to accomplish our mission. You cease and desist or I swear to Christ I'll track you down, I don't care where you are—. All officers and NCOs now hear me, you get to your radios and find this man, make sure you account for all your radios, I don't want a single radio unmanned, I want an officer at every radio in the bat— . . . in this unit and I want this short business to stop. Do you hear me? Now I want you to stay *off* the air, Short. Do you understand? Stay *off* this radio net! Out!"

There was a long pause. Then, plain as day, we heard the static cut out as somebody somewhere keyed a handset. Everyone in the battalion could hear it: soldiers on the guard posts, at the TOC, in the company CPs and in every jeep with a radio; we all listened to dead air until a strange, deep, resonant voice said:

"Three-four, this is Short. Roger, *OUT!*"

I got back to Matta early that evening. From the road below the BOQ where Peters dropped me off, I could hear Harmon's stereo.

> *Flew in from Miami Beach BOAC*
> *Didn't get to bed last night . . .*

Harmon was alone in our room, trying on suits. Sound from his stereo filled the Quonset hut. He had brought in the shaving mirror from the latrine and propped it up on his bunk, and he was checking out a three-piece blue pin stripe suit in the mirror. Trousers and jackets and vests from other suits lay strewn about his bureau and bunk.

> *. . . Man I had a dreadful flight*
> *I'm back in the USSR*
> *You don't know how lucky you are boy*
> *Back in the US, back in the US, back in the USSR.*
> *Well the Ukraine girls really knock me out*
> *They leave the West behind. . . .*

"You want to turn that stereo up some?" I shouted.
He gave me a look.
"I'm going to bed!" I yelled.
"Good for you."
I went into Jack's new room and lay down on his bunk and went to sleep. That was about eleven. At one Jack came in and threw me out. Harmon was still up with the lights blazing; he lay sprawled on his bunk wearing headphones and reading *Playboy*. I managed to sleep. At four I got up, and while getting dressed I dropped my boots on the floor one at a time over and over until I was sure Harmon was awake. I walked the fence, ate, did some

paperwork at the office and then went forward and checked some details. That evening after I walked the fence, Peters drove me into Changpa-ri.

Tammy met me wearing her white kimono. Her dark nipples showed through the cloth, and when she walked, her garment rustled like bedclothes when you climb in. Her black hair looked almost blue. She had opened the windows over the bed, and the murmur of voices and the clank of pots and pans drifted into the room from the courtyards across the street. It was a peaceful, warm evening in early spring and my awareness that I would soon lose Tammy made her tremendously appealing. We stood in the middle of the room and I held her without moving. I imagined her body under the kimono and remembered the texture of her skin and knew my hand would find warm skin and soft hair beneath the folds of her robe. She was there with me and I already missed her.

We made love and afterward I rolled over and looked out the window and thought about leaving. I would lose everything I had here: Tammy, my friends, my rank in the army and even my identity as a soldier and an officer. What would civilian life be like? What would I do? I had no idea. What could I do? Walk a fence, shoot a pistol, a grenade launcher, a machine gun. My only plans were for a motorcycle and a long trip—two months, maybe three. What then? I had no future. The things by which I had come to identify myself—experience, rank, girlfriend, friends —would no longer mean anything because I would not have them anymore. I had thought they didn't matter, yet now I didn't know what it would be like to do without them. Now they seemed to matter. It was almost enough to make one consider extending. Almost.

Outside the window it had become dark and there was a wind that pushed heavy clouds across the sky. It would rain soon. There weren't many lights but I could make out the shapes of the tile roofs and the street and the white concrete homes close together and the courtyards behind them and their walls with broken glass set along the tops. I couldn't see the glass shards in the dark but I knew they were there on the top of every wall.

Behind me I heard Tammy stir, and she put her hand on my shoulder. I felt her cheek against my back. I missed her terribly.

The next few days it rained steadily and the roads turned to deep mud. It took twice as long to get from one place to another. It seemed Peters and I were always in the jeep, splashing through puddles or skidding to avoid them. No one in the mess hall or the BOQ had a kind word to say to anybody. All our clothing got wet and stayed wet. There was no way to keep dry; we couldn't put the tops on our jeeps and trucks, and we were soaking wet and cold most of the time. We all felt tense, waiting for the rain to stop, expecting it to stop. The pervasive attitude seemed to be: "If we can only get through the present, the future will be better." But the future never came, and the present dragged on. The rain continued to fall and there was no relief.

In Changpa-ri, things deteriorated between Tammy and me. We were living out a doomed relationship, and a feeling of despair, or dread—a sense of imminent loss—hung about the place like the smell of a dead animal. It became impossible for us to talk to one another, except to bicker. Our fights were never resolved, our anger never dissipated. It got so that I hated her, and yet I couldn't stay away from her. I needed her very much.

I decided one morning, as Peters drove through the rain toward Changpa-ri, that I would leave it up to her. She was going to have to decide whether or not to go on seeing me. I did not know what was best for her, but I suspected she might be better off if we broke up sooner rather than later. She could go right out and find another man. I wanted to do what was best for her. Why drag out the process of saying good bye? Perhaps there would be less pain if we ended it now.

Peters dropped me off and drove away in the rain without a word. He had spent hours behind the wheel during the past few days and seemed near exhaustion. I struggled with my poncho and wet boots in the hall. I went upstairs and said hello to Tammy and she fixed some hot soup that we shared. Then I brought up what was on my mind. I told her it might be better if we stopped seeing each other soon and I asked her whether she agreed. I said I wanted her to decide.

She remained silent while I talked. When I was done she finished her soup and then calmly said to me, "I want you to stay."

I said, "You don't think it's better that I leave now?"

"Why? You will leave anyway."

"But you could find somebody better. Someone who'll be here much longer."

"No, I won't."

"Sure you will. You've probably started looking already."

"Don't say such things!"

"You're a whore," I said. I waved my soup spoon at her. "You've *got* to find somebody new. And fast, too."

Her face darkened and her lower lip trembled. "So you want to leave it up to me? That's what a weak person does. Leaves it up to the woman."

I realized then what I was doing, and I felt foolish. These were *my* choices. I couldn't avoid hurting her and I couldn't avoid making my own decisions. If I wanted out now—did I?—she was not going to throw me out. I'd have to leave under my own steam.

How long did I have? Two weeks? Three? I wasn't sure. I knew approximately when I'd be leaving, but my orders wouldn't come till a week or so before I left. And the date I was to leave might fall anywhere within a period of about ten days.

I picked up my bowl of soup and drained it. I went over to the bed. The wind gusted and blew rain against the window. There was water inside on the sill.

From the table, Tammy said to me, "Anyhow, I'm pregnant."

I turned and gaped at her. We stayed that way for a few moments, she looking at me from the table, her hands in her lap, and I staring at her from near the bed. The new fact sunk in. It became real.

Finally Tammy said, "I don't know what to do."

"I don't either," I said. "I don't even know how I feel. How do you feel?"

She smiled. "I feel good," she said. Then her smile faded and she looked away. "I'm scared, too. And lonely."

That's great, I thought. I miss you and you feel lonely and we're together in the same room.

I didn't feel like comforting her just then. I said, "I think it'll take me some time to sort this out." I climbed into bed, pulled up the covers and fell asleep almost immediately.

When I awoke it was afternoon and I had a strange feeling. I was in a place that was familiar to me, yet everything was different. I was different and the room seemed different. Outside the wet landscape had changed: the roofs gleamed wetly and the light was soft. I looked up and saw patches of blue sky and clouds that looked white, not gray, and knew the weather had broken. Yet I had a strange feeling in my stomach, an ache that felt ominously permanent. I knew things would never be the same again. Something had changed, and it had changed for good.

I rolled over and looked at Tammy. She was sitting at the table exactly as she had been when I went to sleep.

"Are you going to keep it?" I asked.

"I don't know."

"I could take you with me. I could marry you. You could come back to the States with me if you were my wife. We could have the baby there."

"I know."

"What do you think?"

"I think you're crazy. I think I would hate it. So would you."

"I'm not so sure."

"You're serious, aren't you?"

I thought for a moment. "I'm not exactly proposing. Just going over the possibilities."

She rose and came over to the bed and sat down. She gazed into my eyes. "Arthur, listen to me. I have no status here. It's true, most Korean people despise girls like me. But I have family here. And friends, people I love. I'm Korean. This is my home, it's all I know. No. I could not go to the United States with you. I am Korean." She put her hand on mine. "You really do love me, don't you?"

"Yes."

"It would not work for us in your country. Never."

"Don't condescend to me."

"I did not mean to. I'm sorry." She held my hand. "Thank you for thinking of taking me with you. I am deeply touched. But let's not speak of it again."

We didn't.

On the way to the fence that night, Peters spotted a small deer. The sunset had been gorgeous —the first one we'd seen in days—and now in the fading light Peters slowed the jeep and pointed. The deer stood on a small rise, just off an old trail. It was feeding. Peters stopped the jeep and I stepped onto the road. I took out my pistol.

"Think I can hit him at this range, Peters?"

"You ought to, sir."

260

"Provide a little venison for Headquarters Company."

I cocked the pistol and sighted over the top. My hand was holding the weapon fairly steady. "What do you figure the range is?"

"I dunno. Fifty yards?"

I imagined what would happen to the deer if the huge bullet from the .45 hit it. Or what if it only wounded him? I didn't have the time or the skill to track a wounded deer. But once my pistol was out of the holster and cocked, it was awfully hard to put it away without using it. The deer looked very small at that range but I had no difficulty holding it in my sights. I hesitated, then squeezed off a round. The pistol kicked and the deer raised its head and sprang away and was gone.

"Missed," I said insightfully. "What the hell? I thought I was pretty good with this thing."

"Buck fever," said Peters.

"I should have made that shot." I looked around for another target, any object that I might shoot at. I spotted a Coke bottle lying about twenty meters away in the ditch by the road. I raised the pistol and fired. The bottle exploded.

I grinned at Peters, and he grinned back. "Well fuck it," I said. "Maybe we'll see a man soon. A North Korean." I holstered my pistol and went back to the jeep. I picked up the radio mike and depressed the push-to-talk switch. I cupped my mouth with my hand to give my voice resonance, and I drew out the word like a foghorn:

"SHO-O-O-O-R-R-R-R-R-R-T!"

A few days later, Peters DEROSed. I gave him a couple bottles of good bourbon and we swapped home addresses. The battalion executive officer, Captain Lopez, told me at lunch my new driver would be a guy named Lyons. Lyons turned out to be a tall, dark-haired man with thick glasses who was older than me. He'd been drafted out of graduate school. On our first trip to the fence, that afternoon, he hit all the potholes Peters had learned to avoid. He seemed to seek them out; he must have hit every pothole between Camp Matta and the fence, and he ran the wheels on the right side of the jeep through them all.

I was furious. "If you're going to hit every Goddamn open-pit mine between here and the fence," I shouted, "hit 'em on *your* side!"

Lyons looked at me like I was crazy, and I guess by then I was.

One day soon after that Colonel Brody told me to take the helicopter up. He wanted me to fly reconnaissance in our rear area and look for movement, a trail —anything. "Especially the minefields," he said. "Go in low over the minefields. You won't see the North Korean himself, if he's in there, but you'll see where he's walked or crawled through the grass." He wasn't referring to a specific North Korean; he meant any North Korean.

I picked up a map from the Operations Sergeant and waited for the chopper in front of the battalion headquarters building. It was about eleven o'clock and the sun was high and I sat in the warm grass and rolled up my sleeves and took off my helmet. I felt the sun on my face and arms. In front of me, the stone sentinels stared at one another across their grave mound. No one had mown the grass, and tall stalks were growing up around the bases of the stone figures. I wondered how long it would be before the grass overgrew the figures and the stone crumbled and disappeared. Ten years? Fifty? A few hundred?

Everything was still. There was no wind and the flag on the pole hung straight down. A truck went by; the dust followed it for a while and then lazily drifted straight up.

I stretched and yawned and lay back, shading my eyes with my arm. The sky was a clear blue. The grass prickled the back of my neck, and another yawn welled up in my throat. I suppose under other circumstances I might have fallen asleep, but I had become suspicious of these quiet, pastoral moments. They made me nervous. Shortly on the heels of every one of them seemed to come disaster. I was happier in the thick of a crisis.

The helicopter arrived in a few minutes, and I climbed into it. I recognized the pilot and nodded to him; he grinned at me. He was the one who liked to go fishing in the Imjin. I put on the flight helmet.

"You again," he said.

"Just fly this thing," I replied.

He lifted the machine off the helipad. "Where to?"

"Reconnaissance," I said. I unfolded my map. The minefields were outlined in red ink. "Head down toward the Imjin."

He gave me an eager look.

"But no fishing," I said. I held the map so he could see it and pointed to a red mark in a loop of the river. "Let's check out this minefield first."

He raised his eyebrows. "Minefield?"

"Yes. I want to take a look at them all."

He shrugged. "Your funeral."

"Yours too," I said.

We flew down to the Imjin and began to make long, swooping passes over the ground. We flew low. We crisscrossed the minefields from a height of a hundred feet or so, looking not so much for a man as for a trail or a matted-down place where someone might have rested.

The task soon became tedious. After half an hour, as we were on our way from the fourth minefield to the fifth, the pilot said: "Look up. Twelve o'clock."

I looked straight up through the plastic bubble and the whirling rotor blades. There was a bird, a big one, riding a breeze or a thermal high above us. It looked awesome against the huge blue sky.

"Can you catch it in this contraption?" I asked.

The pilot grinned at me. "Now you're talking." He hit the throttle and the engine revved up. We began to climb. We headed directly toward the soaring bird.

"What is it?" I asked.

"Eagle."

We reached an altitude near that of the bird and began to close on it. The eagle, which had been circling lazily, probably doing a reconnaissance not unlike our own, made a series of graceful turns. We followed. Then, as if it suddenly realized it was being followed, the bird straightened its flight path and began to beat its wide wings with a purpose. Below and behind, unable to take our eyes off it, we pursued the eagle. It was magnificent, a huge brown bird, and from a distance of a hundred meters or so we could make out its tail feathers and the long, finger-like feathers at the edges of its wings. Its whole body seemed to partake of the act of flying, and as it flapped, its feathered wings flowed like liquid. The bird was not stiff and noisy and vibrating like our machine, but silent, flexible, smooth, graceful. We rattled and shook and pounded along, traveling in a noisy straight line, while we watched the muscular flight of the eagle. It was a beautiful sight.

The helicopter gained on the bird, overtaking it gradually. When we got within forty or fifty feet, it suddenly folded its wings, paused, tilted, then dropped like an air-to-ground missile. It disappeared below us. We started to follow it down. The pilot lowered the nose of the chopper and we dived, and I suppose both of us saw the same thing at the same time: mountains—high, blue, jagged ones—and a wide valley, and none of the terrain features I was used to—although the mountains were hauntingly familiar—and I knew immediately where we were even before I looked at the compass, its needle firmly fixed on 'N.' My scalp prickled. We began to turn as we dived.

"North-fucking-Korea!" the pilot shouted. "Hang on!"

The chopper screamed and shook as it dived and I dug my boots into the floor and the seat belt nearly cut me in two. The mountains rushed up toward us but when he got the machine moving as fast as it could go, the pilot leveled off and raced toward the nearest guard post. It looked miles away.

"Can you get below radar range?" I yelled.

"Too late for that. We've already lit up every radar screen in North Korea. It's a pony race from here on out, us against the MiGs. I don't think they can scramble 'em that fast."

"Hope not." I looked down. "What about ground fire?"

He looked too. "They got troops down there?"

"Hell yes."

"Well, let's hope they can't shoot."

We were right on top of the purple mountains I'd been seeing to the north every morning and every evening for months. From the fence I'd found them beautiful, even alluring, but from close above they looked neither mysterious nor attractive but foreboding, ugly, barren: all rock ledges and sheer drops. I would not have wanted to walk on them, much less crash-land.

We flew over them in a straight line toward the most obvious landmark we could see to the south. GP Hendrix stood out clearly in the distance on its bald and barren hilltop—the hill stripped of brush and grass to create fields of fire in front of its bunkers and trenches—and we beat it back as fast as the old machine would go. That chopper may not have been an eagle, but it was fast enough. When we buzzed the guard post for good measure, the troops came out of their bunkers and waved their helmets and grinned up at us. They'd probably never seen a helicopter come flying straight at them out of North Korea before, and it wasn't till later that I began to wonder why they hadn't taken a few shots at us. But then again, perhaps they did. Bravo Company was not known for its marksmanship.

We didn't reconnoiter any more minefields. The pilot landed back at the helipad at Matta. As I was taking off my flight helmet, he said: "What to go fishing tomorrow, Lieutenant?"

I grinned at him. "Some other time. I don't think I'll be flying for a while."

He grinned back. "Yeah. Me too."

I laid the flight helmet on the seat, climbed down, and walked away unsteadily.

The North Koreans lodged a protest the next day at Panmunjom. But they were embarrassed about not having shot us down, and they did not press the issue. I don't know what became of the eagle.

Colonel Brody got chewed out for allowing one of his officers to take a helicopter into North Korea, and he passed that along to me. He called me into his office and ate me alive. He yelled and his face turned purple and he leapt up from his desk and kicked the gray metal wastebasket across the room. But for once I was feeling thankful simply to be alive, south of the MDL, a free man. Besides, I was short. So his anger didn't phase me. What was he going to do, send me to Vietnam? I'd been to worse places.

I stood there with an impertinent expression on my face and took all the abuse he could dish out. He got angrier and angrier. "You better be sorry," he told me. "You better be damn sorry. You're not unpunishable just because you're going home soon and going off active duty status. You can be dealt with. Don't you fuck up again, Richardson. I'm warning you."

By the time he let me go, I no longer felt cocky.

TWENTY-THREE

U P AT THE FORWARD CP THAT
night, talk turned to hand grenades. One went off down the line
somewhere, and I said, "Glad I'm not within range of that."

"Nothing to be afraid of," Colonel Brody said.

"What?" I said.

"Jesus Christ, Colonel," Jack said. "Aren't you afraid of anything?"

"Not a grenade. Least effective weapon the infantry has. All
noise. They bounce and roll till they fall into something, like a
depression in the ground, or a gulley—then bang, nothing. Big
noise and so results. The shrapnel goes straight up. That night we
killed that North Korean, Richardson—how many grenades did
he throw?"

"Four or five, Colonel. The North Korean threw two or three
and Sergeant Love and Sergeant Toomey threw a couple. Then
there was the last one, the one in the chest."

"See? He should have used that PPS. Died with it strapped to
his back."

"I think he did use it, sir," I said.

"And he had a bullet wound in his thigh." Colonel Brody

continued as though I hadn't spoken. "None of those grenades inflicted so much as a scratch. Now a hand grenade'll raise hell in an enclosed place, no doubt about that. Grenades're good for small places like houses, tunnels, a pillbox or a machine gun nest. A mess hall, for Christ's sake. We've seen that, haven't we?" The Colonel paused. I couldn't see his face in the dark. "But they're not worth a shit in the open. Nothing to be afraid of. Just get down on one knee, keep your eyes open for a target. Bullets, artillery fire, that's different. You can't get close enough to the ground when there's artillery shrapnel and effective small-arms fire in the air."

Colonel Brody droned on, talking to himself now. "But the M-14—now there's a weapon. Even beats the M-1, the rifle that won this war twenty years ago. We had thirty or forty yards on the Chinese rifle. We could bring effective fire at least thirty yards before they could. Shit, we'd get 'em pinned down and we could chop 'em up with artillery and aircraft. They couldn't bring effective fire on us at that range. They'd try to move up and we could hit 'em, one at a time. There isn't a lot of cover in this terrain, in case you hadn't noticed. Now that M-14, it's got at least twenty-five meters on the M-16, and that's a hell of a big difference in this terrain. They say they're going to change over to the M-16 here. They think if it works in Vietnam it'll work here. That would be a mistake. You don't want your average rifleman firing on automatic here, you need him to shoot accurately at long range. You got to get him to make that first round count, hit a specific target, not an area. You can see what you're shooting at in this country. The automatic rifle won't do shit for you here. We'll lose the next war here with the M-16. Mark my words."

Going home that night, my new driver took a wrong turn. I was dozing. The jeep bounced through a pothole and then I thought I heard somebody yelling and I opened my eyes and saw a couple flame pots, and then suddenly the fence loomed up in front of us, illuminated at the last second by our blackout lights. Lyons slammed on the brakes.

"Jesus Christ!" I shouted. "Turn this fucking thing around!" Flustered, Lyons had difficulty maneuvering on the narrow road. He backed into the ditch and couldn't get out. I almost took the wheel and drove myself. The jeep roared and whined, its gears grinding as Lyons shifted from first to reverse and back. Some GIs wandered over to watch. "Get back to your positions!" I shouted. "What the fuck do you think this is, a Christmas pageant?"

I went to see Tammy and she told me what she intended to do about the baby. She said she'd decided to have it. Her telling me had a peculiar effect: I was relieved. I made love to her and she was especially warm and sweet and sexy. I was strangely aware that I was making love to a growing fetus as well as to Tammy. Afterward we lay naked in bed and I touched her belly and felt a new firmness to it. At least I thought I did. She was about four months along then.

I wondered why she intended to have the baby, and I asked her. She tried to explain.

"Last time when Jim Anderson left me, I had nothing, nothing. Next time I told myself I would have something. Next time I love a man. I love you, Arthur Richardson. You are a much better man than Jim Anderson, but you are going to leave too. I want to have something of you. And now I do. I will have our baby."

I lay next to her and stared into her brown eyes. She'd have it and I wouldn't, which made me feel jealous. Perhaps she saw something in my eyes, because she put her arm around my neck and drew me to her, cuddling me.

I pulled away. "Tammy, now look, I've been saving money, and I—"

"Shhh," she said, and she placed two fingers over my mouth. "Don't talk about money. This isn't business anymore, you know? I love you, and we are having a baby."

I shut up, and we made love another time.

May 23
I've done something worthwhile—given life to somebody. That is, I've contributed toward a life, played a part in the process. I have taken no life and have given life. Perhaps that is enough.

The baby will be ½ Korean, ½ American, a blend of our two selves.

I don't know what'll become of it. It'll be an orphan, have to fend for itself. But Tammy will keep it, so it'll have a mother. It's me who'll be alone soon. Its mother is a whore. I won't be there. If it's a girl, it'll most likely turn into a whore too. If a boy, it'll probably become a slicky boy. Or a soldier.

But that baby will at least have life. You can look at life as a gift or a curse. I'd rather think I've done her or him a favor.

Over the next couple days I thought about money. I thought about money while I walked the fence and while I rode in the jeep back and forth from the fence to Matta, from Matta to the fence, from the fence to Changpa-ri. I had been paid more and more money as time went on. I was promoted to first lieutenant; then the entire U.S. Army got a pay increase from Congress; then I got a raise after a certain amount of time in grade; and all along I was drawing combat pay as well. I had saved money because there was nothing worth spending it on, except Tammy. I had saved over eight thousand dollars. And now Tammy was pregnant with my baby and I had to make a choice.

I'd wanted to take that cross-country trip. Buy a motorcycle and wheel from Hartford to San Francisco. It was a wonderful fantasy and I'd looked into ordering a Honda through the Seoul PX, but decided I'd rather buy a Harley-Davidson when I got home.

In the end, though, it was not a difficult choice. I wanted Tammy and the baby to have all of it.

I went to Brody and asked him for permission to go down to Seoul.

He told me to forget it. "After that stunt you pulled with the helicopter? You must have your head up your ass."

"I've got some leave time coming, sir. I only want two days. Jack says—"

"What in the hell do you want to go to Seoul for, this close to your DEROS."

"I want to take my girlfriend down with me, sir. Kind of a farewell."

"No."

"Sir, I—"

"No."

"But—"

"Shut up! I don't want my officers falling in love, marrying Korean girls."

"I'm not marrying her."

"Well I don't care. You've grown too attached to that whore. Now leave her alone. One more word out of you and I'll confine you to Camp Matta. You've passed your PCOD anyhow, haven't you?"

"Yes."

"All right then. I don't want to hear another word. Dismissed."

I walked out of his office and went over to Vandenberg's desk. "Hey Ron, you have forms for extending?"

The new sergeant major looked up from his desk across the room. The clerk stopped typing.

Ron said, "Yeah, sure. Officer or enlisted?"

"For me."

Elbows on his desk, he folded his hands together and rested his chin on them. "You'll have to re-up too, you know."

"For how long?"

"A year."

"Do I have to extend in Korea for a year?"

"Minimum's six months. One-year active duty commitment, six-month overseas extension, promotion to captain."

"Let me have the papers."

I filled them out before I left the office.

A couple days later I walked back over to headquarters to check on the paperwork. When Vandenberg saw me walk in he put down his pen, raised his eyebrows, and drew in a long breath.

"Well?" I said.

He looked around. The clerk and the sergeant major were working diligently. Vandenberg leaned back. "Lost," he said.

"What?"

"Your paperwork's been misplaced. No one seems to be able to find it."

"Give me some more."

"Art." He lowered his voice. "The Colonel told me to lose the paperwork for a few days. It's in this drawer here—" he kicked a bottom drawer—"and I can't find the key." He grinned. "Why don't you forget the whole thing? Your orders'll be here any day."

Colonel Brody wasn't in. I walked out of the building and up to the BOQ. Lying on my bunk, I thought it over. I didn't know whether I had the guts to disobey Brody. He could court-martial me. I'd have to be willing to take the consequences.

That night I waited up for Jack. After he returned from the fence around two in the morning, we talked quietly in his room.

"I've got to go AWOL," I told him. "I hate asking you this. I've got to take Tammy down to Seoul, but I can't just leave. Can you get somebody to walk the fence for me? That's all I ask."

He shook his head. "I can't, Art. Who could I get to do it? What the hell is all this?"

"Let your new assistant—what's his name? MacMillan—let him do it."

"It's not that easy. Look, what's—"

"I could have left without telling you. You'd have been up shit's creek."

"Tell me what the fuck's going on!"

"Brody won't give me permission to go down to Seoul. But I've got to go."

"Why?"

I told him about Tammy.

"Oh," he said. "Well." He nodded. "How're you getting down to Seoul if you don't have permission?"

"I'll get a lift into Changpa-ri. We'll take a *kimchi* bus from there."

He shook his head. "It's insanity, Art."

"I know."

"You're far gone, boy."

"Maybe so. But I'm going to do what I think's right."

"Is it true, or is Vandenberg spreading lies about you?"

"What?"

"Did you try to extend?"

"Yeah."

"Brody blocked it?"

"Yeah. He wants me out of here."

"Okay. I'll help you fight the bastard. When push comes to shove, though, you told me you had permission to go, right?"

"You bet!" We grinned at each other. I got up and went over to where he was sitting and shook his hand.

"By the way," he said. "Sergeant Lewis has to run into

Changpa-ri tomorrow morning and pick up some Korean carpenters. He's taking a three-quarter ton. Why don't I make sure he leaves from out front here shortly after you get back from the fence?"

"Stand up," I said. He did. I hugged him, and he hugged me back.

I met Tammy the following morning and we took a bus to Seoul. The bus was small, dirty, and crowded. I asked a middle-aged Korean man to give Tammy his seat, and he pretended not to understand. After I lifted him out of the seat, he understood. Tammy sat down, her cheeks pink, her eyes staring at the floor.

In Seoul we got a hotel room without difficulty. I made a few phone calls. In two hours, we met with an American attorney and a Korean banker. A translator sat in too, a Korean woman not much older than Tammy. We sat in a room with a high ceiling, a long walnut table surrounded by leather-upholstered chairs, and books that rose from floor to ceiling. Walls of books. I hadn't seen so many books in one place in months. Maybe years.

It was late afternoon and sunlight streamed in through tall windows. I told the attorney and the banker what I wanted. The five of us discussed it for a few minutes, and then we broke up. There was a lot of handshaking, and they went off to draw up the papers. Tammy and I went back to our hotel. The next afternoon we met once more in the room with the walls of books, and Tammy and I signed the papers. The bank paid my legal fees, so the transaction cost me nothing. The papers were written in both English and Korean. They created a trust fund for the baby, effective at its birth, and one for its mother as well. I wrote the banker a huge check, and it was done.

They would not be rich, not even by Korean standards. But they would be better off. Almost comfortable. The kid would not wind up in a whorehouse. Tammy would not have to find another boyfriend, at least not immediately—at least not a stranger. Perhaps her next boyfriend would not be an American and would not have to pay her for what she would want to give freely. That was what I hoped. I did not want her to have to screw any more Americans from the 1st Battalion, 31st Infantry.

That night, Tammy and I had a quiet dinner at our hotel. She looked radiant, her hair glistening and her cheeks full of color. But she seemed sad. She ate almost nothing, and we hardly spoke.

The DMZ seemed far away. I thought of the MOOM and The Firecracker Lounge. They weren't far away, but they seemed long ago.

I was standing in front of Colonel Brody's desk. He put me at attention and paced angrily about the room.

"I should throw your ass in the stockade. You could get ten years hard labor for this. Who else knows you went to Seoul? Besides me."

"Jack Evans, sir. And anyone in the next room."

"Don't get smart! You have no concept of how miserable I could make your life. No idea." He continued pacing. "You signed extension papers?"

"Yes sir."

"I might just forward them. Want to serve in my battalion for six more months?"

"There's no reason to extend now, sir."

He stopped pacing. "Then I've got you, don't I?"

"You've got me about eight ways, Colonel."

He looked at me and said, "Why don't we cut the shit. Sit down." He walked around his desk and wearily lowered himself into his desk chair.

Surprised, I sat down in the metal chair facing his desk.

He said, "Let's be honest with each other. And decent. I'm tired of yelling, and you don't hear me anyway. Cigaret?"

"No thanks, sir."

He lit one. "You know, I was once your age. Sure. You may not believe it, but I was. I know what you're going through."

I thought: No you don't. I also thought: Where have I heard this before?

"I have two daughters. Did you know that? That's right. My wife is fifty years old. She turned fifty a few days ago. I wrote her a letter. That's military life for you. We married when I was a lieutenant. She was a colonel's daughter. My second daughter looks just like her. What does all this have to do with you? What are you doing after you get out, Art?"

I shook my head. "I don't know exactly, sir."

He nodded. "I thought so. Purposeless, random, indecisive. No religion, no career. No sense of morality or patriotism."

I sat forward. "What kind of an attack is that? I joined the army, didn't I?"

"To avoid the draft. Don't think I don't know you. I know everything about you. It's my business to. That's why Vandenberg has all those files out there in his office." He gestured toward the door. "Now I'll be frank. You're as good as dead to me. You disobeyed a direct order, went AWOL. If I court-martialed you, you wouldn't get out of the army this week or next, but five years, ten years from now—out of the stockade."

He paused to let that sink in. Then he said, "But frankly, I don't want to bother." He closed his eyes and rubbed his hand down his face. It was a gesture of exhaustion. Finally he leaned forward across his desk.

"Look, Art, you've made a big mistake. Take it from me. You've put your efforts into a lost cause. That girl isn't worth shit. You're far from home, you're lonely. Don't do anything else dumb. A year from now you'll have forgotten her. You'll be going with some lovely American girl, thinking about marriage, a family. . . .

"You know, the army is one big family. It feeds you, clothes you, puts a roof over your head. It *works*. But the trouble is, you went and disobeyed an order. An order, Art—do you know what that means? Without orders, why. . . ." He shrugged. "It would break down, all of it. We might as well all go home. You violated the big one, and for what? Huh? Some lousy little personal affair, some insignificant administrative detail you probably could have taken care of by phone.

"But I can be understanding. I can. And I understand *you*. What I want to convince you of is this: your reason isn't worth it. You picked the wrong cause for your disobedience. A whore from Changpa-ri—what is she? Is she worth risking ten years of your life for? Answer me."

"Okay," I said. "We're supposed to be frank, right? She's a person, like you and me, like your wife, like your daughters. She's worth it, all right. She's worth it if anyone is. What makes you think your daughters are any better than my girl?"

He turned red. "You have no perspective!" he said angrily. He stubbed out his cigaret.

"That's not true, sir. I have *my* perspective. And you have yours. They're equally right."

"I've got thirty years on you."

"Granted. But thirty years doesn't render my point of view invalid."

"All right. That's enough." He raised his hands. "No more argument. We've heard each other out, we won't be swayed. But you hear this, and hear it good: no more trips to Seoul. No more trips to Changpa-ri. You are confined as of this minute to Camp Matta until you leave for the States. Is that clear?"

I didn't say anything.

"Acknowledge, Richardson."

I stood up. "Sir," I said, trying to sound as contrite as I could, "I appreciate that I'm getting off fairly light for going down to Seoul without permission—"

"Against my explicit order," he interrupted.

"Yes sir, but I've got to just ask you one thing. I've gotta see her once more, sir," I pleaded. "Just once. That's all I ask. I'll check out and check in with you personally, if you want. Of course I'll perform all my duties. But I just want to see her once more before I go, to say good bye to her. Please."

I knew I'd see Tammy again whether I had his permission or not. Maybe he knew it too.

"Granted," he said. "Now get the hell out of here."

TWENTY-FOUR

M<small>AY 30TH</small>
Harmon left a few days ago. Quite a production: two cameras, some large boxes filled with stereo components, a huge carton containing six or eight custom-made suits. Packed and shipped by Uncle Sam.

It seems he has a job all lined up for when he gets back to Baltimore.

Today my replacement arrived. He's a short fucker, I don't even know his name. I don't think his legs are long enough to walk the fence. Four companies now. Six miles. On the way to the mess hall this afternoon he took those little steps of his so fast his legs were a blur. I'm going to teach him how to walk the fence in the best tradition. I'm going to initiate the son of a bitch in the finest tradition established by my predecessor Anderson. I'm going to walk his ass off.

May 31
Last night the North Koreans again attempted an infiltration, this time over in the left-flank company attached to us from the 2nd of the 32nd. A team of three cut the fence and then backed off when two GIs made an unscheduled fence check. The hole was discovered and everyone was alerted, pa-

trols and GPs as well as the barrier force and stake-outs. This morning we determined from tracks that no one had gotten through.

It is not us. They are not ourselves, they are not a reflection of ourselves. They are an *other*. *They* are keeping the pressure on. *They* have created this adversary relationship. *They* refuse to be at peace within themselves and with their neighbor.

Who knows what their reasons are? Their agitation and aggression, their national distress and greed and fear are what result in these infiltration attempts. We do not cross their border. They cross ours.

June 1

Curt Davis came and said good bye to me today. He found me in my room. Well, Art, he said, I just wanted to say good bye. It's been great knowin ya.

Has it really? I said.

Yeah, really. You're a good man. I always thought so. You did your job, and you used initiative. You led that QRF platoon real well that night. Love and Toomey told me about it. You should have gotten a medal for that. You should have had a platoon or a company. You were wasted as fence-walker.

Thanks, I said. It's good of you to come say that. I don't think I'd have thought to tell you, but you're the best company commander this battalion's had. I mean that. I've known them all.

Thanks. I guess I agree, but it's nice to hear you say it. So long.

So long, Curt.

We shook hands.

Maybe we'll meet someday in the States, he said.

Yeah, maybe. I hope so. You're from Philly, right?

Yeah. Hartford?

Bloomfield, right outside.

I'll see you.

I'm looking forward to it already.

June 2

They're defoliating along the fence again, using the old, slow but reliable Korean DMZ defoliant: diesel fuel and matches. They're burning all along the fence; black smoke billows into the sky on two horizons. Wherever a few green shoots come up, they burn 'em down. Clear those fields of fire, those killing zones.

Many of us are due to leave at roughly the same time. At the Officers' Club and the mess hall and the BOQ, the spirit is subdued. It's a spirit of suppressed elation, I think, combined with fear. There have been too many deaths. No one wants to tempt fate by being joyous.

The new guys walk around the compound looking frightened. Their eyes shift rapidly about, and when they're spoken to, they reply in staccato sentences. They really are amusing.

I look at the trucks and mortars and recoilless rifles, the fence, the towers and foxholes—not with my old amazement and excitement, but with nothing. No feeling. They've lost their enchantment; they're boring relics. I've seen them hundreds of times and now I'm seeing them for the last time, and I couldn't care less.

But I miss the men.

Captain Stewart is gone; Peters is gone; Klein's dead, shot through the gut on the GP by his best friend; Colonel Curtis is gone, relieved; Major Nichols is gone; and Sellers and Wilson and Harris got sent down a long time ago. Bobby Green and John Harmon have DEROSed, left without a farewell. Baines and Williams are dead. Sergeant Waters was flown out on a stretcher. He got sent home. The men who've come to replace them—Lopez, Lyons, MacMillan, all the rest—seem inadequate and stupid by comparison. Clumsy. What do they know? What can they do? I suppose they'll learn, but learning is such a slow and painful process, and we know so much more.

I don't know these new guys. There're so damn many of them I can't even keep up with their names. I eat meals with them but I don't talk to them. I don't care.

I remember the men who are gone, and despise those who take their places.

June 3

There is so much to lose. I'm losing everything: Tammy, the money I've saved, the experience I've gained. What does an infantryman learn that he can use in the real world? Walking a fence? Firing a machine gun? Terrific. Writing Hostile Contact reports. It's all been for nothing, I'm leaving it here. Tammy, the money, the experience. I've acquired so much—a life, a family in the village, my job, my friends. I'm walking away from it all.

Things go on. You leave, and things continue without you. Fourteen months from now nobody here will be the same.

It'll be the same battalion with different men, running pretty much as it does now.

And we'll cease to exist for each other. They'll all cease to exist for me, these friends and enemies of mine. I'll probably never see any of them again.

That's the thing about leaving. It's as if I'd never been here.

Late that night one of our patrols found a tunnel entrance. The point man stumbled into it and broke his ankle. This was in the A Company sector—where else?—and the patrol leader was Crandall. He radioed it in immediately, in code.

At two in the morning the TOC woke Evans and he woke Colonel Brody. They got me up and we went over to the TOC and Colonel Brody contacted the brigade commander. Then Brody and Evans and MacMillan and I planned and coordinated the operation. At 4:30 a Huey arrived with the dogs and an engineer major, and we headed north toward the fence, the APCs leading the way.

It was dark and cool, and Jack and I rode in the back of Colonel Brody's jeep and I knew already that this would be the one morning out of all my mornings on the DMZ that I wouldn't walk the damn fence. I thought about the rotten irony of it, my last week in this rock pile and here was the biggest operation we'd geared up for in more than a year: the dogs up from I Corps again, two squads of the Quick Reaction Force, a squad of Recon, an engineer major and his assistant up from Seoul, Colonel Brody himself—and the bridade commander sitting back at his headquarters by a radio, as eager for news as an expectant father in a maternity ward.

The convoy moved through the A Company gate just as the sky began to lighten. We wound our way out through the fence and down the road, past the southern boundary and on into the DMZ, the armored personnel carriers with their big .50s manned and loaded, then a long string of jeeps, an ambulance, a gun jeep bringing up the rear—too early to raise much dust and moving fast, too fast, blowing right past the patrol until one of them stood up and shouted and nearly got killed. The column halted and two squads of the reaction force dismounted their tracks while a couple of medics put the kid with the broken ankle into the aid vehicle. When we were ready we headed into the tall grass and rocks, up and down a couple small hills and then the dogs started quivering and barking and there it was: four GIs staked out around it and Al Crandall showing us how they'd camouflaged the opening with a small bush that it had been too dark to see. The entrance situated a ways up a hill, the hole going nearly straight down.

There was a debate as to who was going to go down into it. We stood around while Colonel Brody took out his flashlight, and it was a question of who he was going to give it to.

"I'll go, Colonel," Linderman said.

Brody looked at Evans and me, and Jack shoved his way past me and said, "Let me do it, Colonel." He didn't say it convincingly, but he said it. He started taking off his web gear.

I kept my mouth firmly shut.

Brody said, "Evans. Your last name's easier to pronounce than his," gesturing at Dave with the crook-necked flashlight.

Dave said, "But I spoke up first, sir," and started taking off his flak jacket and web gear too. He stepped forward to take the flashlight, but Colonel Brody hesitated.

Sergeant Small was standing off a little way, his rifle slung over his shoulder as usual, paying more attention to his men than to us but right then he caught my eye. He smiled thinly and I saw in his face at last (it had probably been there all the time) the acknowledgement of what I finally understood, that I was in a drama I did not write the script of. It was a show for people who did not care whether they saw a show or not. But this time I was in the audience, not up on the stage, so I could see what was going on. Evans and Linderman had stepped forward and made the gesture, they'd done it even though they probably knew by now that there was no good reason to. Like mine, their conviction was gone and what was left was habit, the habit of action: or maybe only the husk of action, like the skin a snake leaves after it sheds it.

We were all standing around and the grass had a wet smell to it and the dogs whined and tugged at their leads. Colonel Brody was slapping the flashlight into the palm of his hand. He looked at the two lieutenants, Evans and Linderman, both of them due to get out of the army in a matter of days or at most weeks—this had nothing to do with career or promotion. He didn't know which one to pick. Then his eyes met mine. They suddenly lit up and glittered with joyful malice. He'd found a way out of his dilemma.

"You wanted to go to North Korea so bad, Art," he said. "Here's your chance to see Pyongyang from underground." He walked over and handed me the flashlight.

I took off my web gear and flak jacket and checked my pistol. I sat down on the wet grass, wondering what a tunnel rat did to stay alive, trying to remember my training and thinking Am I ever goddamnit ever going to do something in my life not for the first time?

Pistol cocked and ready in my right hand, flashlight in my left. They wrapped a rope around my ankles—Evans and Linderman, and Brody standing in the background, and behind him Sergeant Small.

Jack squatted down beside me. "Go slow," he said. "Watch out for trip wires. Feel for 'em. And if you see a North Korean this time, shoot the bastard."

"I will." I looked up at Colonel Brody. "What exactly am I looking for?"

"Reconnaissance. You're doing reconnaissance, that's all. See what's down there. Observe. Do not engage."

The engineer major was hovering somewhere above me. "We want to know how big it is, Lieutenant. What kind of movement they can achieve through there. How many troops, how fast. Get dimensions. And which direction it goes. You got a compass?"

"No."

"Here." He pulled one from a case clipped to his pistol belt and buttoned it into my fatigue shirt pocket.

"Okay," I said, and crawled over to the hole.

"Give the rope a couple jerks if you want us to extract you," Jack said. "Or holler." He took hold of the rope.

Colonel Brody said, "Look out for trip wires, Richardson. Bobby traps are for boobies."

I started down head-first. It got dark, and then it got quiet. I went down a ways with roots brushing my face and the light off, paused to let my eyes adjust to the darkness, and then I continued on, nearly upside-down, crawling on my elbows and knees, frustrated because the rope dragged, and restricted my feet. Often I stopped and listened. I was afraid to use the flashlight: it'd do more harm than good, make me a target. As I moved forward, I felt ahead gently with my hand. I couldn't see anything but I kept the light off and trusted my hands as more reliable than my eyes for finding a wire. The air was cool and the earth around me was moist. It would have been impossible to turn around. I was up-side-down and the blood was in my face and ears and sometimes I had to use my elbows to keep from falling too fast. Loose dirt rolled into my hair and shirt and nose and mouth, and breathing became a struggle. I stopped and listened, and heard nothing but dirt and stones rolling. The overwhelming sensations were dizzi-ness and terror and the cool sweet smell of earth.

The tunnel leveled off some and then I sensed a change in the air. It got cooler and wetter. Groping in front of me with my left hand I felt a hole. There was cold air coming up out of it. I crawled forward and reached into the hole and felt nothing, so I closed one eye and blinked the flashlight once down the hole.

The flashlight beam picked up nothing—just blackness—or was that something way ahead? I'd lost the sense of direction, of up and down, of distance. I gently felt around and my hand found something hard, maybe handholds of some kind, like ladder rungs; I swung down and got my feet under me (I thought) and then remembered the danger—wires—and I turned on the light. I was on a ladder and I could see no wires, so I continued down —hopping from rung to rung, the rope still tight around my an-kles, holding the light and the pistol in one hand—until suddenly I was standing on what felt like solid ground, and the weak beam of the light picked up walls—high, shining wet and dripping— and then I realized I was *standing*—it was impossible!— this wasn't a tunnel, it was a thoroughfare, an interstate below ground and I listened and all I could hear was water dripping, its noise echoing vast distances in both directions and I stood there shining the light at the walls and the ceiling and the floor, my mouth wide open, the tunnel mostly rock, with some dirt, and I unbuttoned my pocket and was reaching for the compass when I heard something. I flicked off the light and stood in the darkness and heard voices and footsteps running and then shouting in a language I could not understand, but I understood the tone all right—queries and challenges—and I began to hop toward the ladder but I tripped and fell hard, dropping the flashlight, and that was when the first shot cracked past me.

I started yanking on the rope and hugged the ground. The voices got closer, and then the rope tightened and swung me around and dragged me over something and I felt around until I knew for sure—it *was* a railroad track—and then my feet were lifted off the ground and I was suspended upside-down in the air. I felt dizzy and nauseous. Suddenly a light came on and my body was rotating slowly and moving upward toward the hole and I was suspended upside-down, rising from the floor toward the hole I'd come down and I was perfectly visible and absolutely vulnerable, twisting on the rope—Pull, you bastards, PULL! I was thinking—and I continued to rise (though it seemed like I was sinking, moving as I was in the direction of my feet) while bullets cracked and whined past me like crazy exploding insects. I could see muzzle flashes all around the light and sound was a huge, great reverberation on the threshold of hearing. They were firing pistols I think not automatic weapons and yelling excitedly and I raised my pistol and fired at the light but that only made me swing and rotate all the more and then I thought, More difficult target to hit so I shot at the light and the muzzle flashes every time they came around and there were shadows in front of the light and behind the flashes and I saw some fall and I was glad and then the light flamed and went out and I hoped I'd hit a couple of the bastards. Then my legs entered the tunnel and I tried to accordian up and dirt poured up the waist of my shirt and my bare skin scraped against the walls of the entrance hole and finally my ears and head were in the dirt and I was moving backwards through the tunnel. The walls ripped and tore at every part of my body, my knuckles felt as if they were being scraped to the bone and something hit my stomach and I couldn't breathe and there was dirt in my nose and mouth and ears and I was moving backwards up the tunnel fast, very fast and my ankles burned where the rope attached to them and suddenly: daylight.

I lay on my back and didn't move. I tried to breathe. Half the QRF had been pulling on that rope. They were all sitting in a line, still holding the rope.

Jack leaned over me and shouted "Are you hit? Art, are you hit?"

"No, I'm not hit."

Four or five people stared down at me. I was bleeding from my knees and ankles and elbows and hands.

I lay there breathing and bleeding and I put my forearm over my eyes to keep the sweat out and my stomach bobbed up and down and hiccuping sounds welled up from my chest and throat. It was funny. I said "I killed 'em, Jack. I shot a few of the bastards for you. The fools had a light on and they were perfect targets. I saw 'em fall."

A medic began to bandage the worst cuts. Sergeant Small pulled a grenade off his belt, and walked over to the hole, but the engineer major said "Don't do that, Sergeant," and he unclipped a white phosphorous grenade, pulled the pin, and rolled it in. It went off with a dull thump. White smoke rose from the hole.

"That won't cave in our entrance," said the major. "But it'll discourage 'em from using it for a while."

When I could I told them what I'd seen. It was the railroad tracks and the sheer size of it that seemed impossible: a tunnel twice as tall as me.

The major said, "Did you get a compass bearing?"

"No."

"Why not? Someone'll have to go back down there."

"Why don't you go, Major?" I said. "Your compass is down there. Why don't you go fetch it?"

"Easy, Art," said Colonel Brody.

Colonel Brody and the major took a squad of the QRF and headed back to the vehicles. I went with them, on a stretcher. While they coded a radio message to the brigade commander, I was put into the aid vehicle next to the man with the broken ankle. I fell asleep before we started moving, and I awoke back at Camp Matta.

Sometime after I left, Colonel Brody got his orders: stake out the entrance and stand by. They waited around all morning, but in the afternoon, higher headquarters cancelled further searches for the day. The A Company patrol staked out the tunnel entrance.

I never went down into that tunnel again nor ever again set foot in the DMZ.

I was working at my desk in the S-3 shop, trying to put the files in order. My hands were bandaged and I was having a difficult time writing. Camp Matta was quiet; just about everyone was up at the fence, or all the way out at the tunnel. They were systematically searching, mapping, and destroying the tunnel, but it wasn't my operation, or Jack's, or any of ours. The operation belonged to the new guys. One of the new lieutenants had already been killed in the tunnel.

The AM radio in the S-2 shop next door was tuned to the Armed Forces network station in Seoul. I could hear it clearly.

. . . has anybody here seen my old friend Bobby?
Can you tell me where he's gone?
I thought I saw him walkin'
up over the hill—
with Abraham and Martin and John.

Two reporters were making themselves at home in my office: one from Sweden and the other from the States. The TOC was off-limits to them and so was the forward area: the fence and the DMZ. One reporter was sitting on Jack's desk—the American—and the other sat in a chair opposite me and never took his eyes off me.

From across the room, the American said, "Hey Lieutenant, you sure you're the one who went down in that tunnel first?"

I didn't look up. "Maybe I dreamt it."

"How'd your hands get so cut up then?"

I looked down at the bandages on my hands. "The hazards of jerking off," I said.

The Swedish journalist said, "Lieutenant Richardson, why are you in Korea, anyway? Why are you not in Vietnam?"

I gave him a long look. "How come you're not in Sweden, friend?"

Jack came in through the outside door, grinning from ear to ear, and handed me my orders.

"Present from Vandenberg," he said. "You're gone."

I tore open the envelope. Two days.

"Did you get yours?" I asked.

"Yeah. I fly out tomorrow night."

"You're shorter than me."

He grabbed my orders and looked at them. "Son of a bitch."

"It would have been nice to fly back together."

"Oh well." He shrugged his shoulders. "C'est la vie."

"Yeah, it's la vie, all right," I said. "It's la finie de la vie."

"No," said Jack. "La commencement."

"Whatever. Look, maybe we can ride down to Seoul together tomorrow morning. I could spend the night at the MOOM or something."

Jack raised his eyebrows. "Nice idea, but Brody won't let you do it. I'd bet on it."

"You're probably right, but I'll ask anyway."

That afternoon I managed to catch Colonel Brody alone at the BOQ. He'd been with one general or another all morning, and he looked exhausted. I asked him to let me leave one day early. He told me I was still restricted to Camp Matta until the day I was due to fly home. With the exception of one trip to Chang-pa-ri, I reminded him, and he said Yeah, with one exception. He also told me I'd done a lousy job of breaking in the new fence-walker, so the guy would need an extra day of training. I told him about the way Anderson broke me in and suggested we stick to precedent. Brody waved his hand at me and said, Yeah, look where precedent got us. I said, Thank you, Colonel Brody, it's been a pleasure working with you too.

Jack was on duty that night and also had to pack, so I picked that evening to go into Changpa-ri for the last time. Tammy fed me, and afterwards we lay in the dark on the bed with the curtains open. A hot wind swirled through the village, blowing dust and refuse down the street and up over the rooftops.

Tammy rolled over on her back and stared up at me. "I never thought you would leave," she said. "Until we went to Seoul. Then I knew."

"I don't want to talk about it," I said.

"I do. You must talk about it."

"Why?"

She grinned. "To torture you for leaving."

I laughed. "Of course I knew all along I'd leave. Only I didn't think it would come this soon. Or be this difficult. I didn't think it would be any problem at all."

"You Americans are funny," she said. "You can't wait to go home, and then when it's time, you want to stay. Very crazy."

"It's all your fault. You Korean women."

She smiled, but suddenly her face lost all trace of amusement. She turned her eyes away from me.

I kissed her. "What's the matter?"

"Part of you wants to go very much. I feel that in you, and understand. This place is not real to you. But it's all I know. It hurts," she said. "Like a bullet right here." She touched me just below my sternum.

"I love you, Tammy. I'll always love you."

She moved her finger up to my lips. "Shhh. No you won't. You'll forget me very soon. Only take one American girl to make you forget me. But I will always remember you."

"Maybe someday I'll come back."

"I think not. But it's a nice thought."

I laid my head on one of her breasts, my hand on the other. I squirmed my body around until my knee was snug between her thighs. I murmured, "I'll just stay like this. They'll never find me. I'll stay here forever."

She kissed my forehead and rubbed my neck with her fingertips.

In the morning she cooked while I threw a few things into a laundry bag. We ate, and then she walked with me down the stairs. Lyons was meeting me at four. It was five past. At the bottom of the stairs I held her. I could feel her breath through my fatigue shirt, hot and moist. It seemed incredible that I'd never see her again. She was carrying my child. I felt as if we'd lived a lifetime together, but it had been only a few months. It was a lifetime together that I was giving up.

She began to sob, and I rocked her from side to side, and then I felt tears of my own spilling over.

"Tammy," I said. "I love you and I'll miss you."

"I want to keep you," she said.

"Take care of our baby," I said. "Take good care of it."

She nodded against my chest. At last she pulled away and ran up the stairs. It took me a moment to get control of myself before I opened the door and walked out into the dark morning.

June 7

I didn't volunteer and I enjoyed the killing though quite frankly I would have preferred it if they hadn't been shooting back.

Maybe it was the violence. Even before I joined up. Violence and killing. King and the Kennedys, first John then Robert, and before them Joe. A dead Korean on a hillside and finding pleasure in strangling a man I could smell but not see. It was hate. In Seoul I had it right. In Seoul I took shit without giving in or giving it back and then in the bar I neutralized that punk without destroying anyone. But that was an individual act not a collective one, maybe that's what it's been about all these years is the collectiveness of my life, how I've been a cog on a wheel, one smoothly working part in the huge death monster called an infantry battalion—which is only a small part of a division, etc. etc. *ad infinitum*. Somebody ought to dump a monkey wrench into the armies of the world, but who? A soldiers' rebellion? Not likely.

And what'll come next? Nuclear war? More riots in cities and soldiers and police firing on unarmed people and finally no elections? Where will the violence stop? Will it stop?

I've participated. I felt I had no choice but I did have choices only I made the wrong ones. They sentenced Ali to 5 yrs in prison and a $10,000 fine—would I have gotten more, or less? Is that worse than this? Is it worse than dying?

I had an *alternative*. Prison. Or Canada. Is prison that bad? Would my parents have understood, and supported me? Some of my friends would have, and others wouldn't.

Idle speculation. It's too late now. Alternatives become regrets.

This morning I said good bye to Tammy. Jack left today, before lunch. We swapped addresses. I've settled my affairs and I'm ready to leave. I've said good bye. For me this place is no more. I'll never return. Perhaps I'll see some of these people again, but I doubt it.

To Mom and Dad it'll be as if I never left. It'll be summer; we'll go to the lake. But things at home will never be the same again.

We're all leaving, all of us who've been here thirteen months. How many are we? America is a big place: it will absorb us like on ocean, without thinking, without changing, absorb us as though we did not matter. Extinguish us.

June 8th
Flight Out

Short hop from Kimpo to Tokyo. A few passengers disembark, and they're replaced by others. Most of us remain shut up in the plane while it's refueled. Then the aircraft taxis to the end of the runway, wheels around and lines up. Roar of jet engines; press of acceleration. We begin to roll. We start slowly, and slowly we pick up speed. We roll and roll. We should be lifting off, but we're not. The plane just rolls, doesn't seem to pick up speed, is rolling and rolling and rolling. . . .

We don't leave the ground. I'm certain we're going to crash in the bay. The plane rolls and keeps rolling. The ground flows past the window, doesn't drop away. I wait to feel the kick of brakes and flaps and reversed engines, expect the violent pull of an emergency stop. But we keep rolling.

Then, after I've given up all hope, the airliner struggles off the concrete. Immediately we're over water—barely a few feet above the bay—but now we're rising.

It needed that long run. All that fuel for the trans-Pacific flight. We'd flown from Seoul to Tokyo with little fuel aboard, and in Tokyo they'd topped off our tanks. We needed every inch of runway.

Memorabilia

I pull down the tray and reach into my jacket pocket. Spread them out.

A bullet, 7.62mm, the copper tarnished, rifling grooves plainly visible. The one that hit me.

A pin from a hand grenade.

(The guy sitting next to me, a lieutenant wearing an Eighth Army patch, is pretending to read but his eyes keep shifing over to my seat-back tray.)

An unfired round from the PPS. Small. No markings. Harmon gave it to me, the one decent thing he ever did. Besides introduce me to T.

Some dirt and a pebble from a pocket after they pulled me out of the tunnel.

And a dark, leathery object, about the size and shape of a dried apricot. Still needs a shave.

The Pacific
    journey: we chase the sun westward across the
Pacific—moving toward the light
    nearly cloudless. And above—too bright to see—
    expanse of blue. Vast expanse of blue, far below—endless
miles of ocean, limitless, unbroken sea, rolling, blue, a shining vastness stretching on forever and ever. A shimmering
plane of blue and white. Flat light. A plane of blue and white
light, an ocean of light.
    And after we cross it, if the airliner stays up, if we do cross
it—after we impossibly cross it, what then? Will my parents
and aunts and cousins and old friends welcome me home,
make a fuss, honor me? Will they badger me for stories? Will
they thank me for this year? Will they understand, will they
care?

    What happens next? What will I do?
    I don't know what will become of me at all.